CHOCOLATE-BOX DOUBLE HEARTS

JOSIE RIVIERA

5 STAR READER REVIEWS

"Holiday romance boxed set with a variety of characters, twist and turn plots, believable resolutions, bargain price and all featuring delectable CHOCOLATE! Josie Riviera weaves wonderful stories that delight the soul of the reader."- Amazon Reviewer

A CHOCOLATE-BOX CHRISTMAS

"A unique Christmas Chocolatey short story with delightful characters, a twist and turn plot. A great start for this unique premise to a series - a food critic who dislikes chocolate. Mmmm- interesting."- Amazon Reviewer

A CHOCOLATE-BOX NEW YEARS

"Fresh pasta, star gazing, old movies and more. How many times would you bake a dessert for love? *A Chocolate-Box New Years* is unique that Lorenzo Rossi is a weatherman. As a reader and foodie, I wanted to visit and eat at Julie Elliot's The Pasta Junction restaurant. Together can they plan a perfect celebration."- Amazon Reviewer

A CHOCOLATE-BOX VALENTINE

"As a retired English teacher I loved all the mixed up aphorisms and the reference to Byron's poem about the best laid plans of mice and men. Some other favorite quotes: It's the journey that matters. (Very true.) It's your last love who truly matters. Spontaneous people have more fun. (My sentiments. After years of living on a schedule, so glad retirement leaves room for spontaneity.)" - Amazon Reviewer

A CHOCOLATE-BOX SUMMER BREEZE

"Sometimes the older you get, the more it seems like you've disappeared. So very true. As a 70 year old retiree who loves chocolate and the beach, I could relate with Emily. This retiree also enjoys eating at diners and remembering musicals, the Beatles and a car with an eight-track player. Yes, eight-track cassettes are antiques, just like us. Nostalgia were the beckoning of a summer breeze, lighting the landscape of one's life. Recipe for Peanut Butter Oatmeal Chocolate Bars included." - Amazon Reviewer

A CHOCOLATE-BOX CHRISTMAS WISH

"Mr. Big Shot Anchorman Patrick meets home town child care provider Cora and sparks fly. This avid reader identified with both characters in this riveting page turning novella, having lived in metropolitan and small town communities. Certainly understand the draw to a budget friendly, slower pace, loads of living space to sprawl out, the comfort of driving with no sirens blaring in the middle of the night town. This mother's heart identified with Patrick's tumultuous life with his ex-wife - feeling manipulated and constantly off-balance. Josie Riviera imparts wisdom about Christmas, life and marriage in this inspiring novella. Choosing a unique present that will bring joy. As a German, I enjoyed the German connection and Tara's Church Window

Cookie recipe, reminded me of Great Aunt Ella who made the delectable chocolate delights every Christmas and Easter." - Amazon Reviewer

A CHOCOLATE-BOX IRISH WEDDING

"*A Chocolate -Box Irish Wedding* is a Second Chance at Love HEA fairy tale. I enjoyed Josie Riviera's descriptive passage of the Wexford Irish country side. Enjoyed the Irish folklore with leprechauns, dreams, love, and blessings. Keira and Colum are brought together by their widowed parents finding love. Recipe for Irish Soda Bread included." - Amazon Reviewer

INTRODUCTION

To keep up on newly released ebooks, paperbacks, Large Print Paperbacks, audiobooks, as well as exclusive sales, sign up for Josie's Newsletter today.

As a thank you, I'll send you a Free PDF ... The Beauty Of ...

Josie's Newsletter

Did you know that according to a Yale University study, people who read books live longer?

CONTENTS

A CHOCOLATE-BOX SUMMER BREEZE

A CHOCOLATE-BOX CHRISTMAS WISH

A CHOCOLATE-BOX IRISH WEDDING

PRAISE AND AWARDS

USA TODAY bestselling author

ACKNOWLEDGMENTS

An appreciative thank you to my patient husband, Dave, and our three wonderful children.

DEAR FRIENDS

Dear Friends,

A heartwarming story is the hallmark of a romantic read. Savor the magic of this collection with six heartwarming, clean and wholesome romances.

Find out why readers are falling in love with **Chocolate-Box Double Hearts** & staying up all night reading! These stories will warm your heart. Available in ebook, paperback, and large print paperback. Individual books and corresponding audiobooks are also available separately

Cozy up with your favorite beverage, and lose yourself in the joyful seasons of love.

This bundle contains 6 books.

A Chocolate-Box Christmas

This short and sweet romance is a #1 Amazon Bestseller. Love is sweeter with a touch of mischief.

Judging a chocolate-making competition for the women's shelter's annual fundraiser should be an easy, even pleasurable, assignment for Maise, new food critic for the *Blooming-*

field Daily Dispatch. Too bad just the smell of chocolate makes her stomach roil.

By the time she reaches the last table, she hopes her face isn't as green as her holiday sweater. But the tall, square-jawed man behind piles of fudge makes her want to linger, even savor the moment along with his chocolate-coffee-flavored confection.

Except there's something Ben Elliot is hiding behind his piercing blue eyes and lazy grin, and her reporter's nose senses a story worth exploring. She finds herself longing to discover the secret ingredient sweetening their mutual attraction.

A Chocolate-Box New Years

This holiday story is a top 100 Amazon bestseller in clean and wholesome, as well as holiday fiction romance.

Some recipes don't turn out quite as you predicted…

The extra time and expense of Julie Elliot's old-school cooking methods are worth it, but that means The Pasta Junction's bottom line is often stretched thin—much like herself. Even during the holidays, the restaurant's busiest season.

When she carves out time in her brutal schedule to meet with Bloomingfield weatherman Lorenzo Rossi, she crushes her reaction to the tall, blue-eyed charmer quicker and harder than a clove of roasted garlic. Lorenzo may be sweet as Italian cassata and hot as a red pepper, but *planning an anniversary dinner* means *married,* and she needs another disaster like that like she needs another olive oil stain on her shirt.

But as she and Lorenzo assemble the ingredients for a perfect celebration, she discovers something completely unexpected. And her heart may not withstand the storm of emotion she never saw coming.

A Chocolate-Box Valentine

It's your last love who truly matters.

Owning a candy store should be a fun and delightful profession. Besides, what candy could beat Sally Elliot's signature coffee chocolate fudge?

None, except for the unique infusion candy she designed for Valentine's Day.

Unfortunately, the signature chocolate required for the candy won't be delivered on time.

No problem. She'll pick up the order herself.

When she reaches the diner where the delivery man is stranded, she retrieves the chocolate and intends to return to her shop. But a downed tree detains her. And the handsome, kind man who owns the diner makes her want to stay, especially after she accepts his challenge to prepare homemade delectable chocolates with him.

There's something about Oliver Menroe's gentle mannerisms, his genuine interest in his customers, that ignites a hope Sally had extinguished long ago. As a disillusioned single mother, she knows from experience that love doesn't last forever.

But can she allow herself to believe that one simple ingredient can sweeten their mutual attraction and ... for the first time in her life ... create a lasting love?

A Chocolate-Box Summer Breeze

A disillusioned widow longing for a change. A hard-working truck driver looking for love. Will Emily and Joe find their happily-ever-after in a forgotten summer breeze?

Widow Emily Varon doesn't believe in love anymore, and she isn't wasting her time trying to find it. At her age, she's learned that life is a daily routine. Rinse and repeat. Safe and secure. And she's not about to change her ways now. With her hard-won affluence, succumbing to a truck-driver's invitation to spend a summer weekend together means only one thing. Friendship.

Widower Joe Vertucci has never met any difficulties he couldn't overcome, and work is all he's ever known. But when the chance for romance with Emily beckons in a little seaside town, will a dilapidated cottage wind up becoming a refuge for their hearts?

The waft of a summer breeze can bring summer rain. Or create new memories. Sometimes you have to leave what's familiar in order to discover where home truly is. Because for love, anything is possible.

A Chocolate-Box Christmas Wish

He's been all over the world. She's a home-town girl. Can a holiday wish bridge the gap?

In Cora Carpenter's small California hometown, Christmas is tailor-made for couples. Unfortunately, Cora is a party of one, thanks to a con man who stole her heart, then bilked her out of thousands of dollars.

What's on her Christmas wish list this year? Nothing whimsical. She'll take a new vacuum cleaner, thanks—and no dating for the foreseeable future. But when she meets a stranger with a broken-down car, his warm smile and perilously blue eyes almost make her want to tweak that list. If only she could get over the pain and humiliation of her past.

A double whammy of betrayal and a broken heart sent anchorman Patrick Gervez thousands of miles west looking for a fresh start. But the pretty child care provider's unforgettable amber eyes and deft hand with a set of jumper cables does funny things to his heart—and makes him wonder if she's a forgotten dream come true.

Except she's as skittish as a piece of tinsel in a windstorm.

And the only way to help her forget her heartbreak, is to convince her to forgive. Especially herself.

A Chocolate-Box Irish Wedding

Travel to Ireland with this short and sweet holiday romance.

A woman who wanted more. A man who wanted her. Can they rediscover their love in the seaside town where it all began?

Colum O' Brien, a professional ballet dancer, is still hurt from a break-up four decades earlier. All this time, his heart has gravitated toward the woman who left him behind.

Sure, he's moved on with his life, but he's never forgotten his childhood sweetheart, Keira Murphy.That is, until he meets her again. Because his father is marrying her mother.

Keira was a famous runway model who moved away from her seaside Irish town with dreams of becoming a superstar. She left everything behind, including Colum.

With her skills as a seamstress, she's now determined to return and open her own shop. Only she never expected to see Colum again—or to be instantly connected to him, just like when they were next-door neighbors and childhood sweethearts.

But when the pressures of demanding work schedules and living miles apart prevail, will it make their second chance at love impossible?

Or will their individual journeys lead them right back to where it all began?

USA TODAY BESTSELLING AUTHOR
JOSIE RIVIERA
a Chocolate-Box Christmas

PRAISE AND AWARDS

USA TODAY bestselling author

#1 Bestseller 90 minute short romance
#1 Bestseller Single Authors Short Stories
#1 Bestseller Contemporary Short Stories

CHAPTER 1

$\mathcal{M}$aise Anderson stood at the entrance to the women's shelter in her new hometown, her gaze fastened on the front door. The weather was a typical mid-December afternoon in California, but she was accustomed to cooler temperatures.

However, this wasn't about winter. This was about chocolate.

Under normal circumstances, she would have admired the magnificent landscape surrounding the town of Bloomingfield—the imposing snow-capped mountains, the towering ponderosa pines—but she couldn't, because all she focused on was reaching for the metal door handle and turning it.

With a nervous inhale, she gave herself a stern reminder.

You can accomplish this simple assignment. Candy is a sweet holiday treat. Besides, everyone loves chocolate.

Maybe. Maybe not.

She hadn't eaten chocolate in over two years because of a nasty bout of food poisoning.

Nonetheless, she hadn't gotten sick because of the chocolate, she rationalized, as she recalled that particular dining assignment. Most likely, she'd gotten sick because of her entrée.

She flicked a glance toward the leaden sky, grimacing when a brisk wind blew misty rain across her face. A chill rose up her neck and she shivered.

She tucked her small umbrella under her arm and pressed her lips together.

Outwardly, she passed for the ideal food critic. Her shoulder-length chestnut hair was pulled into a classic chignon, her beige leather pumps sported a sensible heel, and her camel-colored blazer was tasteful and practical. She'd opted for tailored navy-blue slacks, topped with an emerald-green turtleneck sweater, holiday looking but conservative. She'd kept her makeup to a minimum—muted pink lipstick, a light rosy blush, and mascara to highlight her green eyes.

Confidence and expertise on the outside. Foreboding and anxiety on the inside.

She blew out a whoosh of air, straightened her shoulders, and pushed open the door to the shelter. "Here we go," she said under her breath. "I can withstand anything for an hour."

"Happy holidays, Miss Anderson." The mayor, Ed Johnson, a thin man but with a wide grin to make up for it, hailed her as she stepped inside. They'd met at a Hometown Holiday event at the County Museum the previous weekend. "There's a cold front coming in. I'm pleased you agreed to judge our annual fund-raiser."

"I'm happy to participate," she lied. In reality, she had no choice. Her boss, the editor of *Bloomingfield Daily Dispatch*, had given her the assignment with a gruff, "There's no food budget for this affair. Take a couple of pictures with your phone camera, sample the weirdest piece of chocolate you can find, and follow up with a full-of-praise article."

Such was the job of a food-writer reporter. No extravagant feast or fancy sushi. Just pure, sweet chocolate.

At the thought, her stomach roiled.

"Are you settling into your role as our town's newest food critic?" Ed asked.

"Yes." She tempered her voice to sound calm and professional. "There's a wealth of fine restaurants here."

"You're originally from Anchorage, Alaska, correct?" He accepted her blazer as she shrugged it off, hanging it on a coat rack and placing her umbrella beneath it. "California's weather must feel quite warm compared to the frozen north."

"Anchorage winters are certainly memorable." She smiled, well remembering the freezing temperatures and shortened daytime hours that descended on the city from September to May.

"My wife saved your piece in the newspaper about preparing a week's worth of meals ahead of time. She prefers to eat out, but she actually cooked and froze five dinners." Ed reached for a piece of peanut butter fudge on a side table and popped it into his mouth.

"I'm glad my article was helpful." Maise followed him into the dining hall. Eight tables were set up, each covered with a red velvet tablecloth and laden with silver-plated chocolate displays. The entrants, men and women of all ages, stood behind their respective tables and eyed the mayor, then Maise, nervously.

An undecorated Scotch pine soared in the corner of the large room. Beneath the tree, gaily wrapped packages donated by the community were earmarked for the children. The previous day, Ed explained, the shelter had held a Christmas caroling party. Today, most of the women were out job hunting while their children attended school.

Though Maise tried to maintain a semblance of composure, the scents of sweet and bittersweet chocolate filled the air, and she choked back the nausea in her throat.

"Smell that?" Ed inhaled deeply and smacked his lips. "Peppermint fudge, my favorite. This fund-raiser is a choco-holic's dream."

Or nightmare.

She extended a gamely smile, sending a stern command to her queasy stomach to settle.

"All the candies are handmade from the local shops and restaurants," Ed continued. "From my experience, all women love chocolate, so you must have jumped at this assignment."

Jumped? Umm, no. Actually, she'd cringed.

But she couldn't refuse. She'd been on the job less than a month and had finally settled into her comfortable second-floor apartment at the edge of town. She had no intention of moving back to Alaska and hoped to make Bloomingfield her permanent home.

In Anchorage, her five older brothers had doted on her, while she'd been suffocated by controlling parents who constantly argued. She'd moved away, much to her brothers' dismay, but she wanted to prove to herself that she could manage her life independently.

"Well, I didn't really jump," she said.

"Watching the waistline, right? If I was paid to eat out, I'd gain a pound a week."

She fumbled to say more, but he'd turned to welcome the two other judges. The man and woman, who appeared to be in their early sixties, regarded Maise with smug superiority.

Maise understood that she was in a competitive business, and the unspoken truth that came with it. In food journalism, as in most professions, it was necessary to prove oneself in order to establish a distinguished reputation.

A cheerful rendition of "Rudolph the Red-Nosed Reindeer," sung by Gene Autry, played on repeat, and Ed sang along for a few measures. She grinned as he enhanced his singing with a little dance.

When the song began another loop, Ed led the judges to the tables.

"Here are the eight hopeful candymakers." He exchanged a grin with the woman behind the first table, then motioned to an adjacent counter. "Judges, if you want water or coffee in between bites, it's here."

Coffee. Her favorite beverage. Maise regarded the steaming foam cups set on the counter and whispered an appreciative thank you.

As they went down the line of tables, Ed presented the judges to the candymakers, and Maise realized that she already knew two entrants from her recent assignments. Both were restaurateurs, and both acknowledged her. But the other six entrants were strangers. As she tried to remember all the names Ed recited, she paused at the last table. A tall, lean man with a strong, square jawline and solemn demeanor was being introduced.

He was startlingly handsome, with piercing blue eyes and dark curly hair.

"This serious guy is Ben Elliot." Ed surveyed Ben's table, the glass apothecary jars bursting with peanut butter brittle, and the red bento boxes labeled Bean-to-Bar Chocolate. "Everything looks good, Ben."

"Thanks." Ben gave a quiet sigh and tossed aside a cardboard bento box he'd been trying to put together.

The mayor and judges started back to the first table, but Maise lingered. "Aren't you happy you're here, Mr. Elliot?" she asked. "You don't look as thrilled as the other candymakers."

"Like you, I couldn't be more delighted to be here." He met her gaze, and a lazy smile swept across his face. He'd obviously been watching her and had noticed her apprehensive scan of the displays.

She pulled a notepad and pen from her tote bag and flashed him a polite smile. "And what exactly is bean-to-bar chocolate?"

"Why? Is this an interrogation?"

She frowned. "Isn't this a chocolate contest? I'm a judge and—"

"I don't believe the contest has started yet." He glanced at his watch. "Would you like to try a chocolate-covered almond while you wait?"

"No. No, thank you." She angled away from him. She knew her complexion had gone pale at the mention of chocolate. Nevertheless, his admiring stare roved over her face, then glided down her body to her feet, which were shifting restlessly.

"And your name is—" he inquired.

"Maise Anderson. The mayor just introduced me."

"Right." His lips quirked. "You're a bit nervous this afternoon, Miss Anderson. Brand-new on the job, I take it? I read your recent critique in the newspaper about The Pasta Junction, an established restaurant in town. Apparently you don't like pasta?"

"Pasta is my favorite food."

"Really? You certainly didn't mince words in the article. What were some phrases you used …? Oh yes, the sun-dried tomatoes were too dry, and the pasta stuck together."

She stiffened. "I give my honest opinion, without malice. Most restaurants want feedback so that they can get better."

"You recommended that The Pasta Junction add pizza to their menu."

"Because they serve Italian cuisine, I assumed pizza might be offered, perhaps for lunch, if not for dinner."

"I can assure you that pizza hasn't been added. My sister, Julie, owns that restaurant." He regarded Maise in impassive silence. "If she wanted to sell pizza, she'd open a corner pizzeria, not an upscale Italian restaurant that's been in business for ten years."

Maise kept her posture strong, although inwardly her chest felt like it was caving in. She truly wanted diners to discover new restaurants because of her articles. "I realize the word 'critic' may have a negative connotation, but I write honestly and fairly."

"Let's not forget that it's all through your perspective and therefore colored by your opinion. It's up to the reader whether to agree or disagree with you."

Curtly, she nodded. "Correct." She kept her gaze steady and her chin high. Her self-assurance came partly because he'd laced his voice with a teasing tone, and partly because of his good-natured grin.

"Mr. Elliot, please tell your sister that the antipasto was delicious and I look forward to visiting her restaurant again."

"Ben."

She tipped her head. "Excuse me?"

"My name is Ben. May I call you by your first name, Maise?"

"Of course. There's no need for formality." She met his stare. "Rest assured, Ben, I strive to judge restaurants impartially. Surely you must realize my critiques can't be all fluff."

"An impartial food judge." Mayor Ed had returned and gazed at her with a gratified grin. "You're exactly what our little town needs to put it on the map. I read about your writing expertise in Anchorage, a city five times the size of Bloomingfield. Your stellar review of The Moose's Pad helped launch that restaurant. Diners wouldn't have discovered it otherwise."

She winced, remembering the nasty emails she'd received. "Not everyone agreed with my review."

"Apparently enough people did. Your article was picked up by several major newspapers."

Which had been the problem. In a big city, she'd been expected to write ten to twenty posts a week, plus restaurant reviews, plus handle the social media that came with it. After her article exploded, the workload had doubled.

A thoughtful, well-reported piece took time, and she'd begun to burn out. A small town like Bloomingfield was just what she needed to decompress. She'd still do what she loved, but at a slower pace.

Nevertheless, Ed was a skillful politician, strategically spinning the conversation in order to praise her, and the realization made Maise grin.

Ben grinned at the same time, and they shared a chuckle. Belatedly realizing that he might be flirting with her, she took a guarded step backward. He stood only a few feet away, casually dressed in dark pants and a white polo shirt, and became far more handsome the longer she stared at him. His blue eyes were bringing unexpected changes to her heartbeat.

And there it was. An unanticipated magnetism. An attraction that drew her wholly by surprise.

Mayor Ed tossed a piece of peppermint fudge into his mouth and chewed while he spoke. "Ben Elliot is the owner of Bloomingfield Candy Shop."

"All that?" Maise looked directly at Ben.

"All that and more," Ben quipped, then met the mayor's gaze. "Correction, Ed. I'm the co-owner."

"The man behind the scenes. Don't let his unassuming manner fool you, Maise. This guy is our very own small-town hero."

Why, she wanted to ask, but Ed was ushering her back to the coffee table, where the other judges waited.

He addressed the three of them. "Folks, the directions

are simple. Sample the candies and write down your thoughts and criticisms. You can visit the tables in whichever order you choose. Give the candy a score between one and ten—ten being the most delicious." He eyed the sturdy wooden clock hung on a bare wall. "It's two o'clock, everyone is here and we'll begin. By three o'clock, you should be finished. Bring your comments and scores to me. Ready?"

"Ready!" Maise forced an upbeat tone and made her way to the first table while the other judges dispersed.

"This is a pepper truffle," the wiry ginger-haired candy-maker said, quickly enlightening her. He handed her a piece set on a red lace napkin. "Try it."

"You mean a *peppermint* truffle?"

He gave her a knowing look and didn't reply.

She took a deep breath and sampled a bite. Immediately, her eyes watered. She'd expected something sweet with a cooling aftertaste. This candy wasn't sweet. It was flaming hot.

"No, I mean pepper," the man replied. "It's made with red pepper flakes and a dash of pepper oil. A light tang to chocolate candy gives it a punch, wouldn't you agree? It packs a hint of unexpected spicy heat."

Jerkily, Maise bobbed her head, although she wanted to point out that the heat level was more than a hint. While he went on to describe the process of tempering chocolate, she grabbed some water from the counter and greedily drank. Then she switched to a cup of black coffee and sipped appreciatively.

"I worked in France as an assistant chocolatier before opening my own shop," he said. "No doubt a person like you is aware that candy making requires a special skill."

She nodded as she jotted notes on her notepad. "Anything else?"

"Don't get water in the chocolate while you're heating it, because the process will be ruined."

"Thank you." Her stomach rebelled, and she eyed the other seven tables. She snapped a picture and stepped unsteadily to table number two.

She hoped the dark lemon crème candy, charmingly showcased on a linen napkin, might soothe her stomach. It didn't. Maise thanked the chocolatier, took a quick picture, and moved on.

At table three, a blond woman presented Maise with a piece of white chocolate shaped like a candy bar.

"What are the red specks?" Maise asked.

"Strawberries and rose petals, and the petals are edible," the woman replied. "Taste it."

Maise inhaled, then nibbled. "Delicious," she assured. The woman didn't seem to notice Maise's shudder while she explained the difference between pure white chocolate and dark chocolate.

"Did you know that white chocolate is simply cocoa butter and sugar?" the woman quizzed.

"I know now." Maise thanked her, then swiveled to the counter, pondering if she should grab another cup of coffee. The caffeine rush seemed to help her to carry on.

She did, and it helped again.

That is, until she tried the candy at the next four tables.

It was a struggle, and she knew that the fixed, objective expression on her face was slowly disintegrating.

By the time she neared Ben's table, she only had one thought. How could she get out of there? Wildly, her gaze searched for the exit, and she peered at the clock on the wall.

Only a few more minutes. Would it really matter if she skipped his table? He probably wouldn't even notice.

She started toward Mayor Ed, intending to leave. She'd hand in her notes and give Ben's chocolate a score of ...

"Hello, Miss Maise. Or is it Mrs.?" Ben called out to her.

Her lips parted, and she spun to regard him.

That was his greeting? *That* was his question?

She squinted against the sickness in her throat and treated his remark with dull courtesy. "I'm not married."

She'd been engaged when she lived in Alaska, but had decided to break it off. Now, in her early thirties, love didn't come easy for her. Perhaps because she was commitment shy after her argumentative parents had finally divorced once Maise and her brothers had gone off to college.

"Good." He lifted a dark eyebrow. "Were you going somewhere and trying to skip me?"

She stepped to his table, heat flooding her face. "No, I … Well, yes." She sighed. "It's been a long day." She braced herself for his reprimand.

Instead, he offered a simple, tender smile. "Sorry. I've watched you since you walked in, and I wanted to chat."

So he had been watching her. Her cheeks warmed, and a thrill of excitement heightened her senses as he openly admired her.

"Then you have more than one intrusive question?" she asked.

Her reproof brought a smile to his lips. "Many more."

"May I ask a question too?"

"About me? Sure. I'm an open book."

"Are you married?"

"Divorced. Two years ago," he said quietly. "And a bachelor at thirty-five."

She hung back. *So he was single too.*

"I'm glad you're here," he went on. "Our town prides itself on its good taste." Ben laughed at his pun and Maise's heart did a surprising leap. He threw her totally off-balance, and the composure she'd desperately tried to maintain tumbled a notch.

"I was thrilled by the newspaper's generous job offer," she said.

"All this opportunity in one small California town." Again, she was taken aback by his fine features. His thick hair was a tad too long, those deep-set eyes a vivid blue, and he sported the physique of a well-toned athlete.

Maise stalled and took a sip of her coffee. "Will you explain your candy-making process, Ben?"

He shuffled his feet. "What would you like to know?"

"All the other contestants expounded on their delicious candy. I assumed you would do the same."

"I don't want to oversell my product."

"I find that remarkably refreshing and humble." With laughing relentlessness, she continued, "But I'm still interested."

"Would you like a piece of our shop's signature chocolate coffee fudge?" His gaze drifted to her lips, then to the cup she'd set on the corner of the table. His deep tone had a persuasive gentle quality. "I've noticed that you like coffee. Isn't that your second cup?"

"My third, if you count this morning." She pulled her gaze from his and stared at the cup, anything to delay eating another bite of candy.

She took another sip of coffee, and the most surprising thing happened. Here, amidst all this chocolate, her nausea seemed to dissipate, and she began to relax.

Was it the coffee? Or the man standing a few feet away, his gaze riveted on her?

Shakily, she chuckled. "I'll jot down your comments." Noting that his head drooped ever-so-slightly, she asked, "That is, if it's okay?"

"Of course." He avoided eye contact, or maybe she was imagining it.

"Good." She poised her pen on the notepad. "Can you begin by explaining your candy-making process?"

BEN FELT HIS MUSCLES TENSE. He wanted to answer her, but he couldn't follow through if her questions became too exacting.

"For instance," she was saying, "what are the exact ingredients in your signature chocolate coffee fudge?"

"Let me think about it." He swallowed hard, trying to remember what Gee, an excellent employee who had given his sister the recipe, had told him numerous times.

"Still thinking?" Maise prodded after a lengthy beat. Her enchanting features, a clear, porcelain complexion with a smattering of freckles, a pert, upturned nose, and her full pink lips holding a hint of a smile, made him hesitate.

Was she on to him?

Absolutely not. How could she be? They'd only just met.

He glanced at her profile as she scribbled on the notepad —the profile he'd admired ever since she entered the room. Her tall, slender figure was model-like, and her huge green eyes—enhanced by full black lashes and a touch of mischief —were magnificent.

A touch of mischief.

"What are you writing?" he asked, finally breaking the silence. "I haven't said anything."

"I'm writing my grocery list."

Her reply made him laugh.

"I'm still waiting," she reminded, pen poised on the notepad.

He wet his lips and combed through his mind for any details that might be helpful. "Well, our secret ingredient is … coffee."

"In coffee fudge, I wouldn't call coffee a secret ingredient."

"And marshmallows," he hastened to assure her. Gee had mentioned marshmallows in the recipe, hadn't she?

"Chocolate too, I suppose?"

"Yes, yes, of course." Ignoring Maise's furrowed eyebrows, he placed a chunk of fudge on a white lacy napkin and presented it to her. "The final test is in the tasting, don't you agree?"

She lowered her gaze and muttered something that sounded like, "I'm finally beginning to feel better, and I can't eat another piece of chocolate."

But she didn't look sick.

He reached across the table and lightly touched her arm. "The candy from Bloomingfield Candy Shop is the best. I genuinely believe that to be true."

"Which is through your perspective and therefore colored by your opinion?" She echoed his earlier remark. "Please clarify so that my readers will understand."

"Because our … chocolate chips are … sweet."

Her face glowed with laughter. "You mean semisweet?"

He squirmed. "Yes, yes, that's it." With an apologetic grin, he lifted the candy toward her. "Take a bite."

There was something about her over-bright smile that made him suspicious.

"You don't like chocolate, do you?"

A rosy blush stole up her cheeks, and she bent her head, shoving a wayward strand of thick chestnut hair behind her ear.

"You don't like chocolate?" he repeated. Desperately, he struggled to keep his features straight.

"Not today."

He crossed his arms. "A food critic judging a chocolate candy event who doesn't like chocolate."

"I said not today."

"What about tomorrow?"

She fumbled with her bag, her movements both graceful and endearingly awkward. "Two years ago, I had a bout of food poisoning after eating stinkhead and then topped the meal with chocolate for dessert. The memory stuck with me."

"What on earth is stinkhead?"

"It's the mushy fermented head of a king salmon and a delicacy in Alaska. I wrote a review of my experience in the Anchorage newspaper, minus the food-poisoning incident."

Despite her professional tone, her voice quivered. He had the uneasy feeling that he had somehow hit a nerve.

"So, the article wasn't a success?"

"That's putting it mildly." She bit on her lower lip and looked down at her hands.

"Look, I'm sorry about what I said earlier. Your review of my sister's restaurant has actually brought in more diners."

"Apology accepted." Slowly, the embarrassment drained from Maise's face.

Across the room, Mayor Ed was conversing with the other judges.

"Enough about me." Maise plunked her hands on her slim hips. "Let's have a heart-to-heart about you, Mr. Chocolatier. Admit that you have no idea what you're talking about."

"You discovered my secret." He chuckled with relief. "What I know about chocolate could fit into a peanut butter cup. I'm just the businessman who owns the shop. My sister, Sally, makes all the candy. I'm covering for her today, as her daughter is home sick. She's a single parent."

"So you have two sisters? Julie owns The Pasta Junction, and Sally runs Bloomingfield Candy Shop?"

"And a third, Katie, who is a lawyer." Ruefully, he shrugged. "I'm besieged by females."

Maise laughed. "In Alaska, I was surrounded by five brothers."

"So why did you leave?"

"Many reasons. You listened to one of them."

"I'd like to hear the others." Because he wanted to get to know her better.

"I started to lose my readership and credibility," she replied, "after patrons complained that a restaurant I wrote a glowing review for served sub-par food."

He heard the disheartened tone in her voice. "Don't take it to heart." He smiled as Gene Autry began singing again about knowing Dasher and Dancer and Prancer and Vixen.

"This song has been in the same loop at least nineteen times."

"Twenty by my count," Maise said.

"Are you feeling any better? Will you try a taste of my shop's signature chocolate?"

Hesitantly, she accepted his offering, then closed her eyes as she took a bite. Her eyes popped open. "Ben, this is delicious."

"It's my favorite."

"Mmm. I forgot how much I love the combination of coffee and chocolate."

"So, Bloomingfield Candy Shop gets a perfect score?"

"Are you trying to sway me? I'm the judge, you're the contestant." She wrote a number on her notepad, then leaned over the table and whispered, "Is there any way I can make a clean getaway?"

He nodded toward the exit and gave a cheerful wave to Ed, who eyed them warily.

"Thanks." Maise snatched another piece of coffee chocolate fudge, then stepped toward Ed. She handed him her notes, grabbed her blazer and umbrella, and studiously avoided Ben's gaze as she departed.

Still, he laughed when he saw that she'd finished his chocolate.

CHAPTER 2

Christmas Eve came a week later. As usual, Maise hadn't completed her shopping, because buying for five adult brothers and her parents was more than difficult.

It was impossible.

She parked her Volkswagen at the curb of Main Street and stepped out of the car, smoothing her red-and white-striped dress. California weather was mild, almost balmy, and she loved it.

She peered around. Hopefully, a few shops were open, and she'd know the right gift when she came upon it.

A sign in the window of Bloomingfield Candy Shop caught her attention.

Winner of the Women's Shelter Annual Fund-raiser for best candy. Come in for a free taste of flavor-rich fudge.

The shop's red canopied entrance welcomed her as she entered, and she admired the tin pails and decorative boxes tied with exquisite satin bows. The scents of high-quality hand-made chocolates combined with the aromas of butter, vanilla, and sugar. Truly, this shop was a chocolate lovers dream.

She'd pondered her conversation with Ben that day at the shelter. At first, she'd thought he was just schmoozing her to win her vote. But no, he'd been sincere. And besides, his candy had deserved to win.

"Maise!" A handsome, familiar man behind the counter greeted her as she stood at the end of a long line. When it was her turn, he quickly filled her order for seven boxes of chocolate.

"Do you ship to Alaska?" she asked.

"We ship all over the world."

"Can you put a rush on it? It's for my five brothers and my divorced parents who live separately."

"Chocolate is sent two-day air, so it won't be overexposed to the elements. However, your family won't receive the candy in time for Christmas."

"I always run behind. I'll call them on Christmas Day and explain."

Ben added a complimentary cup of hot chocolate and an extra box of signature fudge to her order and placed them on the counter.

"I'll help you drink the hot chocolate," he replied as she raised her eyebrows. "I wasn't supposed to be here tonight, but wanted to lend a hand because of the last-minute rush. My sister left a few minutes ago to be with her child. You just missed her."

"It's Christmas Eve and completely understandable."

He gazed at her for a long moment. Around them, the shop began closing down, and he bid his employees a joyful holiday.

He raised the cup of hot chocolate to her. "Merry Christmas, Maise."

"Merry Christmas, Ben."

"What are you doing this evening?"

"I'm attending a church service at the little chapel in town, then will order a pizza and going home."

"I'll accompany you." His infectious smile made her immediately agree. "But I planned to make a stop at a military service family's home. I'm a volunteer for the USO."

"Is that part of your small-town hero story?"

He nodded.

"I'm fascinated." She swallowed a sip of hot chocolate, then put the cup aside on the counter. "What do you do for the USO?"

"Anything and everything. I'm dedicated to our service members. But mostly, I provide a listening ear."

"Can I visit them with you?"

"I'd like that very much." He took an easy breath and placed her candy in a bag. "Afterward, we can dine at a distinguished Italian restaurant."

"And what's the name of this distinguished restaurant?"

"The Pasta Junction." He caught her hand and led her out the door. "My sister's restaurant stays open late on Christmas Eve."

Maise grinned. "Does she offer pizza?"

"Nope. But I have it on excellent authority that she serves a delicious antipasto."

THE END

A NOTE FROM JOSIE

Dear Friends,

Thank you for reading *A Chocolate-Box Christmas*.

I wanted to write a short, sweet holiday story centering around chocolate.

Please help other people find *A Chocolate-Box Christmas* by posting your review.

A Chocolate-Box Christmas is available in ebook, paperback, audiobook, and Large Print paperback.

I'd love to meet you in person someday, but in the meantime, all I can offer is a sincere and grateful thank you. Without your support, my books would not be possible.

As I write my next sweet or inspirational romance, remember this: Have you ever tried something you were afraid to try because it mattered so much to you? I did, when I started writing. Take the chance, and just do something you love.

Happy Reading!

My Spotify Play List for A Chocolate-Box Christmas is here.

With sincere appreciation,
Josie Riviera

Love sweet romance holiday stories?

Be sure to check out these book bundles:
    Holiday Hearts Volume One
    Holiday Hearts Volume Two
    Holiday Hearts Book Bundle Volume Three
    Holiday Hearts Volume Four

Want the individual books of the Chocolate-Box Series? Click here.

RECIPE FOR CHOCOLATE COFFEE FUDGE

From Gee's Kitchen

<u>Ingredients</u>

¼ cup freeze dried coffee granules (Can use decaf)

2/3 cup canned evaporated milk

½ cup (1 stick) butter

2 ounces baking bar chocolate – broken

1 ½ cups white granulated sugar

2 cups mini marshmallows

1 cup real chocolate chips (semisweet)

½ teaspoon vanilla extract

Prepare a rectangle cake pan lined with parchment paper or aluminum foil with enough overhang that you can lift fudge out for cutting. For thicker fudge use an 8 inch x 8 inch pan.

Large pot (or use a wok)

Place milk and coffee in pot over medium heat, stirring to dissolve the coffee.

Now add the butter, sugar, and baking chocolate with the pot on medium high heat and stir occasionally while they melt adding the marshmallows next. Bring contents to a boil and boil for 5 minutes stirring constantly.

Remove the pot from the heat and add the chocolate chips stirring to dissolve. Add the vanilla extract (it will bubble) stirring till glossy.

Pour into prepared pan and smooth top. Let set on a flat surface for an hour and then refrigerate.

Remove from refrigerator, lift up paper/foil and place on a cutting board. Cut into squares.

Store in an airtight container.

Don't forget to sample the crumbs.

Enjoy!

USA TODAY BESTSELLING AUTHOR

Josie Riviera

a Chocolate-Box New Years

PRAISE AND AWARDS

USA TODAY bestselling author

Top 100 Amazon Bestseller Clean and Wholesome Romance (Books)

Top 100 Amazon Bestseller Holiday Fiction (Books)

CHAPTER 1

In the intricate process of making fresh pasta, the dough has to be kneaded, rolled, and then sliced. Every morning Julie Elliot made the flour and egg base, portioned it, and stored it in her cooler. In this way, she could quickly create satisfying meals for her customers, which was of utmost importance in the restaurant business.

Consequently, it made sense that her linguine and fettuccini were the starring attractions of her Italian restaurant, The Pasta Junction. She liked that, being celebrated for her delectable pasta versus the parboil method other restaurants used.

As expected, many rival chefs told her she was foolish, because preparing pasta every day required a tremendous amount of effort. She realized that and was okay with it. She'd set her standards high and strove to serve her diners only the finest products.

On a typical busy Friday evening in mid-December, she stood by the commercial cooktop of her kitchen's workstation and stirred an enormous pot of minestrone soup. When she finished, she'd chat with patrons in the dining room. She loved people, loved interacting with them. Loved it so much, in fact, her older brother, Ben, often called her an extrovert. As a business owner, that was a good thing. Striking up conversations and conversing with her customers kept them coming back.

Because she didn't stay in the kitchen all night, she made sure she looked attractive and professional. Tonight, she'd pulled her heavy blond tresses into a tight bun, and wore her usual black slacks and a fitted collared blouse. As always, she'd tied a white apron around her slender waist.

She lowered the fire under the soup so it would simmer, then swung to the stainless steel counter to sort green beans. After a few minutes of discarding the beans that weren't fresh, she paused to scan the other workstations. In an adjacent corner a newbie created salads. Nearby, a grill cook prepared chicken dishes. He held his tongs and grill brushes high, flicking dashes of red pepper and sea salt onto the sizzling chicken.

Her gaze traveled to Antonio, the sous chef, who stood across from her. His bald head was covered by a pleated white toque hat—starched, round, and ten inches high—and a white coat. Antonio subscribed to a kitchen hierarchy and believed the head chef should wear the tallest hat, and he took his job very seriously. As she observed him, he flash-fried shrimp in garlic butter, tossing the mixture with a flamboyance rivaling any celebrity chef.

With a tolerant smile, she began snapping the stems off the beans.

Certainly homemade pasta, homemade anything, really, was twice the effort, and her employees often struggled to keep up with orders on fast-paced nights. But it was worth it.

With a sigh, she blew a wisp of hair off her forehead.

Or was it?

Earlier in the evening, a part-time employee had quit

with no notice, and Julie had asked—okay, begged—a member of her prep team to put in a double shift. Not long afterward, a server spilled olive oil on a woman's silk dress, a cook burned his fingers on a steamer, and a waiter tripped over a loose wire in the foyer, dropping an armload of ceramic dishes that had crashed to the floor and shattered into hundreds of pieces.

A glance at her watch prompted her to wryly shake her head. Quite an eventful evening, considering it was only seven o'clock. Already exhausted with an impending headache, she scraped up an armful of beans, intending to rinse them in cold water to remove any dust and dirt.

The phone buzzed, and Julie frowned. No one in the front of the house called the back unless there was a problem.

She set down the beans, snapped off her sanitary gloves, and answered the phone. "Yes?"

"A guy on line three insists on speaking with you," the hostess said.

"We're in the middle of the dinner hour and swamped with orders."

"It's Lorenzo Rossi."

"The meteorologist from the six o'clock news? Why? Is he forecasting another thunderstorm?" Julie asked. "Two weeks ago he panicked the entire community when he raised an alarm about a dangerous storm with potential flood warning, and his forecast was incorrect. We closed early, and the storm bypassed our area."

"Give him credit. He gets the weather right some of the time." The hostess giggled, which was odd. Usually, she was proper and polite, but Julie attributed the giggling to the fact that Lorenzo Rossi was drop-dead gorgeous.

"Shall I tell him to phone back after we close at ten?" the hostess suggested.

Rapidly, Julie considered her options.

Perhaps he was calling to promote her restaurant on TV? After The Pasta Junction's recent less-than-stellar review by the new food critic in Bloomingfield, the positive endorsement from Lorenzo might be a bonus.

"Put him through," Julie said.

"Anything you say, boss."

Julie grinned and accepted the call.

"Julie Elliot?" Lorenzo's voice was deep and familiar, sounding exactly like the man she watched at the end of the day on the television station's website. Instantly, her mind conjured up his handsome face, the black wavy hair and his vivid blue eyes. Similar to his fellow newsmen who wore sport coats and dress pants, Lorenzo clicked it up a notch and wore classic, three-piece suits. And his tone—strong and masculine, with a slight Italian accent.

Julie cupped the phone to her ear. "Yes, this is she."

"My name is Lorenzo Rossi."

"What can I do for you, Mr. Rossi?"

"I'm calling about New Year's Day. Your restaurant is one of the few places in town that are open."

"Christmas and New Years are special occasions. I'm happy to give families and friends the opportunity to dine out together." Plus, the decision to remain open on those holidays had proved profitable. "We'd love to have you join us here at The Pasta Junction. I'll switch you back to the hostess to make a reservation."

"I'd like to book a first-wedding-anniversary dinner."

"The front desk will confirm the number of people in your party."

"Also, I want to serve a special dessert, my grandma Gloria's Italian Cassata."

"My pastry chef can accommodate you." Although the chef had recently quit too, and the restaurant had begun outsourcing their desserts. She didn't have the heart to tell Mr. Rossi that bit of news. She didn't have the heart to tell herself it would cost $2000 to train a new chef.

"Do you know what a cassata is?"

Julie bristled. "A cassata is an Italian cheesecake."

"You're recognized for making genuine homemade pasta."

"Correct."

"Because of your commitment to authenticity, I expect you'll be able to replicate my grandmother's cassata recipe."

"Can you supply us with the recipe, Mr. Rossi?"

"Gladly." Silence prevailed for a beat. "I remember her cheesecake overflowed with chocolate. May I set up an appointment to discuss it?"

He requested an appointment to discuss a cheesecake?

She stared at the phone. "Certainly."

"Excellent," he said. "People rave about your professionalism."

"That's our motto. Professionalism."

Now why had she professed such a thing? Professionalism wasn't the motto, although it was a goal she tried hard to achieve.

However, he could easily reserve online, and email her the recipe. She told him as much, giving him the restaurant's website.

"I've checked it, but I'd still like to meet with you."

Julie's gaze wandered to Antonio as he chopped garlic for another shrimp dinner. An overabundance of garlic would overpower the meal, she thought. Frazzled, she cradled the phone and took a step forward to stop him.

"Miss Elliot?"

Julie nodded into the phone, a silly gesture because Mr. Rossi couldn't see it. "Yes?"

"Will tomorrow morning be agreeable? I need to be at the television studio by noon."

"Mornings are best for me too." *And he apparently wasn't giving her any choice.* Still, she prided herself on excellent customer service and quickly agreed. He expected professionalism, and she would comply.

"Nine o'clock?" he asked.

"Sure. I'll show you several catering menus, and you can choose which meal will suit your party best."

"Thank you, Miss Elliot." He hesitated. "I assume it's Miss—"

"It is." She'd never married, never really dated, except the one occasion when she'd fallen hard for a guy who'd made it a habit to dine alone at her restaurant. He'd flirted with her, and at first she'd enjoyed the attention. Then she'd found out he was married and studiously ignored him until he'd gotten the hint and not come around anymore.

A two-timer. A cheater. No thank you.

Nowadays she was wed to her work, anyway. She kept the barrier shielding her heart intact and secure. Getting involved with a man had proven to be a bad idea.

"Please call me Julie, Mr. Rossi," she said.

"Thank you, Julie, and Mr. Rossi is too formal. I'm Lorenzo."

"See you in the morning, Lorenzo. Remember to bring your grandmother's recipe."

After assuring that he would, he thanked her and hung up.

For a minute she was quiet, ignoring the chattering cooks and hurried footsteps as they scurried through the wide kitchen.

So the gorgeous Lorenzo Rossi was celebrating his first wedding anniversary? As far as she knew, he'd never revealed anything about his personal life on television, but then, why would he? To her knowledge, his marriage hadn't been announced in the local newspaper, either.

Naturally, his career was forecasting the weather, often-times focusing on catastrophic events. California's severe storms and the ever-present threat of wildfires had lately made headline news.

But there were times when his forecasts were light-hearted. She recalled one particular forecast when the temperatures on his weather map were in the negatives—minus 50 degrees Fahrenheit in Anaheim, minus 75 in Los Angeles. Lorenzo had kept his cool, (literally), smiling and pointing out the temperatures with a quip.

"Folks, you may wish to bundle up if you're traveling to these cities today, as well as bring an extra stockpile of gloves. I wouldn't plan on getting my car washed in either place, and I'm anticipating school will be canceled." He'd laughed. "Or better yet, just wait until the spring thaw."

He'd thought quickly and on his feet during the live broadcast. He evidently had a sense of humor.

Grinning with the remembrance, she scooped up the beans and carried them to the sink.

There must be a reasonable explanation why Lorenzo Rossi requested a meeting in person, rather than an online reservation. Surely, this wasn't because of a cheesecake recipe.

Either way, a wonderful surprise was in store for the undoubtedly stunning Mrs. Rossi. Lorenzo was apparently a thoughtful husband who planned ahead, intending to create a perfect anniversary for his wife.

Julie smiled. The wedded bliss of newlyweds was a fanciful prospect. Too bad falling in love was something she never intended to do again. The sting of a disastrous rela-tionship was too great a price to bear.

CHAPTER 2

The following morning, Julie entered The Pasta Junction an hour later than she'd intended. She'd scheduled an interview for a new hire at eight and then planned to review vast amounts of paperwork with her manager before Lorenzo arrived.

Because of her lateness, she'd canceled both the interview and the paperwork review. The previous evening's disasters had required her to remain at the restaurant until well past midnight.

When her alarm woke her at half past seven, she'd hastily showered, dressed in her customary black blouse and slacks, then tugged on a pair of skid-resistant work shoes. Around her neck she tied an emerald-green silk scarf, flicking the lace edging over her shoulder. She styled her hair in pin curls and finger waves, dusted translucent powder on her face, then added dark mascara and red lipstick.

She rushed through the rain into the restaurant, shaking the raindrops from her slick yellow jacket and signature black fedora. She hung both on a coat rack. She'd don the fedora later that evening when she chatted with guests.

Tonight she intended to devote only a few minutes to the kitchen. Large crowds energized her, and reservations were at a max. This was typical for a Saturday, and since this was the holiday season, people were on vacation and eating out more often with family and friends.

She stepped through the silent dining room and quickly arranged pink roses in bud vases, placing one at each table. She'd kept the festive décor to a tasteful minimum—fragrant evergreens draped on the fireplace mantel, and tiny colored lights along the stairwell. She'd preserved an old world Italian atmosphere, complete with classic white tablecloths and huge murals of Italy's countryside. Scenic Tuscany vineyards exuded true European charm.

The Pasta Junction had had several name changes throughout its half century and recently had been declared a Bloomingfield historic landmark.

At this hour, the space was quiet. The servers had set up the tables the night before for the luncheon crowd, and the doors would open at eleven o'clock.

She ducked into the kitchen and brewed a pot of coffee, noting the burrs had begun to dull, a reminder the commercial coffee grinder needed repair.

Money was tight, though. Despite the extra traffic, the additional staffing during the holidays came with a price tag.

As she did every morning, she went through the leftover pasta and made a mental note to donate it to the local charity.

Delicious food, particularly pasta, was an obsession of hers, and through the years she'd perfected her craft. Nothing beat the thrill of her customers' compliments and return visits, the smiles on their faces when they experienced the light, delicate flavor of her specialty fettuccini. She was passionate about her work and enjoyed adding new dishes. Sometimes she started with a recipe, sometimes only an idea, and followed her instincts as often as any written directions.

Nonetheless, a continuous loss of product and thus, revenue, was a growing concern. She had costed out the ingredients and knew she was financially ahead by making her own pasta. However, a waitress had told her that several patrons had walked out the evening before because of the over-long wait. That had been happening too much lately, and Julie rebuked herself. She'd been too busy and was ignoring her staff's feedback.

She began boxing the leftover pasta, trying to understand why she was so driven. Pasta making was not only time-consuming, it was a risky venture. Her updated waste log pinpointed the main revenue problem was the pasta, along with her sous chef over-ordering fresh garlic, which often went bad. And come January, when business slowed, she frequently faced difficulty meeting payroll.

But for the month of December, profits were excellent.

With a satisfied sigh, she dismissed her reservations and plucked a marinated shrimp from the reach-in cooler. A whiff of garlic pinched her nostrils. Just as she feared, the sous chef was overpowering the food with garlic. As she placed the shrimp on a plate to sample later, a glob of congealed butter landed on her blouse.

"Oh, no," she muttered. Rushing to the sink, she snatched a clean towel and moistened it with water. A hard scrub on the grease mark soon left a prominent wet stain. She fanned the stain, trying to recall if she had a spare blouse at the restaurant, or if she had the time to go home and change before lunch.

The doorbell jingled, and she peered at her watch.

Lorenzo? Already? She washed her hands, hastened to the foyer and opened the door.

It was indeed him, standing on the steps, prompting her heart to do an unexpected flip.

Why this strange reaction? She was familiar with his appearance. But in person? Well, that was another story entirely.

He was easily over six feet tall, slim, and wonderfully fit. She'd heard television added pounds to a person's frame. In his case, he looked exactly the same.

"Julie?" He snapped his umbrella closed, then removed his eyeglasses and tucked them into the pocket of his worn leather jacket.

"Yes. Hello, Lorenzo. Please come in." He was early, but she wasn't going to hold that against him, a wet spot on her blouse or not. She admired punctuality, although she was seriously lacking in that department. She rationalized it was because she tried to do too much by herself and refused to delegate.

"Thank you." He stepped into the flagstone-tiled foyer and looked around, his gaze settling on the chalkboard where she wrote the day's specialties. Fettuccini was always on the board, as were the two entrees from the previous night: a creamy risotto and veal flank steak with red-hot peppers.

He considered the restaurant's interior. Then his gaze rested on Julie's face. "Nice." He beamed his approval. He didn't seem to notice the conspicuous stain.

She flushed.

"Everything exceeds my expectations. You run a highly professional establishment."

She shifted, avoiding his stare to hide her discomfiture. He'd been referring to the restaurant and not her when he'd said *nice.*

She ushered him to a table by the mullioned window where he stood while she hunted for the catering menus. Not only was she not exuding professionalism, she hadn't had time to prepare properly for their meeting.

Thrilled to find the menus on a vacant chair, she displayed them. "You've never dined here before?"

"The opportunity never came up, although a number of my friends eat here often and sing your praises. Your website is excellent too, and extremely user friendly. I thoroughly checked every detail." It was on the tip of her tongue to ask him why he hadn't used her website to book his reservation, but then he grinned and continued, "You're much prettier in person than the picture of you on your website."

This time his flattery was specifically meant for her. She took a moment to digest his compliment and decided the best response was a simple "Thank you."

In any case, her photo on The Pasta Junction's website was a few years old. Lorenzo might be admiring her, but in truth he was probably disillusioned upon seeing her in person.

She was ten years younger in the photo which had been taken when she'd first purchased the restaurant. She'd worn a form-fitting white dress, her makeup professionally done to emphasize her blue eyes, her face powdered to a porcelain finish. Her trademark fedora hat was slanted to one side.

"Blond hair, expressive eyes ..." Lorenzo was saying. "And your old-school Hollywood style is lovely. You exude understated elegance."

Hold on. Had he said lovely? Understated elegance?

Yes, both. He'd said both. *The charisma of an Italian man.*

She considered setting him in his place once and for all. Compliments were appreciated, but he was married. Hastily, she reminded herself that this was a business meeting, and he was a customer.

Keep the conversation efficient and quick.

"My restaurant has been open for ten years," she replied. "That's an old photo of me on the website."

"You haven't changed."

Her cheeks were most likely flaming scarlet by now, shining through the translucent powder. She smoothed her shirt, adjusted the collar. "Hardly."

"And I can't believe I've never dined here," he said.

She offered a polite smile. He reciprocated the smile, then shifted to stare out the window at passing traffic. Across the street, a sparkly gold Christmas angel hanging on a lamppost whipped in a gust of wind.

The restaurant was located in a revitalized area of Bloomingfield that featured, among other attractions, a café, bookstore and antique shop. All the buildings were brick, and a steepled white church and covered bridge in the distance completed the idyllic small-town atmosphere.

"Is that yours?" She gestured to a sporty SUV parked in front of her restaurant.

"Yes."

The SUV looked brand new. Evidently, he was generously paid at the television station.

He seemed to notice her appraisal of him, of the car, and pounced on an explanation. "Any degree of success in the broadcasting arena comes with a tall ladder to climb."

She nodded. They both stared outdoors again.

The weather was a typical morning in winter—chilly, windy and rainy. Julie didn't mind. She liked the rain, the scent of wet leaves and grass, the coolness of a clean breeze. Besides, in California the sunshine was likely to stream through the clouds before the day was over.

While Lorenzo stood quiet, she studied his profile—his straight nose and well-carved features. He could have stepped out of a Tuscany painting, and she visualized him laboring in a vineyard, his face streaked with dirt. Beneath his polished television exterior and three-piece suits, there was definitely a ruggedness that went beyond his solid masculinity.

She gave herself a firm mental scolding. What was she doing, fantasizing about a married man?

She yanked her thoughts back to the present and to business.

An eye-catching weatherman who fluttered hearts every night on television might attract other women, but this man was entirely off limits.

"I forgot my manners." His gaze shifted from the window to her and he extended his hand. "I appreciate you taking an hour out of your hectic schedule."

She wiped her hands on her slacks, hoping the garlic odor had been washed away, and accepted his handshake. His fingers were warm and strong and strangely callused for a man who worked indoors and studied weather charts.

"I'm delighted to help you plan your special event," she said with a smile.

Something glimmered in his gaze, and he held her hand for a second longer than she expected. "A successful woman like yourself must be extremely busy this time of year."

Wow, he was an enchanter.

"I am, and I'm grateful for the busyness." The feel of his hand stirred a tingling sensation, and she yanked it away. She kept her smile, but refined it to a cool and distant one. "Will you take coffee, Lorenzo? Or cappuccino?"

He shrugged off his jacket and draped it over a chair. "Is your coffee served with a traditional flaky pastry like they serve in Italy?"

"I didn't know flaky pastries were customary there." His question sidetracked her. "Have you ever visited?"

"Often. I inherited an ancient ancestral home in Calitri.

My parents moved to America when I was quite young. They are Italian immigrants."

"Your home must be beautiful."

"A century ago, it probably was. Now, the stone is decaying, and it's no longer livable, so I purchased a modest apartment in the center of town." He gazed at her. "Have you ever visited Italy?" he asked again.

"No. Hopefully, someday."

"Someday." He smiled. "Someday, we all hope to accomplish a great many things."

What, exactly, did that mean? Did he have dreams he hadn't yet fulfilled, or was he referring to people in general? Or her?

No, definitely not her. He hardly knew her.

"Well, do you?" he was asking.

"Do I what?"

"Have any flaky pastries on hand?"

Not until she hired the new pastry chef, she almost told him. Instead, she answered, "Today I'm serving biscotti with your coffee." Fortunately, the restaurant had a score of the crunchy almond cookies packed airtight in the kitchen.

His thoughtful gaze continued to study her, and she self-consciously twirled a pin curl.

He grinned. "I'll stick with coffee Americano, though I expect your biscotti is delicious."

Yes, definitely a charmer.

An awkward beat passed. "Sugar and cream?" she asked.

"Black."

"Me too." She set down the menus. In the kitchen, she poured two cups of coffee and brought them to the table.

"Are you interested in seeing the separate room we use for parties?" She nodded toward the cocktail lounge. "It's decorated the same as the main dining room."

"Nope. I'm sure it's ideal." He was standing precisely

where she'd left him. His jeans looked faded and the gray T-shirt, emblazoned with the words Trust Me, I Know Everything About the Weather, enhanced his muscled, tanned physique.

"I love the smell of coffee," he said softly.

She swallowed and offered a brief affirmation. His manner was unassuming, his compelling blue eyes bringing to mind an impossibly blue sky. And interest. Unmistakable interest.

Why? Wasn't this a celebratory dinner for his wife?

The knowledge gave Julie pause, and she stepped back. Charmer or not, this type of man wasn't at all to her liking.

She placed the coffees on the table and slid onto a wooden chair.

He grabbed a seat across from her and sipped his coffee. "Excellent. You can always determine the quality of a restaurant by the coffee."

"Among other things," she murmured.

"Needless to say, the meal is important too."

"And the atmosphere."

"Right."

"And the freshness of the food."

"Point taken." He held up his hands. "I summarized the entire restaurant business to a cup of coffee, when there's plenty more to consider." He leaned forward. "Care to enlighten me on the successful approach to running a restaurant? From personal knowledge, it's an expensive venture."

"You owned a restaurant?" she asked.

Feigning interest in the crystal salt and pepper shakers in the middle of the table, he replied, "Nothing hands-on."

Was he making small talk? How much should she elaborate, because she could converse for hours about her restaurant.

"I'm interested in creating fine cuisine." She steepled her

fingers. "I leave the actual operation to my accounting manager. He specializes in the food industry, and before I employed him my invoices were a muddled mess. Attention to detail isn't my forte."

"I'm all about detail, which is why I'm here."

"I understand." She slid the menus across the table. "Please take a look. We offer numerous selections to accommodate the most discerning diner, at a cost suitable for every budget."

"You sound like a commercial."

"I'm a businesswoman."

He took a swallow of coffee, and so did she. His gaze skimmed the menus before he set them aside. "Why don't you choose?"

"Me?" She eyed him over the rim of her cup. "I don't presume to know your tastes."

"Probably not in food," he replied. "But you can make an educated guess about my other tastes."

Surely he wasn't coming on to her again.

Ignoring his remark, she pointedly stacked the menus from appetizer to entrees and pushed them back toward him. "I suggest trays of meatballs, baked chicken, and pasta for your main dishes."

"Whatever you think best."

"Or you might prefer a plated sit-down, which is more expensive. However, then each guest can choose whichever entrée they wish."

He shook his head. "Let's avoid the whole perusal of the menu thing."

Perusal of the menu thing? Wasn't he planning this dinner?

Julie kept her chin high. "May I ask why?"

"All that negotiating—who's ordering which entrée and side dishes—takes time."

"Perhaps consider a limited menu with fewer selections?"

Another head shake. "Too distracting."

"Part of the fun of going out to eat is the cuisine choices."

"For me, the importance of a meal is family and friends sharing the experience together." His sincere smile revealed the dimple on his chin, and her heart did a turn. She almost excused herself to scurry into the kitchen so that she could draw a deep breath and collect herself.

Whenever she'd watched his weather reports, she assumed the camera, lighting, and makeup enhanced his good looks. He couldn't be *that* attractive in person.

But he was.

His thick black hair was shiny, with glints of golden brown at the temples. The warmth in his tone as he talked about friends and family prompted her to nod her head in agreement. Time spent with the people you loved was what mattered most.

His reply was a lazy smile.

Her cheeks burned, and she tamped down the hazardous leap in her pulse. She was staring at him with an expression befitting a sixteen-year-old.

She sat straighter and focused on the stack of menus. *All right, Mr. handsome Two-Timing Meteorologist. Back to business.*

"How about a buffet?" she suggested. "We can serve the typical Italian fare of meatballs in a marinara sauce, a tray of my signature fettuccini, sausage and peppers, baked chicken, and garlic bread." She numbered the selections with her fingers. "That way, no one needs to spend a second on any food decisions. We'll set up the buffet on a side table and guests can help themselves."

His gaze flicked over the menus. "Sounds good." For a guy so focused on details, her list of options didn't seem to hold his attention for long. "Don't forget Grandma Gloria's cassata for dessert."

"Did you bring the recipe?"

"Indeed." He reached into his jacket pocket and handed her a folded sheet of paper. "I'd never forget such an important feature of the party."

Along with his stunning wife, Julie thought. She darted a glance at his left hand. He wasn't wearing a wedding band, but many men didn't, and he'd mentioned he was reporting to the television studio afterwards. Perhaps he had a rule of not wearing jewelry on the air.

Or perhaps he was a double-crossing cad who flirted with women regardless of his marital status.

She unfolded the yellowed paper and perused the directions. Nothing too difficult. In fact, the recipe called for a basic cake mix found in any supermarket. Nonetheless, everything was handwritten, and the ingredients were listed in vague amounts. Her kind of recipe, without numerous restrictions.

"Offhand, do you know how many people the recipe serves?" she asked.

"You're the cook."

"Haven't you eaten this dessert before?"

He sighed and rubbed a hand on his heart. "When I was young, I remember my grandmother preparing the cheesecake for special family occasions."

He didn't answer her question, but Julie let it pass.

His cell phone buzzed, and he pulled it out of his pocket and looked at the caller ID. With an apology to Julie for the interruption, he answered the call.

"Hey, yes, Regina, I'm meeting with the owner right now." Lorenzo laughed. "I don't have a crystal ball, only Doppler radar, so I can't answer your weather question. I'll text you later. *Ciao.*" He disconnected, tucked the phone into his pocket and gave a rueful shrug. "That was my sister joking about my storm prediction last month."

"You mean the storm that never materialized?"

He glanced out the window, then back at her. "Aren't you glad I was wrong?"

"Absolutely, but …your warning flashed across my phone screen and unnerved me. I debated whether to close my restaurant or remain open."

"I take it you didn't close?"

She bit back a smirk. "No, but I did close early."

"Wait." He grinned. "You subscribe to my weather app?"

"Doesn't everyone in town? Your presence is well known."

A flicker of annoyance, or something she couldn't determine, caused him to look away. "I've asked the television station to ease up on advertising, but the studio managers are obsessed with high ratings. I can't argue. They're right about social media."

"I focus my advertising on the newspaper and my website," Julie said.

"You're missing limitless opportunities. Technology is the key to a successful operation, including a restaurant."

"You seem to know a lot about the restaurant business."

"Some." His tone became subdued. "Regarding technology and my forecasting, I heed the advice of my station managers. They're the experts."

She propped her chin on her hands. "You're admitting that your breathless melodramas during storm coverages are over hyped?"

"Whoa, you get right to the point."

"Twice, I almost closed because of your severe storm watch. You made it sound as if disaster was imminent, and I should rush to the grocery store and purchase all the bottled water on the shelves." She kept her posture rigid. "The first time, I actually did. This time, I thought better."

"So you disregarded my forecast." His voice deepened. "Why would you put your patrons in danger?"

"A watch means a storm *may* occur."

"Very good. And a warning means conditions are imminent. So again, why not heed a meteorologist's advice?"

"Because you tend to be wrong more than you're right." She twisted a button on her sleeve. "I'm sorry, I didn't mean to sound negative. We joke about your forecasts … sometimes."

"You joke …" Through narrowed eyes, he studied her. "Who are *we*?"

"Employees, friends, family—"

"On a seven-day forecast, I'm right 80 percent of the time."

"How about a five-day forecast?"

He took a gulp of coffee. "Ninety percent."

"Ten-day?"

"Now you're pushing it." He leaned back and folded his arms. "I'm right half the time on a ten-day. Long-range forecasts are challenging because there are numerous variables." He peered at his watch. "At any rate, I'm not here to discuss the weather."

"And your forecast for today is …?"

He grinned and gestured outside, where raindrops bucketed down. "Rainy."

She shared his grin and then, reminding herself there was business to be discussed, asked if the people coming to the dinner were local.

"My sister Regina lives here in Bloomingfield. Be prepared, though." He grimaced. "Her twin girls, Ella and Emma, are adorable but mischievous."

"I can handle mischievous."

"How about energetic?"

"That too. How old are the girls?"

"Seven." He rolled his eyes. "Their favorite activities are jumping off things and chasing each other."

Julie laughed. "Typical child behavior. So how many people in your party, total?"

"There's Regina, my brother-in-law, and their twin daughters, and my brother John in Wyoming. He's not married. Altogether," Lorenzo finished, "we're eight people. That includes my mother and her husband, of course."

"Of course." Julie skimmed the recipe again. "The cassata recipe is manageable, plus it gives me leeway."

"Leeway to do what?"

"Leeway to experiment." Noting his frown, she continued, "I'll double the recipe to ensure there'll be enough for every-one, and extra to take home."

"I'd like a replica."

"Yes, so you've said. I'll do my best," Julie replied. "Just as there are variables in predicting the weather, the same holds true for baked goods. Cassata consists of ricotta cheese and chocolate and cherries, and these ingredients react differ-ently to oven temperatures. In fact, sometimes it all boils down to what factory the boxed cake mix came from."

"If you measure every ingredient exactly, it should taste the same as my grandmother's."

She pointed to the scribbles on the recipe. "A pinch of this and a little of that isn't exact. Besides, each person's taste isn't the same. Baking is subjective."

"Baking is all about measuring the ingredients correctly and accurately," he said. "Unfortunately, my mother wasn't much of a baker and always failed to recreate her mother's prized dessert. Fortunately, you are an excellent cook."

He didn't know that for certain. He hadn't even eaten at her restaurant. He just assumed she was a good cook because her restaurant was successful.

She shifted. "Is your grandmother still alive?"

"Sadly, no. She passed many years ago. She never spoke a word of English and insisted I only speak Italian when I was with her." He offered a stoic shrug. "When you lose someone special in your life, you come to realize you miss them more with each passing day."

"A dear cousin of mine moved away," Julie responded. "We used to go to the cinema together on Monday afternoon."

"What did you see?" he asked.

"See where?"

"At the cinema. What were your favorite movies?"

"You probably never heard of them."

"Try me."

"Just black and white films. Filled with flashbacks and stark lighting."

Slowly, he nodded. "Film noir."

"You recognize the term?"

"Certainly. I like it too. The run-down Grover Theater features those old movies."

"I haven't been there since my cousin moved away."

He caught her gaze and held it. "Sometimes film noir movies are pessimistic."

"Sometimes not." She savored her coffee. Even cold, it was good. "Usually, the heroes are cynical."

"Do you like cynical heroes?"

"I prefer guys who are genuinely good, honest, and sincere." Although she hadn't met a man with those qualities and oftentimes wondered if such a man truly existed.

She flashed a glimpse at Lorenzo, who was considering her intently. Another reason why she had pledged not to date again. Because of two-timing cads like him.

And yet, her endless hours devoted to her restaurant had led to worried discussions with her brother, Ben, and her sisters, Sally and Katie, who had all told Julie her apartment was too lonely. She'd placated their concerns by promising to get a dog, although when a dog might happen was beyond her.

Maybe when the new year started …

"All the actors in film noir movies are smokers," Lorenzo wrapped his hands around his coffee cup. Sturdy and firm hands, she noticed. "Do you?"

"Do I smoke? I own a cigarette holder. Does that count?"

He laughed. "Nope."

"Then no." She shook her head. "You?"

"Not me, although my grandmother did. I remember spending rainy afternoons baking with her. She'd take a cigarette break every so often, and she always smoked outdoors no matter the weather. The aromas of chocolate and cherries coming from her kitchen when her cassata was in the oven are some of my best memories."

"Along with cigarette smoke?' Julie teased.

"Chesterfield."

"I had an aunt who smoked Chesterfield cigarettes too."

She paused, considering the pensive look on his face before he regarded the yellowed recipe. It seemed as if he sought to replicate the joyful times he'd spent with his grandmother, the satisfying aromas and pleasant feelings, and not the actual cheesecake.

Julie kept the thought to herself, although it was becoming clear that the recipe's relevance to this anniversary was no coincidence.

"This cassata is important to me," he said, "because it's important to my mother. I want it to be perfect for her. She went through a lot when my father died, and she's finally found happiness."

"I'm glad for her," Julie said, puzzled.

"Me too." Again, he smiled. Again, his blue eyes glinted with undisguised attraction.

And again, she stiffened. The eyes, the flirty smile. Where was he going with this?

Good-natured laughter sounded from the kitchen, meaning the waitstaff was arriving.

She tapped her heels, then pushed back her chair and stood.

Lorenzo came instantly to his feet. "I want to taste the cassata you bake before the actual event."

"I assumed so. However, my waking hours between now and the beginning of January are jam-packed."

Briefly, he touched her arm. Again, the tingle. Again, she pulled back.

"I'll pay you for your efforts," he said. "I don't expect you to work for free."

She picked up the menus. "It's not so much the money, it's the time."

"I'm hoping you can squeeze me into your schedule."

Right.

His statement began with a hope, but sounded suspiciously like a demand.

With a sigh, she mulled over their mutual interest in film noir, black coffee, their shared fondness of fine food. And sure, the Chesterfield cigarettes.

"Less than two weeks before New Year's ..." she muttered, half to herself.

"I'm visiting my mother and stepfather in Wyoming for Christmas. They live near my brother and the big excitement of the trip is the holiday concert with the Wyoming Symphony Orchestra. We're all big symphony lovers."

"I love full orchestras. Over a decade ago, I played the violin." Now why was she telling him more personal information about herself? If she spent another minute with this man, she'd be pouring out her life story.

"I was first chair trumpet in the high school band," he said.

"Are you bragging?"

He laughed. "No. Well, yes, maybe I was, but by my senior year I became more fascinated by the weather than the band. So I quit, much to my music teacher's dismay." He kept her gaze. "You?"

"Much the same, although my teacher was probably thrilled because I hardly ever practiced. By then, my attention shifted to fine cuisine and experimenting with recipes."

"It seems we share a number of commonalities."

She forced herself to keep her attention on the menus clutched in her hand.

"At any rate," he went on, "I'll be back in Bloomingfield the day after Christmas. May I contact you then?"

"Phone the restaurant to schedule a taste test, but allow me a few hours' lead time."

If he caught on that her reply was evasive he made no mention, nor did he press for her personal cellphone number.

"I'll look forward to our first cassata sampling together," he said.

"First?"

"Unless you get it right."

"I will."

He smiled. "We'll see."

She walked him to the front door, and he gestured to her fedora, still drying on the coat rack. "Fine hat."

"Thanks."

"Well, Merry Christmas, Julie." With a nod, he departed.

"Merry Christmas, Lorenzo," she said as the door swung closed behind him.

She'd spend another lonely Christmas working. He'd

settle in at the symphony, listening to classical music and relaxing with his family and wife.

CHAPTER 3

The perfect dessert.

Julie grabbed an oven mitt and removed an exquisitely baked cassata from the oven. Pleased with herself, she eyed the smooth, even texture as she set it on the stainless-steel cooktop in her restaurant's kitchen.

It was the Monday after Christmas, the only day The Pasta Junction was closed. Although weary from the flow of never-ending diners on Christmas Eve and Christmas Day, she was satisfied. Profits were excellent, and her employees had been pleased with big-hearted tips from customers and the year-end bonus Julie annually presented. She and her staff were a team, and the addition of several new waiters had lessened the job strain.

However, the search for a proficient pastry chef had yielded no results, and she continued to outsource her desserts to a local bakery.

To be sure, Lorenzo would have none of it.

With a quiet groan, she reflected on their last phone conversation. He'd rung the restaurant on Christmas Eve, apparently timing his call for when she closed at ten o'clock.

"I wanted to wish you a Merry Christmas, Julie," he said. "Will you be able to spend any time with your family?"

"My brother, Ben, and Maise stopped in for a late dinner tonight. She's a new food editor in town, and Ben co-owns Bloomingfield Candy Shop, along with my sister Sally. Their shop won first place in a chocolate contest."

"Yes, I remember reading the article in the newspaper."

"If you're ever in the market for the finest chocolate in Bloomingfield, be sure to visit."

"Chocolate is a weakness of mine, and so is ..." She waited, half-expecting him to rattle off his favorite fudge flavor, but silence sat in the open and he didn't elaborate.

Naturally, they chatted about the weather and then the holiday, before the subject veered to Lorenzo's upcoming party.

"I'll arrive in Bloomingfield the day after Christmas," he said. "Can we arrange a time to meet?"

"To taste test the cassata, you mean."

"Right."

"It might be better to assign the cassata to a true baker," she said. "I'm in the process of looking for a pastry chef. In the meantime, the bakery my restaurant outsources to is excellent, and your recipe is easy."

"I want only the best restauranteur in Bloomingfield to prepare it." His response was swift and firm. "And please wish your brother and sisters a Merry Christmas from me and my family."

Apparently that was the conclusion of their discussion.

They set a day and time, agreed to meet at her restaurant, exchanged Merry Christmases, and clicked off.

AND THAT DAY and time had arrived on a rainy Monday morning.

Julie cast a critical appraisal of herself in her restaurant's full-length mirror. A couple days had passed since she'd spoken with Lorenzo, and she couldn't control her thoughts about him—his friendly smiles, the deep timbre of his voice.

She'd run late, as usual, and opted for casual clothes—dark skinny jeans and a vintage T-shirt—her makeup a raisin-colored lipstick and porcelain finishing powder. She'd brushed her hair into soft waves, rolling it to the side in a bun and pinning it in place.

She perched on a stool in the restaurant kitchen, massaging her temples and rereading the recipe. The directions and ingredients were unclear, so she'd taken some liberties. Being a chocoholic, she preferred a larger quantity of chocolate and a smaller amount of maraschino cherries.

A soft knock on the front door had her hurrying to the entrance.

Lorenzo stood in the doorway, tall and handsome, his captivating blue eyes holding her gaze. His broad shoulders filled out his gray trench coat to perfection. The other day, he looked as if he could have been toiling in an olive field. Today, he resembled a man who had just stepped off the set of film noir. All he lacked was a dimly lit bar, and a foggy evening.

Her heart skipped a beat which seemed to be the recent norm when it came to Lorenzo Rossi.

"Hi, Julie." He grinned and brandished an oversized tube in the air. "I bought you something."

She ushered him inside. "Why?"

"Because it's Christmas."

"Lorenzo, thank you. I didn't buy you anything."

"You're the key to my successful party, which is a magnificent gift in itself." He regarded her with frank admiration. "And you look beautiful on this lovely California day."

"It's another rainy day." She gazed outside, listening to the gentle tapping of raindrops on the sidewalk.

"I like the rain and take comfort in it," he said. "For me, it's relaxing. And you are beautiful."

Self-conscious because he'd repeated his compliment, Julie adjusted her white apron and murmured a thank you.

Beautiful was a term no one used to describe her. Attractive, cute and pretty, but never beautiful, though she had been blessed with her mother's high cheekbones and plump lips. Nonetheless, when Julie peered at herself in the mirror, the woman who stared back at her looked stressed, in a never-ending cycle of work that defined her life.

"I discovered a quaint boutique in Wyoming, and thought of you," Lorenzo said. He pulled off his coat and slung it over his shoulder. Again, he wore a T-shirt and jeans that looked comfortable and lived-in, yet emphasized his strong physique.

"You shouldn't have bought me anything. We hardly know each other."

"But I did, because I hope to get to know you better." He handed her the tube and stepped to an empty table. "I'm hoping you'll hang my gift in your kitchen."

Should she? She wondered, viewing the oversized tube with uncertainty.

Why not? she argued with herself and then backtracked.

Understandably, it depended on the poster. If it was suitable for her restaurant, perhaps an inspiring photo depicting Italian pastries, then the gift wasn't personal.

"Go on," Lorenzo prodded, gesturing her to stand next to him. "I want to see you smile when you open it."

Her curiosity piqued, she arranged the poster on the table and unrolled it.

And then she smiled. And so did he.

The black and white poster portrayed a woman wearing a black dress, fedora, and shiny lipstick.

But it was the words on the poster that prompted Julie to step back.

A beautiful woman has strolled into my peaceful life.

"Do you like it?" he asked.

"Are you joking?" Her smile died. "Lorenzo, I can't possibly accept this."

"Why not?"

"The words are too ... too personal."

"And that's because ...?"

She folded her hands together and frowned. "To begin with, what about your wife?" It hurt to even say the words aloud, because Julie's pulse kicked up a notch every minute she looked at him. But she'd heard the old adage and agreed with it: *The truth hurts, but it's better than an untruth.*

Eyes wide with astonishment, he stared at her. "What wife?"

"The woman you wed a year ago?" Julie's lips pursed. "Mrs. Rossi? The reason you're planning this fabulous party?"

He chuckled. Chuckled of all things. "You're right. There was a Mrs. Rossi."

"So consequently—"

"Consequently ..." His blue eyes gleamed with mirth. "Consequently there was a Mrs. Rossi before my mother remarried, but now her name is Mrs. Talley."

"I'm not referring to your mother." Julie's tone sharpened. "I'm referring to your wife."

Her statement seemed to amuse him all the more. "Whatever gave you that idea? I'm not married."

"You're not ..." For the first time since he'd spoken, his response finally penetrated her brain. "Then who is this party for?"

"My mother and her husband, my stepfather, Joe Talley. I spent the holiday with them and managed to keep their surprise a secret, which was difficult because I'm terrible at keeping secrets. My sister invited them to Bloomingfield for New Year's Day to celebrate their first anniversary, which is how this party all came together." He paused. "Did you think I was flirting with you even though I was married?" He shook his head and scowled. "I see from your expression that's exactly what you thought."

A slice of guilt pierced her. She'd fixed him on an imaginary jury stand and judged him guilty without the facts. No wonder he was scowling.

"The thought crossed my mind," she said quietly. "I apologize."

"Apology accepted on one condition." His tone was so reasonable, she nearly consented without hearing what the condition was.

Nearly consented.

"Which is?" she asked.

"You'll smile and accept my gift."

"I already smiled."

"I'll wait for your smile again when you hang the poster in your kitchen."

"My entire staff will click their tongues for a year if I hang this poster in there." She gestured toward the kitchen.

"I wasn't referring to your restaurant kitchen. I was hoping you'd bring the poster home."

With him? Was that what he was implying?

"I'll think about it," she hedged. "But what are you trying to say? These words are ..."

His gaze slid tellingly from the poster to her face. "You know exactly what I'm saying, although the poster states the fact better than I do."

She felt a rosy blush tinting her cheeks and tried to make

light of his comment with a nod. "Thank you," she whispered, pondering the madness that seemed to overtake her whenever Lorenzo was near.

"You're forgetting to smile," he reminded.

She managed a grin, and his gaze softened.

"From the delicious aroma I smelled as soon as I walked in, I presume you've been baking." He extended his hand. "Shall we begin our first taste test?"

She accepted and led the way to the kitchen. "The cheesecake isn't cool enough to cut yet," she warned.

"How long?"

She couldn't resist teasing him. "Oh, we'll probably have to wait three or four hours."

He tilted his head. "I'll phone the station to tell them I'll be late. I'm not on television until the six o'clock news."

Would he really stay for cheesecake? Or was it more … perhaps to spend more time with her?

"Lorenzo, I'm joking." They were still holding hands. Quickly, she let go.

He set his coat on a stool, then removed his cell phone from his jeans pocket. "How long, then?"

"Probably an hour, although the cheesecake is heavy and thick, so possibly longer."

He quirked a dark eyebrow and grinned. "I have time if you do."

There were a million matters calling for her attention, but spending an extra hour with this captivating man was suddenly more important.

He pulled out a stool by the counter for her. "I planned to work in my office, but my job can wait," he said.

"My job never can." She glanced at the coffee maker. She must order a new grinder soon. And she still lacked a pastry chef.

She eyed leftover dough sitting on a tray near a workstation. Perhaps she'd spin it into pizza. If so, she was forced to use her conventional oven, though she'd recently considered purchasing a brick pizza oven.

She shifted to Lorenzo. "Maise, the new food critic, reviewed my restaurant in the newspaper."

"Yes, I read the article."

Julie nodded. At first, Maise's article had upset Julie, but then she'd pondered Maise's suggestion and was seriously considering it.

"Maise was surprised The Pasta Junction didn't serve pizza," she said.

"I thought the same. Because this is an Italian restaurant. I assumed pizza was on your menu."

"The Pasta Junction is high-end, not a corner pizzeria. They have an entirely different clientele."

"Do they?" he asked. "Everyone likes pizza, even the fancy clientele."

"Like you?"

"I may come across as posh on television because I wear a three-piece suit. But believe me, I'm a regular, stay-at-home kind of guy."

Julie tapped her fingers and pushed out a breath. He and Maise were probably correct about serving pizza, and no doubt a variety of pizzas with different toppings—pepperoni, assorted vegetables, grilled chicken—would quickly become restaurant favorites.

She grabbed her laptop computer from its shelf and flipped it open. "A pizza oven is the first step." Intent on her task, she surfed the internet before pointing to the screen. "This oven is top notch, but it costs ten thousand dollars."

"Wow. You'll need to sell a lot of pizzas to make a profit." Lorenzo reached for his glasses in his pocket and put them on. "Did you calculate the cost of labor and ingredients?"

"Several times, and the price comes out to approximately six dollars per pizza."

"Can't you outsource pizzas like you outsource desserts?"

"Outsourcing desserts is temporary," she reminded as she viewed the computer screen. The oven price was prohibitive. However, she could charge by the slice. Two dollars per slice and eight servings in one pizza equaled …

She fiddled with a pin that came loose from her bun. Somewhere in the back of her head, a headache began to erupt. Stress seemed to produce that more and more lately, along with a constant money worry.

"Are you a workaholic?" Lorenzo asked, interrupting her reflections. His gaze was probing yet caring, and some of her frustration evaporated.

"My siblings, Ben and Sally and Katie, certainly think I am. Still, Sally is as driven as I am. She throws every bit of effort into her chocolate shop."

"Perhaps you might consider less time on the job or more people to share your workload? Did any of your siblings offer a solution?"

"Yes, and they also suggested I get a dog."

His lips rounded into a smile. "A dog offers unconditional love. What type are you considering?"

"*I'm* not considering a dog. *They* are. For me."

"Big or little? If you have allergies—"

"I told you, no dog. I can't devote the care he might need."

"He?"

"*If* I ever get a dog, which I'm not, I've considered naming him Buddy."

"I'm partial to beagles. I'm available any time if you want to stop by the local animal shelter." He acted as if he hadn't heard her. "There are countless animals begging to be adopted."

Her legs were tired from standing, and Lorenzo's

unswerving gaze flustered her. He was looking for an assurance that she would visit the animal shelter with him, and she couldn't guarantee it. Besides, she didn't want to leave a dog alone for extended periods while she worked.

For lack of anything else to say, she asked Lorenzo if he would like a cup of coffee.

He leaned against the counter. "Will the coffee be as good as the other day?"

"Absolutely not." She cut her gaze to the overworked coffee machine. "This coffee has sat out for a couple hours. It might taste stale, but I can brew a fresh pot."

"I'm easy. Old coffee works for me."

Easy about coffee maybe, but certainly not about his grandmother's recipe.

She went to the coffeemaker and poured him a cup, then lifted the lid of a glass bin overflowing with biscotti. "The cookies are hard, but excellent for dunking in a hot drink."

"Or breaking a tooth." He sipped the coffee she set beside him and slightly grimaced. "Considering the coffee is lukewarm, I better not take my chances."

She grinned. "You might look odd on television with a missing front tooth."

"It wouldn't be the first time."

She blinked. Her lips parted. "You're kidding, right?"

"Nope." He pulled in a breath. "Before I worked in Bloomingfield, I was a weatherman at a prestigious Atlanta television station. In college, I'd decided on a dual degree in meteorology and journalism, and began my career in smaller markets. After several years, I was hired as the anchor weatherman on the evening news. Finally, I thought, I'm in a big city and snagged my dream job. Everything was ideal. At least, so I assumed."

"And?"

"I'd worked at the station three years. One afternoon, I

had a run-in with a guy who had been my best friend at college."

"Your friend came into the television station to speak with you?"

"Yes, on a business matter that ended up being personal. He'd needed help, and I'd given it." Lorenzo pressed his lips together. "Our conversation escalated to a disagreement, and he punched me in the jaw."

"Why? What was the business matter?"

"I'd lent him some money, which apparently wasn't enough, because he wanted more. I refused, and he wasn't happy."

"The personal matter?"

"My supposed girlfriend who was actually dating both of us." He refused to meet her stare. "During our heated disagreement, I lost a tooth. After my TV segment was over, I was served my walking papers. It was wrong of me to argue publicly with him, especially at my job."

"Who threw the first punch?"

"He did. I threw the second. There were only two."

She bit her lip. "Who broke up the fight?"

"The station manager." Lorenzo shook his head. "Honestly, none of this matters. The primary requirement in media is to present an accomplished image, and I failed."

"You were trying to protect yourself."

"I've never struck anyone in my life, either before or after that incident. It was instinctive, but it was wrong."

A silence filled the air. Lorenzo had owned up to his mistake. In summary, he'd been stripped of his job and title because of it. Still, admitting wrongness took courage and conviction.

Julie waited a beat until his gaze rested on her. He gave a heavy sigh.

"What happened doesn't seem fair." Her tone softened.

"Your supposed friend was clearly looking for a fight. Losing your dream job must have been devastating."

Lorenzo took off his eyeglasses and rubbed his eyes. "In the end, it was for the best. I found a job I love here in Bloomingfield, and because the town is small, the hours aren't as demanding. The managers matched my Atlanta salary, so I'm not complaining. Thus, I can pursue other interests, like baking." He chucked her under the chin.

"Uh-huh." She smiled. "As if you like to bake."

"I'm starting to enjoy baking a great deal." He leaned over and pressed a light kiss on her mouth. His lips were warm, the flavor of dark coffee.

She should have pulled away. Instead, her heart did a little flip in her chest.

"Truthfully," he whispered, "I'm growing fonder and fonder of …"

"Baking?"

"Spending time with you."

"Lorenzo," she murmured, "I'm not interested in dating."

"Surely a woman—"

"A *businesswoman*. The restaurant is always on my mind, and I don't have room in my life for anyone or anything else." She drew away and didn't meet his gaze.

Such a feathery, brief kiss, but it had been perilously comfortable, as if they had kissed before and would again.

No, no. This entire cassata taste testing was a bad idea. She couldn't get entangled in a relationship. *Wouldn't* get entangled in a relationship. Determinedly, she erected the safe barricade around her heart and reverted to her practical self.

"I have no flaky pastry to offer you today, either. Sorry."

"How about a bottle of water?" he asked.

"Certainly." A quick reach in the cooler, and she placed the water beside him.

"Thanks." He downed the water. "Someday, I'd like you to come to Italy with me to savor the finest pastry in the world."

She hesitated. He was full of surprises.

He observed her closely, as if interested in her response.

"Are you offering an invitation?" she asked.

He grinned. "Of the most blatant kind."

"I've never flown." Her explanation came out more like an embarrassed confession than an excuse.

"Are you afraid?"

"The opportunity never presented itself. When I was young, my parents hardly traveled. And the past few years I've been trying to succeed in this challenging restaurant business."

"Are you … succeeding?"

"Sometimes yes." She sagged onto the stool, a kaleidoscope of stressful nights filing through her mind. "Sometimes no. The workload is tremendous."

He sat beside her. "Are you enjoying your life?"

"I can't get philosophical in the daytime."

"Good excuse, and even more of a reason that you deserve a break." He reached out to take her hands, his grip firm and reassuring. "If it's your first experience, you might as well fly with someone you trust."

"I never consented to go with you. Furthermore, I'm supposed to trust you? These are early days in our friendship."

"Yes, we're definitely friends, Julie, and I'm hoping we'll become more than friends. I find you truly amazing."

She was in new territory, too fresh and unfamiliar, and she didn't know whether to respond with a smile or a scoff.

"I've always dreamed of seeing Italy," she murmured. "It's just not possible between my restaurant and financial demands."

"Since you own an Italian restaurant, you can draw upon

old-country techniques and innovative recipes, so it's a business trip. I visit my relatives there often."

"Is that why you're inviting me? To help me improve my business?"

"Yes, and because, as you stated, we are friends."

Just two friends traveling to Italy together.

She envisioned the scenario. Warm Mediterranean sunshine, scents of olives and garlic, appreciating the gorgeous architecture, dining on local cuisine every day.

She swallowed the knot in her throat, conscious of her tight schedule and realizing she'd never be able to visit. Going forward, she would be wise to keep that cold realization in her mind when dealing with Lorenzo. They were two experts in their fields, and this was a business relationship.

"But in the meantime, my *friend*, while we're here in California?" She tugged her hands from his, rolled to her feet and motioned toward the tin. "Would you like a biscotti?"

"I'm set. Thanks." He glanced at the stovetop. "I'm a patient man."

"I was late getting the cassata in the oven, and when I inserted a knife to check if it came out clean, it didn't. So I left the cheesecake in for another ten minutes."

"Is that good or bad?"

"We'll see." She refilled his coffee cup and perched on the stool. "So, what should we chat about while we wait for the cassata to cool?"

He had stood when she did. Now he propped on his stool once more, his feet resting on the bottom rung. "The weather?"

She laughed. "No sensationalism for New Year's Eve, I hope?"

"I returned to Bloomingfield a short time ago. Tune in to my segment tonight to hear the complete forecast."

"Because I'm a busy restaurant owner, I might not have time." She flashed him a smile. "Although I'll try."

Oh, she'd do more than try. Lorenzo's funny, endearing style captivated her. He made the weather forecast humorous, almost as if he told a story each night. She said as much and received a satisfied grin in reply. "Thank you, Julie. Your kind words mean a lot to me."

CHAPTER 4

*L*orenzo drank more of his water, forcing himself not to stare at the striking woman sitting next to him. Her sparkling gaze and sweet smile made his pulse race.

He slanted her a glance, unsurprised that she had switched into businesslike mode again. Already, he was beginning to know her.

They sat so near their knees touched, and his heartbeat accelerated. Julie's face was as close to perfection as any woman he'd ever seen, especially when she smiled.

He'd examined several restaurants' websites when he was first organizing this anniversary party. It was his way of showing his mother he approved of her new relationship, and that by marrying Joe, Lorenzo understood she wasn't abandoning Lorenzo's father. She was embarking on a different season in her life, and his father's memory would always be cherished. The cassata was an extra bonus—a sharing of remarkable memories.

The oddest thing had happened when he came across The Pasta Junction's website. He saw the photo of the owner, Julie

Elliot, and he couldn't stop staring. Her blue eyes were enticing, yet mysterious, inspiring him to learn more about her. Her full red lips were pouty and curved. And, by the choice of her outfit and matching fedora, he realized she enjoyed film noir.

Exactly like him.

Before he phoned her, he'd double-checked to be certain she wasn't married, although gazing at her now, he wondered why she hadn't been scooped up years ago. What were all the single men in this town doing? Was the California sunshine making them blind?

Certainly he loved his grandmother and the marvelous memories they'd made together. Admittedly, though, he'd also used the recipe as a way to meet Julie in person, rather than simply booking the party on her website. Once they met, his decision became firm. He wanted to see her again, and couldn't wait until New Year's Day.

Okay, the poster had blatantly blared his interest, although he'd deemed it romantic when he purchased it. Now, for a man who earned his living by speaking into a camera to thousands of viewers, he found that expressing his feelings was surprisingly difficult.

"Lorenzo," she was saying, "there's a new movie playing at the Grover Theater. Or rather, I should say it's an old movie."

"Which one?"

"*The Big Sleep.*"

"The movie starring Humphrey Bogart and Lauren Bacall?"

"The very same." Julie rewarded him with a wide grin.

"Private detective Philip Marlowe." Lorenzo paused. Did Julie hope he would ask her for a date? She was regarding him with anticipation in her eyes.

"Our finest film noir movie," she said.

Our film noir, because they shared a commonality. He

debated correcting her with a teasing *Our?*, but kept the question to himself. "I love the line from that movie, you know, the book shop scene," he said. "'You intrigue me.'"

"I believe Bogart used the word 'interest.'"

"'Interest me,'" Lorenzo corrected.

"Vaguely. Bogart said 'vaguely' at the end."

Lorenzo's gaze lingered on Julie's face. Yes, she certainly did interest him, and a whole lot more than vaguely.

Faintly, she smiled, as if reading his mind.

He cupped her chin, so she was forced to stare at him, and her smile warmed.

There were times when he wasn't certain how best to respond, and this became one of those moments. Should he kiss her?

She answered his silent question by drawing back. "Shall we try the cassata?" Her words tumbled out.

"Absolutely." He pushed back his stool and followed her lead.

"It may fall apart because it hasn't cooled long enough," she warned as he took her hand and led her to the cooktop.

Excellent. Then he'd have the excuse that it wasn't perfect, and he'd be able to see her again.

"We'll begin with a nibble." He hoped his grin flashed plenty of persuasion.

She pulled two dessert plates from a shelf, two forks and napkins, and sliced the cassata. She placed a portion on his plate and a second serving for herself.

He carried the plates to the counter as, with an apologetic murmur about hoping the coffee hadn't changed to mud yet, she poured them both more.

When they were once again perched on their stools, she bowed her head and recited a blessing. When the prayer ended, he murmured "Amen." Then he took a bite of the cassata.

As Julie predicted, the ricotta cheese separated from the still-steaming chocolate chips and fell to pieces.

He ignored her "I'm right" stare, shrugged, and forked another piece.

The cassata was good. Very good. The blending of chocolate and cheese melted in his mouth.

"Well?" she prompted.

He gestured to her plate. "You're the restaurant owner. What do you think?"

Slowly, she forked a sampling. "The combination is—"

She didn't finish and began coughing.

For an instant, he smiled, assuming she was elaborating her response with an exaggerated cough. Then her eyes widened.

He hesitated, then grasped her shoulders as his heart dropped. Surely she couldn't be choking on a small piece of cheesecake? She'd hardly eaten a bite. "Julie, can you speak?"

She didn't reply and continued coughing.

He slapped her across the back, attempting to dislodge any food stuck in her windpipe. With his other hand, which had begun to shake, he grabbed his cell phone, intending to call 911.

"Lorenzo—" Julie sputtered. "Don't. I'm okay."

His jaw clenched, and he grasped her forearm. "Are you certain?"

She nodded and dabbed at her watering eyes with the edge of her ruffled apron.

"I feared you ... you were smoking," he said.

"You mean choking."

"Right." He licked his lips, grabbed his bottle of water and drained it.

"I wasn't." She eyed his fingers clasped around her arm, the crumbs of cassata on her plate. "Okay, maybe I was. But I own a restaurant and have come to the rescue of many diners."

"What did you do?"

"Precisely what you did."

"So, in a way, I'm glad I was here, in case you needed medical assistance." His voice was still raspy with fright. He usually took charge during an emergency, but Julie in peril had had an odd effect on him. He'd almost been paralyzed for a frightening moment.

"In a way?" she asked.

"It's like in a movie. The hero saves the heroine in the end."

"Or vice versa."

His laugh nearly drowned out her next observation.

"This restaurant kitchen is hardly the setting for a crime drama," she pointed out.

Undeterred, he rummaged through the cabinets and found a glass. Filling it with water, he set it beside her. "Drink. Plus, I know why you choked."

Quickly, she drank. "Now you're a hard-boiled detective?"

"Only when it comes to cheesecake, which was too crumbly. Therefore ..." He watched her carefully as she chewed.

"Therefore?" she prompted.

"Therefore, you're clearly gifted." Inwardly, he congratulated himself on his adept subject change. He glanced at her hands, soft and delicate, as she grasped her fork. She accomplished so much with her hands, creating wonderful meals and, subsequently, memories.

"So, because I'm so gifted, we're all set?" She inclined her head in a slight nod and picked up her fork. "Can we agree the cassata is delicious?"

He directed a slow, meaningful gaze at the crumbs left on their plates. "Are you willing to bake another?"

She set her fork down. "Why?"

"Unfortunately, it's not as delicious as my grandmother's cassata." He affected a long sigh. "I suggest an extra cup of cherries and a half cup less of chocolate."

He should tell her the truth. But he couldn't. He'd already given her a poster declaring his feelings. They'd only just met, and he might come across as a love sick pudding-head. He'd done that once in his life and once was enough.

When she began to object, he said, "Therefore, can we meet again for another taste test?"

"Therefore?" She shook her head. "Lorenzo, these few days after Christmas were slow, but the restaurant is already booked for New Year's Eve and nearly full for the next few days."

He flashed a charismatic smile, hoping it so infectious she would immediately concur. "I can come by early tomorrow afternoon and assist you."

"Don't you work?"

"Morning meetings should be finished by noon. As long as I'm back at the station by four o'clock, I'm available."

"On Tuesday, we're only open for dinner."

He knew her restaurant's hours, but didn't want to confess he'd perused her website so often, he'd almost memorized it.

"Excellent. I'll pick up the ingredients beforehand." He smoothed out his grandmother's recipe and made a great show of producing a pen and paper from the pocket of his coat.

"I purchase most ingredients at a chef's food supply store," she said. "They're located on the other side of the bridge."

"I don't mind the extra distance. Didn't you mention the

flavor might change depending on what factory produced the boxed cake mix? I'll stop by the grocer's in town."

"The corner grocer is not a factory, nor a chef's store," she replied. "Plus, this grocer wouldn't be the same as the one your grandmother shopped in years ago, would it?"

"True." He scooped up the last bit of crumbs on his plate.

An hour later, after nonstop animated conversation, he reluctantly glanced at the clock on the wall and sighed. "I should get to the studio."

"I'll watch your weather report tonight."

"You won't be working?"

"I usually watch it on the station's website."

His delighted gaze met hers. "Since when?"

"Since you became Bloomingfield's premier meteorologist." The tip of her tongue moistened her lips. Captivating him.

He cleared his throat. "Don't forget my gift."

Her gaze drifted to the poster and then to him. By her softened expression, she apparently knew why he'd selected that particular poster, and their love for film noir was only part of the reason. The real reason was the words.

He was falling for her. And he hoped that whenever she looked at the poster, she'd think of him.

"Shall we say twelve o'clock?" he asked.

She nodded. "Thank you for thinking of me, and for making my Christmas special." Her smile lit her entire beautiful face and twisted his insides upside down.

CHAPTER 5

The next morning, Julie spent a few hectic hours making pasta dough, receiving a food delivery, reviewing the accounts with her manager, and waiting for a pastry chef who never showed for his interview. With nothing more to do before Lorenzo arrived, Julie walked back to her third-floor apartment. The apartment was located on a tree-lined neighborhood only two blocks away from the restaurant.

Spurred by Lorenzo's invitation to fly to Italy with him, she'd done something the night before she rarely did. She'd surfed the internet, most notably the town of Calitri in Italy.

She wasn't stalking him, she told herself, she was researching Italy. The vivid descriptions of castle ruins and ancient cathedrals opened a realm of possibilities she hadn't considered before.

When she retired to her apartment, she entered her cheerful kitchen, painted a bright yellow, and brewed a mug of peppermint tea. She carried the mug into the living room, which she'd decorated in calming shades of green. French doors offered a panoramic view of Bloomingfield and opened onto an outdoor balcony with a wrought-iron railing. On sunny days, the room flooded with natural light, and on cool, rainy evenings, the wood-burning fireplace provided cozy warmth.

The previous evening, she'd rolled Lorenzo's poster out on the coffee table, anchoring it with books. Now as she stood in the living room, she deliberated on where to hang it.

"For what it's worth," she said aloud, "the poster is beautiful."

Once more reflecting on the words, she fastened it to a plain wall by the fireplace.

Taking her tea over to the couch, she phoned Sally at Bloomingfield Chocolate Shop. The shop was extremely popular and boasted a steady stream of devoted patrons. At a recent candy-making contest held in a local women's shelter, the shop's chocolate coffee fudge was voted first place. Since then, business had doubled.

"Are you busy?" Julie inquired when Sally answered the phone. "I know that's a silly question, considering how conscientious you are."

"Conscientious is overrated." Sally chuckled. Despite the trying work hours, the mischievous giggle of Sally's youth was still there.

As a tangle-haired imp, Sally had constantly teased Julie when they were children. Once they'd reached their teens, they'd become fast friends, and their conversations often lasted for hours. A few years younger than Julie, Sally's curly hair gave her a pixie look, while Julie preferred to style her hair in classic buns and pin curls.

"Overrated?" Julie repeated. "Being conscientious is how you get things done."

"Unfortunately, or fortunately, however you want to view it, our jobs, including Katie's as a lawyer, are demanding,"

Sally confirmed. "Even Ben. He's at the cash register cashing out customers. I'll wave to him for you."

Julie suppressed the urge to playfully inquire if Ben had ventured into the shop's kitchen, for he knew nothing about the candy-making process. Their older brother was a silent partner, but he often stepped into the chocolate shop to help.

"I'm sorting red bento boxes," Sally continued. "Believe it or not, I'm already planning Valentine's Day, a popular chocolate day in my candy part of town."

Julie chuckled. "Well, in my restaurant part of town, I'm managing the overbooked reservations for the New Year's holiday."

"Sounds like you had a profitable Christmas. You mentioned people waited in line for a table."

"Thankfully, we were able to accommodate every patient diner," Julie replied. "Although that's not the problem."

"There's a problem?"

Julie set her cell phone to speaker, placing it beside her, and picked up her mug of tea. "Yes, and it's Lorenzo Rossi."

After a thoughtful silence, Sally asked, "The good-looking meteorologist on the evening news?"

"He booked a first anniversary party for his mother and step-father at The Pasta Junction for New Year's Day."

"Gosh, that man is dazzling."

"Gosh? Dazzling?" Sally's statement earned a giggle from Julie. "You're not helping."

"Explain, please."

"I met with him yesterday. And I'm seeing him again today."

"Why? Is he pulling out of the booking and, for some odd reason, chooses to tell you in person?" Sally asked. "I guarantee you'll fill his table quickly."

"No, he's not canceling. Actually, it's just the opposite. Lorenzo is obsessed with his Italian grandmother's cheesecake recipe and wants to serve it at the party." A warm tingling coursed through Julie's body as she remembered sharing the cheesecake with him. She shook it off. "Can I also say that he is completely impossible?"

"We both encounter difficult customers. We're used to it."

After Julie's brief explanation regarding the taste testing, Sally's musical laugh erupted. "Why didn't you explain sooner? He's not interested in the cassata. He's interested in you."

"We just met."

"Love at first sight. It happens all the time, although I've never experienced anything of the sort."

Julie refrained from commenting. Her sister had endured a painful divorce and was now happily raising Clarissa, her beautiful daughter, as a single mother. Julie loved spending time with the little girl and taking her for sweets at the local ice cream parlor, which always earned her a cuddle and a "You're the best, Aunt Julie."

Julie glanced at the poster. "We're talking about Lorenzo Rossi."

"That's what I said. Love at first sight."

Shaking her head, Julie picked up her cell phone and stepped to the poster, and the eye-catching portrayal of a mysterious, beautiful woman. She'd read that the noir films of the 1940s had reflected the world weariness of the era after the war. Cool, businesslike heroines and nonchalant heroes, along with subdued lighting, embodied the sense of uncertain times. As she viewed the poster, her stomach tensed. Had she become an emotionless, efficient adult like the insouciant woman in the poster, thrusting all her energy into work and no longer taking precious opportunities to genuinely appreciate life?

"Hey?" Sally inquired. "Are you still there?"

"Yes, I'm here. I'm starting to suspect that any cassata I

bake for him will not be satisfactory," Julie said in a hushed voice.

And was that a bad thing? Then she'd get to see Lorenzo again.

She blinked. Is that what Lorenzo had intended all along?

"When will you meet him next?" Sally asked.

Julie peered at her watch. "In about an hour. He wants another taste test."

"Uh-huh. Because he wants to see you again." Sally voiced Julie's contemplations aloud. "And I can see through the phone that you're blushing."

"I'm not," Julie refuted, although her heated cheeks contradicted her.

"I bet you are," Sally said. "You always blush when you're attracted to a guy."

It went without saying that Sally was alluding to the time when Julie had been charmed by the married man. She'd gushed nonstop about him for weeks. That is, until she'd learned the truth.

Beyond a doubt, Lorenzo was different. The warmth in his eyes when they'd chatted about the scene from the movie *The Big Sleep*, the determination in his deep voice when he decided to phone the television station to inform them he'd be late, assured Julie he was sincere.

"I wonder if I should continue to meet with him alone at my restaurant," she said aloud. "It's not professional."

"You're being ridiculous," Sally scolded. "He isn't married, is he?"

"No."

"Divorced?"

"Not that I'm aware." Julie tried to suppress the images of the supermodels Lorenzo probably dated and chided herself for speculating. Based on his exceptional looks and charisma, she could only imagine. "But I haven't asked him."

"Does he know anything about your dating past?"

"I don't have a dating past."

"Then push your concerns aside and enjoy his gorgeousness." Sally paused. "Hang on. All the customers have left and Ben is quizzically watching me. I'll tell him I'm talking to you."

Sally cupped the phone. After several seconds of muted conversation, she laughed.

"I'm back," Sally said a moment later. "Ben spouted the funniest joke about a weatherman."

Julie shook her head in disbelief. "You told him about Lorenzo in under a minute?"

"Affirmative. What are siblings for, except to cheer each other on? Do you want to hear Ben's joke?"

"Do I have a choice?"

"Not really," Sally said. "So why was the old meteorologist worried?"

"I'm supposed to ask why, correct?"

"Of course."

Julie blew out a breath. "Why?"

"Because he was fearful the new weatherman would steal his thunder. Get it? Thunder?"

Julie chuckled. "I'll try to remember to pass along the joke to Lorenzo."

"Good. One more thing. Julie?"

"Yes?"

"I can't judge from watching Lorenzo on television if his persona is the real deal or not, but he comes across as a good guy. He seems genuine."

And he likes film noir, Julie thought. And black coffee. He also reacted quickly when he was afraid I was choking …

"I feared you … you were smoking."

"You mean choking."

His ashen face appeared in her mind as he'd mixed up his

words. His brilliant blue eyes had been overly bright. He'd been honestly concerned about her.

She sought to tear herself away from her reflections, yet she daydreamed about him. His slow easy smile, his tender kiss. Softly, she smoothed her fingers over her lips, remembering.

"Hello, Julie? Did I lose you again?" Sally asked.

She must stop thinking about him. "I'm here. Thank Ben for the joke."

"He's delighted to tell more whenever asked."

"Then we need to be certain we never ask." Despite herself, Julie giggled. "I love you both and we'll talk soon."

"We love you too. Oh, and Julie, Ben and I and Katie look forward to meeting your guy."

"He's not my guy, Sally."

"You're smitten. Admit it. Bring him into the chocolate shop."

Murmuring an agreement she assumed would never happen, Julie clicked off and studied the poster.

A beautiful woman has strolled into my peaceful life.

The words were a mirror of her own thoughts, although she reversed them.

A handsome man has strolled into my peaceful life.

CHAPTER 6

*L*orenzo walked into Julie's restaurant at precisely one o'clock.

Elated anticipation had grown inside him all morning. The cassata excuse, which he'd originally intended as a means to get to know her better, was the highlight of his day. He'd spent his waking hours remembering each of their moments together and speculated on when he could introduce Julie to his family.

Certainly there was no better opportunity than New Year's Day, when everyone was present and he could introduce her as his …?

His what? Date? Girlfriend? Perhaps more.

Perhaps less. They'd only just met, and relationships took stages to mature as people learned more about each other.

Nevertheless, with inborn optimism, he smiled. The promise of a delightful afternoon with Julie beckoned.

After he knocked on The Pasta Junction's green wooden door, she'd called out to him to come inside. "The door's unlocked," she added.

"I bought the ingredients at the corner grocer's." He

strode into the dining room and they acknowledged each other with cheerful greetings.

He followed her into the kitchen.

He set down the brown grocery bag, removed his beat-up leather jacket, damp from the rain, and draped it over a stool.

With a sigh, she busied herself with tidying cutlery.

"Anything the matter?" he asked with a smile. He hoped the smile hid his concern. She looked pale and tired. Although her resilience amazed him, her work responsibility was a challenging burden to carry on her own.

"A headache is coming on, and I realize it's stress because of the holiday season." She rubbed her temples, then her tight shoulders. "I'm grateful for my patrons, but also hoping my life calms down after the first of the year."

"Will it? Calm down?"

Uncertainly, she gazed at him. "Maybe."

"Some of those choices are up to you." He reached into the grocery bag and placed the cake mix, ricotta cheese, chocolate chips, and maraschino cherries on the counter. "I presume this is the correct boxed mix. It looks the same as the one I remember from my grandmother's house."

She quirked a delicate eyebrow. "How long is it since you baked a cassata?"

"Well, I'm thirty-two, and spent many afternoons with her throughout my childhood." He perused the label on the box. "Thus, over twenty years ago."

"It's highly doubtful the packaging stayed the same." Julie grinned, went to the cooler and brought back two bottles of water. He stepped aside as she poured the water into glasses.

He'd phoned her from the store to ask what type of ricotta he should purchase—low fat, fat free, or regular—and she'd instructed that regular ricotta was fine, and then remarked that the restaurant's coffee machine had broken down. She expected it would be repaired before the dinner crowd arrived and was concerned the fix might be costly. Still, she'd explained, a repair was better than purchasing a brand new machine.

As she started pulling out bowls and a wooden spoon, he couldn't stop admiring her. Her tight black denims, topped with a red holiday sweater, enhanced her slim curves. He gave her an appreciative appraisal from the tips of her blond hair, which was clipped into a side bun by a shiny gold barrette, to her sensible work shoes.

When she turned and picked up her water glass, he clinked his glass with hers. "Good afternoon, gorgeous."

Her shoulders relaxed. "Good afternoon, Lorenzo." She set down her glass and considered him. "I guessed you were younger than thirty-two years old."

"Thank you. I'm assuming you're complimenting me." He viewed her smooth complexion, the light sprinkling of freckles on the bridge of her nose, her glossy red lipstick. "May I ask how old you are?"

"Let's just say somewhere in my thirties. Not all women reveal their ages and I'm one of those women."

"I'm intrigued by a woman with a hint of mystery."

She batted her long dark eyelashes and laughed out loud. He laughed with her.

She was enchanting.

What if he arranged a trip to Italy and persuaded her to travel with him? He pictured them together in his beloved Calitri, wandering the narrow streets, while he translated Italian words and phrases and showed her his ancestral home nestled in the olive groves.

She touched her mouth, and he had the urge to step forward and kiss her. Instead, he set down his glass and embraced her. The feel of her warm, delicate body against his unexpectedly shook him.

. . .

TWO HOURS LATER, the cassata had been baked and was cooling. During the preparation, he'd hummed a venerable Italian melody, "O Sole Mio," theatrically flinging out his arms while he belted out the chorus, first in Italian, again in English.

Afterward, they sat at the counter, talking and laughing. Between mixing the ricotta and chopping maraschino cherries, she'd folded countless white napkins and polished the silverware to a gleaming finish. Today, the restaurant was only open for dinner beginning at six o'clock, she informed him, but he already knew that.

Soon afterward, she declared that she needed to make her trademark pasta for dinner.

"I can watch, can't I?" Lorenzo asked.

"Nope."

He grimaced. "Is pasta making some kind of trademark secret? Can't I even take notes?"

"No watching or taking notes." At his inquiring protest, she flashed a dazzling smile. "You can do better, because you can help me." She moved to a cabinet and brandished a frilly red apron.

"I like you a lot," he said. *Okay, more than a lot.* "But under no condition am I wearing an apron."

She drew out a white apron and tied it around herself. "See? Now we match."

With a muffled laugh, she gestured to the empty kitchen. "No one else is here, and I'm not anticipating a television crew arriving to film your weather report. Are you?"

He noted she was correct. With a sigh, he stood and held up his arms as she tied the red apron around his waist. He tucked the ends into the waistband of his jeans.

"Ideal," she teased when he twirled for her approval. "I admire a man who doesn't object to working in the kitchen."

"For you, I'll do anything." He stepped within inches of

her and slid an arm around her waist. Gently, he swept a pin curl from her cheek. "And I do mean anything."

She turned, smiling up at him as her gaze warmed.

He felt happier than he'd been in a long time, and the reason stood clearly in his arms.

Julie was tall and slim, near his height, and a single word appeared in his mind as he gazed at her.

Knockout. Julie Elliott was a knockout.

She swung from him and he followed her to an open area in the rear room. There, she dragged out a large piece of stainless steel equipment.

"This is how I make fresh pasta," she said, "and this is a pasta machine."

Boy, was she ever proficient.

"How many pounds of pasta do you produce in a day?" he inquired.

"Five to six." She took out a bowl of dough from a cooler, placed a substantial amount on the flat counter, and began kneading. "Truly, there is a distinguishable taste difference between dry pasta and fresh," she said.

"What are the ingredients for your dough?" He brought out his cell phone and snapped a picture of her. "For me," he assured at her distracted expression.

The photo on her website depicted a playful, yet sultry, Julie. This photo, Julie preparing her beloved pasta, was the real Julie, the working Julie.

Although, wasn't she a combination of both women? Didn't everyone have multiple characteristics, multiple selves?

"Eggs, flour, olive oil, and kosher salt," she was saying. "I made the dough earlier, covered it with plastic wrap and let it rest. Today is a happy day because you're here to help."

"A happy day and a happy man who is happy to oblige," he quipped as he put away his cell phone. "What comes next?"

"Let's wash our hands. After we dry them thoroughly, we'll dust them with flour."

After their hands were clean and white with flour, they doubled back to the counter. "First, I flatten the dough." She wielded her rolling pin. "Next, I roll it."

"Fascinating."

"And this is where you come in."

He stiffened. "Me?"

She fitted the pasta machine to the counter and adjusted the clamp, demonstrating that it kept the machine steady. "Keep adjusting the knob until the dough becomes thin."

He worked cautiously at first, turning the crank with one hand while feeding dough into the machine with the other. After more than a dozen tries and several sheets of ruined pasta, he began turning out expertly thin sheets.

"Your dough is pliable," he remarked. "If I weren't so diligent, I'd applaud your talents, but I can't let go of the crank."

"Applause is always appreciated," she laughed, and bobbed her head toward the pasta machine. "Don't forget to keep dusting the dough with flour, or else it will stick."

"You're being bossy."

"That's because I'm the boss."

He chuckled, shaking his head at the discarded pasta. "I'm guessing your noodles are amazing, and that you're thrilled I don't actually work here."

"Similar to any art, pasta making takes time and patience. You're doing splendid." She paused. "I forgot you've never eaten here."

"That will change," he assured her. "Because we're a couple."

Her lips parted. "We're a couple?"

He was intensely aware of his own heartbeat. "That is, if you agree."

"I'm tied up countless hours every day." Ruefully, she

shook her head and placed her hand over his. The tender gesture caused his thoughts to whirl.

"Is that a yes or a no?" he asked.

"It's a cautious … yes."

"Good," he replied. "We'll make it work."

She made an impressive show of delight by displaying a wide grin, and any frustration at his failed pasta attempts, or whether she reciprocated his feelings, quickly evaporated. Already, she was filling his days with enchantment.

"My 'famous,'" she finger quoted, "fettuccini uses the same dough. For lasagna, I would double the recipe." She quickly sliced his long pasta sheets into smaller sheets of equal length. "This pasta will boil in under a minute."

"But it takes a substantial number of hours to make, not to mention the daily commitment," he said. He finished cranking the last portion of the dough. Then he floured sheet pans as she instructed, laying out the strips to dry.

"Once you start making fresh, it's tough to reintroduce dried," she remarked. "Fresh pasta tastes silkier and creamier."

"Plus, you're saving money."

"Perhaps. But when you factor in the cost of this machine and my labor …" She set down the rolling pin. "Then not so much."

"Are you strapped financially?" he asked.

"Money is always tight."

He avoided eye contact with her. He knew from firsthand experience the expense of investing in a restaurant and subsequently losing it when the restaurant shuttered. Ironically, he could even recite the statistics. Sixty percent of restaurants failed, even if they were excellent.

She nodded toward the main kitchen. "Ready to try the cassata?"

"Absolutely."

After all that cranking, he was starving. Welcoming scents of chocolate and cherries greeted him as they stepped into the kitchen. He remembered where she kept the dishes and forks and brought them to the counter.

She plated their servings. As she'd done the previous day, she bent her head and murmured a quiet blessing, and he followed her lead.

Then he savored a bite of cassata. The texture was heavenly, the sweetness of the cherries blending seamlessly with the chocolate.

"Well?" She scooped up another bite. "I assume you're satisfied, because this is delicious."

His first instinct was to take her in his arms and declare that in order to be satisfied, he needed to see her again.

He thought quickly and didn't rely on his instincts. Yes, they were now "a couple," but their bond was still fragile. After his hurtful relationship with a cheater who had ultimately betrayed him, he'd vowed never to fall in love again. Casual dating? Certainly, and with more women than he cared to count. Anything more? Absolutely not.

And yet, in merely a few days he'd fallen for a sharp-witted, ambitious beauty who softened his heart with her contagious smile.

So here he stood, confronting a dilemma. If he admitted the cassata was perfect, he wouldn't see Julie again until he was a customer at her restaurant, surrounded by his family. She was too busy to actually date him until after the holidays.

"It's good," he replied hesitantly. "However ..."

She subjected him to a narrowed gaze. "Is that the only word in your vocabulary when it comes to describing this cassata?"

He untied his frilly apron and draped it over a chair, taking his time to formulate his reply. "As you instructed, I bought whole milk ricotta for this recipe. However, I just remembered my mother specifically told me she is watching her waistline."

"You just remembered?"

He shifted and shrugged on his jacket. "Therefore, let's try the recipe with low-fat ricotta."

"You're the person who bought the ingredients."

"Remember? I forgot."

"Convenient," she countered. "May I point out that your Italian buffet will consist of hundreds of calories between the pasta, garlic bread, and meatballs?"

"Still, I'd like to test the recipe using low-fat ricotta," he said. "In addition, this time you should measure the quantities exactly. Level off the cinnamon and cocoa in the measuring cup."

She plunked her hands on her hips. "*Therefore,* you're suggesting I measure exact amounts of ingredients which aren't listed?"

He grinned. "Something like that."

"Lorenzo, you can't rely on math for baking or cooking, because the process is creative and subjective." Her spine stiffened. "And I prefer to do things my way."

He strode to her and tipped up her chin. "One more taste test?"

"Why?"

"Because I want to see you again," he said softly. He cuddled her close for a lengthy, thorough kiss.

When he lifted his head, her soft blue eyes gazed up at him. "I'd like to see you too."

His attention was diverted by his buzzing cell phone. He reviewed the message flashing across his screen, and an idea took hold.

"Tonight there is a meteor shower that should turn into an outburst," he said.

She stepped away from him and tugged off her apron. "I have no idea what you're talking about."

"The meteor shower comes from the constellation Ursa Major," he explained. "Most people recognize it as the Big Dipper, although it's technically not a constellation."

He studied her blank smile, her tentative nod.

"Do you know what a constellation is?"

"Naturally," she replied. "A chance grouping of stars, although you're clearly better versed on the subject than I am."

"That's because I'm a meteorologist, constantly studying weather patterns and the sky. Astronomy has a noteworthy effect on climate."

Her eyes sparkled. "I find astronomy fascinating."

"Excellent. Now we share another commonality." He opened the Star Tracker app on his phone and cited the stars blanketed by a black sky. "Are you interested in seeing meteors tonight?"

She hesitated. "I'm interested, sure. But—"

"A group of amateur astronomers meets twice a month at a field behind Bloomingfield High School. They're called the Stargazers. Ever hear of them?"

She accompanied him to the door. "No."

"The high school field is ideal for star watching, because the mountains block the city lights. Oftentimes, the Stargazers are there."

"Perhaps some other time." She sighed. "Tonight is a busy night at the restaurant."

"You can't work constantly, Julie. Besides, sky conditions are ideal." Desperately, he tried to keep his features straight, because he recognized her interest by her intent gaze. "I'll even bring my telescope."

She shook her head. "Impossible. Maybe after the holidays …" At her head shake, blond wisps broke free from her bun and fell across her cheek. "The restaurant can't operate without me."

"I'll pick you up after work at ten o'clock. Better yet, I'll come earlier." He deliberately ignored her observation about being indispensable. Once, he'd harbored the same mindset and had discovered a surprising awakening. The Pasta Junction could indeed function without her for a few hours, just as another weatherman had neatly and quickly filled Lorenzo's weatherman position in Atlanta.

Tenderly, he kissed her cheek. "This event only happens every twenty-four years. You don't want to miss it."

"I can't commit. After the restaurant closes, there's cleanup—"

"I'll help you. The best viewing for the meteor shower is around eleven o'clock until midnight. Thus you won't be out long, and I promise to deliver you home safely."

She glanced at his phone. "I've never allowed myself the time to study the stars."

"They're predicting hundreds of meteors. The outburst will last about fifteen minutes and promises an extraordinary show." He paused, then reminded, "Once every twenty-four years…"

"You are very persuasive." She granted him a flirtatious smile, presenting such a charming image he was torn between kissing her again or the correspondingly pleasant prospect of feasting his gaze on her.

"You were the expert when it came to pasta making. Although truth be told," he reminded, "you were a little bossy."

She shot a quick gaze toward the ceiling. "I was not because—" She broke off and frowned. "Was I?"

"A tad." He chuckled. "Anyway, tonight is an opportunity for me to demonstrate my knowledge."

"All these exciting adventures," she murmured. "You bring

the charming Italian man charisma thing to a whole new level."

"If I can persuade you to come with me, then I'm doing my job." He pocketed his phone and kissed her temple. "I'll pack a blanket and thermos of coffee."

"I'd honestly love to go." She wavered. "Should I bring food? I invariably have leftovers."

"Does your restaurant have a takeout or delivery service?"

"No," she replied. "I'm missing out on a profitable opportunity, right?"

"A service would provide a positive monthly addition to your income."

"I may try your recommendation. Mr. Rossi, you're a wizard."

"Hardly." He laughed, then sobered. "Where does the excess restaurant food end up?"

"I donate everything to a soup kitchen in town."

"Do you usually have pasta leftovers?"

"More often than not."

"Wow, I'll finally get to taste the pasta I toiled over." He lifted stray strands of her hair and nuzzled her neck, her chin, her lips.

"The pasta you toiled over for all of thirty minutes," she joked.

"With my knowledge and your expertise ..." he murmured, changing a line from a film he suspected she knew.

"We might go places," she finished, instantly proving that she did. "Although you're misquoting Frank Chambers from *The Postman Always Rings Twice.*"

"Did you know the movie was made in 1946?"

"I did. And I loved every minute of it."

And I love you.

The revelation startled him. Obviously, he couldn't be in

love with her. Their shared experiences had just begun. Plus they were on completely different tracks. She was immersed in her work while he'd learned to slow down and enjoy life. She was a true workaholic, and sometimes that got tiresome. Lately, it seemed everyone he knew was on the job 24/7. The way of the world, he supposed.

Stop analyzing, he ordered himself. They were simply *a couple*.

"Has anyone ever refused you?" She opened the front door to the rush of a warm breeze. The rain had stopped. Energetic sounds drifted from the street—the clink of coffee cups from people sitting outside at the nearby café, the whisper of tree branches, pedestrians chatting as they wandered in and out of the bookstore.

An occasional car was the only traffic. The restaurant's historic building was positioned in an ideal location, exuding traditional appeal in an intimate neighborhood.

"I don't remember." He gave a quiet chuckle. "Furthermore, I'll never refuse any of your requests, so we're even."

"That's encouraging." Her lilting laughter lit her entire face.

He laughed, enjoying the exhilaration of relishing every available second with this extraordinary woman.

CHAPTER 7

Star gazing. She'd actually gone star gazing.

Julie flopped on her living room couch and went over the previous evening in her mind.

True to his word, Lorenzo had arrived at The Pasta Junction well before ten o'clock. He'd worn his usual jeans, weathered chukka boots and scruffy leather jacket. Upon seeing her, he greeted her with a kiss. His chiseled features were all male, and her pulse leaped at the sound of his rich voice, his enthusiastic, "Hello, gorgeous."

Immediately, he went to work wherever she directed, assisting the bus boys and waiters and waitresses with an agreeable smile while they exchanged pleased looks with one another.

The restaurant's vibe was different from the quiet space he'd seen the last two days, he informed Julie. Now it purred with efficiency, as all the employees got down to the issue of cleanup.

She and Lorenzo decided to dine inside the restaurant, sliding into a booth in the formal dining area. The adjoining lounge featured a bar and large-screen television. Idly, they followed the news while enjoying a hasty meal of homemade fettuccini and crusty Italian bread.

"Delicious," Lorenzo pronounced, lifting his gaze now and then to the wall clock before focusing on the bowl, heaped with pasta, in the center of the table.

"Enjoy another helping," Julie encouraged.

"It's getting late." Reluctantly, he pushed back his chair. "I'm torn between eating more or stargazing, but we don't want to miss the meteor shower."

"The heavens won't wait for pasta?"

He exhaled. "Unfortunately not."

"Well then, return here tomorrow. I guarantee there will be more pasta."

"Are you extending an invitation?"

"You bet." She tugged off her apron and declared that she ought to freshen up. He immediately stood to stack their dinner plates and carry them to the kitchen. When she circled back, his slow, appreciative grin filled her with pleasure.

In the restroom, she brushed her hair until it snapped, leaving it loose and spilling over her shoulders. When she gazed in the mirror to apply a touch of red lipstick, she smiled at her reflection. Despite the many hours on her feet, her smile was genuine, and her complexion positively glowed.

"You are gorgeous," he said when she returned to the dining area. He brought a tender smile to his intent gaze. "And I like when you wear your hair down."

There was no denying that her pulse tingled every time he complimented her.

"Thanks." With a last fluff of her hair, she added water bottles to his backpack while he shrugged on his jacket. While the day's temperatures had been comfortable, a night in a large, open field would be chilly, and she donned a coral suede coat for extra warmth.

When they reached the open field, he set up two folding chairs, a tray table, a blanket on the ground, and then adjusted his telescope. Inky blackness enveloped them, and even though Lorenzo stood near, his figure blurred.

"Conditions are ideal for star gazing," he explained. "No rain is in the forecast and the sky is clear and not hazy."

She peered around. "Is this a good viewing spot?"

"Excellent. I'm here often. A while back, I instructed the astronomer's club on the various constellations."

Absently listening while he described why the best time to go star gazing was when the moon wasn't visible because moonlight washed out fainter stars, she dug into his backpack, poured two cups of coffee into cups and set them on the table.

He always remembered everything. In addition, he displayed gentlemanly characteristics she appreciated—holding doors open for her, standing when she stood, and complete absorption in her words whenever she spoke. Already, she was appreciating his insight and wisdom when she described a problem at the restaurant and he came up with a thoughtful solution.

Bighearted yet humble, he'd mentioned he volunteered weekly at a national park close by and cleaned up litter.

He loved nature. And because he was a meteorologist, a scientist who studied weather, he was also a perfectionist. She welcomed perfection, though food and creativity were her strong suits.

"Do you recognize the constellations?" he asked as he clicked his coffee cup against hers with a smile and a toast.

"Raise your cup to the extraordinary night sky," he said.

And she did. Here on this field, exuding enthusiasm and exuberance, he created a celebratory event.

She sipped her coffee and set down her cup. "A little."

"Where's Gemini?" He gestured upward, and a slight breeze caught his question. "You can see the constellation with your naked eye."

She shivered. "Perhaps if I knew where to look."

He glided his arm around her, and murmured, "There."

She leaned against his muscled chest and fixated on the pitch-black sky and brilliant pricks of stars, following his forefinger as he connected the stars with an imaginary line forming recognizable stick figures.

Together, they sat on the woolen blanket, and he suggested she lie back and peer upward. "The horizon will be at the edge of your peripheral vision," he said, "and the sky will fill everything you see."

She did as he directed, lying beside him on the woolen blanket. He waited until her eyes adjusted to the dark, then pointed out each star of the Little Dipper. Meteors streaking through the sky immediately captured her attention.

In awe was the only term she could use to describe the next fifteen minutes. The meteors' tiny sizes and penetrating brilliance, along with Lorenzo's throaty laugh as she excitedly gasped whenever she identified one, prompted her to forget everything except the extraordinary thrill of the moment.

"This entire evening is magical," she said.

He pulled her tight and cupped her face in his hands. "You're magical."

Her heart beat so hard and fast in her chest, she thought surely he must hear it.

When the meteor shower ended, she fully faced him. "What is the difference between a shooting star and a falling star?"

"They are the same," he replied. "Meteors travel at tens of

thousands miles per hour and burn because of the powerful atmospheric friction."

"Such a technical answer," she teased.

He smiled. "Occasionally you'll be lucky enough to witness a meteor plunge to earth. Thus, your falling star."

"Do you consider yourself a lucky man?" She gazed at his handsome face. Although the night was dark, she could discern the intense blueness of his eyes. Pausing, she surveyed his expression. "And why are you grinning like a Cheshire cat?"

"Because since I met you," he whispered, his face inches from hers, "I'm feeling fortunate and truly blessed."

Caught between joy and affection at his admission, she quietly stated, "So am I."

He shot her a gratified glance and skimmed his lips across her temple. "I intend to make you very, very happy."

Beneath a black velvet sky and twinkling stars, he drew her close and kissed her. His scent was the outdoors, mixed with a whiff of leather.

Close by, a chorus of high-pitched katydids serenaded them with their buzzing. He held her for a long while, his arms enfolding her.

Briefly, he closed his eyes, and she studied his features. His eyebrows were dark, his lashes thick and black and spiky. She shifted, and he gathered her closer. His response was unconscious, she assumed, but she was pleased with the idea that he wished her near.

It wasn't necessary, she dreamily reflected. She harbored no intention of drawing away, for she was falling in love with him. And she was surprised, because her love for him had developed so swiftly. When it came to her affections, she'd hidden behind a sturdy shield that had protected her. She'd been hurt once, and recovery took time.

But the moment had come to let down her shield, she decided, and she embraced the feelings of love and trust.

Lorenzo's second kiss was deeper, lengthier, and she responded by laying her hand on his cheek and responding with desire and certainty. With him, she could hardly contain the emotions welling inside her. She knew this vital, intelligent man was quickly winning a permanent place in her heart.

After their hour together had drifted to two, they packed their things and prepared to leave. Several people waved and shouted greetings as they started for Lorenzo's car.

"The amateur astronomers I mentioned," he murmured. "I assumed they were somewhere in this field tonight." He returned their waves and grinned.

"Lorenzo, what is your reaction to tonight's meteor display?" a stocky fellow called out. He wore binoculars around his neck and carried a telescope.

"I'm humbled by the universe," Lorenzo responded.

"Will we hear about the meteors on tomorrow's evening news?"

"Possibly, if my managers give me the go-ahead."

"Will you speak at one of our meetings again?" someone else asked. "You were sensational in October. Our members are still discussing the information you presented."

"I'm glad to oblige," Lorenzo replied.

"Your girlfriend is lovely," an older woman said.

Julie gazed up at him. Without question, he was a favored television personality among the townspeople of Bloomingfield, and their regard for him seemed to cautiously embrace her too.

With his arm securely around her, Lorenzo agreed with the woman, then tipped up Julie's chin.

"You can't kiss me in front of the entire astronomer's

club," she whispered, knowing her face heated and feeling eternally grateful for the darkness.

"With your permission I can." He waited a beat. "Permission granted?"

Seeing his affectionate gaze, she smiled. "No one can refuse your Italian—"

"Charm," he finished with a mischievous gleam. He bent his head and soundly kissed her.

Somewhere in the distance, a cheer rose up. In response, Lorenzo locked her in a tight embrace and kissed her again.

CHAPTER 8

As the following days merged into a frenzy of activity, New Year's Eve arrived.

Julie stood in the foyer of The Pasta Junction and cradled her cell phone to her ear.

"I need your help," she told Sally while she hung a broad white sign with black lettering on the front door.

"'I was thinking about that dame upstairs.'" Julie quoted the sign aloud.

"Huh?" Sally asked.

"I'm citing Fred MacMurray's words in *Double Indemnity*. Anyone familiar with film noir will recognize the famous line immediately."

"I've never watched those movies," Sally said.

"Once you start, you'll be hooked." Julie circled her attention to the never-ending business at hand—organizing and preparing an outstanding gala. Three days earlier, on the spur of the moment, she'd decided to offer a glamorous, film noir theme. She posted the event on her website, inviting women to wear sleek gowns, elegant gloves and saucy hats. *Dress up or dress down*, she wrote. *All are welcome.*

She listed three-piece pin-striped suits as an option for men.

"So you require my help because …?" Sally reverted their conversation back to the reason Julie had phoned. As usual, Sally was ringing out customers in her chocolate shop, and the simultaneous chime of the cash register and chatting people brought a smile to Julie's face. Ben and his girlfriend, Maise, had taken Clarissa, Sally's daughter, to an afternoon matinee.

Katie, their lawyer sister, as Ben teasingly called her, was out of town for the holidays and vacationing in Colorado.

"I need your help because you're the chocolate expert, Sally," Julie replied. She stepped back to peruse the dining room. For late-night munchies, she'd serve popcorn in striped containers, arrayed on black linen tablecloths. Beverages included festive bubbly cocktails, both alcoholic and nonalcoholic, and dinner would be served on gleaming white plates offset by black chargers. After a balloon drop and confetti at midnight, she'd added a one o'clock a.m. supper buffet, expecting her guests might be hungry again. She'd also partnered with a local cab company to offer free rides home to revelers after the festivities ended.

Easygoing background music, moody jazz arrangements featuring a saxophonist accompanied by a string quartet, enhanced the setting, and Lorenzo's poster hung prominently on one wall.

Lorenzo. She stared at the poster, recalling so many images of him.

His shoulders quaking with laughter at her exclamations upon seeing hundreds of meteors, the attractive white smile that flew across his face whenever he gazed at her, the stubborn way he crossed his arms when he declared yet another baking session was in order.

Since her flirtation with the married guy a few years ago,

she'd held every man at arm's length. Her emotions hadn't seemed alive.

But with Lorenzo …Around him she melted. When they weren't together, she struggled to focus on her job. However, work didn't seem as important anymore. Perhaps she was suffering from burnout. More likely, she was deeply in love with a man she'd only met less than two weeks ago.

And the reality of the situation sent a heated pulse through her body.

"Hello?" Sally asked.

"Sorry."

"You do that a lot these days."

Julie flinched. "Do what?"

"Daydream, and it has something to do with a certain drop-dead gorgeous weatherman who'll be on TV at six o'clock tonight. You're still seeing him, correct?"

"Every day," Julie replied. "And I just wanted to tell someone that the last cassata he and I baked came out just as delectable as the previous two."

"Okay, good. So again, my help is needed because …"

Julie spun on her heels for the kitchen, realizing her buffet table lacked champagne flutes. "Because *I* declared the cassata delicious."

"Then I think I know where this conversation is going." Sally laughed. "Somehow I get the impression that Lorenzo didn't share your enthusiasm?"

"Maybe I should add more chocolate chips to the recipe to appease him?" Julie stopped in mid step. "This time, he claimed there was something not quite right about the taste."

"Uh huh. Look, I'm a chocolate candy expert, not a baker. Pouring chocolate chips into a cheesecake isn't my forte."

"Get this." Julie peered at the evening menu and lost her train of thought. The Pasta Junction would serve a la carte dining from five until eight, and a toast from ten o'clock until the early morning buffet.

"Get what?" Sally prompted.

"Lorenzo claimed he suddenly realized that a first wedding anniversary is a paper anniversary," Julie said.

"Suddenly?"

"Yes. Therefore, he wants the cassata brought to his mother's anniversary table in a box."

"Like … a cardboard box?"

"Cardboard, paper. He didn't say."

"I display my chocolate candy in bento boxes. What size is the cassata?"

"We're doubling the recipe. Thus, a sizable box is preferable."

"I'll look around and bring something tonight and leave it in your back office. Ben and I and Maise plan on dining at your restaurant around seven. Clarissa is coming too, obviously."

"Excellent. Don't forget the theme is black and white."

"My daughter and I are matchy-matchy. Black poodle skirts and starchy white blouses."

"You nailed it. Talk to you later."

AT FIRST WHEN Lorenzo walked into The Pasta Junction at ten o'clock that evening, Julie didn't see him. Instead she sensed his presence when heads swung toward the door. He had a tangible, confident personality that filled the room.

Clearing empty glasses on her path to the kitchen, she swiveled.

For a second he remained in the lobby, conversing with the maître d' who accepted his black leather jacket. All the while, Lorenzo's gaze skimmed the dining room. With a flush of excitement, she knew he searched for her.

Their gazes connected, and she set down the glasses.

Quickly, he fixed his dinner jacket on an empty chair, weaved around the candlelit tables and swept her into his arms for a kiss.

"You've outdone yourself tonight, Julie," he said. "The restaurant looks spectacular and you are …" He stepped back, frankly admiring her glamorous V-neck black gown, slinky and flaring at the hem, with scalloped lace embellished sleeves. Tiny diamond earrings, strappy sandals and her trademark fedora hat completed the outfit. She'd brought her white faux fur coat and black opera gloves to wear later when Lorenzo drove her home.

She lifted an eyebrow at his loss for words. "I am …?"

"Exquisite. A femme fatale."

Her breath caught at the gentleness in his voice. "Thank you."

She took in his powerful shoulders fitted in a snowy-white shirt, his narrow waist and long legs encased in black pants topped with black suspenders. Her heart did a flip, and she battled to keep her emotions in check. He'd dressed the part, emanating masculinity, and it was clear that every woman in the dining room had set down her fork to marvel at his exceptional looks.

"I hoped to arrive sooner," he said. "But the second my TV segment was over, the station held a staff party to celebrate the holiday … All the while, 'I was thinking about that dame upstairs.'"

She chuckled, burying her escalating attraction behind a jest. "If you mean me, I'm not upstairs."

His gaze fixed intently on her. The buoyant mood grew serious. "Good. I like you near me."

She swallowed. "I'm thrilled you're here. We'll ring in the new year together." She gestured to the packed dining room, the waiters traveling from table to table. "As you can see, it's one of the busiest nights of the year."

He grimaced. "Duly noted."

"Don't you like big crowds?"

"Not a bit," he softly replied.

"You're an extrovert, so I'm surprised to hear you say that."

Sharply, he glanced at her. "Why would you assume I'm an extrovert?"

"You're a public figure and on television every day where you're viewed by thousands."

"You're describing me in front of the camera in a closed-off area with people I know and trust, and where I'm comfortable." He reached for her hand and steered her into a quiet corner. "In truth, I'm an extroverted introvert."

"What does that mean? You're friendly and outgoing. You spoke at the astronomer's meeting."

"On television and in a setting I can control," he said. "Nonetheless, what people don't see is that I go home afterwards to recharge my batteries in solitude."

"Julie?" From a nearby table, a familiar woman's voice called out to them. "Aren't you going to introduce us?" Sally gaily waved, then attempted to pat her springy curls back into place. She'd declared years ago that no matter how many straightening products she used, in the end it was futile.

She and her daughter Clarissa displayed matching outfits, although Clarissa kept pulling at the collar of her starched blouse. Dark-haired Ben sported a suit and was smiling at his date, chestnut-haired and green-eyed Maise, who wore a broad-brimmed hat that dipped over one eye.

Julie shot Lorenzo a rueful glance. "My family wants to meet you."

There was a noticeable pause before he responded.

"Right." He picked up a non-alcoholic cocktail from a

passing waiter, took a gulp, and kept a death grip on his glass. "Okay."

She felt his guard go up and couldn't understand why. He was so upbeat and witty. Why would he greet meeting her family with such unease, just because he was an introvert? They were merely four people, and one was a little girl.

She gave his hand a squeeze and led him over to them.

After introductions, Sally grabbed Lorenzo's arm and led him into the lounge to see the holiday decorations. Odd, yes, but Sally had been eager to talk with Lorenzo, and they were hardly gone a couple minutes.

When they returned, Ben merrily declared to Lorenzo that he had a stack of weatherman jokes, and inquired whether Lorenzo wanted to hear one. "Did you tell him my other joke?" he asked Julie.

"I'm sorry. I forgot."

"Well, this one is better." Ben angled toward Lorenzo.

"I can't wait," Lorenzo informed him. Still standing with Julie while the others sat, he set his drink on the table.

"A weatherman broke both of his arms and his legs," Ben began, "and he phoned the television station from the hospital. Guess what he told them?"

Laughing, Julie held up a hand. "The weatherman couldn't report to work because of his injuries?"

Ben grinned. "Nope. He informed the station about his four casts. Get it? Forecasts."

All three women, Julie, Maise, and Sally, dissolved into exaggerated laughter, and Clarissa giggled and clapped her hands. Her rosy red cheeks and sweet personality had brought abundant joy to the Elliot family, and Julie bent to hug her.

Lorenzo reached for his drink. "I get it, yes." He smiled, although his smile didn't seem sincere. "Your joke is … amusing."

"Have you heard that joke before?" Julie murmured to him as they walked away.

"About a thousand times," he replied.

After her family left, Lorenzo helped Julie wherever she asked, which was mostly keeping the patrons happy. In fact, he demonstrated a sixth sense regarding restaurant management, working out details with the staff before they became readily apparent.

All the while, she was absorbed in speculation. Although he'd acted personable with her family, he'd also seemed dismissive. When Sally had suggested they all get together soon, Lorenzo's posture had stiffened.

Okay, he was uncomfortable, an introvert, although no one would suspect by watching him. His smile remained in place, his manner relaxed and sociable.

She peered around. How could an enormous crowd, or an impromptu meeting with her family, not invigorate him?

THE NEW YEAR countdown began a short while later, and Lorenzo assisted Julie and the waitstaff in distributing leis and noisemakers to the guests.

"Oh no!" Julie grabbed a noisemaker, whirled, and brought a shaky hand to her forehead. "Where are the party hats? It's almost midnight!" She rushed to a side table and bent to search beneath the tablecloth for the feather tiaras and light-up fedoras. "I must have left them in the back room."

"You did, and I found them." Lorenzo edged her toward the waiters who were distributing the hats.

Amazed and touched to realize he'd taken care of another detail for her, she straightened and beamed into his handsome, smiling face.

When they'd first met, she'd been uneasy because she'd

assumed he was married. Afterward, because he was so lethally good-looking and well-regarded, she'd been reluctant to admit her feelings. Now, as the clock was about to herald a new year, she had a strong urge to tell him how much she cared. But, she warned herself, she was perched dangerously close to the edge of a perilous cliff, and she'd already been hurt once in love.

She pushed aside her reservations and spoke aloud what she'd been thinking ever since he'd gifted her the poster. "A handsome man has strolled into my peaceful life."

He tipped up her chin. "And a beautiful woman has strolled into mine."

They angled toward the television screen in the lounge area. Along with a tide of revelers, they counted off the seconds until midnight.

"Ten, nine, eight, seven, six, five, four, three, two, one … Happy New Year!"

Lorenzo embraced her. On cue, the waiter in charge of the sound system put on "Auld Lang Syne," sung by a lone Scottish man. Tears pricked Julie's eyes.

Lorenzo held her close, swaying with the music.

"I've always loved that song," she whispered.

"And I love you," he said quietly.

Her gaze flew to his face. Wait, what? He said he loved her.

A tremble of excitement quickened her pulse. And yet she couldn't respond to his heartfelt declaration. It was too soon. Too soon to put herself out there and become vulnerable to …

To what?

Still, she didn't reply.

She stole a look at his shuttered expression before a waitress apologized for the interruption and declared they were out of popcorn.

Julie hightailed it into the kitchen to solve the minor crisis by substituting the popcorn with pretzels.

Lorenzo came up behind her. "I have an awesome idea." He wrapped his arms around her waist. "Let's take in a movie at the Grover Theater tonight."

She wheeled around. "The cinema is showing a movie tonight?"

"Yes, remember? One of the most popular film noir movies."

"*The Big Sleep?*"

Lorenzo grinned. "There's a showing at one. If we hurry, we'll make it."

"One o'clock in the morning? Who would go to a movie at that time?"

"We would."

"Lorenzo, I can't leave my staff to fend for themselves."

He perused the kitchen and half-dozen employees, the babble of cheery voices as they moved about their tasks preparing for the supper buffet. "They seem extremely efficient to me."

"I've never attended a movie at this time of night. Or day, depending on how you view it. Plus, I have an anniversary party to prepare for tomorrow."

"*My* party doesn't begin until three."

"Which is when my restaurant opens," she reminded. In addition, she planned to bake the cassata *without* his assistance. Intent on facilitating the early morning supper preparations, she attempted to scurry past him.

He braced his hands on either side of the door frame, blocking her way. "Tonight is special. It's New Year's Eve."

"The clock chimed midnight a half hour ago." Despite her protests, she knew she couldn't refuse him, and admitted as much. She dashed to the back office to retrieve her coat and gloves.

By the time she came back, he'd reclaimed his leather jacket.

He helped her on with her coat and extended his arm. "Ready?"

"You are impossible." She couldn't resist smoothing a lock of black hair from his forehead.

He smiled. "My SUV is parked a block away. Wait in the lobby. The weather is cold tonight."

"I can brave the cold."

"I'll pick you up. Wait here."

"Does anyone ever refuse you?" With a laugh in her voice, she placed her hand in the crook of his arm and walked with him to the lobby. A waft of wind teased her hair as he opened the door, and he gently swept the stray strands from her cheek.

Slowly, languorously, he appraised her. "Not on a marvelous night like this," he murmured, and sealed his statement with a kiss.

CHAPTER 9

New Year's Eve with Lorenzo should have ended marvelously, the way Lorenzo had described it.

It didn't.

The following morning arrived prematurely for Julie, and she'd overslept. Still tired from the night before, she showered quickly and got dressed. As she paused at the French doors in her apartment and gazed out at a dazzlingly bright day, her thoughts veered to the previous evening.

After the movie had let out at three a.m., she and Lorenzo had strolled hand in hand toward his SUV, laughing and chatting. Save for the streetlights, the darkness was dense, the air cool. She looked around at her beloved hometown of Bloomingfield, the thick Ponderosa pines, the mountains soaring in the distance, and felt utter serenity. Soon, the sun would streak through the tree boughs in bright beams of daylight, and the mountain peaks would overshadow the horizon.

"What we're doing is called a *passeggiata* in Italy," Lorenzo said.

"Which means?"

"It's an Italian tradition, and everyone in the town participates. People dress up and take a leisurely stroll. Usually on Sunday evenings or a holiday."

"Today is a holiday," she said. "And I can grow accustomed to that tradition."

She stepped lightly as they continued, a weightlessness in her limbs, a sense of breathlessness she couldn't describe. Or maybe she could. She was content. Truly content.

She tilted her head. "Although I've watched *The Big Sleep* at least a half dozen times, I never tire of watching it."

He nodded, seeming to know precisely what she meant.

Pausing at a street corner, he gestured upward and pointed out Orion, the hunter, the brightest constellation in the sky. He shared his enthusiasm for the stars with her, just as he had the night they went star gazing, bringing to mind an amazing memory and poignant tears. She loved everything about this man.

He tipped up her chin. "Why are you crying? Is anything wrong?"

"I'm not crying because I'm sad." She leaned into his chest. "I'm crying because I'm happy."

As they went on, he asked, "What was your favorite scene in the film?"

"There are several, but I always chuckle when Philip Marlowe first meets his daughter, Vivien. He mentions not being very tall and walking on stilts."

"And Vivien coolly informs him that stilts won't help." Lorenzo chuckled. "The dialogue in the entire film is flawless."

Julie nodded in agreement. Perhaps it was the late hour, or the exhaustion from an incredibly busy day, or the fact that she felt so close to him, but it struck her that she should be totally honest with him. Therefore, she decided to challenge him with a question she'd reflected on all evening.

"Don't you like my family?"

He stopped and regarded her with a slight frown. "Why on earth would you ask me that question?"

"Because you were … standoffish with them."

"I'm a loner, Julie. I told you that."

"But if you don't want to be with my family, then that affects me."

"I never said I didn't want to hang out with your family."

You acted it, she thought, but didn't express her observation aloud. Most likely, she was reading into actions and words that weren't there. Again, she blamed her reservations on weariness. Why had she brought up the subject? The evening had been perfect until then.

"What did you think of my sister, Sally?" she asked.

"She seems nice. We only chatted alone for a couple minutes."

"Yes." Julie raised an eyebrow.

He paused, apparently choosing his words carefully. "From our discussion, she's totally invested in her daughter, her family and the chocolate shop."

"She's an entrepreneur and a hard worker."

"Another word to describe a workaholic."

She shot him an uneasy glance. "What's wrong with being a workaholic?"

"I'm tired of hearing about work, work, work. There's considerable more to life. When I'm in Italy, the pace is slower. Italians take their time eating, drinking and socializing."

"Well, some of us haven't had the opportunity to travel to Italy."

"And others," he firmly reminded, "were specifically invited. I believe I'm still waiting for a favorable response."

She rubbed her forehead, realizing she should answer him. "I'll know more after the first of the year." Her reply was noncommittal. She knew it, and so did he. "Let's see how it goes."

How what goes? Their relationship? How her restaurant fared? She didn't elaborate.

He offered a cool smile, his posture stiff and proud. "Right."

BY NOON, Julie stopped into The Pasta Junction's kitchen, soon flanked by two of her finest cooks, one being Antonio, her sous chef. While they engaged in the preparation of meatballs, baked chicken, and fried sausage and peppers for Lorenzo's party, she readied her homemade fettuccini.

She insisted on preparing the cassata herself, cracking eggs, chopping maraschino cherries, stirring the ingredients together, and applying some of Lorenzo's suggestions for interpreting his grandmother's recipe by using exact measurements.

But then she resisted. He used math to figure precise quantities, but they'd tested his method and he still hadn't been satisfied. The man was never content when it came to this dessert.

Sally had insinuated that it was more—his excuse to see Julie.

Perhaps. She set down the mixing spoon and stared at the cake mix box.

But there was more.

When he'd described his grandmother's cassata, waxing poetic about her cozy kitchen, the rich scent of chocolate chips, he'd actually hummed and begun singing in Italian.

Realistically, however, he wouldn't remember how the

dessert tasted. He was seeking to recapture an ideal moment from his childhood. That's what he was after.

The memories. The good times framed forever in his mind.

A HALF HOUR before Lorenzo's family was scheduled to arrive, nervous anticipation brought an emptiness to the pit of Julie's stomach.

Suppose his mother didn't approve of her? Or what if his family didn't like her restaurant, or the special buffet and dessert she'd prepared?

Quickly, she changed out of her work attire. Lorenzo had invited her to the party, insisting she attend as a guest, and not a hostess who would serve them. This caused even more of a panic. She'd literally be sitting down to a meal with them.

She closed her eyes and breathed a calming breath.

For the event, she'd chosen a knee-length dress in a shimmering silver and high heel pumps. She left her hair loose, the way Lorenzo preferred, and it fell over her shoulders in loose waves.

Of course, there was also a feeling of panic because of the man himself, she thought, as she clipped on a pair of sparkly earrings. They hadn't parted on good terms. He usually texted her in the morning, and his texts, which she'd read with a racing heart, had been short:

Happy New Year, Julie.

She responded with the same greeting.

Do you need any help today? I'm happy to come to the restaurant early. I'm done at the station by noon. I can assist you with the cassata preparation.

Thanks. I'm all set. She'd cringed after she'd sent the message. Did it sound like she didn't need his help … that she didn't need *him?*

Okay, came his response.

She wondered if he was really okay with her answer.

My staff volunteered to come in early, she quickly texted, as a way to assuage her reply with an explanation. *Thanks anyway.*

See you at three o'clock, then.

She typed *Great,* changed it to *Good,* and hit send.

After she freshened her lipstick, she read through his texts again. Their exchange had been systematic. Dejectedly, she blew out a sigh, remembering the slightly sour ending to their evening. She didn't have enough experience with relationships, and as swift as their attraction had been, there was plenty yet to learn about each other.

With a final determined breath, she inspected herself in the full-length mirror in the restroom, and headed for the private dining area for the final arrangements.

When Lorenzo's family arrived a few minutes later, his mother, a tiny slim woman, swept into the room, surrounded by four men, one woman, and two giggling children.

The way Lorenzo's mother carried herself brought poise to her effortless beauty. As Lorenzo took the lead, presenting his mother as Mrs. Eleanor Talley to Julie, her motions were graceful.

She held Julie's hand firmly for several seconds before letting go. "I've heard a great deal about you." Her gray eyes, with flecks of gold and brown, emanated warm kindness. "My son spoke about you nonstop when he visited my husband and me in Wyoming."

"Did he?" Bewildered laughter stole into Julie's tone.

"Thanks for giving away all my secrets," Lorenzo said before focusing on Julie. "Happy New Year."

The husky resonance in his tone drew a sharp wrench to her heart.

"Happy New Year, Lorenzo."

"You are beautiful."

"Thank you. And you are dashing."

Already, he'd taken off his suit jacket and rolled his white shirtsleeves back.

"Lorenzo, we haven't taken any pictures yet," his mother chided.

"I'll put my jacket back on for pictures, Ma," he replied.

From beneath her long lashes, Julie studied him. He caught her gaze and smiled, and she was fully aware of the magnetism drawing them together.

He broke the spell by doubling back to an elderly balding man with a neat white mustache. "May I introduce my stepfather, Joe Talley? He's brought my mother tremendous happiness and we're pleased to all be present for their first wedding anniversary."

"Julie, your restaurant is magnificent," Eleanor remarked, as Lorenzo rushed away to dash after the twins, who were taking turns jumping off a side chair. "Believe me, my family knows a lot about running a restaurant."

"You do?" Julie asked.

"Yes, my late husband owned a restaurant for a short spell. Didn't Lorenzo mention it to you?"

Unpleasantly surprised, Julie shook her head. "No, he never breathed a word."

"It was only for a matter of months. Just long enough to ensure we all lost money before his next venture." With a dismissive wave, Eleanor redirected her attention to the group. "Thank you, Lorenzo, for all your planning, and to my lovely daughter and her husband and children, and my son, John."

Regina, Lorenzo's sister, gave a friendly wave, then attempted to catch up to her twin girls who were chasing each other around the room.

Lorenzo returned and guided his mother and stepfather to the head of the table, which Julie had decorated in gold. The table featured a large pansy flower bouquet centerpiece, the vivid purple and bright yellow blossoms brilliantly displayed in an antique cream-colored teapot. From the ceiling, Julie's staff had hung gold balloons and streamers. The traditional colors and flowers celebrated a first anniversary.

John stepped up to Julie and took her cold hands in his. "Now that wasn't so bad, was it?" he teased.

"I'm thrilled to meet your family."

"Good, because we're happy to meet you too." Like his older brother, John was tall and slim, and his dark good looks heightened the similarity between them. However, John's eyes were a soft gray, the same color as his mother's, and his presence wasn't as powerful as Lorenzo's. He possessed a tranquil quality, but still exuded his brother's charm in equal measure.

"I hope to make a good impression," Julie admitted.

"For Lorenzo's sake."

"For all of you," she clarified.

At the sound of Eleanor's voice, everyone swung toward her in unison. "And now," she declared as the waitstaff set up the buffet's silver trays, "*mangiamo*. Let's eat."

Tempting aromas of basil, garlic, peppers, and tomato sauce filled the intimate room, and everyone heartily agreed.

LORENZO INVITED Julie to sit next to him at the round table they all shared. He was confused by the distance she maintained between them, which seemed odd considering her delighted expression when his mother had remarked that he'd spoken about Julie nonstop.

Throughout dinner, he methodically reexamined their

whirlwind courtship, seeking a clue, a detail in one of their conversations. Perhaps he'd miscalculated the deepness of her feelings for him, although she'd responded to his kisses with sweet abandonment, and consistently seemed pleased to see him.

By the time the meal was finished, he'd only come up with pleasant images of their moments together. Julie was kind and good-hearted, radiating a generous spirit.

Was she afraid of a commitment? If so, he understood. Sally had revealed to him in their short two minutes together that Julie had been hurt by a married man.

"We're ready for dessert!" His sister's twin girls interrupted his musings, loudly chanting when the waitresses brought out two perfect cassatas arranged on white bento boxes. The staff placed both boxes by Lorenzo's mother.

He grinned, reveling in her exclamations of delight. When she tasted the cassata, she'd remember …

Emma—her curly hair the only distinguishable characteristic between her and her straight-haired twin, Ella—raced from her seat. Before anyone could react, she reached up to the table and yanked one of the boxes. The cassata landed on the floor and split in two.

Julie quickly rose, and he drew her back down. "Allow your staff to handle it. We'll eat the other cassata."

As one waitress cleaned up the mess, the other sliced the cheesecake and delivered the first piece to his mother on a gleaming plate. Lorenzo watched her intently, waiting for her reaction.

"Delicious!" She smiled at Julie. "You baked this?"

Julie blushed gorgeously. "Yes. Do you like it?"

"I love it!"

His mother took another bite, but didn't dissolve into tears, as he'd half-expected. Maybe her mother's cassata hadn't been as important to her as it had been to him.

"Is anything the matter?" Julie asked him, as she accepted her plated cassata from a server.

"I'm surprised," he said.

"Are you surprised the cassata turned out so well?"

"You're a mastermind in the kitchen." He sampled a bite and closed his eyes, almost dropping his fork. Yes, whatever Julie had created, she'd managed to bring alive the memories of his youth.

"Is this the part where I'm supposed to offer a clever rejoinder?" she teased. "Perhaps another weatherman joke?"

He laughed. "I'll wait for your brother for that."

Much to his relief, her eyes twinkled. Slowly, he felt her tenseness begin to melt away.

He set his fork beside his plate as the lights dimmed, and a 1940s song began to play, *I'm in the Mood For Love*. His heart burst with pride. Julie had organized every detail to ensure the party's success.

Lorenzo's stepfather and mother found a modest space on the floor to dance. The twins gleefully joined in, holding hands and twirling round and round.

Julie chuckled. "They're adorable and exactly how you described."

He glimpsed her profile. Her head was turned away, her hands folded in her lap.

"And so are you." He placed an arm around her shoulders.

"I'm adorable?"

"Absolutely."

She granted him a sidelong glance and sidled closer. "And you're the most charming man I've ever met."

"Excellent, because I hope to occupy many hours of your time." Gently, he stroked her hair. "That is, if it's okay."

"It's okay."

"Look, I'm sorry about what I said … about your family. They're a fun bunch."

She gazed up at him. "They mean the world to me. I love every minute with them and want to share those moments with you."

Because she cared.

"Only on one condition," he warned.

"What's that?"

"You'll spend time with my family as well. Agreed?"

She brought a heartwarming smile to her nod. "Agreed."

"And there's another thing," he added.

"What's that?"

"How about a little trip to Italy with me?"

She gave him a questioning look. "You still want me to go?"

"Absolutely."

"Then I gladly accept. I'm looking forward to knowing you better in the new year. Everything about you."

"I feel the same way about you." He smoothed a kiss on her temple. "Any more good news?"

Her beautiful eyes widened. "I'm adopting a dog."

"A male?"

"Yes. His name will be Buddy."

This was his Julie. Taking time to mull things over, then coming to a decision when she was ready.

"I love you," he softly said.

Her reaction was thoughtful, bringing a firm tug to his heart. "I love you too."

"You know," he said, "I was thinking about that dame upstairs."

"Think no more. I'm right beside you."

And that's where he intended her to stay. Beside him, where she belonged.

Their new beginning, a fresh start, brought a mistiness to his eyes.

Because a beautiful, precious woman, the woman he loved, had strolled into his peaceful life.

And she had brought with her a bright future, full of limitless possibilities.

THE END

A NOTE FROM JOSIE

Dear Friends,

Thank you for reading *A Chocolate-Box New Years.*

I wanted to write a holiday romance centering around chocolate.

If you loved this sweet romance as much as I loved writing it, please help other people find *A Chocolate-Box New Years* by posting your review.

A Chocolate-Box New Years is available in ebook, paperback, Hardcover, Audiobook, and Large Print paperback.

My Spotify Play List for A Chocolate-Box New Years is here.

RECIPE FOR GRANDMA GLORIA'S CHEESECAKE CASSATA

Ingredients:

Marble Cake Mix

2 lbs. coarse ricotta cheese (use low or non-fat if you prefer)

½ cup sugar

4 eggs

1 cup chocolate chips, or more.

1 cup maraschino cherries-chopped, or less.

Instructions:

Follow recipe on cake mix box. Place in a greased cassata or sturdy angel food cake pan.

Blend the rest of the ingredients together and place on top of prepared cake mix.

Bake at 350 degrees for 1 ½ hours.

Let set for 2 hours. Better when refrigerated.

Enjoy!

JOSIE RIVIERA

a Chocolate-Box Valentine

PRAISE AND AWARDS

USA TODAY bestselling author

Top 15 Amazon Bestseller Family Life Fiction

Top 20 Amazon Bestseller Saga Fiction

Top 20 Amazon Bestseller Romance Anthologies

CHAPTER 1

It was raining. Again. Hard and relentless.

Sally Elliot gazed out the window of Bloomingfield Candy Shop, the shop that she'd owned for nearly a decade.

From high school onward, she'd become passionate about candy making and dedicated all her efforts into turning her dream into a reality. She'd prided herself on her strong work ethic, because surely success would follow. And her shop wasn't a franchise. The shop was her *own* business, started from scratch.

However, as in the case of many newbie business owners, she'd overestimated her sales and underestimated her costs.

Yet, her perseverance had eventually paid off.

Or rather, her perseverance *usually* paid off, except that … Well, except that if today was any indication of candy sales for the month of February, she was skating directly toward a patch of thin ice. If she plunged through, she'd be out of funds within six months.

With a nervous sigh, she glanced out the front window of her shop.

Anxious thoughts clustered in her mind, as they invariably did when sales were slow, and she did her best to banish them. It was a gray, rainy and steely afternoon. Therefore, she attributed the lack of sales to the bad weather.

Okay, fine. She turned away from the window. She could deal with bad weather.

However, she couldn't deal with the fact that the delivery of the specialty chocolate she'd ordered, in fact, *needed*, was late. Not thirty minutes late, or an hour, but an entire half day. And this was a rush supply, because she had underestimated the amount of candy that customers would pre-order for Valentine's Day.

She'd read in a business magazine that fifty-eight billion pounds of chocolate were purchased during Valentine's week. Well, she was nowhere near selling that amount.

Still, her store sold a lot of candy.

Ben, her older brother, stood beside a white display case in the middle of the store, holding his cellphone to his ear. He offered a trace of a smile, then sobered. His gaze flicked from her to the free foil-wrapped candy kisses they offered to customers near the cash register. Gift cards were also conveniently stacked for last-minute buyers, who were mostly men.

Sally shook her head. Surely there was some psychology behind that. Perhaps men didn't embrace the shopping experience like women did. Or perhaps they were procrastinators, because they didn't have the right mindset to shop.

She wouldn't know. She hadn't been part of the dating scene for many years. In fact, because she'd married so young, had she ever been part of the scene?

Ben muttered into his cellphone, glanced at her, and then away again. She blinked in confusion at his somber expression, pressing away the prickle of awareness that something might be wrong.

No. This day couldn't possibly get any worse.

She walked to the front of the store. The vibrant red lollipops, balloons and gaily packaged gifts she'd added to the entryway brought a grin to her face. Several displays enhanced the different types of chocolate in the shiny cases lining the walls, and all reflected the upcoming Valentine celebration. As a savvy businesswoman, she recognized that placing beautiful and enticingly wrapped candy boxes where they would easily be seen resulted in impulse buys.

She'd been pleased with the result, though now she wasn't so sure.

Was the staging too white? Too red? Too cutesy? Had the displays put buyers off from entering the store today?

Thoughtfully, she nibbled on her lower lip as she second-guessed herself.

Ben ended his conversation, then jammed his cellphone into his pocket.

She turned to him. "Are you finally finished with your conversation?"

"Yep." His voice was quiet, his gaze probing. "And can you do anything else besides look worried?"

Her seasoned eyes took in his uneasy expression. "Can you do something besides acting so secretive?"

"Okay, that's a fair question," he said, "but I expect an answer from you first."

"Why?"

"Because I asked you first."

"Alright." She shifted. "Does my nervousness show because of our lack of customers today?"

"A little. Actually, more than a little." His unswerving stare unnerved her. "You don't seem to enjoy anything fun anymore. Often, Maise and I have invited you to dinner, and you consistently refuse."

"What does that have to do with my looking nervous?"

"Everything. Your business shouldn't be the focus of your entire life."

"It isn't," she answered with a self-conscious laugh. "My daughter is."

"Along with your business."

"This conversation isn't fair, Ben. The biggest candy holiday of the year is looming and I can't deal with any more guilt. I'm extremely busy right now."

"You're always busy because you're a workaholic."

"Please, Ben, not again, although I realize you mean well." Sally stood straight in open rebellion, using the cool business tone she usually reserved for her suppliers when she haggled over snagging the best prices. "You and Maise can invite me when Valentine's Day is over. I guarantee I'll say yes."

"We'll see."

Despite the five-year age difference between them, their features were similar—both blue eyed, tall and lean. However, that was where the similarities ended, because Sally had been a tangle-haired blond adventurer in her youth, whereas dark-haired Ben was a stickler for following rules.

Nonetheless, Ben was her financial as well as emotional support. When her daughter, Clarissa, had been born prematurely, so tiny and swaddled in pink chenille blankets in a hospital isolette, her husband, Leon, had deserted them. At the tender age of twenty, Sally had become a single mother and consequently depended on Ben and her two sisters, because Leon had disappeared from her life. Several years later, nothing had changed except for her hasty divorce.

Once, as a teenage girl harboring romantic fantasies, she'd assumed that she and Leon shared a love that endured forever. After all, they'd dated since high school.

She'd been wrong.

For better or for worse. She shook her head in mock disgust at her naïve illusions.

"So on February fifteenth," Ben said, "you'll revert back to the optimistic sister I formally knew?"

"You've known me all your life."

"I mean the fun-loving adventurous girl before you became an entrepreneur." At her frown, he hastily explained, "Which will be great, because I've never seen you this jumpy and anxious, not even during the Christmas holiday candy season."

Sally stooped to rearrange the trail of pink and lavender paper hearts she'd secured to the front window. With dismay, she realized that one of the hearts had torn. Did she have any extra hearts left? She scrambled to her feet, intending to rummage through the back storage room.

"I'm jumpy and anxious," she clarified, "because I need that case of specialty chocolate for my newest candy-making project. And you still haven't answered *my* question, Ben. You're looking so … secretive." Ben's gaze was downcast as she rushed past him. He didn't reply, but her mind was already racing toward the next task. "Moonglow Chocolatiers supplies the finest chocolate and I'm depending on them to come through with my rush order."

"You don't *need* specialty chocolate," Ben said. "You *want* specialty chocolate."

She swung around. "I've advertised my new chocolate creations since January, and there are outstanding orders. Not to mention our walk-in customers between now and February fourteenth. I can't produce dark shells for salted caramel infusion candy without bittersweet chocolate."

"What is infusion candy, anyway?"

"I explained to you yesterday. It's—"

"I remember."

"Do you, truly?"

"Well, I remember the candy part." He threw up his hands. "I admit my knowledge of candy would fit into—"

"A peanut butter cup."

"Right." He smirked. "But as co-owner of your shop, I have permission to be concerned about you. You're spending excessive time and energy focusing on your latest product and you're exhausted and overwhelmed."

"Once I hire the two additional new employees—"

"Both of whom you haven't found yet."

She pushed out a breath. "Then I'll be able to relax."

He quirked a dark eyebrow. "You're a go-getter, but lately you've taken on too much of the workload yourself."

"We own a candy shop, Ben. Valentine's Day is a significant holiday in our world."

"Why not promote our signature chocolate coffee fudge, instead?" He scanned the row of sugar-coated candy apples and the popcorn machine she'd recently placed next to the fudge presentation. "Our fudge won first place at the women's shelter candy-making contest in December, and since then sales have doubled."

Sally eyed the red and white bento boxes chock-full of their number one selling fudge positioned at the entrance. "Thanks to your fiancée, Maise."

"I attribute our success to your candy-making skills. Maise simply wrote an outstanding newspaper article that helped bring in customers."

"She also awarded our fudge first place."

"Maise wasn't the only judge at the women's shelter contest. The other two judges voted for our chocolate too."

Ben's cellphone rang, and he fished in his pocket.

"Again?" Sally asked.

With a quick nod, Ben flipped open the phone and swiveled from her.

When he finished speaking, he fidgeted, placed his phone on the counter next to the cash register, then unwrapped a candy kiss.

Sally's gaze shifted from the candy kiss to Ben. "Who called this time?"

"The same person as last time."

"And that same person is—?"

He popped the candy kiss into his mouth. "Do you want to sit down first?"

Her response was an exasperated glance. "I'd rather stand."

"Your specialty chocolate shipment is delayed. That was Joe, the delivery man. He phoned earlier too."

"Joe? Why? What happened?"

"We were trying to work out a plan, unfortunately without success." Ben chewed the candy, swallowed, then displayed a bright smile. "No use in fretting, though. Our store has plenty of chocolate to carry us through Valentine's Day."

Fretting? *Fretting*? Ben never used words like that. This was his way of avoiding, then softening the news she didn't want to hear. She stepped to the counter and concealed her distress by taking a brisk swallow of coffee that had turned cold. She grimaced. "Exactly how late is the shipment?"

"Joe's truck broke down in Evanville and he's grounded at a diner called Olive's. More significant is an update that the major highways are flooding."

She frowned and drew her cellphone from the pocket of her black slacks, scrutinizing the weather map. "Heavy rain is in the forecast, but the storm is west of here."

Her brother's penetrating blue eyes leveled on her. "Which means?"

"I'll get the order myself. That way, I can return to the

shop tonight and begin making infusion candy." As he shook his head she reminded, "Outstanding orders to fill, remember?"

He didn't bother to assure her that she was right. He merely blew out a sigh.

"Will you pick up Clarissa?" Sally grabbed her pink water-repellent jacket from the coat rack and slid on a pair of yellow rain boots. "School dismisses at three o'clock."

"Certainly." Ben nodded. "Provided you give Maise and me permission to take her to dinner. We may head to The Pasta Junction and see Julie. Lorenzo will be there after he gets off work at the television station."

Julie, their sister, owned The Pasta Junction. Lorenzo Rossi was the local weatherman, and they'd been dating for a few weeks. They'd met when he booked her restaurant for a first wedding anniversary dinner, a surprise for his mother and new husband. Over the excuse of baking the perfect Italian cassata cheesecake, Lorenzo had seen Julie several times, and they'd dated ever since.

They both shared a variety of commonalties—their appreciation for fine food, all things Italian, and film noir, which Sally had never watched, although Julie and Lorenzo raved about the stylistic black-and-white films.

Someday, perhaps, when she had more time, Sally promised herself.

Pulling her attention to the present, she said, "Dinner for my daughter is mac and cheese. Nothing fancy. Believe it or not, Clarissa also likes steamed broccoli."

"Can you repeat where you're headed?" Ben asked.

"Olive's Diner." Sally caught her brother's concerned stare. "I'll return by eight o'clock tonight."

"Stick to the main route, 29A. And check Lorenzo's weather forecasts."

"I will. And stop worrying, big brother. I'll call Joe and meet him at the diner." Sally schooled her features into a reassuring smile, waved her cellphone in the air, and scurried out the door.

CHAPTER 2

If there was one thing Sally loved about Valentine's Day, it was chocolate. She sold the idea, the rich, velvety taste, to her customers—celebrating romance by gifting exquisite candy to a spouse or partner, or any loved one.

The entire holiday was appealing, although a man's love was something she hadn't experienced in ages. If ever, if she was honest with herself. The holiday had lost all significance when her ex-husband had bailed on her and their daughter. He'd gotten a preview of the responsibility of caring for a premature infant, which meant little sleep and a selfless attitude, and he'd wanted no part of it.

So much for a dedicated partner and lifelong commitment.

She sighed as she surveyed the wet roads ahead.

Lorenzo had predicted rough weather, the message flashing across her cellphone screen. Sometimes he was right, other times wrong. This time, unfortunately, he was right.

The lengthy day was taking its toll, and six o'clock showed on her car's dashboard by the time she neared the diner. Joe, the delivery driver, had acknowledged her phone call with gratefulness, and assured he'd meet her in the parking lot.

Dusk fell early on a chilly, rainy day in California, and the evening had darkened sooner than Sally anticipated. A slow-moving thunderstorm had followed her, and there had been no break in the icy-gray clouds. Mercilessly, rain pounded her windshield, and the concrete highway became slick, then muddied. As she drove, her gaze flicked repeatedly to the edge of the road as she dodged sizable tree branches.

She gripped the steering wheel tight against the blustery wind swaying her car, tuned her car radio to a traffic station and was immediately bombarded by a series of flash-flood warnings.

"Travelers on route 29A are advised to choose another route." The announcer issued the advisory in a somber tone.

Her car crested the last hill. A neon sign back-lit in green blinked *Olive's Diner*, and soft light beckoned from the large paneled windows. The exterior walls in reflective silver reminded her of a favorite 1950s diner she'd frequented as a child, and she anticipated a blue plate special of savory meat loaf and creamy mashed potatoes, topped with homemade brown gravy.

She drove into the parking lot, relieved to spot the Moon-glow Chocolatiers truck. The driver's door snapped open and a short, stocky man slid out. Wearing eyeglasses and a jovial expression, he hailed her. "Sally Elliot?"

She zippered up her raincoat, secured the hood, and stepped from her car. Several other vehicles, including an outdated pickup truck, were parked nearby.

"I'm here!" she called as he darted toward her. Horizontal, icy pellets of rain whirled around them.

"I'm Joe." He gestured upward. "The tree branches are

swinging like crazy. I heard on the radio that the wind gusts could reach forty miles per hour."

She brushed away the cold raindrops hitting her cheeks, tightened the raincoat's hood sheltering her head, then jammed her hands into her pockets. "Yes, I heard the same."

"I'll hurry and load the chocolate into your car, ma'am. Thanks for driving here."

"You're welcome." *Really, she'd had no choice, because she needed the chocolate now.* "I didn't want this shipment delayed another day." She peered toward the road. Here in the blinding rainstorm, everything blurred.

"As soon as you're finished, I'll be on my way back to Bloomingfield," she said. "If it's okay, I'll stay in my car to avoid the rain."

A cracking sound, then a creak, prompted them both to spin. A gigantic tree fell across the highway with a crash resembling a thunderous roar. It was so close that, for several seconds, Sally feared the diner had been hit.

Fortunately it hadn't.

However, the tree blocked her way home.

In the ensuing seconds of stunned silence, she heard herself gasp, scarcely audible above the whistling wind. A chill shivered up her spine as noise and chaos erupted around her.

A young couple rushed out of the diner. They gaped in disbelief at the fallen tree, shouting in shrill voices that they were phoning the police while signaling to Sally and Joe to hurry inside.

Joe's eyes widened as he gaped at the wide tree limbs spread across the road. "Wow, that's a huge tree. You won't be returning to Bloomingfield tonight," he said. "Let's get inside with the other stranded folks."

For a few seconds, Sally lacked the ability to utter a

coherent sentence. Absently, she rubbed her arms, then reached inside her car to retrieve her tote bag.

The only word she'd heard was *stranded.* With an unfocused stare, she darted a gaze toward the tree, then Joe, then the diner. The neon green sign was still blinking, so the diner hadn't lost power.

"You'll like the cook," Joe was saying. "We chatted before you arrived, and he's a good guy."

No, no, no. Good guy or not, this tree had to fall now? The same question raced over and over in her mind.

"The cook. Right," she tonelessly replied, realizing her voice shook. "Where is he? Didn't he hear the noise?" She dragged her thoughts from a situation she couldn't control and sprinted with Joe across the parking lot.

"Okay, Olive," she muttered to herself as they entered and stamped their wet boots in the entryway. "I hope you serve meat loaf." She envisioned a burly cook sporting a straggly white beard, a dirty apron tied around his protruding belly.

Joe shrugged off his jacket and swung it over a coat rack. He beamed at a well-dressed woman and slid into her booth. Eagerly, his voice raised above Elvis Presley crooning from the wall-mounted juke box, as Joe embellished the events that had taken place. The young couple that had raced outside were already snuggled in a corner booth. They bid Sally a quick wave.

"Are you all right?" the young woman asked. Her mid-length chestnut-colored hair was damp from the rain. On her porcelain cheeks was a hint of red blusher.

"Yes, yes, I'm fine." Sally offered a nervous laugh, then raised her voice for the benefit of the man who had emerged from the kitchen and had begun brewing coffee behind the counter. "Oh, hello."

He curved around. "Hi. Glad you were able to get out of the rain."

Rain? His calm statement snapped the last thread of her reserve. "Are you aware a tree fell in front of the diner?"

"Yes. I was in the back room when it happened. The police have been called. You're safe here."

"Safe?" she parroted, surveying the oversized booths with seats covered in green plastic. The pink lights shining over each booth cast the diners in rose-colored puddles of light. "This diner could blow ... all the way to Kansas."

"No wicked witches here, and I assure you that you're not in Oz," the man countered. "This building has been standing here for a hundred years, and will be here long after we're gone."

"Now that's reassuring."

"No worries." His tone was composed, his manner amiable.

The first thing she noticed about him was his eyes. They were a wonderful hazelnut brown, shining and welcoming. He wore a smile which he freely extended. He was tall, muscular, and well-toned.

"I assume you're the cook?" she asked.

"Yes."

"Is the owner here?"

He sent her a brief grin. "You're looking at him."

Her lips parted. He looked too young to own a restaurant. She guessed him to be in his midthirties. But then again, she was young too, approaching thirty, having opened her shop several years earlier.

She tugged off her raincoat and draped it over a stool, apologizing for the puddle pooling on the black-and-white square tile flooring beneath her feet.

"It's all right. Tile is easy to clean." He gestured outside to the incessant rain. "I'm surprised anyone is out driving on a night like this."

"Well, I had no choice." She again glanced about the diner,

at the youthful couple nestled close together in their booth and the smartly dressed older woman wearing camel wool slacks and a cream-colored cardigan. She'd been sitting alone before Joe took a seat across from her. Now they were thoroughly engaged in conversation and didn't seem to notice anyone else.

"I don't know about the others," Sally continued. "I'm sure they have their reasons for being here."

"It's probably because of my food." The owner's lips quirked into a smile. "Why else would anyone venture out in a severe storm?"

"Chocolate," Sally murmured. "If they desperately needed a shipment of chocolate."

"Ah, chocolate, the ideal sweet treat." Amusement laced his deep voice. She noted that he didn't remark on her use of the word *desperately*. "But you can't beat a diner for a plentiful, wholesome American meal."

"Oh, but you can," she said.

"Excuse me?"

"I beg to differ. My sister, Julie, owns a fine dining establishment called The Pasta Junction. She serves homemade fettuccini."

"The restaurant is located in Bloomingfield, correct?"

"Yes, have you ever visited?"

"This diner keeps me in Evanville most days."

"My sister's latest addition is a brick pizza oven."

The result had been pizzas with a smoky wood flavor and charred crust that had quickly become a town favorite. Certainly, authentic Italian food beat a greasy diner any day.

When her gaze flew to his, she could tell by his smile that, to her intense relief, he hadn't read her thoughts.

"Emily comes here every evening and eats dinner." He gestured toward the booth where Joe and Emily sat.

"Rain or shine, apparently," Sally said.

"Apparently." He chuckled. "The kissing couple are on their honeymoon and were passing through town when the storm hit. They said they wanted to drive across America and discover new places—wherever their travels took them."

"They obviously aren't planners," Sally said.

"They told me they love being spontaneous."

"I prefer an organized agenda. I'm more productive and efficient that way." Sally turned toward the couple, then back to him. He was studying her with a concerned frown.

"Spontaneous individuals have more fun," he said.

"But planning ahead yields better results."

"Like encountering fallen trees, for instance?" he asked. "The best laid plans of mice and men often …"

"Often go astray," she finished.

"Awry."

"Yes, well, I'm familiar with that saying." To avoid the debate, she shifted. "Do you have many steady customers?"

"Thankfully, yes."

"So it gets busy here at times?"

"At times." That smile again. For a long moment he studied her, a warm look in his eyes.

Without warning, her heart began beating uncontrollably.

"A calm and deliberate pace wins the race," he continued.

"Another saying?"

"One of my own. And, a well-fed, contented customer will return."

"That's two sayings."

He shrugged. "I suppose, but they're both important."

She started to contradict him. A quick pace wins the race, she wanted to inform him. Instead, she toyed with the leather tote bag slung over her shoulder.

"Do you agree?" he inquired.

"No, sorry, I don't. At least, not with your first saying.

Calm and deliberate won't fly in our fast-paced world where customers are constantly in a hurry."

"We'll just have to agree to disagree, then."

This time she didn't respond immediately, her attention captivated by his tousled rich-brown hair and the shadow of a dark beard. High cheekbones and an angular jaw brought one thought to mind: he was beyond handsome, and because of her preoccupation with the fallen tree and her plans going off-center, she hadn't noticed his athletic good looks until now.

She flushed as they locked gazes. "If the saying applies to your diner, that's all that matters."

For you. Not for me.

She squinted at her watch, then at the bakery case filled with a selection of breads, including sourdough and whole wheat; a coconut layered cake and cherry pie; and a dozen chocolate chip cookies. She surveyed the fake potted lilacs adorning each booth, the thick tan-colored curtains hanging from the windows. An antique cash register was situated at the far end of the counter. Coins from the young couple jingled into the juke box as they picked out songs, and Dolly Parton replaced Elvis, singing about working nine to five.

"This is a nice highway for a diner," Sally remarked. Again, she shifted. Brilliant, Sally, just brilliant. Who used the word *nice* to describe a highway? She put on a smile. "Did you decorate the place yourself?"

"Hardly. My sister helped me." With an easy grace, he collected her coat and hung it on the rack by the door. "Please forgive my manners. I should have taken your coat sooner."

That wasn't his job, which she voiced aloud.

"My pleasure," he responded.

She trailed him and stole a glance in the mirror near the doorway, critically appraising her hair, which always curled when wet. She was forced to wait and see how it behaved when it dried and hoped that tonight it wouldn't spin into a super frizzy mess. Scrutinizing her reflection, she knew that the endless nights she'd worked late had deprived her of much-needed sleep, subsequently leaving shadows beneath her eyes.

The man turned, his smile ever-present.

She felt her cheeks heat.

"Is your name … Olive?" she asked. *Another stroke of brilliant conversation, Sally. Surely he'd named the diner after his sister.*

"Nope. I'm Oliver Menroe."

"And your sister?"

"Her name is Amy." Those brown eyes of his, so cordial and reassuring. She couldn't drag her gaze away. "And you are …?"

"Sally. Sally Elliot."

"*Miss* Sally Elliott?"

"Yes."

"I'm glad to hear that."

She paused, surprised by his remark, but decided it was nothing more than courteous flirtation with a potential customer. Still, her mind scrambled for a subject change. "So the name Olive is …?"

"The name from the previous owners. They were Italian and thought *Olive* had a nice ring to it."

"Didn't you want to add the *r* to the end of the word when you bought the place? There's a big difference between Olive and Oliver."

"The customers don't mind. It's a standing joke around here." Oliver wiped his hands on his clean white apron. *Clean,* completely shattering her preconceived notions of a short-order cook working at a diner in the middle of nowhere.

She pulled her cellphone from her bag and dashed off a text to Ben, explaining she was detained because of a fallen tree, had met Joe, the delivery man, and that they were both safely inside Olive's Diner.

Give Clarissa my love, she finished. *Is she having fun?*

A blast, Ben replied. *She's devouring a box of specialty infusion chocolates. (Kidding, kidding.) Let me know when you get back on the road. Maise and I will take care of Clarissa tonight and put her to bed. I have a key to your apartment, so don't fret.*

Fret again. Sally grinned and thanked him.

She snapped the phone shut and excused herself to freshen up in the restroom, then reentered the dining room. Although the diner was somewhat rundown and the fan above her didn't appear to spin, none of this took away from the inviting interior. Enticing whiffs of freshly ground coffee and buttery yeast rolls made her mouth water. She hadn't eaten since noon, an eggplant parmigiana takeout sandwich from her sister Julie's restaurant, and a cup of cold coffee.

Oliver strode into the open adjoining kitchen and stirred an enormous pot on the stove. Then he returned to stand behind the counter.

Sally indicated the display case, because she loved sweets. "Do you bake, Oliver?"

"I outsource to a woman in town because I realized my limitations early on. Would you like a chocolate chip cookie?"

"Certainly." She settled on a stool. "Thank you."

"I have a Greek salad in the cooler that's all made up."

"Perfect." Gratefully, she accepted the cookie while he arranged and garnished the salad, then set it, a glass of water, and a white paper napkin from the dispenser in front of her.

She flattened the napkin on her lap and bowed her head to offer a prayer of thanks to God. "How long have you been in business?" she asked.

"Five years." He shifted and switched on the grill. "Do you like your eggs over easy? I use fresh ingredients from the locals. Farm-to-home is a term I employed before it became trendy."

"Scrambled eggs are my favorite, but I'm already enjoying a salad and cookie, remember?

"Indulge me."

Sally wasn't up to disputing with him. Besides, she was still hungry, and it was hard to resist the intoxicating aromas of fresh coffee, grilled hamburgers, and butter-topped biscuits. She took a swallow of water. "I like my eggs with toast. I love toast."

"Wheat or white bread?"

"Do you have rye bread?"

"Of course." An enigmatic lazy smile crossed his lips while he scanned her features. She had the surprising notion that he was delighted she was sitting and talking with him, a notion that was highlighted when he lifted a loaf of rye bread in the form of a salute. "May I say, Sally, that you look lovely when your blond curls frame your face."

Her pulse fluttered. She'd never been complimented by a man waving a loaf of rye bread, but somehow his comment meant a great deal.

Somehow, she knew his compliment was heartfelt.

Wait. She set down her glass. Her curls framed her face? That meant her hair was a mass of oversized, wiry waves. She yanked at a curl near her cheek and watched it spring back into place. She really needed to look into purchasing a hair straightener.

"Well, okay, thank you," she said softly, then dug into her salad.

"Can you give me a minute before I cook your eggs?" he asked.

"Absolutely. I need more than a minute to digest."

Oliver started toward the dining room with a pot of coffee, refilling cups and talking with the customers. There were only a handful, Joe and Emily and the newlyweds, but he treated each person as if they were the most important one in the room, stopping to listen, nodding and optimistically commenting.

"You don't employ anyone else, Oliver?" Sally asked when he came back behind the counter. As he poured coffee for himself, then set the pot on the burner, she noticed the way his white T-shirt fit across his broad shoulders. He was strong and muscular, as if he routinely exercised each day.

"I have a dishwasher, hostess, and several local waitresses," he replied. "Because those raindrops were getting as big as hailstones, I sent everyone home early."

Five minutes later, he set a plateful of steaming scrambled eggs, two slices of buttered rye toast, and a mug of coffee next to her salad. She eyed the mug, and he smiled. "I assumed you may want coffee, because it might be a long night."

"Thanks."

"Cream and sugar?"

"Black is fine."

"Me too." He rolled his coffee mug between his palms. "Joe and I chatted a while before you arrived. He told me you own a candy store, and he was on his way to deliver wholesale chocolate to you."

"Then you know my story."

"Yes, I expect I do, but I'm always interested in learning more."

About her?

She fell silent, sipping her coffee, and evaded questioning why he might be so interested. Perhaps he simply craved conversation. Long hours in a diner might cause him to become lonely and disconnected. Sometimes in her candy shop, a sense of isolation would sweep over her, prompting her to phone one of her siblings. She wondered if Oliver felt the same.

"There isn't much else to say," she replied.

He splashed more coffee into her mug. "I didn't mean about your business. I meant about you."

She gave a little laugh and decided to talk about her business again. "When Joe's truck broke down, he phoned my brother Ben. I drove here to pick up the chocolate for my special infusion candy, because I couldn't wait another day for the delivery."

Oliver popped two more slices of toast into the toaster, then regarded her. "Ironic, because the tree fell unexpectedly and you're delayed, anyway."

There was something about the matter-of-fact way he described her situation, something about his easy manner and intoxicating grin that triggered a sudden, irrepressible, and, considering the turn of events, curious response from Sally. She began chuckling. And then she began laughing so hard, tears coursed down her cheeks. Her ribs still hurt from laughing when Oliver walked over carrying another plate of buttered rye toast.

A minute later, he seated himself on a stool next to her with a second mug of coffee, joking with her because she couldn't choose between a slice of coconut layered cake or cherry pie for dessert.

"Try both." He swallowed some coffee and put the mug aside.

Deliberately, she turned to gaze at him. "Honestly, Oliver, you believe in feeding your customers extraordinarily well."

His gaze never left hers. "That's my saying, remember?" She smiled at his contagious good nature and attempted to match his humor. "One of your many sayings," she reminded.

He stood to clear away her dishes. "By the way, being that

you seem to want to focus only on business, what is infusion candy?"

She laughed and dismissed his inquiry with a wave. "Never mind. Let's just say it's a fancy specialty candy."

With the plates in his hands, he paused to consider her—from the top of her wavy hair which surely resembled a lion's mane by now, to the toes of her rain boots.

Another bewildering tingle went through her. She shook her head, mystified at her reaction to this man.

"You own Bloomingfield's Candy Shop," he said.

"Yes. I assumed you knew that from your conversation with Joe."

"I didn't piece everything together until now. Your picture and an article were featured in the newspaper at Christmastime. I thought I recognized you from some-where." Across the two feet between them, their gazes held, the silence punctuated by the newlyweds giggling and smooching, Joe and Emily chatting quietly, and Patsy Cline singing from the juke box about falling to pieces. "In any event, we're both in the food service industry, so we can commiserate about the long hours. And speaking of which, I'd better put more coffee on."

Sally smiled as he stepped behind the counter, and she stood to wander to the window. Through the rain-streaked glass, she located the large tree, the lifeless limbs lying across the road. Fortunately, the Department of Transportation, truck lights flashing a dull yellow, had arrived.

After a few moments, Oliver walked over to join her.

"How long does it take to remove a tree?" she asked.

"First, the DOT will check to be sure the tree hasn't hit any power lines," he said. "We have power, so the electric company won't be called in."

"How long?" she repeated.

"Are you in a hurry?"

"You know I have a candy shop to run. More important, my seven-year-old daughter is at home. My brother and his fiancée are watching her tonight."

"You didn't mention you had a daughter. What's her name?"

"Clarissa." Sally pulled her cellphone from her pocket and scrolled through the pictures, opening a recent one where Clarissa, pink-cheeked and giggling, was sliding down a slide in the town park. Her hands were raised in utter delight. She'd skinned her knee that day, and Sally had held and comforted her in a steady grip, never wanting to let go.

"She's adorable." Oliver peered over her shoulder as she pointed to the photo. "As an aside, I thought you were a *miss.*"

"I am." Sally slipped the cellphone back into her pocket. "I'm divorced."

"Me too. No kids for me, unfortunately."

Unfortunately? This tall, handsome man liked children? She couldn't stop from voicing her inquiry aloud.

"Of course. Who doesn't like children?" His expression gentled. "I wanted kids desperately. My ex-wife, however, had other plans, which included running off with my best friend."

"I'm sorry. Were you married long?"

"Two years. You?"

"I married my high school sweetheart." She sighed. "We were young, and when Clarissa came along … It's complicated."

"That's life. In the end, it's all about living life and appreciating every moment."

This was the time for her to utter something profound and witty, but all she did was nod in agreement.

"Even if life is chaotic and unpredictable?" she asked.

"It's the journey that matters," he said softly.

She stared out the window at the rain streaming down

the glass, the blinking yellow truck lights as crewmen moved debris to the grassy shoulder.

"At any rate," Oliver continued, "the DOT will cut the tree into pieces and stack it on the side of the road, which will be challenging, because this road isn't very wide. To answer your question, plan on a two-or three-hour wait, depending on how quickly the work progresses. The police must have directed traffic off the last exit."

Frustrated, she expelled an impatient breath.

"Can I get you more coffee?" He headed toward the counter.

"Thank you." She trailed him and reclaimed a stool.

He replenished her mug, then again carried the coffee pot from customer to customer, refilling their mugs, chatting, offering food. His manner was jovial and inviting. He focused his attention outward, on his customers, ensuring they were satisfied.

"Still hungry?" he asked, when he returned to Sally. "Can I get you anything else? I'm used to preparing a lot of orders quickly, but apparently not tonight."

"Honestly, I'm stuffed." She raised her mug in a toast. "My sincere compliments. Oliver. Everything you served is delicious."

"My world-famous vegetable soup will be done in a few hours. You can have a bowl then."

"World-famous?" she teased.

"Well, in this town, anyway."

"I'd love some, but I expect I'll be long gone by the time it's finished." She peered at her watch. "I meant to ask you earlier—no meat loaf and mashed potatoes on your menu?"

"Of course." He grinned. "It's not on the menu because customers know I have it."

"Telepathy?"

"Something like that." He laughed out loud, full and hearty. "I can heat a plateful, if you'd like."

She chuckled and patted her stomach. "Perhaps another day."

"I'll prepare any meal, if I have the ingredients on hand. That's my saying."

"I thought your saying was 'Calm and deliberate wins the race'?"

He shrugged.

Comically, she raised her eyebrows. "How about your other saying that a well-fed, contented customer will return?"

He seemed to be trying to keep his features straight. "I suppose I have three sayings, then."

She chuckled. "What's in your soup?"

"You name the vegetable—"

"Onions, celery …" she began.

"And my homemade beef broth, potatoes and carrots." Lightly, he touched her arm before pointing to the kitchen. It was friendly and casual, yet her pulse fired into a tailspin. "Can you guess the best thing about my soup?"

"Oliver, I'm not good at guessing."

"Tonight, the soup is on the house." His grin was boyish for such a confident, compelling man. "In fact, everything I've provided is on the house."

"Absolutely not. I can pay for my own food."

"I insist."

"Why?"

"Because you're the prettiest woman I've seen all day." He dragged up a stool to perch closer to her. "Correction. You're the most beautiful woman I've ever met."

"And you're staring at me because—"

"I told you why."

Self-consciously, she patted her hair. Sure enough, it had

frizzed. "Thank you," she murmured, although she suspected she'd never looked worse.

"Tell me again why you're so eager to get back to Bloomingfield?" he asked.

"My daughter Clarissa is reason number one."

However, contemplating the hundreds of jobs awaiting her made Sally anxious. She chewed her bottom lip and took in the diner's coziness, the patrons sipping coffee and speaking quietly among themselves. The unhurried pace was quiet and relaxing.

"From what I understand," Oliver said, "your daughter is safe with your brother and his date. So again, what's your hurry to travel on these unsafe roads?"

"My candy shop's orders have exploded since the December newspaper article, and I've publicized a unique new product, which is why I came here tonight. Joe's truck—"

Oliver's quick nod interrupted her. "I was delighted to hear his story."

He was a good listener. Not many men possessed that quality. Not many *folks* possessed that quality. Most wanted to talk only about themselves. But with Oliver, she felt like she could chat with him for hours.

"In summary, I have hundreds of orders." She stared at him, stared down at her coffee. She hadn't intended to talk about her shop, but the shop was always on her mind.

"Therefore, it's a bad thing to have all this new business and the subsequent profits that go along with it?"

"No, of course not." She grabbed a napkin from the dispenser and dabbed at her mouth. "You're an entrepreneur. You of all people should understand."

"Aren't you thrilled to earn a living doing what you love?"

"I'm extremely grateful. It's just that so many rely on me

—my employees, my customers, and everyone else along the supply chain. It's an enormous responsibility."

He scrubbed a hand over his face. "Your candy shop sounds tremendously successful."

She paused, realizing her unintended implication—that because his diner was modest, he didn't have the same pressures she did.

"Oliver, I apologize," she said.

He eased the awkward moment with a smile, then answered the cellphone buzzing in his jean pocket. After an abrupt conversation, he clicked off the phone.

"Excuse me. I need to pull together an order for takeout."

"Go ahead. I'll attend to the customers."

"Thanks, Sally." Oliver excused himself and hastened into the kitchen.

CHAPTER 3

*E*mily, who had been sitting with Joe, stood. She flattened the creases in her tailored slacks, and her booted heels assertively clicked on the tile floor as she made her way to Sally. Joe grabbed a newspaper and sank back into the booth.

"I'm Emily Varon, as you probably know." She accompanied her introduction with a vibrant smile and direct eye contact. Something about her understated beauty, the cream-colored wool cardigan contrasting with her dark skin, her friendly mannerisms and overall interest, made Sally feel at home.

"I'm Sally Elliot."

"It's lovely to formally meet you, Sally."

In view of Emily's gracious greeting, Sally extended a smile in return. "I admired your outfit when I walked in," she said. "You are stunning and entirely put together."

With a toss of perfectly coiffed platinum-silver hair, Emily chuckled and sat straight and proper on the stool next to Sally, her hands clasped neatly on her lap. "You mean for a woman of a certain age."

"What I meant was … you carry an aura of self-confidence."

"At seventy years old, I'm finally content with myself. Along the way, I've learned that women are beautiful no matter their age." Emily motioned toward the honeymooners cuddling and kissing, whispering and laughing. Once in a while, they paused to take a selfie. "Earlier, those two told me they've been together from the time they were in high school. They'll share many joys and sorrows." Wistfully, she exhaled. "There's something magical about a first love."

Sally flinched. For her, the couple was a painful reminder of her own marriage gone wrong, and the emptiness that had followed her for years. Not once since the final evening when Leon left had she wept, but in turn, a massive weight of sadness and heartache had accumulated inside her.

"My experience with first love didn't work out," she said quietly.

"You were married?" Emily inquired.

"And divorced. I took my maiden surname. I'm an Elliot again."

"It's your last love who truly matters." Emily's blue-eyed gaze fixed on Sally, as if she were seeking something. "He's the man to treasure."

Sitting on the sidelines of love, Sally attempted a serene smile.

"I overheard some of your conversation with Oliver. I wanted to come over earlier, but you two were so intent on each other, I didn't want to interrupt."

Sally rolled her eyes, an attempt at dismissing any attraction she might feel for Oliver. "I wouldn't say that."

"I would." Emily flicked a glance toward the kitchen. "At my age, I don't apologize for eavesdropping. Perhaps you should get to know a person before deciding who they are."

"I agree." Sally pinched the bridge of her nose and briefly

closed her eyes. "My comments to him about my candy shop being so busy were thoughtless."

In all honesty, his remarks to her were insightful—about being grateful and connecting with men and women and families. He stirred her to reflect on where she put her energy these days. Orders were at an all-time high. So why was she stressed and unhappy?

An older couple wandered into the diner, and Sally stood, excusing herself from Emily and taking it upon herself to greet the couple. The man, she noted, walked with a shuffle and used a cane.

"Hello, and welcome to Olive's Diner. Please sit anywhere." Sally gestured to an empty booth near the juke box.

"We were stopped by the fallen tree." The woman shrugged off her tan-colored raincoat and draped it on the seat beside her. "We came off a side road, and the police refused to wave us any farther."

"Can I get you anything?" Sally asked. "Coffee? Food?"

"I'm starved." The man's spotted, aged hands splayed across his chest. "We drove quite a while."

"Harold, we were on the road ten minutes. We've been married over thirty years and rarely agree on anything." His wife snorted with dismissive amusement, then leaned back and pulled her thin mouth into a scowl. "I'll just have coffee."

There was no similarity between them, Sally thought, as sometimes happened when men and women were married a long time. The wife was thin, gray-haired, and under five feet tall, whereas her husband was a solid foot taller and at least one hundred pounds heavier.

"What do you have to eat?" the man asked.

"You've eaten too much today already," came his wife's reply.

He set his cane beside him and removed his cap, revealing

the polished brilliance of his bald head. "You call that bowl of cereal this morning a meal?"

"You're forgetting you ate a massive lunch."

"Let me see what the owner recommends." Sally held up the couple's bickering with a smile. "I'll return shortly."

When Sally stepped into the spotless kitchen, the mouth-watering aroma of vegetable soup flooded her nostrils. On a large stainless steel table, Oliver was arranging a dozen sandwiches, some with meat and cheese, others peanut butter and jelly, as well as apple slices and shortbread cookies. On the side were twelve bottles of water.

"That's quite a takeout order," she said.

"Cora, the friend who phoned, runs a daycare center not far from here," he replied. "She's in a frenzy because of the storm. I wanted to prepare food that appealed to everyone."

"Wow, I'm impressed at how quickly you worked."

"Thanks. That's why I'm called a short-order cook." A lazy smile swept over his face. "Everything under control out there?"

"Two more customers arrived. Can you suggest what I can serve? They can't decide."

"How about a couple of deli sandwiches and two slices of cherry pie?"

"I'll check." Sally scurried to the couple, got their drink orders and served them, then rushed back into the kitchen.

"They actually agreed," she joked. Quickly, she made up the two plates.

Meanwhile, Oliver, without rushing, deftly finished the sandwich preparation and began wrapping each in brown paper bags.

With a businesslike tenor in her voice, Sally asked, "Are you always this efficient?"

"Like everyone, I try my best."

This was Oliver, believing the good in everyone. She

studied him surreptitiously as she plated the couple's sandwiches, then sliced two pieces of cherry pie.

Their mood of quiet camaraderie as they worked together, along with his heart-stopping grin and relaxed bantering, left her oddly unwilling to leave the confines of the kitchen. She was drawn to him, more and more for every minute they spent together. She knew he was thoughtful and considerate, his actions compassionate and kind-hearted. Beyond his handsome physique was an innate quality—a genuine caring about people.

Reluctantly, she placed the sandwich plates and slices of pie on a tray and headed for the dining room.

"I'll be in as soon as these sandwiches are wrapped," Oliver said. "Thanks for taking care of the orders for me."

"Absolutely."

A car pulled into the parking lot, stopping in front of the door. A thirty-something woman rushed inside as Oliver appeared with an armload of brown bags.

"I'm almost done, Cora. Give me a couple more minutes." He gestured to Sally. "But first, let me introduce you."

"I know Cora and I'll take it from here." Emily slid from her stool and walked over to Cora and Sally as Oliver returned to the kitchen. "Cora runs the daycare in town, and all the children love her. My neighbor's kids are always thrilled when they're dropped off there."

Cora raked a hand through her glossy brown hair, the short pixie cut accentuating her vivid amber eyes and creamy complexion. "I love watching these kids, they're like family to me. Some of them were a little frightened when the storm hit, but most are excited."

"Where are they now?" Sally asked.

"With my brother at the daycare. He helps me out sometimes."

"I have a daughter. Her name is Clarissa," Sally said. "She's not afraid of anything, except fireworks on the Fourth of July. Then she cries and puts her hands over her ears."

"What do you do to calm her down?"

"I give her a piece of fudge and tell her that it has a magical ingredient which will make her happy."

"Does it work?" Emily inquired.

"Most of the time. If anything, the candy distracts her," Sally said. "You see, I own a candy shop, thus a supply of chocolate fudge is usually in a box on my kitchen counter. Don't worry, Clarissa brushes her teeth afterward."

From the corner of her eye, Sally noted that a smiling Oliver had surfaced from the kitchen.

"Oliver, thank you," Cora said as he slipped the takeout containers into several bags. "The kids can't return home yet since their parents are trapped on the other side of that downed tree."

"Glad I can help. I'll carry these to the car for you."

"I'm fine, but thanks for your support." Cora drew a wallet from her purse. "How much do I owe you?"

"Nothing. My treat and my pleasure." As she left, his lips curved upward into a dazzling smile that he directed toward Sally. That smile—honest and sincere, with exactly the right touch of straightforwardness—prompted a warmth in the pit of her stomach. She was getting it: he had his community too. Moreover, his heart was generous and empathetic.

She returned his thoughtfulness with her own twinkling smile.

Emily swiveled to face Sally. "Explain what is so vitally important about this chocolate of yours that you had to come fetch it yourself."

"I'm creating an infusion candy which requires a certain type of bittersweet chocolate."

"What's infusion candy?" Emily crossed her arms. "Some sort of millennial fad?"

"No, it's not a fad. The process is somewhat complex, but the design is important. However, I'm not sure I'll get back to my store in time to produce all the candy."

"How about a trade?" Oliver still stood by the doorway with them. "You can use my kitchen to create your candy. Afterwards, you can try my soup, which I guarantee is the most delicious taste in the world."

"Better than my signature fudge?"

"Yup."

She shook her head. "I doubt you have everything I need for my specialty chocolates."

"How about regular candy?" He grinned. "Specialty is overrated."

"We like peanut butter cups," the honeymooners chimed from their booth. Apparently the patrons were delighted to listen to each other's conversations, Sally mused.

"I stock jars of peanut butter," Oliver said. "And I have a recipe from my sister that calls for margarine and graham crackers and semisweet chocolate chips."

"I'm a candymaker."

"Peanut butter cups are candy," Emily pointed out.

"But my infusion candy uses high-quality bittersweet chocolate."

"Yes, yes, so we've heard." Emily looked so determined that Sally peered at her with a mixture of laughter and surrender.

"I prefer store-bought chocolate chips, of which I have plenty," Oliver broke in. Gently, he touched Sally's cheek, guiding her to gaze at him. "Sally Elliot, I challenge you to prepare a batch of peanut butter cups in my kitchen. In fact, I predict our candy will be better than your infusion … whatever."

"*Our* candy?"

"A blending of two magnificent cooks' expertise."

His blunt response made her laugh. Her spirit crazily soared. Despite the exhausting workdays, he'd thrown down a gauntlet she couldn't resist picking up.

Tamping down her smile, she quickly texted her brother, telling him she would be late. She looked up at Oliver. "In that case, I accept your challenge."

This was a decisive decision for her, and she could feel herself poised on the threshold of an unforgettable evening. Granted, she wouldn't be making specialty chocolate, but she was creating something better. Memories.

Since Leon, she'd held men at a distance, but with Oliver she felt safe. She enjoyed being near him—the way he put others before himself, his selfless manner, his witty responses. And the way he looked, as if he'd materialized from a Hollywood magazine with his effortlessly attractive features.

"Good. I'll help you." Oliver's mouth quirked in a smile. "We can enhance the semisweet with a few pieces of your fancy bittersweet candy if you'd like."

"And I'll pour our little group of diners more coffee while Joe gets your chocolate," Emily said.

Joe returned with a pound of chocolate and handed it to Sally, but Emily stopped him from continuing on into the kitchen by grabbing his hand and leading him to a booth. "You two go ahead," she directed Sally and Oliver. "We'll be your taste testers when you're done."

"Shall we?" Oliver affectionately rumpled Sally's hair, then showed her the kitchen. The effect of his strong hand on her arm sparked sudden tears, and she swallowed the surge of grateful emotion in her throat.

Here in Evanville, this tiny diner and everyone in it had welcomed her, and she felt happier than she'd been in ages.

A few minutes later, she tugged her hair back with a

ponytail holder, rolled up her sleeves, and faced him at the sink while they washed their hands.

"I can't wait to watch you doing what you do best." He handed her a clean apron. "I never imagined the most prominent candymaker in Bloomingfield would be in my diner."

As she tied the apron about her waist, she quipped, "Be prepared to taste the finest candy Evanville has ever experienced. But only if you promise to help me with cleanup afterward."

He chuckled. "It's a deal."

CHAPTER 4

Cooking with Sally in his cozy diner proved strangely intimate, Oliver thought.

Hyper focused, Sally concentrated on melting and stirring chips and margarine, while Oliver spread thick chocolate into mini-muffin tins. He seldom spoke, allowing his cooking companion to work with no interruptions.

He attempted to concentrate, but in the comfortable ambiance of his kitchen, he was more absorbed in pondering the remarkable turn of fate that had caused Sally Elliot to wind up at his diner. For many reasons, beginning with his failed marriage, his first consideration was that it would have been better if Sally hadn't been stranded at his diner, because of his instant attraction to her.

However, after the last few hours establishing a friendship, she was compelling him to acknowledge and contemplate everything he'd missed since his divorce, and the fact that he'd hidden behind the familiar confines of his small-town diner.

A safe refuge. Not that there was anything wrong with that.

He gave himself a firm mental shake.

Nonetheless, he wanted to experience life again. And all this reflection had begun with a beautiful, vivacious, and intelligent woman who was busily creating candy across from him. She stopped in the process of stirring chocolate and raised her gaze to his, the color of her soft eyes reminding him of colorful blue cornflowers. Shiny, golden highlights around her face accentuated her ivory skin. Her lips were full, the perfect shade of pink.

"You're not spreading," she reminded.

"Sorry." He laughed. "By the way, do you want to sit down?"

"I'm okay." She hesitated, but remained doggedly standing. "Thank you for asking, though."

They exchanged cheerful nods and went quietly back to their tasks.

Deep in contemplation, he studied her.

What if she'd entered his diner two years ago, when his divorce was still raw? Would he have noticed her then, or would he have been wallowing in the hurt and disappointment, the mistrust of his once-wife leaving him for his best friend?

Would he have admired her high cheekbones and soft lips, her slim figure and gorgeous, thick hair?

He blew out a silent sigh. Yes, he concluded, he would have admired her charm, her straightforwardness, her work ethic. However, he wouldn't have taken the relationship any further.

Absently, he grinned at her offhand remark that if he chose to cook, he was also slated for cleanup duty. This woman drove a hard bargain.

She slanted him a teasing smile, gazing at him with those incredibly striking eyes. "Cat got your tongue, Mr. Oliver?"

He was so lost in his reflections, he jumped at her question.

"Some people like more chocolate, some less," he advised, waving his wooden spoon jokingly in the air.

"Shouldn't you use a measuring cup so that all the candy is even?"

He raised an eyebrow. "Nope."

"Well we're about out of semisweet chips." Sally plunked her hands on her hips. "What should we do with the leftover peanut butter mixture?"

"That's where your specialty chocolate comes in." He opened the box of bittersweet chocolate and spooned a modest amount into the semisweet chips. Deftly, he stirred, then heated the remainder.

"Innovation is the mother of—" he began.

"The saying is, 'Necessity is the mother of invention,'" she corrected, a smile flickering across her face. "However, you are an impressive innovator."

"A trait learned from my father. We were poor, so he learned to make do with what we had—simple, wholesome food. Although, observing and listening to you inspires me to want to pursue more formal chef training."

She beamed, the sort of beam that begins from within and cannot be contained. "You're an expert in your own right, Oliver."

She stood by his side while they continued to portion and bake. Continuously distracted by her, he admired the easy, natural way she handled herself in the kitchen—a pinch of this, a shake of that, then meticulously measuring the key ingredients. As he did his own mixing, he reminisced about his boyhood in Evanville and the happy-go-lucky days of his youth before his mother got sick, then his father, leaving him at an inexperienced age to raise a twelve-year-old sister.

Sally chatted about her daughter and touched on the piercing defeat of losing her husband when she'd needed him most, and Oliver's heart squeezed.

"Ben came to my rescue." Tears welled in her eyes, and she wiped them away with the back of her hand. "I'm sorry for getting so emotional."

"Please don't apologize," he said.

"All these years I've numbed my emotions and immersed myself in work."

"I completely understand," he commiserated. "Much the same happened to me." He was silent for a beat before setting down his spoon and tipping up her chin. "I imagine being a single mother isn't easy, but I bet you're the best mother in the world."

"Clarissa is my greatest reward." Sally's flawless complexion fairly glowed whenever she mentioned her daughter. Without hesitation, she continued, "Oliver, I was thinking."

"Forever dangerous where women are concerned." At her frown, he prodded, "Thinking about what?"

"When I leave here tonight, who will shower me with compliments?"

"Compliments will definitely be forthcoming." His heartbeat doubled as he shifted closer. For a moment, he debated. Should he kiss her? Was it too soon? They'd only met a few hours earlier.

He did kiss her, but opted for a sweet brush of his lips on her forehead.

"Hey, you two lovebirds! It's not Valentine's Day yet!" Emily burst into the kitchen with the others in tow. "How long does it take to make a few peanut butter cups?"

"The first batch is ready," Sally said.

Emily snatched one up. "Delicious," she declared, and the

newlyweds agreed as they shared bites. Joe grabbed two, stating that he deserved more than the others because he'd delivered the chocolate.

"Not quite all the way to my shop," Sally reminded him.

"Close enough," came his response.

"Too sweet," the older woman proclaimed, refusing to eat another bite.

"Not sweet enough," her husband declared, devouring an entire peanut butter cup and then seizing the rest of hers.

Oliver split a peanut butter cup with Sally. They stood closer together, his arm brushing against hers, the air between them fairly charged with an electrical current. He knew she recognized the change in their relationship from when she'd first scurried into the diner. He knew that as surely as he knew that he wanted to see her again, *planned* on seeing her again.

He wanted to appreciate the contagious ring of her laughter, their easy-going banter. He hoped to meet her adorable daughter.

And he wanted to feel her lips pressed against his.

CLOSING hour at the Bloomingfield Candy Shop couldn't arrive soon enough, Sally mused three days later. The last of the customers had picked up their orders, and there was scarcely a piece of candy left in the store.

Valentine's Day sales were a success.

Bone tired, she bent to arrange two red lollipops that had toppled over on the white display case. The chocolate coffee fudge had won out over her infusion salted caramel candies as the store's bestselling Valentine candy.

Her thoughts drifted to Olive's Diner, the night she'd been stranded.

Initially, she'd intended to bring home the peanut butter cups she'd prepared, but the candy hadn't made it out of the diner. The newlyweds, Emily, and Joe had waxed poetic about the flavor with every bite. The older couple, not so much.

She grinned. The wonderful people she'd met were the ideal antidote to her crazy work life. Since then, she decided she wanted other people's opinions of her products, that is, people who weren't in her business—her staff and candymakers.

She'd brought up the idea of monthly taste-testings to Ben, who, as she'd anticipated, had scolded her for taking on additional work. Nonetheless, she intended to go ahead with her new idea.

"Spontaneous people have more fun," Oliver had said.

Still, planning was important if a person wished to get things accomplished.

Oliver. She had to put him out of her mind, but even while she told herself that, her musings returned to the diner.

By the time the tree in the middle of the road had been cleared, she hadn't arrived home until after midnight, with a case full of specialty chocolate, minus one pound.

She gathered a deep breath. Oliver hadn't texted her since she left Evanville, although he'd requested her phone number. Perhaps she'd return to his diner with Clarissa and order the meat loaf and mashed potatoes that wasn't on his menu.

"It's not on the menu because customers know I have it," he'd said.

Truly the man needed someone to advise him on how to run a profitable business. And if he didn't contact her by the end of the week, she'd contact him.

No, no, she couldn't do that, a desperate attempt at a relationship with a man who might not be interested. She'd done that once already, and her marriage to Leon had almost destroyed her self-esteem.

She paused, her thoughts circling back to Oliver, as they often did. In the midst of an impromptu candy-making session, she'd found something she'd searched for her entire life.

Contentment. Joy in a simple project.

And maybe, just maybe, a good, sincere man.

"I'M LEAVING," Ben said. "Congratulations on a remarkably successful holiday." He grabbed his jacket. "Maise and I are dining out tonight."

"Is it one of her food critic jobs?" Sally asked.

"No. Although she does it for work, she loves going out for pleasure. Please join us."

"I can't." Sally declined with an apologetic sigh. "I'm committed to mac and cheese with Clarissa."

"Valentine's Day is over."

"I know, but barely."

"We're going to Julie's restaurant, and you love her home-made fettuccini."

"Some other night. Soon. I promise."

"That's what you always say," he reminded.

As he walked out the door, Sally called after him, "We'll take a raincheck."

Five minutes later, as she was rearranging a display that had little candy left, the bell on the door jingled, indicating one more customer. She stifled a groan. Hadn't Ben posted the closed sign?

"Sally?" The deep male voice made her pause.

She hesitated for a second before she spun. Her heart beat double time, taking in his strong, athletic features, his wonderful smile. "Oliver?"

"Your hair looks … different. Wonderful."

There was no mistaking the huskiness in his tone. She couldn't free her stare from his intent gaze. "I used a hair straightener." She fingered a strand that had come loose from her ponytail. "Do you like it?"

"You look gorgeous, whether your hair is curly or straight." He strode to her, bearing a foil-covered plate. "I brought you something for Valentine's Day."

She stepped over to him, peering at the plate as he uncovered it. Peanut butter cups, unevenly spaced, some thicker than others.

"I've been trying these out for the past two days, incorporating some ideas you suggested about working with chocolate." He offered that boyish grin. "I'm not claiming these peanut butter cups are better than your fancy infusion candies, but . . ."

As he chatted, she plucked up a candy and took a bite. "Oliver, this is amazing." She closed her eyes, allowing the flavors of peanut butter and chocolate to melt on her tongue.

"I used more sugar."

"Excellent." She grinned. "Perhaps we can start selling your peanut butter cups in my shop."

"Are they as delicious as my vegetable soup?"

"I don't know. I never had the opportunity to try your soup."

"I'll make it again." He set the candy aside, took her in his arms and brushed a kiss on her mouth. "Just for you."

Just for her. His words swirled around in her mind. His voice lowered, his gaze loving, his lips tasting of chocolate.

She drew a quiet, steadying inhale, shaking her head at

her resolutions to avoid love. With Oliver, there was no need for false pride and relationship games.

Because the truth was, in the short time she'd known him, she had begun to fall in love with him. And by his affectionate gaze, the romantic way he stroked her cheek, he felt the same about her.

"Happy Valentine's Day, Sally," he said. "And thank you."

She cleared her throat to prevent her voice from shaking. "Whatever for?"

"For coming into my diner. For looking beautiful and never missing a single step, no matter the obstacles. And for creating the most delectable candy in the world for me and my customers."

"Not as tasty as your diner food."

"Because diner food is the best." He laughed and linked his fingers through hers. "Miss Sally Elliot, about all that planning you do …"

She tipped back her head, smiling at him with wide-eyed innocence. "Me?"

"I'm available if you can squeeze me into your calendar." His tone was firm. He wouldn't allow otherwise. "And I'd love to meet your daughter."

"How about tonight?"

His gaze searched hers, glinting with amusement. "You're being spontaneous?"

"Absolutely. I'm picking Clarissa up at the sitter's in a few minutes." Quickly, Sally adjusted her plans. "How would you like to go to dinner with us at my sister's restaurant?"

"The Pasta Junction?"

"Everyone will be there. Ben and Maise, and Lorenzo, the TV weatherman. He and Julie are dating."

"Count me in." His deep voice had a precarious effect on her heart beat. "Sounds like the perfect Valentine's Day celebration."

She eyed his handsome features, his poignant smile, the look in his eyes—warm and inviting. He was her Valentine. Now and always.

Because, she realized, it's your last love who truly matters.

THE END

RECIPE FOR AMY'S PEANUT BUTTER CUPS

Bottom layer:
- 2 sticks margarine melted
- 1 18-ounce jar peanut butter
- 2 sleeves graham crackers, crushed
- 1 pound powdered sugar

Mix until well blended

Top layer

1 12-ounce bag semisweet chocolate chips

1 stick margarine

Melt together in the microwave for about 90 seconds, stirring halfway through.

Place bottom layer in the prepared tins and pour the top layer over it.

Prepare in mini muffin or regular sized tins. The thickness of the chocolate can be varied according to your preferences.

Can also be done in a 9x13 dish and cut into squares.

Enjoy!

A NOTE FROM JOSIE

Dear Friends,

Thank you for reading *A Chocolate-Box Valentine.*

This is a short story for a quick, sweet read.

I wanted to write a Valentine romance centering around chocolate, which continues the story of my *Chocolate-Box* books.

If you loved this romance as much as I loved writing it, please help other people find *A Chocolate-Box Valentine* by posting your review.

A Chocolate-Box Valentine is available in ebook, paperback, Large Print paperback, Hardcover, and Audiobook.

My Spotify Play List for A Chocolate-Box Valentine is here.

Love sweet romance Valentine romances?
Be sure to check out:

I Love You More
A Valentine To Cherish
1-800-CUPID
Valentine Hearts: A 3 book Valentine Bundle

USA TODAY BESTSELLING AUTHOR

JOSIE RIVIERA

A Chocolate-Box Summer Breeze

PRAISE AND AWARDS

USA TODAY bestselling author

CHAPTER 1

*A*t seven o'clock on a Thursday evening, Emily Varon sat alone in a corner booth in Olive's Diner. She swallowed some black coffee, pushed the cup aside and checked her watch.

Joe Vertucci was ten minutes late. Odd, because he was always punctual when he phoned her.

Emily bit her bottom lip, drew back the diner's thick tan-colored curtains, and peered out the window at a sultry California evening. The parking lot was empty except for the few cars that belonged to the customers who were dining inside.

She grabbed her cellphone from her leather handbag and read the last words Joe had texted.

After all these months, I'm looking forward to seeing you in person again, Emily.

Her stomach fluttered as she imagined their reunion. She was looking forward to seeing him too and told him as much. He'd responded with a thumbs-up, which had prompted her to smile. She'd attempted to explain different emojis to him, he didn't always have to use a thumbs-up.

However, he couldn't seem to get the hang of new technology.

Of course, emoji stickers weren't new, and he'd beamed on their video chat when she'd assured that she'd teach him how to use them.

Their only disagreement had taken place when Joe had insisted on paying for their meal. Eventually, she'd conceded and offered to leave the tip.

He'd concluded their conversation with a quip. "That's why I'm crazy about you, Emily. You don't take advantage of me."

Frequently, he'd referred to himself as a blue-collar, working-class guy, and she'd heard a trace of disparagement in his voice, as if he was putting himself down. Although people took pride in referring to themselves in that way, she repeatedly wondered if he genuinely believed in himself.

He should. He was a thoughtful, good-natured man.

Again, her gazed flitted to the window. He could have been delayed by rough weather, or unexpected traffic delays. Hazards on the road occurred in seconds, and driver fatigue often caused serious accidents.

Or, perhaps ... Joe wasn't interested in her after all.

She rubbed her cheek with the back of her hand, attempting to pry herself free from the anxious speculations. She hadn't dated in years, and her nerves wavered as if she were a schoolgirl.

This isn't a date, she reminded herself, nor a naïve teenage crush.

She opened the menu and scanned the dinner selections. The special featured grilled chicken, and a baked potato, which suited her nicely. However, the diner's delicious coconut cake would surely ruin her diet.

It was her proper upbringing, she supposed, that kept her focused on the latest fashion trends. Often, though, she pondered if there was a reason to watch her weight anymore. The only people she encountered besides the diners were her son and his family, the weekly grocer, her hair stylist, and Sunday morning churchgoers.

A Moonglow Chocolatiers truck pulled into the lot, and Emily's heart leaped. A man with silver-white hair emerged from the driver's side. Several patrons whispered Emily's name, like the murmurings of a breeze rushing through a forest. Somehow, they knew Joe was here to see Emily.

"I haven't seen Joe in a long time." Oliver, the owner of the diner, stepped over to her booth. He held a steaming pot of coffee.

Emily jumped. She was so focused on Joe's arrival that she hadn't realized Oliver had approached.

"You're eating dinner later than usual." Oliver grinned and gestured toward the window. "Are you waiting for Joe?"

"Yes." Hastily, she jammed her cellphone into her purse. "He's overnighting near here for a couple days."

Oliver refilled her cup. "How did you know Joe was in the area?"

"Why are you asking?" She sat straighter and adjusted her flawlessly creased white slacks. Through all her months at the diner, she'd kept her personal life private. "Sometimes, people need to eat dinner with someone else, rather than all alone."

At the swift, questioning look he shot her, she grimaced. Her response had a breathless, edgy quality. "Sorry."

"No worries, Emily, and you're one hundred percent right. I shouldn't pry." Oliver patted her hand. "I can't help being an old-fashioned Cupid, and I detect a romance is brewing."

"Hardly." She dismissed any further inquiries Oliver poised on his lips with a wave. "Joe and I regularly talk on the phone."

"Ever since you met him here in my diner?"

"Yes," she acknowledged. For an instant, she closed her eyes and relived that stormy February night.

After panicking because she'd never been in a situation like that before—stranded in a diner—her nerves had settled, and she'd enjoyed several hours conversing with Joe. The narratives about his over-the-road travels had made her laugh. It felt good to laugh, especially after she had visited with her son the previous weekend. He, his wife, and her grandchild had been cordial, but their life was hectic and Emily had felt useless and in the way.

She knew they loved her, but they didn't need her.

"May I call you?" Joe had politely inquired that evening, after the road had been cleared and the customers could safely leave the diner.

His request had wrung a reluctant chuckle from Emily, but the sight of his incredible smile had done odd quivery things to her pulse.

She'd agreed and wrote her number on a napkin before handing it to him.

Following an exchange of "safe travels", she'd driven back to her large, empty home in town, and hadn't felt quite so lonely.

"I remember you two got along well." Oliver grabbed a cup and paper placemat from an adjacent table and set them across from Emily. "You never mentioned that your relationship with Joe had blossomed. You eat dinner here nightly."

"Your food is delicious."

"Thanks. I might use your testimonial as advertising." He paused. "However, you're not answering."

"Is this a question or a statement?"

"Both, considering I'm an old-fashioned Cupid," he reminded.

"Joe and I are too timeworn for a romantic relationship."

She tasted the coffee, which was always perfect, then dabbed her lips with a napkin. "Even though I gave him my phone number, I didn't expect him to call me."

"Why not? You're an attractive, classy lady."

She shook her head. She wasn't. She'd continually considered herself plump and the opposite of model-thin, but she wasn't about to introduce a lengthy psychological discussion. Plus, she'd been obsessed with tanning salons, believing a tan made her look younger. However, she'd finally recognized that tanning aged her, and had given that up after she'd met Joe.

One didn't need any more wrinkles at her age.

"Thus," Oliver said, "you've been talking to Joe for—"

"Nearly four months. Joe and I believe in phone calls and occasional video chats," she said.

"There's something about hearing a person's voice. It's more personal."

"Yes, definitely. These days, everyone relies on texting." Emily took another sip of coffee. "Young people stare at their cellphones waiting for bubbles to appear when a phone call accomplishes twice as much in half the time. In addition, there's constantly a risk you'll be misunderstood."

In accord, she and Oliver nodded.

"I'm glad he's here now," Oliver said. "Beneath the flannel shirt and jeans façade, Joe is a romantic guy."

Romantic. The idea brought a funny catch to her chest.

Once, romance had made life worth living.

Now?

She lowered her gaze to concentrate on her cup.

She'd lost all sense of romance after Krandall—her tall, striking husband—had unexpectedly died three years earlier. At the image of his well-heeled demeanor, his poise in the board room, his focus and goal-setting … "I've set my eyes on you, Emily," he'd declared, and the remembrance brought a thickness to her throat. Her moneyed parents had extended not-so-subtle nudges for her to accept his advances so that she could "marry well."

Emily fingered the black-gold and sapphire bracelet, the last piece of jewelry Krandall had bought her before he'd gotten sick.

In fact, he'd purchased many gifts for her, mostly to apologize for his outbursts. He'd been super-critical and continuously chastised her. Sometimes, she believed she was little more than a fixture on his arm that he could show off at high-class fund-raisers.

Glancing up, she realized that Oliver was studying her.

"You're categorizing Joe as a romantic?" she asked him.

"Absolutely. We chatted at length the night he was stranded here, and our conversation was poignant and enlightening."

"Poignant?"

"Guys use fancy words too." He grinned. "From what I gathered, he yearns for a connection with a woman. He was widowed several years ago."

"Companionship … most people are seeking mutual support."

"Joe confided that he longs to feel loved again." Oliver scanned the diner, then set the coffeepot on the table and perched across from her. "Is this a first date? Or a second?"

"Oliver, you're not listening. A widow and widower who are seventy years old don't date."

Although this meeting with Joe was, in every sense of the word, a date. Wasn't it?

No, she repeated to herself.

She fished in her handbag for pink lipstick and a mirrored compact. Ordinarily, she wouldn't fuss as much with her appearance, but the anticipation she'd soon see Joe face to face …

Where is he? the question intruded. It shouldn't take that long to park a truck.

"He's been rummaging for a while." Oliver echoed her thoughts.

Carefully, Emily arranged her silver-blond hair and applied a dab of lipstick. "He keeps track of his hours in a logbook and is doubtlessly making certain the load matches the manifest sheet."

"Manifest sheet?"

"The list of deliveries and shipments." She cast Oliver a sideways smile as he went to the counter to pour two glasses of water.

She'd learned a lot about trucking from her conversations with Joe. What's more, she'd gained an understanding of the man himself. He was frugal, efficient, and fit. He was also sincere, sensible, and because of his job, mechanical.

With an inner sigh, her gaze wandered back to the parking lot.

Tonight was so different compared to the night they'd met. That eventful evening, a severe storm had flattened a tree in front of the diner. Now, four months later, the California rains were nonexistent. Summer bloomed, intense and motionless, the sky a mellow golden hue.

A painter embraced the tints of the sunset, bold tones of orange and crimson. For her, the spectacular evening marked the beginning of another lengthy, desolate season.

Summertime, the potential for light-heartedness and unexpected delight. Days to flaunt straw hats and sundresses, pretty floral blouses, and sandals.

Don't be ridiculous, she scolded herself. The season didn't matter. Not for a grown woman of a particular age.

"What is taking Joe so long?" she blurted, as Oliver returned with two glasses.

"Most likely, he's planning something extraordinary for you."

"From the back of his truck?"

Her thoughts drifted to their conversation the previous evening. As was his custom, he'd phoned at six o'clock, and suggested video-chatting.

"I chuckle whenever I consider Oliver and his diner," Joe had said. "The former owners had named the diner Olive, and Oliver kept the name, declaring it had a nice ring to it."

"Even though we've all told him there's a considerable difference between Olive and Oliver."

Joe laughed. "So let's have dinner together at the diner while I'm in town … the place where it all began."

"Where *what* began?" she'd responded.

"Our … our friendship."

Friendship was a safe word. Although, she'd read in a leading scientific journal that men and women weren't capable of being "just friends" because romance bubbled just around the corner.

Her cellphone buzzed. She pulled the phone from her handbag and checked the screen.

"Who is it?" Oliver stood and plucked up the coffee pot.

Her pulse quickened. "Joe is here. He sent me a thumbs-up."

"I know. We saw him get out of his truck, but now I'm staring at him." Oliver pointed to the doorway as Joe entered. "He looks great. Did he lose weight?"

Indeed he had—twenty pounds and counting. She knew he'd been trying because he'd outlined his nutritious diet, reiterating the calorie and fat content.

And indeed he did. Look great, that is.

Joe's handsome, rugged face was clean-shaven. He adjusted his eyeglasses, then shoved a hand in his jeans, his gaze searching the diner. Searching for *her*, Emily realized with a wide grin.

His manner was comfortable, almost boyish. But it was his genuine, inviting smile, a smile that reached all the way to his blue eyes when he spotted Emily, that encouraged her to grin in return.

She stood, flattened her fine, white linen blouse and hailed him. "His route takes him across the state and back," she informed Oliver.

"Sounds like you're proud of him."

Briefly, she savored the moment as she regarded Joe.

"I am," she said truthfully. "We talk for at least an hour until Jeopardy comes on." Her face sobered. She was showing too much excitement. "Oliver, are you taking note of my social life?"

Oliver chuckled and shook his head. "I can hardly manage my own."

"I imagine that Sally Elliot keeps you on your toes?"

Sally was the woman who owned Bloomingfield Candy Shop. She'd been stranded at the diner that same February night along with Emily, Joe, and several others.

"You're imagining correctly." Oliver wiped a hand on his clean white apron. "I see Sally and her daughter, Clarissa, every weekend. Nevertheless, our busy work schedules produce challenges, because I'm here in Evanville and she's in Bloomingfield."

"Challenges you both are apparently overcoming?" Emily teased.

"For love," Oliver replied, "anything is possible."

*E*mily caught a quick breath as Joe hastened to her table. He carried a package wrapped in blue paper, and she silently groaned, hoping it wasn't another baked good. Thus far, the cupcakes and brownies he'd sent to her had been dry and tasteless.

Joe's bright eyes fixated on her. "My lovely Emily." He laid a hand over his heart, confirming he was as elated about their meeting as she. His voice cracked as he placed the package on the table, then took her hands in his—completely disregarding Oliver except for a brief nod. "Thanks for waiting. I'm sorry I'm late."

"Joe, you're only fifteen minutes late. I'm glad you drive slow and conscientious." She glanced at her watch. Okay, he was twenty minutes late, but that was because he'd spent a few minutes in the back of his truck.

"By the time I finished my deliveries, then sorted the chocolate—"

"Anything on the road can slow your progress," Oliver broke in. "Did you deliver to Bloomingfield?"

"I did, indeed." Joe winked. "Sally said hello. She and her

daughter will see you later this evening when she gets off work. And tomorrow you're both playing hooky in order to take Clarissa to the aquarium at the new mall in Santa Rosa."

"Exactly the plan." A satisfied grin spread across Oliver's features as he wended around the tables, filling cups of coffee for his customers and stopping to chat.

"How are you?" Joe waited for Emily to sit before settling across from her. She appreciated his gentlemanly traits. He was chivalrous in a traditional manner some people labeled as out-of-date.

Emily didn't. Gallant and respectful behaviors never went out of style.

"I'm fine," she replied. "You?"

He beamed, never taking his gaze from hers. "I couldn't be better."

"You're staring at me as though I have food on my chin."

"I was thinking about how gorgeous you are in person. A phone screen doesn't do you justice. And your hair, it's blonder?"

Self-consciously, she touched her hair. Earlier that morning, she'd asked her stylist to color over the platinum silver. After a half hour of consultation and assurances, Emily had decided the two hours in the salon had been worth it.

"What do you think?" she asked. "It's my natural color, minus the years in between."

He chuckled. "I love it."

"I wanted a change."

"It's a marvelous one ... I mean ... I liked your previous hair color too."

"It's not that much different."

He studied her. "No, it's just ... blonder."

Emily tried not to chuckle at how ridiculous their conversation might sound to anyone who happened to listen.

Judging from the patrons eating and conversing, no one had heard them.

Joe nudged the gift toward her. "I brought something for you."

"Chocolates from Sally's shop?" *With any luck*, she thought. Joe was so intent on creating low-fat goodies he'd forgotten that in the end, taste mattered the most.

"Nope," he said. "I baked these German chocolate mini-muffins in my own kitchen."

She kept her grimace at bay. "Are they healthy?"

"Naturally. I substituted unsweetened applesauce for the vegetable oil. The muffins got jostled during the trip, but I re-wrapped them."

Two weeks earlier, he'd mailed her a batch of chocolate chip muffins, followed by brownies. Each time, he used a thin cord of gold ribbon to create a delicate bow. Although stunning to look at, the baked goods inside didn't prove as delicious as the packaging. The last batch had been too sweet, and Emily had tactfully suggested he use real sugar instead of artificial, which frequently left an aftertaste.

He'd agreed, but the following week, his chocolate-coffee muffins had arrived on her doorstep. Those muffins had tasted odd, and she'd (respectfully, of course), urged him to check the expiration dates on the ingredients.

Sure enough, flour had been the culprit.

She glanced up. Expectantly, he watched her as she examined the package.

"Thank you, Joe. You're becoming a baking expert." She smiled.

A little white lie never hurt anyone.

She nudged aside the fake potted lilac plant Oliver always placed on every table, unwrapped the package, and peeped inside. Immediately, she inhaled the aroma of rich, dark chocolate.

"I bought a new bag of flour," Joe said.

She extended a brilliant smile. "Thus you baked two perfect muffins."

Hopefully.

"Maybe not perfect, but I figured that after dinner we'll try them for dessert."

"Joe, you always persevere."

"All I can do is try."

He was sincere and put his whole being into everything.

The knowledge caused her to smile. "Oliver's special dessert tonight is coconut cake," she said.

"My muffins have fewer calories than cake." Absently, Joe perused the menu, then grasped her hands. "Is there anything in the world more captivating than you?" he asked softly.

She moved back. "What brought on that compliment?"

"You. Just seeing your lovely face and new hair style."

"New hair *color,*" she corrected. "My style is the same." With a laughing sigh, she leaned her head against the green vinyl seat. "There are countless subjects more captivating than me."

"You're not a subject. You're my Emily."

She concentrated on his words. Nonetheless, she drew her hands away and clasped them properly on her lap. They were friends, she repeated to herself, and she wasn't about to get cozy in a public diner. She'd grown accustomed to living life alone, although, through Joe's direct and indirect hints, she intuitively knew he craved more from their relationship.

Joe frowned at her response. There was that directness about him she admired, the way he wore his sentiments on his sleeve. Her late, by-the-book husband had controlled his emotions.

Krandall had been a generous provider, fixating on his net worth and savvy with his fortune, believing the money from his investment business liberated them.

Joe remained silent, evidently waiting for her to say more. When she didn't, he said, "We've established dessert. What is your choice for dinner?"

"I've decided on the grilled chicken special and a bowl of Oliver's homemade vegetable soup."

"Low calorie and hearty, but please choose the most expensive meal on the menu." He held out his palms in a generous gesture. "Remember, dinner is my treat."

"The grilled chicken is the most expensive entrée tonight."

He laughed. "Then I'll have the same, because this is a celebratory evening."

After they'd placed their order with an efficient teenage waitress, Emily leaned in. "Do you eat all your meals in diners, Joe?"

"Usually." Yet again, he grasped her hands. "What about you?"

"I never eat out anywhere but here, and only for dinner. I prepare my other meals at home."

"We should dine together more often. When I'm driving, all I can think about is phoning you from my hotel room. You're the highlight of my hours and I love hearing your voice."

The heartfelt attentiveness in his gaze and the enthusiasm in his tone made Emily feel warm and cherished.

"I feel the same," she said. In fact, his calls had become a lifeline, and she looked forward to telling someone about her day. "Although I wish you'd cut back your working hours—for your sake."

"I can't, Emily. I'm paying off my daughter's college tuition loan because she recently lost her job. As a single mother, Lydia is struggling. She applied at the bank for a debt consolidation and seeks employment every day."

You're struggling financially too, Emily thought, but she didn't share her contemplation with him.

The fact that he was compelled to work an exhausting job in order to pay his daughter's bills brought a sadness, an infuriation, to Emily's chest. By now, Joe should be ready to retire.

Managing his route and the truck's contents while staying on schedule was arduous for a younger man, and ever more so for someone Joe's age. Yet, he managed it all while maintaining a courteous demeanor with his suppliers and customers. Even when describing his workdays he never complained, and she innately knew he wouldn't welcome her observations or sympathy.

Emily blew out a breath. "Your actions are admirable. However, your daughter is a grown woman."

"Wouldn't you do the same for your son? From what you've mentioned, he's doing well financially, but if he wasn't—"

"Naturally," she agreed. "But I wish you would relax more."

"Relaxing isn't a word in my vocabulary." Joe downed his water, then fidgeted. "So Emily, where do we go from here?"

"We? Why? Where are we going?"

For the first time, she questioned if there was another purpose for their arranged meeting that Joe was easing into. Since this was a special and upbeat reunion, she followed his lead. Perhaps she'd shift their discussion to small talk, rather than student loans and debts. At cocktail parties in the past, she'd been a pro at engaging people in light conversations.

"It's a figure of speech." Joe cleared his throat and scratched his chin. "I have the next few days off."

"Good. You deserve it."

"How about you?"

"I don't work."

He scanned her face. "I mean, what do you have planned for the weekend?"

"Nothing."

Oliver wandered to the juke-box, and the jingle of coins dropping in the slot followed as he selected a song, throwing a grin at Emily over his shoulder.

Several seconds later, Frank Sinatra's voice crooned the first few measures of *You Make Me Feel So Young*, an upbeat romantic swing jazz piece.

She grinned at Oliver and awarded a wave. There was something about being in a familiar place—with an attractive man who was obviously interested in her sitting across the table—that brought an excitement she hadn't envisioned. Add the music, and the night was magical.

"Are you a Frank Sinatra enthusiast?" Joe inquired.

"I love his music, particularly *Come Fly With Me*."

"I'm a Beatles fan."

"Rock?" She scoffed. "All the music sounds the same —rebellious."

"Not the Beatles. Their music is fresh and innovative. How about country songs?"

"No, but I adore musicals," Emily replied. "Especially *Cats,* by Andrew Lloyd Webber."

"I've never seen a live musical, nor listened to any."

"You've never visited New York city, or strolled on Broadway?"

"Nope." He sat on the edge of his seat. "What's the musical about? A cat?"

"Several cats, and my favorite song is *Memory*." With a soft murmur, she called up the lyrics ... "being alone in the moonlight with remembrances of the past."

"Is there a storyline?"

"Of course. The old cat, Grizabella, is mourning her

youth." Emily tipped her head to the side. "Sometimes the older you get, the more it seems like you've disappeared."

Sometimes, oftentimes, she'd felt that way with her son and his family.

"What's your favorite song?" she asked. "Besides anything by The Beatles."

"Give me any tunes by Journey."

"You're going on a journey?"

"Journey is the band's name, Emily."

She offered an abashed smile. "I'm joking."

"I know." He shifted but didn't grin. "Are you spending the Fourth of July with friends?"

She automatically tensed at the question. Any social life since she became a widow was nonexistent. Her core of socialite friends had avoided calling, and Emily learned that several wives considered her a threat because she was single.

To keep active, she'd tried a sip and paint class before concluding she wasn't good at sipping wine or painting. Hence, she'd given up on a night life, or a day life, or any social life, for that matter.

"No plans," she replied.

Joe kept his features reserved, although the affection in his deep-blue eyes betrayed him. "Will you see your son?"

"He and his wife and my grandson are taking a hiking trip to the mountains."

"They didn't invite you?"

"Not in so many words, but I suppose the invitation was there." She kept her voice a monotone. "I'll call him. That is, if he has cell phone service where they are camping. Oftentimes he doesn't pick up. However, I always leave a message."

Joe extended a half-smile. "I do the same."

"Our adult children and their families lead hectic lives."

"Yes."

Emily focused on the ceiling. "Anyway, I've never slept in

a tent before and informed my son that I'm certainly not starting at my age."

"So you prefer creature comforts?"

"Totally. You?"

"Delicious food, a pleasant home, and a delightful woman by my side is my vision of paradise," Joe said. "I could probably climb into a sleeping bag … however, climbing out is a different matter entirely."

"Because of the zipper?"

"Because I'm seventy." He smirked. "It's not easy for me to get up."

His upbeat banter was so infectious that she grabbed his hand before she could stop herself. "Not exactly a simple task for me, either."

"Unless we're both planning to become Olympic athletes in our seventies, sleeping in bags on the ground probably isn't a satisfactory plan. You're physically fit, though, Emily. I presume you work out."

There was no mistaking the admiration on his features.

Her face flushed. The two-mile walk on the treadmill every morning was tiring, but obviously worth it.

She drew back but didn't release her gaze.

"My daughter and her little girl won't be around either." Joe picked up his coffee cup and smiled at her over the rim. "What I'm trying to ask is … are you interested in riding to Cambria with me? I'm scheduled to pick up another chocolate delivery near there, but not until Monday. Therefore, my days in between are clear, plus I'm paid for the vacation."

"And you choose to spend those days with me?"

"Absolutely."

"You mean … ride with you to Cambria … in your delivery truck?"

"Sure, and we can enjoy the long weekend together. Cambria is a little seaside town. I've visited a number of times because there's a major chocolate distribution center close by. Tourist attractions in Cambria include a castle and a boardwalk, and we can watch the sunsets on Moonstone Beach."

Emily attempted to tamp down her excitement, although her senses reeled. "Where is Cambria?" she hedged.

"About five hours away."

"I'm not sure—"

"No pressure." Joe set down his cup and grasped her hands again. "No expectations. Just two friends taking pleasure in one another's company."

She eyed the Moonglow Chocolatiers truck in the parking lot. "Is there enough room for me?"

"I'm driving a box truck, Emily. There's plenty of space."

"I'm not accustomed to packing lightly."

"Bring whatever is best for a beach trip, especially if it fits into a duffel bag."

She frowned. She couldn't recall if she even owned a duffel bag, but she owned a set of white designer suitcases.

"Fair warning," Joe said. "If I keep any clothes and items in the back, they tend to smell like chocolate."

"Tend?"

"They do. They will."

With a quiet giggle, she assured, "Chocolate is my favorite."

"Me too, or I wouldn't have lasted two decades transporting it across the state."

She pressed her lips together, still debating. "Is there a downside of riding in a truck?"

"Well, dust always lands in the passenger seat."

"Can anything go wrong on the road?"

"Plenty." He caressed her fingers with his thumb. "A punctured tire, a cracked windshield—"

Halfheartedly, she stifled a grin. "Joe, are you trying to talk me into going? If so, you're hardly succeeding."

"Because I saved the best for last." He sat straighter. "My truck has something no other can boast. Besides having you along for the ride, of course."

"Which is?"

"A year ago, I installed an eight-track cassette tape player in the dashboard."

"The proprietor agreed?"

"I leased the truck for five years, and now I own it."

"I commend your entrepreneurial spirit, but where did you find cassettes?"

"Several big-box stores, vintage record shops, and online. It's a niche industry, but many people prefer tapes."

"Therefore, there is no CD player in your truck?"

He quirked a white eyebrow. "What are those?"

"CD's are—" She caught his smirk and joined in. "At any rate, eight-track cassettes are antiques. Like us."

"We're not antiques, Emily. We have an exciting life ahead of us and an entire world to experience."

She shrugged. "Maybe." She wondered exactly where that world was located … sometimes. At other times, she was content in her quiet, daily routine.

Wasn't she?

Of course.

Moreover, repetition was excellent for aiding memory, and her routine was invariably the same. She drove the short distance to the diner for dinner, conversed with the other customers and Oliver, and returned to her comfortable brick house in the center of the small adjacent city.

Rinse and repeat, her conscience chided, noting that her days had become repetitive and dreary. Was Joe's invitation an opportunity for adventure?

"What are the accommodations in Cambria?" she asked. "Are there hotels?"

"There are numerous motels and hotels and quaint bed-and-breakfast spots. At last count, Cambria's population was around six thousand."

"You described a seaside town." Emily envisioned starfish, tumbling waves, and a smart pier harboring million-dollar yachts.

"Cambria is near the Pacific Ocean," Joe continued. "The community boasts an abundance of sea life, including otters and seals. We can book a boat excursion if you'd like. I did once when I was there … by myself." He paused. "We can swim, although parts of the coast are rocky."

Emily's head came up at the swimming reference. "Decades ago, I was a member of my college's swim team."

"What was your best stroke?"

"The backstroke." She met his gaze. "Were you on the swim team in college?"

"I didn't attend college, but I know how to swim. To support my family, I took the first job offered as soon as I graduated from high school. My father had died when I was young, and my mother cleaned houses for a living. We constantly struggled to make ends meet."

When she didn't respond, Joe granted a broad, disarming grin. "May I confess something?"

"Why not?"

"I rented a tiny, quaint cottage by the sea. It's not as fancy as the deluxe resorts where you vacationed when Krandall was alive." He hesitated. "I know you summered in Europe and wintered in the Bahamas."

She shook her head. "Contrary to what you might presume about me—"

"You prefer the finer things in life."

"Admittedly, but Cambria sounds enchanting."

Joe blinked. His eyes rounded. "My tiny cottage will suffice?"

"Nicely." She bit back a smile at his enthusiastic tone. "However, if you've already rented the cottage, then you assumed I'd agree to your invitation?"

"I wasn't certain." He squeezed her hands. "Nonetheless, I was hopeful."

She turned to the window. Night had descended, the golden colors of afternoon had dimmed to twilight, then blackness.

And there was one more subject to resolve.

"Joe, without sounding prudish …" She subjected him to a delicate raise of her eyebrows. "We both were married, but my mother instilled Victorian values in me that I still ascribe to."

"Excellent." He grinned. "Your mother must have known my mother."

When he continued to grin, Emily reiterated with utmost honesty. "Consequently, I won't share a bedroom with you."

"I respect you too much to ask otherwise. The cottage I rented has two bedrooms, and I'll sleep in the smaller of the two."

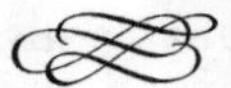

CHAPTER 3

*W*as this beach trip a wise idea?

The following morning, Emily pondered the question while she finished packing. She'd selected casual, comfortable clothes. After all, it was a spur-of-the-moment invitation. For the drive, she opted for a black and white jersey knit sundress, black leather sandals, a thin silver bracelet, and a cardigan sweater to drape over her shoulders.

When had she last gone on a vacation, or anywhere at all since Krandall had died, except to visit her son and his family?

Pausing to rest on the tufted sofa in her cozy sitting room, Emily set the duffel bag on a table and drew a knitted blanket over her lap. Because of the air conditioning, she was often cold.

She leaned her head back. Too excited to sleep the previous evening, she'd risen when stars still flickered in the sky. She hardly ever slept well anymore, waking frequently.

After their dinner at the diner, Joe had phoned when she'd returned to her house, describing in enthusiastic detail the places in Cambria she might be interested in—the charming boutiques lining the boardwalk and an artifacts gallery displaying art painted by local California artists. She envisioned a Nantucket-style cottage, a coastal retreat with lattice greenery growing over the roof. A sunny, gleaming oasis decorated with cane chairs and needlepoint pillows.

A thumbs-up text from Joe brought her to her feet. She stifled the kick in her pulse as his truck rounded the street corner.

A minute later, she was partway across the living room when the doorbell rang. Although she was overjoyed to see him, she was determined to stay poised and attempted to tamp down her enthusiasm as she opened the door.

He stood on her front steps with his hands dug in the pockets of his khaki shorts, wearing a smile that revealed white teeth. His strong pride showed in his rough-hewn features, and the firm mouth that had tenderly kissed her goodnight.

He wore sunglasses, quickly pointing out they were prescription when she complimented him on his appearance.

He held her hands in his, then slanted his head. "How much stuff are you bringing?"

"Stuff?

"Clothes … stuff."

"This and that. Somehow, I managed to fit most of my toiletries into a duffel bag."

"Somehow? Almost?" He peered around. "I don't see a duffel bag, but I do see two large white suitcases."

"My duffel bag is in the sitting room."

"Sitting room?" He shoved up his glasses. "What's that?"

"A place where you … sit. I needed something slightly bigger and couldn't fit all my clothes into one little bag."

"A duffel bag expands."

"Not enough," she countered. Because she'd added another one-piece swimsuit, a cover-up, two more sundresses, nightclothes, a bold pearl necklace, white cotton slacks, and a couple flowery-print blouses. In addition, her makeup and night clothes took up more space than she'd anticipated, which had necessitated the second suitcase.

Joe rubbed his temples. "I'll store your suitcases in the back. Be ready to smell like chocolate when you open them in the morning."

"You warned me already, and I'm prepared." She hung her hands on her hips, opting for a more logical approach. "What woman can fit all her weekend outfits into a duffel bag, anyway?"

"Certainly not anyone as fashionable as you." He placed his arm lightly on her shoulders. "I phoned my daughter. Did you speak with your son?"

"He seemed pleased I had plans for the holiday." *Immensely, overly pleased.*

With a twinge of heartache, Emily had detected her son's relief. Definitely, she was joyful because he had a devoted wife and an adorable son, but oftentimes she felt abandoned.

"Excellent." Joe brought a hand to his forehead and peered toward the hallway. "Are you ready?"

"Whenever you are." She retrieved her duffel bag, secured the windows and snatched her purse, and house keys.

Joe lifted her suitcases and feigned an amplified groan. "Imagine if we traveled for a week. What would you pack then?"

"Enough for at least four suitcases." At his incredulous stare, she quickly inserted, "Just kidding."

As they walked to his truck, he paused to regard her. "I still can't believe I persuaded a fine, wonderful woman like you to come along with me."

"It was the eight-track cassette player," she reminded with a laugh.

He opened the passenger door, then waited as she

climbed in and buckled her seat belt. "Thank you for agreeing to ride with me, Emily. This trip means more than you can imagine."

"Me too," she said quietly.

He was a thoughtful man with a tender heart, and she hardly was able to contain her happiness that she'd met him.

He started the ignition and eased onto the street, then the interstate, while Emily fiddled with the radio stations. When the disc jockey's voice introduced the next song as country/western, a man in an SUV pulled up next to them at the stoplight. His SUV blasted the same station.

"My cassettes are in the glove compartment." Joe had evidently noticed Emily's pained expression as Willie Nelson blared from their twin speakers. A woman, apparently, was always on Willie Nelson's mind.

Emily sifted through the row of cassettes—ranging from The Eagles to an assortment of Beatles collections—and her hand stilled. "Frank Sinatra's Greatest Hits? The soundtrack from *My Fair Lady*?"

"I couldn't find the musical you mentioned … the one about dogs."

"Cats," she corrected. "And I thought you didn't care for—"

"This morning, I patronized an oldies store in town."

"You were searching for music for me?"

"Only for you," he said affectionately.

She was special to him, and the knowledge filled her with delight.

The miles passed rapidly, and Joe remarked on the numerous tourist attractions. Traffic moved at a crawl when they hit construction sites, and he braked slowly and gently. Whenever they picked up speed, acceleration was seldom quick.

"We're in Bloomingfield," Joe announced when they drove

along the main street of a charming town. He angled his steering wheel toward the curb. "This is where Sally Elliot owns her candy shop."

"Don't stop," Emily said. "Sally isn't working today because she and Oliver and her daughter are visiting an aquarium."

"Oh, right." Joe stared out the front window and carefully merged into traffic. "Her sister, Julie, owns The Pasta Junction, a fine Italian restaurant here in town, and she makes her own pasta. Her eatery doesn't open until dinnertime, though. Have you frequented either place?"

"I don't travel much farther than the diner," Emily answered with a broken laugh. She shook off her defeatism and said graciously, "But Oliver's food is tasty."

"His meals are the best in the state," Joe agreed. "We'll stop in Bloomingfield some other time, alright?"

"Alright."

He glanced at her. "Is that a promise?"

"Indeed." Emily nodded and stretched out her legs. Her limbs felt weightless, and her expectations were positive.

Some other time. A promise of a next time.

"I've never ridden in a truck before," she confessed. "I'm up so high."

"There's a first for everything, and the view is better."

"Is driving difficult? The ride is a bit rough, and I noticed you swing wide on your turns."

"Yep, and I take ramps and curves unhurriedly."

For the next half hour, they covered an expansive stretch of highway while serenaded by Frank Sinatra's soothing voice singing, "That's Life." Up ahead, a billboard advertised a fast-food restaurant at an upcoming exit.

"Are we stopping for lunch?" Emily asked. "I'm content eating at a drive-through."

"I packed sandwiches," Joe replied. "Or rather, the deli prepared them. There are several roadside picnic areas."

"I haven't picnicked since … forever."

"The spot where I'm headed is on a riverfront."

"Krandall preferred to dine at the country club," Emily mused.

"Nothing against a country club, although I've never even entered one. I prefer to eat outdoors. Food tastes better, particularly a classic turkey sub with roasted red peppers, which I requested especially for you."

She clutched her fingers together. "How did you know some of my favorite foods?"

"Easy." He chuckled at her reaction. "I phoned Oliver. I ordered the same sub for myself, except I requested mine garnished with green peppers instead of red."

When they broke for lunch, she heartily agreed that food tasted better alfresco, further declaring she was becoming a nature lover. To her surprised pleasure, she wasn't immune to the ambiance of an unassuming meal and devoured an amazingly marvelous lunch. As she reached for a cold bottle of water from the sack of drinks and sandwiches, she marveled at the backdrop of their location—the grove of redwood trees, the rushing river, and the scenic, towering mountains.

They disputed whether green or red peppers were tastier, and she did fun things—simple things—such as sitting by the river and skipping rocks.

"Find the smoothest, flattest rock," Joe instructed, demonstrating that a simple flick of the wrist produced the best bounce. "Also, face the water."

"Where else would I face?" She laughed out loud, relishing the friendly competition as she thrust rapidly and the rock flew airborne.

"Next time, I'll teach you how to spin rocks," he said. "You're certainly a pro."

"My newfound skill," she jested, "is skipping rocks."

"You beat me on every throw."

She shoved the hair off her forehead, her lips twitching with laughter as she embraced the finest, most relaxing day she'd ever experienced.

But of course she was with Joe, and as she'd previously determined during their numerous conversations, he had the ability to change ordinary events in life into memorable ones. No fancy meals for him. Just plain old-fashioned fun that didn't rely on a high-priced atmosphere or over-the-top chef creations.

Afterwards, Emily lounged against the truck while Joe filled the tank with gas. She relished the soothing breeze against her face and the brilliant glow of the afternoon sun, grateful for the straw hat she'd worn to protect her complexion.

In a few short hours, they exited the highway. The day had flown by, and soon they arrived at the cottage. Emily rushed across the stone walkway, taking in the appeal of the classic Cape Cod style—the weathered cedar shingles and white wooden shutters.

And then she stopped.

The cottage looked neglected, as if it hadn't been updated in decades.

"The website stated that the cottage had a run of owners, but the reviews were pretty good," Joe said. "Plus, the rental rate was reasonable."

Pretty good. Reasonable. Emily made a quiet groan in her throat. Half of the dilapidated wrap-around deck faced the shimmering Pacific ocean, and two rusty pink bicycles sat propped against an abandoned rose trellis.

"I haven't ridden a bike since I was a teenager," she

murmured, sidestepping the fact that the bicycles screamed for a major repair, as did the rest of the property.

"Neither have I." Joe gestured to a younger woman who stood on the sandy beach and stared at them. With his arm draped around Emily, he steered her toward the doorway and tipped her chin up. "I bet our neighbor thinks I should kiss you before we enter our weekend escape."

Emily tucked her hands at her sides. "I bet she's not thinking any such thing. She doesn't even know us."

He lowered his head. "Let's show her what two happy people look like … two people on top of the world."

Emily bit back a helpless smile as their lips touched. "Make it quick," she murmured.

"I can't kiss you quick when you're laughing."

"I'm laughing because you are."

As their breaths merged, he extended a friendly wave to their neighbor.

THE MUSTY, dry odor of the cottage's interior hit Emily first.

"This place was advertised as sparkling clean and boasting divine beds," Joe muttered.

"Nothing that an airing can't solve," Emily chirped. "We'll open the doors and windows."

They stepped on creaky, white-washed wooden floors and came upon the larger of the two bedrooms. A red and white buffalo checked quilt covered the single bed. An ancient air-conditioning unit blocked most of the cracked window, and slivers of light shone through. Outside, rolling sand dunes, and tall grass swayed in a wind gust.

"If I owned a cottage in a splendid location like this," Emily said, "I would remodel the bedroom, install central air-conditioning, and let the sunlight in. The view of the ocean is spectacular." She ran her fingers over the dusty oak veneer chest and studied a watercolor depicting a fisherman's boat set against a backdrop of jagged cliffs. Emblazoned in blue letters on the boat's stern was *Summer Breeze*.

"Sometimes, owners name their boat after a pleasant memory," Joe remarked.

"*Summer Breeze* brings to mind hope and joy. It's easy to forget any concerns with the promise of summer to cheer you." Emily balanced on her toes to examine the initials etched in the right-hand corner. "K. S. Who do you suppose that is?"

"There was a Keaton Smith art gallery in town a few months ago when I was here," Joe replied. "Let's include the gallery on our itinerary."

"I like itineraries." Emily offered a smile, then reluctantly returned her attention to the bedroom, particularly the cobwebs. Her smile faded as she pondered how long it had been since the walls had absorbed a fresh coat of paint, or the four rooms had been filled with the aroma of a Sunday pot roast.

"When you stare at the floor," Joe said, "you make me think the cottage is inadequate."

Quickly, she shook her head. "No, no, not at all. It's lovely ...really. Only, I'd anticipated something more modern." Belatedly registering his wounded expression, she focused on a point over his shoulder, regretful for allowing her expectations to prompt her to blurt her reservations aloud.

Several seconds of unpromising silence followed.

She stiffened, expecting a verbal set-down. When Joe didn't respond, she encouraged, "Please talk to me. I'm sorry."

"What would you like me to say?"

"To begin with, you can chastise me about my comment."

"I'd never chastise you."

"Okay, but you can tell me that I was rude and ungracious."

"I won't do that, either." He sighed. "This is a cottage built in the 1920s, Emily. You can't expect modern. I told you it was quaint."

"I realize you tried to find the best place on a budget." She drew a long breath. "Are you upset by my remark?"

"I'm not sure."

"I don't understand."

"When it comes to you, my thoughts haven't been clear since we met. In addition, my insecurity grows heavier every second we're together." He kept his stare downcast, which prompted Emily to smile.

She rattled him because he was attracted to her.

"I'm thrilled to hear that," she declared.

Joe didn't appear nearly as thrilled. He rubbed the back of his neck, sat on the edge of the bed, and invited her to sit beside him. "We should come to a clearer understanding of what is happening between us, and, more importantly, how we should continue."

"Joe, we just arrived. This conversation is too serious."

He steepled his hands. "Shall I speak first, or you?"

She flinched. He'd ignored her statement.

"Go ahead," she relented.

"Fifty percent of the time I shake myself, a reminder that I'm really here with you and this isn't all a dream," he said. "You're too attractive and elegant to devote your days to a guy like me."

"Don't put yourself down. I respect you a great deal."

"We're not having this conversation because I'm fishing for compliments, Emily."

She fingered the silver bracelet on her wrist. "And the other fifty percent?" she prodded.

"Despite how well you may perceive me and my lifestyle,

I'm a galaxy away from being inexperienced. The perfectionism I strove for in my youth, the same perfectionism I believe you still want, disappeared for me many years ago. We're both seventy and should acknowledge our differences. I'm the opposite of a wealthy millionaire. I earn an hourly wage and will never receive a six-figure, end-of-year bonus." The grin had long since vanished from his features. "This isn't a senior prom, and I'm not speculating about whether I'll kiss you, because I already have, and—with your permission—will do so again."

Her cheeks heated. He was frank about expressing his feelings. She liked that.

Politely, she folded her hands. "Are you finished?"

"Should I be?"

"Can't you understand that I'm proud of you and what you've accomplished?"

"I own a delivery truck, Emily, and my house is a quarter of the size of yours."

Their earlier excitement was rapidly disintegrating, and an imperceptible strain slowly descended on the tiny bedroom.

"Those things aren't important to me," she replied.

He tapped his fingers on his knee and didn't look convinced.

She inhaled and smiled. "Well then, everything is settled."

"What's settled?"

"You have my permission."

"For what?"

She peered at the doorway. "It's been nearly a half hour since you kissed me and …"

Realization dawned on his face.

Smiling, he cupped her chin and silenced her next words with his lips. As further proof she was sincere, she flung her arms around his neck and returned his kiss.

Several minutes later, they walked hand in hand through the narrow hallway to inspect the galley kitchen, which was painted a dark cobalt blue and boasted glass cupboard doors.

She scanned the chipped Formica countertop. "Where's the coffee machine and pods?"

"There is a coffee pot on the stove." He indicated a stainless steel percolator, then stepped to the white refrigerator and peeked inside. "I also arranged a grocery delivery for necessities."

Sure enough, a quart of milk, a dozen eggs, a loaf of bread, butter, bottled water, and ground coffee perched on the top two shelves.

"You planned everything." She darted a glance at the shabby surroundings, forcibly reminding herself that this was a beach cottage, not a five-star resort. "Where is the bathroom?"

"It must be through here." As he freed a jammed door, his voice went quiet. Water leaked from the sink's faucet, and the mirror reflected tarnish. Although only one person at a time could fit in the cramped space, the tiles gleamed and fresh white towels hung on the towel bars.

She peered inside. "There's no shower stall."

Joe strode to the living room and grabbed a brochure off the coffee table. "I read about an outdoor shower, but I assumed it was to rinse off the sand after a day at the beach." He swung wide a saloon-style door in the kitchen which led outside.

"Hmm."

"Hmm?" she asked.

"I guess the shower is truly outdoors." He hesitated before facing her. "I assume that's okay … because … because you're a nature-lover, right?"

CHAPTER 4

Nature, Emily soon realized the following morning when she stepped into the outdoor shower, presented a challenge. And clearly she wasn't a nature-lover after all.

Spiders and creepy-crawlies naturally gravitated to a damp area. In addition to the leaves and sand piled in the corner, clouds rolled in while she was soaking wet and the wind picked up, leaving her shivering and taking the fastest shower of her life.

And then there was the bigger problem.

In addition to the compactness of the space, she was *exposed.*

Not to mention that she had to hang her rosy-red sundress and clean undergarments on the door and hoped they didn't fall into the dirt while she quickly scrubbed herself. Thankfully, the warm water, plus the fragrant euca-lyptus spearmint soap she'd brought from home lifted her spirits.

She didn't bother with make-up except for a pastel pink lipstick, foundation, and mascara. She had secured her neatly coiffed hair with a shower cap beforehand so it didn't get wet, and later swept back the ends with a thin, glossy-red headband.

Despite the obstacles, she was determined to impress Joe.

Why did she care about impressing him? she challenged herself. They were two friends sharing a weekend. Romance wasn't part of the equation. Furthermore, there was no attraction between them.

Hah, her conscience chided, and she thrust it aside. Oftentimes, her conscience was an annoyance.

A half hour later, fully dressed and made-up, she slipped on easy, closed-toe shoes and entered the kitchen.

The front door and windows were wide open, and the weather promised a silvery-blue sky and comfortable temperatures. Emily caught a whiff of a salty sea breeze and the echoes of percussive waves hitting rhythmically against the shore.

Joe stood near the stove, brewing coffee and popping bread into the toaster, and his efficient movements made her smile. The attractiveness of his robust physique, his purple polo shirt tucked into navy shorts, hastened her breathing. Feeling suddenly shy, she shoved her hands into her pockets and wished him a cheerful good morning.

"Good morning, beautiful." He met her smile, and her heartbeat doubled at the affection in his gaze. "Red becomes you."

She braced her fingers on the counter and took a slow breath. *Friends, friends, friends,* she reminded herself.

"How was your shower?" he asked.

"Quite an adventure." *Talk about an understatement.* "A stunning sanctuary isn't the first description that comes to mind."

"The second?"

"Um, no. Perhaps airy?"

"Therefore, the experience was …"

"Harrowing. And my clothes smell like a chocolate factory."

"I warned you." He grinned. "I encountered a large spider."

"That's all?" She laughed, then feigned disappointment. "You were lucky."

"Why? What did you see?"

"The better question is … what *didn't* I see?"

He barked with laughter. "I rose before dawn and showered early."

"I didn't hear you."

"You were fast asleep. Did you rest well?"

"Surprisingly, yes. I opened my window and the sound of the ocean waves lulled me to sleep. Usually it takes me a long time to fall asleep."

"Me too, but not last night. It must be those divine beds." She giggled her assent as he reached into the cupboard for mugs and poured two cups of coffee. She inhaled the deep, rich aroma.

"You take your coffee black, right?" he inquired.

She nodded and relished the first sip. Of course he'd remembered her preference.

Standing, she spread butter on their toast, and they worked companionably, bantering while they set their dishes in the sink after a light breakfast.

"No dishwasher," he murmured. "Sorry."

"I can certainly wash and dry a few dishes. There's nothing to apologize for." She glanced his way and her pulse quickened. Her feelings for him multiplied the more hours they spent together.

"Let's venture into town and stock up on more food supplies," Joe suggested. "I want to try a new recipe while we're here."

"Another brownie that promotes weight loss?" Emily teased.

He draped a dishcloth over his shoulder and perched his hip at the edge of the table. "Lydia emailed me a recipe for peanut butter bars. She insists they're delicious." He pulled out his cellphone and scrolled.

Emily eyed the tiny stove, and oven, then peeked over his shoulder. "All my favorite ingredients. Butter, peanut butter, and chocolate."

He frowned. "Hardly low-calorie."

"Excellent news." Emily placed the last of the clean plates in the cupboard. "A modest amount of fat isn't necessarily bad, as long as you balance the foods with a nourishing meal plan."

He didn't appear convinced but tucked his cellphone into his pocket. "This afternoon we can visit William Randolph Hearst's castle. I reserved two tickets for a tour of the grand rooms."

CHAPTER 5

A few hours later, as the tour guide detailed the history of the magnificent Hearst Castle, Joe scanned the gardens, then concentrated on Emily. With her hair pulled back by a red headband and a hint of pink lipstick on her full lips, she presented a stunning vision. Her complexion was clear, and her heavenly blue eyes were framed by black lashes and elegant eyebrows.

"Can you believe the castle took all those years to finish?" Her demeanor was upbeat, and her gaze shone with excitement as she pointed out the architecture surrounding the opulent pool.

Joe nodded. "Right."

"From 1919 to 1947! And building on the mountaintop in order to capture the breathtaking views was brilliant. I am in awe of Mr. Hearst's vision."

Again, Joe nodded.

She squinted and slipped on her sunglasses. "Hence, you agree?"

"Yep."

"Uh, huh. Did you hear what I said?"

"Of course."

She hung her hands on her hips. "Tell me, then, word for word."

"You began with … we're on a mountaintop." He continually lost his train of thought as he gazed at the curves of her figure, her stunning smile, and the sun shining on her face.

"Therefore, you weren't listening. First, I remarked on the views because they are awe-inspiring." She drew in a breath. "I wonder what the rooms that were not included on our tour look like."

"You do?"

"Yes." She paused, and he sensed an uncertainty in her voice. With any luck, she was exploring a dignified way to suggest another road trip with him.

"You'd like to see more of the castle?" he encouraged. "With me?"

"Am I that transparent?" Studiously, she observed the rose bushes and avoided his gaze. "You must realize you're the ideal—"

"Companion?" He drew her nearer and chuckled, the scent of her spearmint fragrance uplifting. Steadying himself, he pondered why she had such an insane effect on him. "You're my ideal companion too."

She hesitated and pulled at the neckline of her dress. "Joe?"

Whenever she uttered his name, her delicate, pure voice had a dreamlike quality that stirred his senses.

"Hmm?"

"I'm glad we met."

"Me too." He held her close. "I believe fate has a hand in these things—how people meet, when they meet. Sometimes events take place that are beyond our control."

Slightly, her lips parted. "Fate is from the Latin word, fatum, which means 'that which has been spoken.'"

"Did you study Latin in college?"

She rested her head on his shoulder and grinned. "I read a lot, but I learned that from Webster's Dictionary."

THE REMAINDER of the day was a blur of shared hugs and a peaceful walk on the beach. Later, a stroll through town revealed that the Keaton Smith Art Gallery had shuttered a few months earlier. However, they appreciated the sense of originality in the flourishing community that especially beckoned to Emily. She stopped often and browsed—particularly at the stalls where local jewelers created white polished necklaces, rings, and matching bracelets, and crafters wove bright-colored quilts.

She purchased a nautical souvenir for her son's home, plus a bag of caramels for her grandchild, and Joe did the same.

When an antique dealer invited them inside his shop, Emily murmured that his pieces seemed ideally suited to the cottage's ambiance.

"You mean because they're old?" Joe jested.

"Nothing can be as old as that cottage," she solemnly returned.

Simultaneously, they both laughed.

He hugged her then, right in the middle of the shop. He couldn't get enough of her, which was a unique experience for him. Since his wife had died a decade before, he'd found little claim in socializing because no woman appealed to him. Sure, his friends arranged double-dates, but Joe had made up his mind. He wasn't interested in anyone or anything except his daughter, his grandchild, and his work. Any dreams before his beloved wife's death had been lost.

That is until now.

Emily fit effortlessly in the curve of his arm. She was

appealing, curious, and captivated him with stories about her experiences traveling around the world—Europe and Asia and Africa—places he'd never envisioned outside of magazines and television. In her enthusiastic style she'd encouraged him to imagine new possibilities again.

He'd also been impressed by her understanding of technology when she'd adeptly showed him where to find the emojis on his phone. That had resulted in a half hour of experimentation as he'd texted her pink hearts, red hearts, dazzling hearts, and an array of golden stars that had prompted her to giggle until tears streamed down her cheeks.

Sometimes she was stubborn, other times she charmed him with her smile. She was refined and elegant, never showy, topped with so much love bottled up that she mesmerized him.

"All my life I've lived for my son," she said.

"Live for yourself, not others," Joe replied. "Although it's entirely understandable when it comes to our children. They are an important part of who we are."

Emily's eyes had glistened with tears. "There are instances when my son is too preoccupied to spend time with me and I miss the noise and clatter of a crowded household. I remember when I believed the outside world was fraught with peril, and my mission was to protect him."

"You describe memories I also hold close to my heart," Joe admitted. "I miss those years too."

He was living proof of that emptiness. It was the main reason why he preferred to be on the road—to avoid going home to a desolate, lonely house.

Although he and Emily were the same age, he was a million times more world-weary, because he had grown up in a poor neighborhood, whereas her life had been one of affluence. Nonetheless, something about her relaxed him, and that was novel.

However, she avoided any discussions about their future, explaining she didn't wish to ruin their hours together with talks about anything other than the present. Besides, they were too old for any of "that foolishness."

The foolishness of love?

Or was she ashamed of him, his modest background and line of work, and too considerate to vocalize her feelings? He was suitable for a fun, light-hearted weekend, but beyond that ... nothing.

He'd always been a plain, unassuming guy, accustomed to simplicity. At eighteen, he had taken the first job that had come along and was grateful. He'd noticed Emily's barely disguised disapproval when he'd mentioned assisting his daughter financially and couldn't understand why it seemed to upset her. At his stage, he was pleased to help his family while they were down on their luck. In addition, he'd managed to tuck away a fair amount of savings.

On Sunday, Joe spent the afternoon assembling ingredients for the recipe his daughter had sent. Emily came and stood beside him in the kitchen and assisted. As a team, they creamed butter, spooned in the peanut butter, and measured the oatmeal.

After the peanut butter bars finished baking, they assembled a tray and two mugs of herbal green tea and headed into the living room. The only TV displayed a makeshift antenna, and they caught tidbits of black and white Andy Griffith Show reruns, which suited them nicely. The everyday activity of passing time—relaxing and watching TV with a special woman—was something he hadn't enjoyed in years.

As Emily placed the half-eaten tray of cookies on the

coffee table, he spoke with a grin. "I decided I prefer regular butter over the low-fat stuff."

"Hurray and don't forget extra chocolate." She stood to brew more tea. As he observed her walking gracefully to the kitchen, he admired her effortless, natural style and the understated sophistication in which she carried herself.

At his insistence, she'd dressed up for their Sunday together. She'd strung a large pearl necklace around her elegant throat, and her deep-blue sundress matched the color of her vivid eyes. With her shiny hair pushed back, her face radiated a sun-kissed glow. After getting ready, they'd found a white-steepled church in town and attended services.

After the service, he'd caressed her cheek and kissed her.

"Tomorrow is our last day," she said, and he detected the conclusiveness in her tone. Or perhaps he imagined it.

"Unfortunately, yes," he replied, his voice shaky. "But we have several hours together while we pick up the delivery, and the ride back home."

He envisioned her attending various social functions when she was married to Krandall—charity balls and Broadway musicals in New York City, and couldn't imagine how he'd forgotten that he'd never be a part of those scenes. He wouldn't escort her to extravagant events because he couldn't afford them. Furthermore, his awkwardness would embarrass her.

In that instant, he understood that not having her in his life was going to be hard, but there was no other choice. Emily deserved better than anything he could offer.

Vacantly, he focused on the paneled wall in the living room as a hollowness filled his chest.

"What are you thinking?" she asked, returning with two steaming mugs.

"Nothing." He shifted. *Nothing he would share with her.*

He offered his best imitation of a smile. "Shall I bake the

next cookie batch using spray butter and artificial sugar?" He suspected that she didn't care for his low-calorie baked goods. She'd never told him, not in so many words, but oftentimes a person conveyed more by what they didn't say, rather than by what they did say.

"No! Please!" Emily sputtered, almost dropping the mugs before setting them on the table.

"I can save several hundred calories—"

"At the expense of taste."

"I've lost weight since I lowered my calorie intake," he loftily responded. "However, this is our vacation, so I'll just sit on the couch and eat more cookies." He gave her a sidelong smirk, snatched a cookie from the tray, and took a bite. "Although the middle is undercooked."

Emily nestled closer, and he shared his cookie with her. "Blame it on the tiniest oven in the universe, not your daughter's recipe."

"Are you saying … never blame the cook?"

She laughed and lifted her lips to his. She tasted of chocolate and sweetness and all that he'd missed for so many years. "Never, ever blame the cook."

"Emily, you're the best thing that has happened to me in a long time," he whispered. "Always remember that."

If she wondered why he'd uttered that last part, she gave no indication. Instead, the bonus for his admission was a dainty brush of her fingers against his chin, and a kiss that stole his breath away.

SEVERAL HOURS LATER, they rode in his truck to Moonglow beach and strolled the planked wooden walkway of the boardwalk. Along the way, they searched for moonstones. Yes, there were really moonstones, he assured Emily, and many people made jewelry with them—such as the necklaces and rings and bracelets they'd admired in town. As they found shiny black pebbles and polished sea glass, they often rested on the benches lining the pathway. Joggers ran past, riders on bicycles flew by at a brisk clip, and a couple stopped to converse—describing the playful seals they'd spotted earlier in the day.

As Joe and Emily continued, an easy summer breeze ruffled Emily's hair, and the tang of the ocean filled his nostrils. Fingers entwined, they admired the rock-strewn cliffs and jaw-dropping coastline.

"We didn't have time to take the boat excursion," he said. "Or to swim."

"Maybe next time."

He turned to gaze at the ocean, his heart heavy, knowing there would be no next time.

One last night together.

He wanted all that they were sharing—tomorrow, the day after that, and the day after that. He longed to paint the town red… would she know that old expression? He suspected she would.

He yearned to embrace life and celebrate every hour with her, because time went by too quickly.

She snuggled against him and he squeezed his eyes shut for a moment. Nearby, people threw red, white, and blue confetti in the air, waved American flags, and cheered.

He soaked in the ambiance of the enchanting pint-size community, its gentler pace, and the way the sun scattered bits of golden sequins on the Pacific Ocean. Fireworks marked the July Fourth celebration, and patriotic music blasted from a loudspeaker in the distance.

A flood of affection, of contentment, radiated through him.

He loved their little cottage. Unquestionably it showed

maturity, but the weather-beaten shingles proved it had lived successfully through another season, despite its age.

Much like him. Much like Emily.

He loved this ageless place that hinted at a kinder lifestyle from a date long forgotten.

And then he realized what he'd known in his heart all along.

He was in love with Emily Varon.

CHAPTER 6

Sunrise came quicker than expected, and Emily snuggled under the buffalo-checked red and white quilt longer than she'd planned. A sea wind whistled through the cracks of the window as she reluctantly opened her eyes.

They were leaving.

Quickly she showered and then packed, appreciative of the coffee and toast Joe had placed on the oak chest in her bedroom. When she tried to swallow, the coffee tasted bitter in her constricted throat, and the toast was dry and flavorless. A disturbing awareness hit her, setting in motion sadness and confusion. She didn't want to return to her private and solitary existence.

Making a concerted effort to maintain her composure, she pondered why this trip with Joe had come to mean so much.

However, she couldn't let him know, choosing not to appear needy. Especially when she suspected that her son and his family considered her clingy and desperate.

She finished arranging the last of her toiletries in the duffel bag and stepped to the doorway. The Moonglow

Chocolatiers truck idled, exhaust coiling densely from the tailpipe into the sultry morning air.

"Good morning, lovely." Joe adjusted the emerald-green silk scarf she'd tied carelessly around her throat. "Are you ready? I brewed an extra thermos of coffee for the ride, and I included leftover peanut butter bars to nibble on before we stop for lunch."

Emily bobbed her head, but her legs refused to move.

"There's rain in the forecast. I'll need to drive slower and keep my lights on." He peered at the gray clouds on the horizon, then hoisted her suitcases.

"Okay. I'm in no hurry." Emily went into the kitchen and slowly picked up the coffee pot, disposing of the coffee grounds and washing the mugs and plates they had used. She held Joe's mug against her heart, tracing the rim with her finger before she placed it back in the cupboard.

With a muffled sigh, she glanced around. Much as the cottage was in disrepair, she would truly miss the place.

After they collected the cases of chocolate at the delivery center outside of town, the rains started. Joe kept the radio volume low and made no mention of playing any cassette tapes. He increased his following distance and kept the truck at a deliberate, safe speed.

After an hour, he pulled into a rest area, and Emily grabbed the thermos and poured them coffee. They stood under a tree, and a car sped past, splashing water against the truck.

Hazardous weather. Rain. Construction. Joe was under a considerable amount of strain, regularly driving under challenging conditions, and this had been his occupation for countless years.

They stopped several more times for gas and food, and the mood remained solemn.

They made it through Bloomingfield an hour later than it

had taken to cover the same distance in sunny weather. Soon, they would be back in her hometown.

As they covered the last stretch, Emily sat straighter and gathered her courage. She'd never declared her feelings openly, certainly not to a man she'd known for mere months.

Nonetheless, the time had come.

She couldn't envision a life without Joe, couldn't accept the agonizing awareness of resorting to repeated phone and Skype calls with him again.

Despite her jittery stomach, she dismissed her reservations and single-mindedly focused on one objective. She didn't care anymore about sounding needy. In truth, she *was* needy when it came to continuing their relationship. And she would tell him, employing her 'small talk' finesse.

"Joe?" she began.

"Hmm?" He kept his gaze forward, the wipers beating a recurring back-and-forth flap against the windshield.

"I'd like a more permanent courtship."

So much for finesse.

He blinked. For a split-second, he took his gaze off the road and regarded her.

"How? I constantly work, Emily."

"Perhaps you can drive less." She took a quick breath. "Or, preferably, not at all."

"I need to continue working, Emily."

She pushed on, crossing and uncrossing her legs. "Move to my town, so we can be together more often."

"You're talking marriage?"

"Well—"

"In summary, I'd have no income and would rely on your money to support me?"

"I didn't say that."

"I noticed you didn't ask to move in with me. I assume you're ashamed of my house, although you've never seen it."

His shoulders curved forward as he concentrated on the road. "Let's face it, Emily, you're ashamed of *me* because I'm a common truck driver."

"You're misconstruing all my words."

"Am I? What would my daughter reckon, and my fellow drivers, if they learned I was with you? They'd suspect I was after your wealth."

"You assume this is about money, and you're worried about your self-esteem?" Letting out a shocked gasp, Emily sat back. "It's about a full-time relationship rather than a part-time one. I deserve better than that."

"You deserve better than *me*," Joe countered. "Someone who fits into your world."

She flinched, and her stomach hardened. As they passed Olive's Diner, she stayed silent. When they arrived at her house, Joe parked the truck and came around to open the door for her.

"Thanks for coming with me," he said briefly, and leaned forward.

In case he wanted to kiss her, she held up her palm to ward him off.

He grimaced, grabbed her suitcases and duffel bag, and carried them into the living room.

"Thanks, Joe. Goodbye. Safe travels." Her chest hitched. She couldn't say more.

His grimace remained. "Goodbye, Emily." He stumbled back a few steps, then spun. Without another word, he got into his truck and drove away.

CHAPTER 7

Seven days went by. Then fourteen.

Despite her efforts to occupy herself, Emily pined for Joe, missing him desperately. He'd sent a brief text saying he was driving to another part of the state and would be gone for a while.

And then, nothing.

Naturally, she was too proud to phone him, and awaited a call that never came. Obsessively, she checked her phone and waited.

The weekend they'd shared had begun like a fairy-tale. Oftentimes, she imagined another scenario, a happier ending. If only their relationship had turned out differently.

Yes, she loved him, and believed he cared for her.

But now it was over.

On a typical Thursday evening a week later, she sat at a corner booth in Olive's Diner, staring out the front window at the sunset. Fresh pink and tangerine orange colors ignited the sky. The month of July was coming to a close, and the days had been reduced to a smudge of summer. She'd gone into town more often, holding on to the breeze as she chatted with people she passed. It felt wonderful not to disconnect from strangers anymore.

She'd even enrolled in a painting class again, surprising herself when she discovered that she did better when she put forth more effort. Her earlier lack of talent had grown from mental obstacles, and she'd been hesitant to try anything new since Krandall's death for fear of failure.

Failure was a matter of one's experience, she supposed. The fear of risking her heart and subsequently losing it, had almost broken her. That is, until she'd relaxed her tight muscles, taken a fortifying breath, and stepped into the art studio again. Her first attempt had produced a watercolor of a fishing boat, which she'd proudly hung on her sitting room wall. On the stern, she'd penned, 'Summer Breeze' in scripted calligraphy. In addition, she'd filled her home with vases of pink and yellow seaside daisies, a display of cheerfulness she seldom felt.

Oliver stepped to her table, bringing her musings to the present.

"The air-conditioning broke," he said.

"I noticed it's warm in here tonight, but I don't care for air-conditioning, anyway."

"Have you seen Joe lately?"

She swallowed hard. "No." They'd been over this every day since she and Joe had parted.

"Are you ordering tonight's special?" He grabbed a pencil from behind his ear and tugged an order pad from his apron. "I'm serving lasagna."

"Excellent. I expect the pasta is loaded with extra ricotta cheese and heaps of calories."

"Guaranteed." He tapped his pencil on the edge of the table and peered at his watch. "Look, Emily. I wanted to surprise you and probably should have told you earlier, but—"

"Lasagna isn't a surprise, Oliver." She gazed at him with frustration. "You serve lasagna on alternate Thursdays." She glanced out the window and her head jerked back as a familiar Moonglow Chocolatiers truck pulled into the parking lot.

"It's about time," Oliver muttered, perching across from her. "He's running late."

She grabbed Oliver's arm. "It can't be … Joe is in town?"

"We've had nightly conversations, and I knew he was coming this evening to see you."

Her heartbeat accelerated as a short, handsome man—carrying a package wrapped in blue paper and a thin gold bow—strode into the diner.

His usually neat flannel shirt puckered at the waist, his white hair was disheveled.

"When did you arrange this?" She squinted at him. "How?"

Oliver set the order pad on the table, a doodling of two hearts in the corner. "I'm an old-fashioned Cupid, and recommended he take action."

"Hi, Emily." Joe strode to her booth. Tears were in his eyes as he hesitantly set the box on the table. "I brought you a gift."

She stared up at him. "Joe, if it's brownies …"

"I think I'm done playing Cupid." Oliver shoved to his feet and moved to the counter. "Shall I prepare two servings of lasagna?"

Emily regarded Joe.

"Absolutely," he agreed.

Still reeling, she said stiffly, "You could have mailed the package, Joe."

"I'm not here to deliver brownies." He settled across from her, gazing at her with boyish eagerness. "I'm here to offer you what's in this box."

"Did you bake another low-calorie recipe?"

He shook his head. "Not low calorie. No calorie."

"What?" She couldn't help herself. She was staring at him.

"Please open it."

She did, and then she gasped. A polished moonstone ring, exquisite in its simple luminous beauty, was set in a magnificent gold setting.

"I wasn't sure of your ring size. However, the jewelry maker in Cambria assured me that the size can be altered."

"You bought this in Cambria?"

"I ordered it ahead, left my house before dawn and picked it up this morning. The way we parted … it's not over. *We're* not over. I traveled halfway across the state to be with you."

"Five hours each way. That's a long drive."

"Not for the woman I love."

He loved her and was uttering the words out loud. The knowledge made her breath catch.

His voice was deep and gripping. She'd longed to hear from him, to see him.

"All this effort … for me." She fixed her hand on top of his. He was warm, animated, dynamic.

"Our life together," he said. "There's a wonderful, exciting world waiting for us to explore."

She opened her mouth, and then closed it, celebrating the upcoming years in her mind.

He pressed his fingers to her lips. "I want to marry you, Emily, and I won't take no for an answer."

"You said you didn't want to be with me. You were

concerned about what your daughter and co-workers might assume."

"I'm ashamed of myself, because it was my own self-esteem and fears that caused the problem. I couldn't allow people to speculate that I was with you for your money. I would never use you."

"Joe, I don't care about other people's opinions."

"But I do, and I will protect you from any disparaging remarks because I love you, Emily."

"And I love you."

"Good. Good." He beamed. "I've spent many hours pondering our situation, and I figured out a workable solution."

She nodded, waiting for him to continue.

"I'll drive part time, and when I go on a trip, you'll come with me."

"But, Joe, where will we live?"

"Anywhere." He paused, then grinned. "I have nowhere to go, though, because I sold my house. However, I managed to purchase a quaint cottage in Cambria with part of my savings. It boasts an outdoor shower and is situated near the sea."

She pressed her fingers to her throat. "You bought our cottage?"

"Yep. It needs a painting, though."

"I can paint."

The infectious grin that had filled her days in Cambria settled on his features, along with a charismatic trace of conscience. "I approached the owner who was more than willing to sell for a fair price. He even threw in the two bicycles at no extra charge."

"Generous." She shared his grin at that. "What about my house?"

"Keep it, sell it. We can discuss the logistics later."

"After living there for thirty years, I'll sell." She gazed up at him with a helpless smile. "I expected to never see you again."

"Yet, here I am." He pushed up his glasses. "Will you marry me, Emily Varon?"

"Yes. Yes. Yes." For the first time, she noticed the stubble of his white beard, the strokes of weariness at the corners of his bright-blue eyes.

He secured the ring on her left hand finger, then leaned over and kissed her, gently and lovingly and expressively. She curved her hand around his nape, and he buried his kisses in her hair. From the corner of her eye, she spotted Oliver placing a cassette tape player on the counter.

"Now?" he asked Joe when they pulled back from their kiss.

Joe turned to Oliver. "Perfect."

The poignant music from Andrew Lloyd Webber's musical, *Cats,* floated through the diner. The handful of patrons looked up from their meals and smiled. Apparently, the entire diner was in on her surprise.

Emily's heart tightened. "That's my favorite song. 'Memory'."

"I found the cassette online, and I've listened to the music ever since."

"You discovered musicals," she said.

"Especially the lyrics to this song. You're not alone, Emily. Not in the moonlight, not in the daylight. We're here, together, living for today and tomorrow. We'll create our own memories."

She glimpsed Oliver opening several windows to let in a flurry of air, and then her gaze settled on Joe.

The man she loved. Their journey in unison.

"We'll create our own life events," Joe was saying.

And the beckoning of a summer breeze, lighting the landscape of their lives.

The End

A NOTE FROM JOSIE

Dear Friends,

Thank you for reading *A Chocolate-Box Summer Breeze*.

I wanted to write another story centering around the characters in the "Chocolate" series, and chose an older couple—Emily and Joe—to share a summer romance with you.

If you loved this sweet romance as much as I loved writing it, please help other people find *A Chocolate-Box Summer Breeze* by posting your review.

A Chocolate-Box Summer Breeze is available in ebook, Paperback, Large Print Paperback, Hardcover, and Audiobook.

My Spotify Play List for A Chocolate-Box Summer Breeze is here.

RECIPE FOR LYDIA'S PEANUT BUTTER BARS

#1 CRUST:

    1 cup margarine

    1 cup brown sugar

    ½ cup white sugar

    4 cups oatmeal

    Mix together, PRESS in an 12 x 18 ungreased pan.

    Bake 375 degrees for 12 minutes. COOL.

#2 Spread over crust.

    1 cup creamy Peanut Butter

    (Place in the garage or outside to harden.)

#3

12 – 18 ounces of chocolate chips

1 ½ - 2 Tablespoon butter

Melt together. Dot evenly over peanut butter and spread out.

260

#4

COOL. Cut into squares. Place into a cookie tin or a plastic container.

Refrigerate. Keeps well for up to a month.

Enjoy!

JOSIE RIVIERA

A Christmas Wish

A Chocolate-Box Christmas Wish

PRAISE AND AWARDS

USA TODAY bestselling author

CHAPTER 1

*H*igh on a rain-drenched hill, Cora Carpenter set down her mug of tea and stared out the kitchen window of her bungalow. The stream of chatter from the children in her day care had ceased, leaving the quiet of a cloudy California afternoon.

She didn't focus on Evanville's town square below, which she easily spotted from her window. Soon, the square would boast hundreds of twinkling white lights as night fell. Or, if she opened her window, the faint sounds of a community concert might drift up to her.

The window remained closed, the concert quiet, because one weekly chore pervaded her thoughts. She dreaded grocery shopping on Thursdays. And today was Thursday.

Never much of cook she found preparing a spread for a single person, namely herself, was disheartening. Not to mention it emphasized she was alone, without anyone to share meals or companionship.

She blew out a sigh. So?

So, it was no big deal, right?

Wrong.

Perhaps it was society's lofty expectations. Every television commercial promoted sharing holiday festivities with a partner.

Not her, though. She wouldn't expose herself to the hurt that inevitably followed.

She turned as Jack, her brother, breezed into the kitchen. Bald, sporting a thin black mustache, and older than she by a decade, he told everyone he was a confirmed bachelor.

"Smells good in here." He made a beeline for the cinnamon cookies on the counter. "Are you holiday baking, already?"

"Cinnamon and cream cheese are key ingredients." She gestured to the trays. "Try one."

"Only one?" He snatched a handful.

"Or take a dozen. A couple of the older children and I baked them for you and the nurses at the hospital."

"Much appreciated." He craned his neck to peer out the window. "By the way, Evanville pulled out all the stops for the holidays, complete with a strolling Christmas tree."

"I don't remember anyone mentioning a strolling tree," Cora said.

"It's an innovative idea by the town council's think tank."

"*Our* town council has a think tank?"

He winked between bites. "More like the mayor and his wife. You'll notice the tree when you visit downtown."

"How … jolly." She lifted a snowman mug to her lips and gave her reindeer earrings a toss. "What's more festive than a walking tree?"

"A *strolling* tree," he corrected. "And, there's something even more exciting."

"The live nativity?"

"The annual *candy-cane-eating contest.*" Dramatically, he enunciated every word.

"A favorite of yours because you've won three years in a row." When he didn't reply, she asked, "Are you entering?"

"I probably should give other people a chance." He sported a smug grin. "But I won't. Besides, all the extra sugar in candy canes leads to only one result."

"Which is?"

He poured a mug of coffee for himself. "Obesity."

Despite herself, Cora laughed at her brother's good humor, his acceptance of himself as an overweight man. Lighthearted, embracing the comedy in life, he pushed away the loneliness in her chest.

"Are you participating in the hospital's 5K charity run?" he asked.

She smoothed her khaki-colored sweatshirt, embroidered with the likeness of a cherry-red cardinal. "Sadly, I'm out of shape."

"You're lanky and lean. Me, on the other hand …" He patted his protruding stomach. At six feet and three hundred pounds, Jack was at a weight many people, including his doctor, labeled as morbidly obese.

"The run is important to me," he went on, "because it benefits Project Nutrition." He grabbed a napkin to wipe his mouth and tossed it in the trash. "Needless to say, I'll be walking."

"I read about the program," Cora replied. "They implement cost-effective strategies, such as adding iron to food to help cut childhood anemia."

"Malnutrition contributes to a number of developmental delays." As always, Jack spoke passionately when talking about kids. He was a nurse in the children's ward at the local hospital. Both he and Cora had chosen child-oriented occupations, and they loved youngsters, although neither of them were married nor had children.

He set down his mug and picked up a paper and pen.

"Are you taking notes on how many candy canes you're required to devour in order to win the contest?" Cora joked.

"Nope. I already know."

"How many?"

He zipped his lips with his fingers.

She chuckled at the image of a secretive Jack sitting at a table piled high with candy canes in the festively decorated town square.

"I'm an organized person and preparing my holiday shopping list," he said.

"Right now?"

"Why not?" Sheepishly, he grinned. "What's your Christmas wish this year, Cora?"

She tapped her fingers on the counter. "I can't think of anything special."

"December twenty-fifth isn't far away. You must have an idea."

"Honestly, I don't." She squinted at the paper as he quickly jotted numbers. "What are you writing?"

"My ideal weight." He presented a guilty smile and set the pen down. "And have you decided whether you'll fly to Nevada with me to visit Mom?"

"Maybe."

He let out a frustrated sigh. "That's not an answer."

Cora turned and began wrapping the cookies for him to take with him. She exhaled, only then recognizing she'd been holding her breath.

In truth, she'd made her choice. Their mother, Zoe, had raved for weeks about her latest beau, and Cora suspected that adult children would be in the way of this fresh romance. Their visit might result in an awkward situation.

Jack, apparently, harbored no such qualms.

"Well?" He counted off the days on his fingers until Christmas.

"I'll stay in town," Cora replied. "If any of my child-care parents are working extra shifts, they'll call for me to watch their kids."

"You deserve a week off."

"I want to be available just in case, but will plan to take time off between Christmas and New Year's." She provided a small smile. "We'll agree on a raincheck for me to visit Mom, okay?"

"Don't you want to accompany me on my first solo flight?"

She stiffened. "You're flying a plane yourself?"

"A commuter plane. I finally earned my pilot's license, and it's an hour flight from California to Nevada." At Cora's frown, he smiled reassuringly. "My instructor offered to fly with me."

"Olivia?" Cora's mind raced with the possibilities. "The woman with curly auburn hair down to her waist who recently graduated from college?"

"One and the same. After sixty hours of flight time, thirty of flight briefings, and forty hours of ground school, I'm ready."

"To date or to fly?"

"Both." He hooked an arm around her waist and twirled her, singing "I'll be Home For Christmas."

Laughing, she leaned against the counter to shake off the dizziness. "Are you abandoning bachelorhood for a woman fifteen years your junior?"

"Me? A man who prizes my unmarried status?" He looked out the window again and cleared his throat. "Have you spoken to Dad? I realize you might still be angry at him, what with his tendency to try to control our lives."

"*Tendency* to control?"

"Yeah, more than a tendency." Jack gave a quick laugh. "Well, have you?"

"I've reached out to him."

She chewed her bottom lip. She had no desire to revisit *that* argument. Her father's vocal opinions had left her panicked and embarrassed. In short, he'd been opposed to her dating the man she'd met online because he believed he was a con. She'd refused to listen. Her father had never liked any of the men she'd dated.

Then he'd chided her for being a silly, desperate fool, and they had quarreled. Wasn't it her decision as a grown woman to date whoever she pleased?

Besides, she wasn't desperate. Was she?

Mentally, she reviewed her childhood. Her father had always criticized her, especially after he and her mother had divorced. Don't wear revealing clothes, don't attend any university except the one he selected. His overbearing demands of how she should behave had become the thread mark of their conversations.

Now she was sorry for the argument because she'd raised her voice to her own father. He'd been right.

She swallowed the lump in her throat.

Weren't most decisions easier in hindsight?

"Don't be offended by Dad's outburst." Jack retrieved a worn teddy bear from the floor and deposited it in a plastic bin. "Refuse to let a scam artist ruin your Christmas."

She accepted Jack's words in the vein they were meant—encouragement from a caring older brother. Thankfully, he didn't press her for more details.

"So what's your wish?" he repeated.

She surveyed the kitchen—the cabinets that hadn't been painted in a decade, the leaky sink faucet, the budget-friendly linoleum.

Grimacing, she finally said, "I'd love a bright and shiny stainless-steel refrigerator."

He chuckled. "A refrigerator is not a Christmas wish."

"When it's twenty years old and formerly belonged to our parents, then it constitutes a wish." She nodded to the pen. "Write that down."

"Mom and Dad split long ago, and you can't break up with your refrigerator." He pinned her with a thoughtful gaze. "Think of something else."

"A dishwasher to replace the one I never had?"

He tapped his foot and snatched another cookie before she could wrap it. "Nope."

"A shelving unit for baby board books?" She stepped into the living room. "Better yet, a chest full of educational toys."

"I meant a special wish for you." Jack peered at the wall clock. "My hospital shift begins at three. Keep thinking and we'll talk soon, okay?"

"Okay. I'm off to complete my least favorite task."

"Grocery shopping?"

"You know me well." She pushed a strand of hair from her face. She didn't fuss with her appearance. She'd always preferred to style her dark hair in a short pixie cut, but lately had let it grow out. Who had hours for fancy grooming while watching youngsters all day?

Jack placed his mug in the sink. "You'll stop at Olive's Diner first?"

"I'm a creature of habit." She shook her ponytail free and dug through her purse for the key to her ten-year-old Chevy. "A meal at the diner definitely brightens my Thursdays."

On the drive to town, she mulled over Jack's Christmas-wish question and chided herself on her responses. Instead of materialistic or self-centered items, she should wish for something that benefitted others.

Her mind wandered, taking inventory of her to-do list:

Home decorating, gift-giving, writing out cards, baking …

Once, she'd treasured the Christmas holiday. The days were thrilling, not demanding. Lately, endless activities screamed to be accomplished. What did it all mean, the frantic rush to accomplish everything by New Year's? Was it acceptable to think of herself?

She switched on her car radio, and the melodic strains of "A Holly Jolly Christmas" came through the speakers. Would she ever reach a place when the holidays didn't retell what had vanished from her life?

She'd believed that Gregory Pansa loved her, and they would spend Christmas together on the beach in Florida. He'd promised. Unfortunately, he never existed.

Burl Ives continued crooning about the best time of the year, and Cora sang along. One constant hadn't changed.

Her love of music.

THIRTY MINUTES LATER, Cora sat at her preferred booth in Olive's Diner, enticed by the scents of buttery mashed potatoes and a pot roast simmering with root vegetables. Comfort-foods, timeless and hearty staples.

She rotated a string of Christmas oldies in the jukebox every week while she ate.

Today was no exception, and she fed the jukebox enough coins so that Elvis Presley repeatedly belted out a tune about his blue Christmas.

Oliver, the owner and an amiable man in his thirties, stepped to the booth and poured her a cup of coffee. "How are the peanut butter cups?" he asked.

She touched her hands to her lips. "Delicious, as always. An ideal end to a wonderful meal."

"Thanks to Sally." The pride in his tone was apparent. "It's her recipe."

"Yes, so you've mentioned." *A million times.*

Oliver's hazelnut-colored eyes lit with warmth whenever he mentioned Sally Elliot. They'd met the previous Valentine's Day when she and several other customers had been stranded at his diner because of a violent storm. She was a chocolatier and owned a candy shop in Bloomingfield, a couple hours' drive from the diner. Sally and Oliver had created the recipe that night.

"I can't make these peanut butter cups fast enough," he said. "Every Thursday, I place two aside for you."

"I admire your thoughtfulness." Cora unwrapped the second candy on her plate. "Have you and Sally planned a wedding date yet?"

"February fourteenth. Her daughter, Clarissa, will be our flower girl."

His ecstatic expression prompted Cora's smile. "Is Sally aware of your plans?"

"Not yet." A wide grin split his face. "I'm surprising her with an engagement ring on Christmas day, and a Valentine wedding is—"

"Romantic." Cora clasped her hands together. The thrill of the romance brought goose bumps to her arms. "Let me add *brilliant* and *delightful.*"

"I show my love on my sleeve, don't I? When it comes to Sally, I'm definitely starry-eyed."

"Don't ever change, Oliver." Despite her encouraging smile, Cora bit back a resigned sigh. When had she last experienced any of those wonderful emotions called love?

She hadn't.

That is, not until she recently met a man on an online dating platform. On a whim, she'd joined the site and uploaded her profile and picture. The man's photo displayed a middle-aged, black-bearded guy in medical scrubs by the name of Gregory Pansa.

Soon after, he'd messaged her. He was a doctor who lived in Egypt, trying desperately to return to America because he was a US citizen. Day after day he endured one obstacle after another. He was out of money because his funds were tied up in a foreign bank account, he'd been in an accident and was in the hospital. Or, the latest, he'd missed his flight to the States.

At first, she had shaken her head in exasperation. But the more he emailed, the more she believed him. Surely he wasn't scamming her, no matter what her father contended.

Not now. Not during the holidays.

Gregory complimented her "soulful amber eyes rimmed by generous black lashes" and her "velvety-smooth complexion." She embraced his poetic words since they brought a rush of exhilaration. Perhaps Gregory was *the one.*

Her father investigated further, drawing her attention to numerous inconsistencies with Gregory's story. Finally, she faced the fact that Gregory Pansa wasn't real.

She'd been a fool. Plus, she was out two thousand dollars.

She sank back in the booth and allowed Elvis Presley's deep voice to carry a note of warmth into a chilly afternoon.

The diner's door swung open and a tall man filled the entrance with his broad shoulders and strong frame. His handsome, sun-kissed face set in a mild frown while he surveyed the diner. Quickly, he strode to the counter as Oliver emerged from the kitchen carrying a tray of red velvet cakes.

Cora turned to watch their exchange. Customer chats around her table stilted.

"Is there a garage nearby?" the man inquired. "My car broke down a mile from here."

Oliver set down the tray. "Were you in a car wreck? Are you all right?"

"No. I'm fine."

"You walked?"

"It isn't far."

"Far enough. Fortunately, the rain never started."

"Right." Grimly, the man looked toward the window, then at Oliver. "Are you the cook?"

Oliver gave a slight bow. "I'm the owner. Oliver."

"Patrick Gervez." The man removed his black leather gloves, shoved them into the pockets of his tan wool coat, and the men shook hands. "I'm on my way to Bloomingfield."

"You're new here?" Oliver asked.

"Brand new. Actually, I was aware of the forecast because Lorenzo Rossi, the meteorologist, called to inform me. I'll be working with him, and he wanted to make certain I arrived in Bloomingfield safely."

"Where are you from?" Oliver set the plated cakes in the bakery case. "California drivers aren't recognized for their competency on wet roads, and we catch plenty of rain in winter."

"I'm off the hook then. I'm relocating from Raleigh, North Carolina."

"Raleigh is a sizable city."

The man pressed his lips together. "Yep."

"And Bloomingfield is a modest town." Slowly, a smile dawned across Oliver's face. "My fiancée, Sally, mentioned you, Patrick. Lorenzo married her sister, Julie."

"I heard." Patrick shifted. "The garage?"

"Harry's Car and Truck Service is open from early morning till about four, so it might be too late. I'll call, just to be certain." Oliver reached for his cellphone.

As Cora and the other patrons looked on, Oliver's unanswered call confirmed that Harry's Garage was clearly closed.

At Patrick's frustrated groan, Oliver signaled to Cora. He didn't need to say anything because she immediately realized what he requested.

She grabbed her purse and hurried to the counter. "I can help you, Patrick," she offered.

Patrick glanced at her. "A pair of jumper cables are called for, miss. Thanks, anyway." He considered Oliver. "Do you have any?"

"Nope," Oliver replied.

"I do," Cora piped in. "I keep jumper cables in my car."

Patrick's dark eyebrows raised. He rubbed the slight beard on his chin. "You do?"

"Doesn't everyone?"

A corner of his full mouth turned up in a self-deprecating smile. "Apparently, I don't."

She gazed into his intense blue eyes and managed a straight face. "Well, the penalty for not being prepared is—"

He bent and whispered in her ear, "A Christmas angel floated to my rescue exactly when I needed her."

His words brought a flush of warmth to her cheeks, and she drew back. The trace of his aftershave, a mild pine scent, filled her nostrils. Clean and heady, bringing to mind a woodsy outdoor fire.

Her hands fluttered. A sidelong glance at a grinning Oliver reminded he was ever the romantic. She sent him a glare, silently stating, *Get that smirk off your face.*

"I'm hardly an angel," she replied to Patrick. "I store jumper cables in my trunk, along with a first aid kit and a flashlight in the glove compartment."

"I like a woman who is always prepared. I'm obviously failing in that department and—" From his expression, he grimly rebuked himself.

She held up a hand before he finished. "You can't anticipate when an emergency will happen." He was easily over six feet tall, a giant compared to her under five feet height. Better responses flooded her brain, but she shifted back to him. "Incidentally, did you shut your car's engine off?"

"I didn't have a choice. The car stalled."

"Does it stall a lot?"

"More and more."

"Then the damage to your battery is already done." She extended a smile. "I'll drive you to your car, and the jump-start should get you on the road to a service station."

"Will I reach Bloomingfield?"

"You should."

"Should?"

"Barring any unforeseen circumstances."

"Like what?"

"A flat tire."

"Thanks, that's reassuring." He didn't appear pleased at her statement, although he held out his hand. "I'm Patrick Gervez."

"I overheard." She stretched out her hand to his. "In Olive's Diner, everyone makes it a point to know everyone else's business."

"I see," Patrick wryly observed. "And you are …?"

"Cora Carpenter."

His fingers were firm, yet warm and gentle, and an unanticipated jolt of attraction sent a fluttering sensation straight through her pulse.

Quickly, she drew her hand away.

"I'm pleased to meet you, Mrs. …." he began.

"It's miss and call me Cora."

He considered her with a smile of open, male interest, so flattering and unsettling that she focused on standing still, fearful of stumbling if she took more than a step.

He tipped his head. "Cora is a beautiful name."

"Thanks." She straightened and gazed up at his outrageously good-looking face. "A pleasure, Mr. Gervez."

"Patrick. I'm new to California."

"I've lived here all my life."

"And you're the first person I've met, aside from Oliver."

"Lucky you," she joked.

"Nice earrings." He drew attention to the miniature reindeers swinging from her ears.

"They glow. Their noses—"

"Like Rudolph."

"Correct."

They shared a smile.

MINUTES LATER, with Patrick in the passenger seat of her Chevy, Cora stopped in front of his stranded car on the side of the road. He might be new to the area, she reflected, but his car was the opposite.

He insisted on her waiting while he scurried around to open the door for her. Although their fingers hardly touched as she got out, her hand tingled. Determined to ignore her reaction, she stroked his classic Mustang's shiny navy-blue exterior. "This is gorgeous. You drive a sleek convertible."

"Do you like it?"

"A Mustang? Definitely."

"So do I, when it runs. Usually, the car is reliable."

She grabbed her jumper cables from her trunk. "You traveled all the way from the Carolinas?"

"A four-day drive that took thirty-nine hours. My Mustang never disappoints. Until this afternoon, that is."

She lifted the hood, grateful she'd dressed casually in dark-washed jeans and the comfortable jean jacket she'd donned over her sweatshirt.

"My father was a mechanic and taught me and my brother everything," she said. "In fact, my father has a weakness for older cars, much like me."

Patrick gave a thumbs-up. "We share a commonality, except all I know about cars is I want them to run."

She chuckled.

"Your father sounds highly competent," Patrick said.

"He is." And she loved her father, their recent argument notwithstanding. She'd phoned to apologize, but he hadn't picked up nor responded to her voice mails.

Patrick studied her. "Are you close?"

"Why do you ask?"

"By the expression on your face, he must mean a great deal to you."

"He's one of the most important people in my life." She walked to her car to prop the hood, aware of his gaze on her back. If she chatted with him any longer, she might divulge the entire, sad story of her failed online dating and the ensuing fight that had severed any last rapport with her father.

Patrick yanked off his coat and placed it in his car. "How can I help, Cora?"

"I'm all set, and this won't take long." Explaining the process, she fastened the clamp on the red jumper cable to her car's battery, and the other red clamp to the positive terminal on Patrick's car and then the black clip to Patrick's negative terminal and to her own car's unpainted metal surface—not near the battery.

"Very impressive," he murmured. "Thank you."

"You're welcome. Wait for a while so my engine can charge your battery." She slid into the driver's seat of her car, lowered the window, and gestured for Patrick to do the same. "Try starting it now," she called.

He spun the ignition and the engine immediately purred

to life. "Wow." He applauded. "You're a wizard."

"Hardly, but thanks."

He strode to her car and bent down to peer at her through the open window. "If I were you, I'd ask me out to dinner to offer my appreciation."

"What?" She blinked. Startled laughter bubbled to the surface. "Say that again?"

"I wanted to get your attention." A grin tugged at his mouth. "Will Saturday evening suit you?"

Somehow, she kept her expression noncommittal. "I can't."

"Why not?"

"I'm … I'm cleaning my refrigerator, but thank you for the invitation."

"Is Sunday night better?"

"I'm considering running a 5K and should practice … running."

"You can advise me on the necessary emergency equipment to store in my trunk while we dine."

"No. Sorry."

"I hoped chatting about cars might attract you."

It did. Spending time with him attracted her even more.

She brought her thoughts back to reality and shifted her attention to the road. "I'm on a dating hiatus."

"Why? A bad breakup?"

Briefly, she nodded.

"When did your hiatus begin?" He brushed a hand across his forehead as a slight drizzle began falling.

"Last month."

"Mine is three years, so I've got you beat." He leaned in. His scent again, a whiff of pine and infinitely appealing.

"I guess you're the winner," she replied.

"Have you heard the phrase, 'a tincture of time'?"

"You mean, 'time heals all wounds'?"

"'A tincture of time refers more to bodily ailments." His voice was deep and entirely too certain. "Whereas 'time heals all wounds' indicates time's healing nature."

"It depends on how you define the word *heal*."

"In time, you will heal." He straightened. "Look, I really appreciate you helping me. You lost an hour of your afternoon."

"It's not a loss. I'm happy to assist."

"Few people extend themselves nowadays."

"You'll discover things are different here."

A spark of pleasure lit his features. "Highly reassuring. Big cities are often uncaring, you know?"

She didn't know. She'd never lived anywhere else—always residing in the tiny town of Evanville, where everyone knew each other by name.

She lifted her face to his and her heart skipped a beat. His brown hair was thick and wavy and a tad too long, his eyes a piercing blue. He'd folded his white shirtsleeves up on his powerful forearms when he offered to help her with the jumper cables, and the masculinity he exuded left her breathless.

And here, on this wet December day, she felt an instant magnetism to a man she just met. She hadn't expected that and wondered if her fair skin concealed the telltale flush of awareness heating her cheeks.

At his perceptive smile, she highly doubted it.

"Where do you work?" An unruly lock fell onto his forehead, damp with the drizzling rain. His hair was naturally wavy, and she resisted the urge to brush it back.

Don't you dare, she reprimanded herself. The gesture would be much too familiar.

"I run a licensed child care from my home," she responded.

"I've heard licensing isn't an easy process."

"Where did you hear that?"

"My wife, I mean my ex-wife, Olympia, and I interviewed numerous daycares. In the end, Olympia decided she didn't want children after all. Her decision, not mine."

So he'd been married and divorced.

"I take my role seriously," Cora replied. "I'm responsible for the health and safety of the kids I watch."

"All ages?"

"Preschoolers in the morning and school-age in the afternoon."

"I suspect you're a wonderful caregiver."

He assessed her with those gorgeous eyes. Up close, specks of gold enhanced the vivid blueness.

"I love children," she said.

"I do too."

For several beats he was silent. His shuttered expression revealed there was more, but it was swiftly replaced with a charismatic smile.

Everyone had a story and oftentimes, a haunted past. She debated. She didn't know him well, but went with her gut instinct. "If you ever choose to talk—"

"About what?"

"Life, children, failed relationships ..." *Had she really suggested that?*

"No. I won't." His gaze swung from hers. "Thanks for the offer, though."

Normally, fine-looking men didn't interest her. In her limited experience, they were generally self-centered. Patrick seemed considerate, genuinely attentive and appreciative.

Stylish, high-profile women probably fell into his arms if he showed the slightest interest.

Cora, though, was neither stylish nor high-profile, and for once she was pleased with her flaws. That way, he wouldn't be interested enough to bring on the full potency of his magnetic appeal.

Belatedly realizing she'd studied him far too long, she blurted, "I've worked from home the past few years."

"You're an entrepreneur. Another admirable trait besides being a beautiful car mechanic." His gaze drifted to her face. "Before I leave, shall I try to ask you out again?"

She shot him an expression of tolerant amusement and shook her head.

"You're getting wet," she pointed out.

"Well, then, I should go." He glanced at his watch. "I anticipate seeing you around."

Around? Around where? And what about his dinner invitation? Had he accepted no for an answer so easily?

He'd asked twice. She'd refused twice.

"Sure," she muttered. "Let me unhitch our cars."

She removed the jumper cables and recommended he purchase a new battery immediately. "Good luck on your move," she said as they each got back into their cars.

As he drove off, she reassured herself he had wreaked enough havoc on her for one afternoon. It was probably for the best if they didn't meet again.

She'd felt an instant, powerful draw to him that he apparently ... didn't feel for her.

She braced her palms on the dashboard and collected a slow, steady breath. Hadn't she learned from painful experience that she was a terrible judge of men?

Nonetheless, the idea of dining with Patrick, sitting across from him in a restaurant as he gazed at her, being held in his arms while he kissed her ... Listening to the community band in the town square, the charm of miniature white lights glowing from boutiques while they strolled through picturesque towns, the creation of Christmas memories ...

Nope. Not going there.

Her encounter with Patrick was happenstance, her daydreams nothing more than fantasies. With that, she forced any further contemplations of him from her mind.

CHAPTER 2

Four days later, Cora and her part-time employee, Molly, spent an early evening cleaning and straightening Cora's living room. Her home was licensed for up to six children, and they all had appeared at dawn.

Now they had departed with their parents, and only two weeks remained until Christmas.

Cora plucked the dead leaves from a pink poinsettia plant a parent had gifted her and arranged it on a side table.

Finished with her tasks, Molly walked into the kitchen. She perched on a stool, her fingers rapidly texting, when Cora entered.

"How did you spend your weekend?" Molly's attempt to disguise a grin failed.

"I jogged on Saturday and Sunday to get in shape for the hospital's charity run."

"Did you have any interesting romantic adventures?"

Cora set down a toy truck she held. "Why do you ask?"

"Because Harry texted me." Molly cut her gaze to her cellphone. "He heard you met a guy in Olive's Diner."

"Who told him?"

"Oliver. He mentioned he had called Harry's garage on Thursday to help a new guy in town because his car had broken down, and you came to his rescue."

"Cars are my specialty." Cora pasted on a bright smile. "The guy owns a gorgeous Mustang."

"Uh huh." Deliberately, Molly set her cellphone to the side. "I wonder who he is?"

"His name is Patrick, and he's relocating to the Bloomingfield area."

"Uh-huh."

"What's with all the 'uh-huh's'?" Idly, Cora spun the tiny wheels of the truck, recalling her racing pulse when she was around Patrick. Flattered he asked her out to dinner, she also feared becoming nothing more than a conquest if she spent another minute with him.

"Why is he in this quiet part of California?" Molly asked.

Cora shrugged. "He's going to work with Lorenzo Rossi. Perhaps he's a newly hired cameraman for the TV station."

"Is he single?"

"Yes. He's divorced." Cora climbed onto the stool across from Molly. "He requested I go on a Saturday night dinner date with him."

"You certainly brightened my Monday." Molly leaned forward. "Ditch the clothes you normally wear that are a size too big and show off the lovely figure you always hide."

"I can't wear tight outfits and high heels running around after children all day."

"But you can on a date with a guy who's got excellent taste in cars. When are you going?"

Molly had been married a year, and assumed everyone should be in a constant, blissful, newlywed state consisting of flowery words and endless kisses. The Christmas season merely heightened her enthusiasm.

"No date." Cora rubbed her neck. "We're not, because—"

"I realize you're in a once-bitten-three-times-shy frame of mind. Don't let that prevent you from pursuing a good life."

"Once bitten, twice shy," Cora corrected. "And thanks for the unsolicited opinion, Ann Landers."

"Who's she?"

Cora offered a bemused grin. "An advice columnist, evidently before your time."

"Move forward and begin real live dating, like your father advised. Have you settled your differences with him?"

Cora vacantly fixed her gaze on the Santa's Village cookie jar on the counter, and didn't reply.

"Forget the online Egyptian stuff," Molly said firmly.

Molly knew about the fictional Gregory Pansa, and the general string of bad luck Cora had experienced with boyfriends. Prior to Gregory, she'd dated infrequently. Nothing had worked out, although she invariably chose to be fair and allow the men a chance. In most cases, her instincts had shouted *no*, but she hadn't listened.

Her instincts had been right on. No man had appealed to her.

And she'd been the biggest chump of all. Even when her father had hired a private investigator, and it turned out that Gregory wasn't a doctor living in a church basement in Egypt—a church that incidentally didn't exist—Cora hadn't accepted the fact that the romance was a hoax.

"Enough about my nonexistent dating life." Dismissively, she flapped her hand, hoping Molly got the hint and dropped the subject of Patrick. "My brother wants me to make a Christmas wish. Any suggestions?"

"Well, duh." Molly drew a laughing breath. "How about a new man? Someone honest, reliable and handsome. Looks aren't all that important, but while we're wishing ..." She included a whimsical sigh.

Cora stood and dragged the vacuum cleaner from the hall closet, intending to vacuum the carpet, the final chore for the day. When she switched it on, sparks flew through the air.

With a last spurted cough, it died.

"There's my wish." Cora half-laughed. "A brand-new vacuum cleaner."

After Molly left, Cora settled on the plaid sofa in her living room and reached for a cup of green tea. The local broadcast was televised every evening, and she took an active interest in the latest news, weather and local sports updates.

She knew Lorenzo, the meteorologist, and appreciated his witty forecasts. Straightaway, he dove into his habit of changing a dismal forecast into a funny, upbeat occurrence.

"Clouds are still hiding our California sun, and precipitation is producing the ideal climate for ducks." He gestured to the weather screen showing rain clouds, then opened an umbrella and whistled the refrain from "Singin' in the Rain." He even twirled.

She laughed out loud. Perhaps she'd contact Lorenzo and inquire about Patrick ...

What? No. She refused to chase after a man she'd met in a diner. Especially one who'd requested she have dinner with him not once but twice, then hadn't seemed interested after all.

A new anchorman was introduced during the next segment, and Patrick Gervez's handsome face appeared on the television screen.

A tentative smile formed on Cora's lips as surprise kicked in.

Patrick was the new anchor? Not a cameraman?

She remained glued to the entire broadcast, entertained

by the clever banter between him and the various announcers.

When Lorenzo returned, he concluded his segment singing "White Christmas," performed with a pair of sleigh bells as accompaniment.

"So, Lorenzo, you're overflowing with props and tunes tonight." Patrick folded his hands on the news desk. "Shall I harmonize?"

"I'm content singing solo." Lorenzo launched into a tuneful "I'm Dreaming of a …"

Cora made the mistake of focusing on Patrick, and noticed the crinkles around his blue eyes, which were perilously appealing when he laughed.

"Lorenzo," he said, "Speaking of holiday tunes, will you enlighten us on the story behind 'Jingle Bells'?"

"The song was published in 1857, right around the year when you were born," Lorenzo joked.

Patrick grinned. "Did you know it was the first song transmitted from space?"

"I know now." Lorenzo strode to the anchor desk and took a seat beside Patrick.

"As our viewers are aware, I'm new to the area," Patrick continued. "Lorenzo, what can you tell me about Bloomingfield?"

"It's the quintessential small town."

"Have you lived here your entire life?"

"Not yet."

At Patrick's chuckle, Lorenzo countered, "Any final words to end your first broadcast?"

Patrick's eyebrows furrowed while he gave the question serious deliberation. His eyes sparkled and a mysterious smile edged his lips. "I'm pleased to be a part of this award-winning station and now residing in this lovely new town."

There was that word, new, Cora thought, as she squeezed

a slice of fresh lemon into her tea. All references regarding Patrick seemed to circle back to that word.

"Everyone I've met this week has been friendly and helpful." He paused, staring directly into the camera. "I particularly want to thank a woman named Cora, who braved the rain to fix my temperamental car."

Cora? He was referring to her? On live television?

Dumbfounded, Cora almost dropped her cup. Hastily, she placed it on the coffee table.

Her cellphone rang. When she picked up, Molly demanded, "Is the dreamboat newscaster who just went off the air your Patrick?"

Cora visualized Molly's self-satisfied grin.

Although filled with joy, she refuted, "He's not *my* Patrick. We just met."

"Well, he's definitely not *my* Patrick. I'm married to Harry, and together we'll dash through the snow in a ten-horse open sleigh."

Cora chuckled, not bothering to correct Molly. She peered out the window, the dark sidewalks illuminated by the colored holiday lights of her neighbors' homes. "What snow?"

"I'm quoting the lyrics to a song."

Well, not exactly. Cora put her head in her hands and sighed.

Molly laughed, then dipped her voice to an amplified whisper. "The woman he referred to was you, correct?"

Cora nodded into the phone. When she clicked off, it immediately rang again.

And again.

First Jack, then Oliver, shadowed by her mother, who Jack had apparently alerted.

As Cora readied for bed, another *new* floated through her mind.

Perhaps she should get a *new* phone number.

The week passed and Cora fended off suggestions from her friends, mother, and brother that she should contact Patrick.

"I'm too busy," she rationalized. "Besides, it's Christmastime."

Which was true. Plus, the kids in her care were in hyper mode. Consequently, she and Molly were exhausted at day's end.

Furthermore, Cora hadn't begun any holiday decorating. Inside, decorating meant setting up a miniature pine tree in the living room, and adding ornaments of the children around the branches.

The outside, though, was a different matter.

On Tuesday evening, she discovered that half the multi-colored icicle lights for her porch railings didn't work, and opted to string clear lights, instead. A twinkle of cheer was exactly what her bungalow lacked, and she anticipated the smiles on the children's faces when they dashed up to her house.

Sparkly, bright and …

Her mind swung to Patrick.

New.

The next morning, she requested that each child bring in a cookie recipe for a reception on December 23, the day before she officially closed for the holidays. It went without saying she'd help any parent who required eleventh-hour child care.

As the demanding days rolled on, Cora gave a grateful sigh when Saturday arrived. Nap hours and feeding routines, arts and crafts, plus the preparation for the children's holiday singalong at the reception meant long hours. Much as she didn't want to admit it, sometimes she wished the holidays were over.

Sure, she embraced the jubilant enthusiasm, the cheerfulness, the merry decorations adorning neighborhood homes. She valued every precious minute.

But still …

"There's no rest for the exhausted," she mumbled at eleven a.m. on Saturday. She'd set aside the day to complete her serious Christmas shopping.

Earlier that morning, she'd been too preoccupied with her holiday list to fuss with her appearance. She'd washed her hair and let it fall naturally over her shoulders. From her closet, she selected dark-wash jeans, a black and red tartan blouse and brown leather boots. A pair of festive Santa Claus earrings completed her ensemble.

List in hand and purse on her arm, she hurried to the front door.

The telltale crunch of car tires on her gravel driveway checked her steps.

Assuming the visitor wasn't her brother, because he was working a double shift at the hospital, she drew back the living room curtains and peered out the window.

A classic navy-blue Mustang sat parked in her driveway.

She opened the front door just as Patrick strode up the walkway.

"Hi, Cora." Clad in black jeans, boots, and a blue polo shirt that enhanced the heavenly deep blue of his eyes, his attractiveness was unquestionably lethal. Over his shoulder, he'd thrown a brown wool jacket.

"Hello, Patrick." She touched her throat. That enticing scent again—pine. "How did you find me?"

"It was easy." He smiled. "Every person I asked knew where you lived."

"In Bloomingfield?"

"I found a place on the outskirts and am almost halfway to Evanville. In any event, your fame covers miles." He kept his smile. "I was frustrated because I had to wait so long to see you again."

"You obviously succeeded, so your frustration has ended." She returned his smile and ushered him inside.

"I'm hoping if I ask you out in person that you won't refuse, since I went through all this trouble to locate you."

"You just said it was easy."

"Did I?" He regarded her from head to toe and smiled approvingly, as if she were the most beautiful woman on the planet. "You look gorgeous."

She ran a self-conscious hand through her hair. "Flattery will do little to persuade me."

"What about sincerity?"

Memories of his politeness while she'd fixed his car flooded back, drowning out the surprise of his arrival.

"Sincerity? In that case, a different story entirely." She hung her purse on the doorknob of the hall closet. "A sincere person is a rare and much-needed commodity these days."

"I agree."

Patrick was kind and treated her with respect. He gave and didn't seem to expect anything in return.

"Sincerity breeds trust," he maintained. "Which is important when establishing a successful relationship."

"You mean between us?"

"Exactly."

"We have a relationship?"

"Hopefully. Successful and otherwise ..."

His unexpected allusion—or was it a compliment?—brought a rush of pleasure to the pit of her stomach.

"Are you working today?" His smile filled the tight confines of the entryway.

"No."

"Wonderful. Neither am I."

"Happy coincidence, I'm sure." She bobbed her head as if she didn't believe him for a minute. "Is that why you're here?"

He opened his mouth, and she thought he'd crack a joke. Instead, he confirmed with a quiet, "I heard you usually had weekends off."

"From whom?"

"Oliver."

"You could have phoned instead of driving all the way from Bloomingfield."

"I didn't have your phone number."

She lifted a skeptical brow. "I'm fairly certain the same people who gave you my address and told you I took the weekends off would have also given you my number."

"Except talking to you in person is infinitely better."

Uncertain if she should agree or disagree, she merely shook her head.

In the limited time they'd spent together, Cora was certain of two things.

First, Patrick was a pro at small talk and compliments. And second, his male charm and persuasive smile were luring her ever closer to him.

Decisively, she took a step backward. She wasn't good at

any of this, and she certainly couldn't handle being so near him.

"Therefore, may I take you to lunch?" he asked.

"Therefore?"

He chuckled and gauged the distance between them before gazing down the hallway. "I'm guessing it isn't necessary to clean your refrigerator again."

"My refrigerator is spic and span."

He threw a teasing smile. "Mine could use a cleaning."

"Not on your life. Good try, though."

He laughed. "So, may I buy you lunch?"

"I admire your kindness and your unshakable effort—"

"Here comes the *but*," he murmured.

"*But* I've earmarked today for all my last-minute holiday shopping."

"Another happy coincidence. I wanted to finish today too, and we can shop together. After lunch."

She was about to speak, but he forestalled her.

"My dinner proposal was shot down twice," he reminded. "Now I'm determined to buy you lunch. If you refuse, I'll extend a breakfast invitation."

"Quite the strategy." She held off a grin. "Though it's kind of late for breakfast."

"Conversely …" He peered at his watch. "It's not too late for lunch or dinner."

She vacillated.

"Let's go to that diner … Olive's?" he suggested. "Allow me to repay you for fixing my car."

"How's the car acting?"

"Like a charm with its new battery. Although, the engine backfires."

"You might have too much fuel running to the cylinders."

"I had that checked. Regardless, if my car breaks down, I'm traveling with an expert mechanic."

Should she refuse again? A rebuff would be rude, and if this was a quick luncheon date, then the setting would be lively and open and hardly intimate. Totally relaxing in a cheery diner, savoring a deli sandwich and a cup of Oliver's delicious coffee.

Nevertheless, she was wary. Her attraction to him had swiftly reappeared, a reminder that Patrick was dangerously appealing.

Lost in thought, she repeated the vow she'd made to herself. After the shattering episode with Gregory, she never wanted to feel that precarious emotion called love again. Love was too painful, and she didn't trust her rash heart, nor her imprudent instincts.

Furthermore, the children in her day care were her main concern. If she allowed it, Patrick could become an all-consuming factor, and she wasn't prepared for a drastic change in her routine, especially one prompted by a compelling stranger.

But …

Another but?

Sure, because he wasn't a stranger. He was a friend.

"My lunches consist of a hurried peanut butter and jelly sandwich." She pitched an additional excuse, anticipating it was enough for him to admit defeat.

"Fortunately, Oliver serves an extensive menu." Patrick smiled and motioned toward the door. "Shall we?"

"Perhaps in January," she hedged, realizing she was quickly running out of excuses. "I'm super busy, and my days are filled with a thousand extra tasks. You know how it is."

"Lunch isn't a task, Cora," Patrick replied as if he hadn't heard her. "Lunch is a necessity."

"I'm finishing my shopping today, remember?"

"Me too. Besides, I'd love to learn more about this quaint area I now call home. And ... I realize you like old cars." He studied her and paused. "The weather is clear so we can drive with the convertible top down. We might get chilly, but the car has an excellent heater."

She hung back on her heels and peered outside. "The weather *is* perfect," she said softly.

"Well?"

His lopsided grin brought a chortle to her lips.

How she loved riding in convertibles. She imagined the rush of wind on her cheeks, the crystal-blue sky, the silvery sun warming her face.

Besides, she liked lunch, she liked Olive's Diner, and she liked Patrick.

Who could refuse?

She grabbed her purse, drew her red parka from the closet, and they headed out the door.

CHAPTER 4

$\mathcal{P}$atrick knew the offer of a ride in his Mustang had steered Cora's decision in his favor. He'd rightfully anticipated she wouldn't refuse, and she hadn't. With that, the negotiation had been sealed, and expectation pulsed through him as he started the car. He was spending the afternoon with the enchanting, entrancing Cora.

She pulled down the visor, nudged aside her hair, and rummaged for an ivory comb in her purse. She tamed a stubborn curl by clipping it back and allowed her luxurious waves to spill over her shoulders.

"You're more stunning than a woman on the cover of a glossy magazine," he said.

"Glossy magazine?"

"Or any magazine."

"Thank you. You're very sweet." She pressed a forefinger to her grinning lips, then flipped the visor back into place.

Her face was clean and glowing, and his heart turned over at her wholesome beauty.

"The red color of the blouse complements your deep eyes," he cited.

"My eyes are deep?"

"Amber is striking and mysterious."

Before she replied, he inserted, "And your Santa earrings bring the finishing touch to a festive look."

His compliment was frank and judging by her smile, delighted her.

"So Santa earrings bring out the color of my eyes?" she challenged. "More than the reindeer earrings I wore the other day?"

He smirked. "Definitely a toss-up.

A short while later, the enticing whiffs of freshly baked bread and slow cooked meat welcomed them as they entered Olive's Diner. Patrick slid his arm casually around Cora as a waitress ushered them to a booth by the window, then promptly returned with two glasses of water.

He flicked a glance at the oversized booths covered in green plastic, the pink lights shining overhead, the fake potted poinsettia plants atop each table. In the corner, a skinny artificial fir tree glittered with silvery bulbs and a sprinkling of tinsel. Festive with a pinch of old-fashioned flair, the diner could have been featured on any iconic movie set depicting a vibrant Christmas scene.

A well-dressed older woman and a man in work clothes sat at the counter and they enthusiastically waved at Cora.

With a cheerful "Hello, how is your cottage by the sea?" Cora returned the wave.

"Fabulous!" they chimed in unison.

Patrick smiled an acknowledgement toward them. "Who are they?" he inquired.

"Emily Varon, or rather, Emily Vertucci and her husband, Joe. Emily frequented Olive's for dinner when she lived in Evanville. She and Joe met here, though now they're married and live in Cambria. Joe delivers chocolate to several shops, including Sally's."

"Sally, as in Oliver's girlfriend?"

"Yes. She co-owns Bloomingfield Candy Shop along with her brother, Ben." Cora indicated the parking lot. "There's Joe's truck, Moonglow Chocolatiers."

Patrick angled toward them. "They're an older couple."

"Both over the age of seventy, which proves love can happen at any age."

"They seem happy," he confirmed.

"Blissfully, judging from Oliver's sometimes long-winded commentaries."

So married people could be happy?

Patrick sat back and folded his arms, recalling the way his coworker Lorenzo beamed about his wife, Julie, but those expectations were shadowed by the memories of Patrick's demanding ex-wife, Olympia. Constant turmoil was the name of her game, and when they'd been married, he'd felt manipulated and constantly off-balance. His suggestions to seek guidance for their marriage had gone unheard.

"I love Christmas music," Cora was saying—no, singing about a button nose and corncob pipe. He grinned. His equilibrium was restored as he listened to her bright voice. "Can you think of a more favorable song for the holidays then 'Frosty the Snowman'?" she asked.

Actually, he could.

All I Want for Christmas Is You came to mind.

Now, why that particular song and that particular title? He kept the question to himself.

He wasn't a stranger to dating beautiful women, except this woman was fascinating, her heartwarming laugh irresistible. He drew a prolonged breath and allowed himself a thorough study of her face—a gorgeous brunette with the delicate features of a cherub.

"I don't hear any music except for your sweet voice," he noted.

"You will. Willie Nelson sings the greatest songs." She headed for the jukebox and dropped coins into the slot. Soon, a gravelly male voice began singing about a snowman called Frosty.

With her hands clasped behind her back and glossy hair framing her captivating face, Cora made her way back to the booth. She looked more like a college freshman than a woman in her thirties. (Patrick had inquired about her age too.)

As he admired her slow easy strides, he was catapulted back to a decade earlier, when, on his climb to the top of the proverbial news ladder, he'd married Olympia. He expected his high-society wife, the country club they joined, the brick mansion with, yep, a white picket fence, were all part of the happily-ever-after he envisioned.

It wasn't. He'd been wrong.

He recalled an adage his grandfather had recited on numerous occasions: "Youth is wasted on the young."

Wise words indeed.

Five years had passed, and Olympia was now a long-gone ex. In the interim, Patrick's imaginings of a carefree family crowded with giggling youngsters had been etched out.

He'd wanted children. Olympia had not. Why hadn't they discussed their priorities before marriage?

"Do you like the song I chose?" Cora slid onto the booth seat across from him.

He shifted his gaze to the jukebox. "Who doesn't wait all year for Willie Nelson to sing carols?"

"Ho, ho, ho." Cora sipped some water from her glass and gazed at him over the rim. "What's your favorite carol?"

"Hmm." He tapped his fingers on his bearded chin. "Difficult to choose."

"Surely one carol rises above the rest. A melody you never tire of."

He didn't particularly like Christmas carols and rarely sang, except in the shower where no one heard him. At the age of thirty-eight, he was jaded. Christmas had lost its spirit —somewhat because of the commercialism and never-ending media pressure to buy, buy, buy.

He expressed his observances aloud, and Cora quickly concurred.

"One benefit is that this season encourages people to help others," he said.

"Yes. Christmas is truly magical," she replied. "Or, rather, it used to be."

He settled his hands behind his head. "Why do you say that?"

"Lately, the season is a juggling act to accomplish more than I can ever get done."

"True," he agreed.

She pursed her lips. Nodded.

He drank more water.

"For countless families, the religious sentiment is forgotten." She clutched her fingers together. "Many children believe Christmas is mainly about presents. Too much money can be a bad thing."

"I like the giving gifts part." Patrick gazed down at his glass. "However, Christmas isn't really my thing."

Despite his response, she replied, "Even Mr. Scrooge came around in the end."

"Bah, humbug." Patrick flashed his most amiable grin. "Perhaps there's a chance for me after all."

"Most definitely."

Her words created an unexpected sense of optimism that flowed through his veins like a soothing balm.

"Choosing a unique present for someone you love is the best feeling, especially if you know it will bring them joy."

"A thoughtful sentiment behind the gift makes it even more special," he granted.

He left it at that. She acknowledged his statement with an adamant nod.

When he was married, he'd kept a running list on his computer of items Olympia wanted—mostly designer purses and shoes and costly perfume. Conversely, when it was a gift-giving occasion, she accepted his offerings with tightened lips. Soon afterwards, he'd learned why. She'd been having an affair with their next-door neighbor, a man twice her age.

His chest tightened. Their marriage had been built on lies and pretenses, and motherhood hadn't been part of the package.

"The children's parents and I want to observe the true Christian significance of Christmas," Cora was saying.

He drank some water. "I haven't been inside a church in years."

"I'm a churchgoer."

"Not me."

"Oh," she answered softly.

Oh?

A trace of sadness coupled with resignation crept into that one word, giving him the distinct impression that attending church was important to her.

"At any rate," he adeptly shifted the topic, "I prefer classical hymns. They're sung in church, correct?"

"All the time. Any hymn in particular?"

"Handel's *Messiah*." He suggested the first piece that came to mind.

"Hmm. Not exactly a hymn, but certainly inspirational. I'd categorize the *Messiah* as a large orchestral work."

"True." He preferred to watch hockey games or football over a concert. Nonetheless, he'd *heard* of Handel's *Messiah*.

Surely that counted, although he couldn't pinpoint how large a *large orchestral work* actually was.

Fortunately, she nodded as if she was completely satisfied by his claim.

Then she added, "Handel originally intended the composition for Easter week, not Christmas."

"Really?"

"Yes. He feared a London audience might not accept the piece because it was unorthodox, so he moved the premiere to Dublin, Ireland. He'd determined that the Irish audience was more sophisticated and elite than London."

"I never knew that. I'm spellbound."

"Are you now?" She laughed, and he laughed with her. He liked the sound of them laughing together.

"I love music," she reminded. "The *Messiah* is a true masterpiece."

"And you know a lot about it." *Apparently, much more than he did.* "On the other hand, I love facts, and I'll share these facts about the *Messiah* with Lorenzo. He's been singing Christmas melodies every day since I arrived at the studio."

"I'm aware." She laughed. "On the air, and both before and after your news reports."

"That's my job."

"You're an expert." She smiled, earnest and tender.

And there it was again. The tug on his heart.

He was hopelessly drawn to her sunny disposition, her never-ending enthusiasm, her appreciation for all things uplifting.

ONCE THEY HAD ORDERED the luncheon special—a covered turkey sandwich drenched in brown gravy with a side of cranberry sauce—from their feisty middle-aged waitress who somehow pulled off calling Patrick "darlin'" and Cora "honey pie" without offending them; Patrick let the atmosphere of chrome and Formica countertops, and a rehash of Willie Nelson singing "Pretty Paper," to wash over him.

"So, you two are together once again." Oliver came to their booth wearing a red and white velvet Santa Claus hat. Across the front was embroidered the name *Sally*.

"Isn't your name, Oliver?" Patrick jested.

"Last I knew." Oliver bequeathed an all-encompassing smile as if he were truly Santa Claus catering to his customers. "But we all agree that Sally is prettier."

"The name or the person?" Cora teased.

"Both." Displaying his customary coffee pot, Oliver filled their cups, then placed sugar packets and a creamer on the table. He chatted with a combination of kindness and affable teasing. "I assumed Patrick intended to knock on every door from Bloomingfield to Evanville until he found you, Cora."

Patrick shifted and drew a bracing sip of hot black coffee. So absorbed in looking at her, he'd forgotten to load up his cup with cream and sugar.

"Enjoy lunch, you two." With a playful salute, Oliver marched to another table.

Cora lifted a dainty eyebrow. "What's this about knocking on every door?"

Patrick swallowed an unfamiliar constriction in his throat. "You want honest?"

"Absolutely. I believe in truth and honesty, remember?"

"I wanted to see you. How's that for honest?" He touched her palm. "Obviously, I'm not a pro on the best way to go about it. I didn't intend—"

"To declare it on local television?"

"Something like that." He fiddled with the plastic salt and pepper shakers, a vintage pair of reindeers with bright-green bows.

"I'm flattered, Patrick," Cora said quietly.

He looked up at her. "You are?"

A rosy blush tinted her high cheekbones. "More than flattered."

He took several seconds to appreciate the lovely vision she created. The vivid tartan blouse enhanced her creamy complexion. Her lips, a rosy pink from the hot coffee, tempted him almost beyond reason. He could think of little else except kissing her.

Right there. In the diner. With Willie Nelson's raspy rendition of a Christmas carol in the background. He didn't regard Willie Nelson's music as romantic, but Cora probably did.

Patrick peered around, then gazed upward. Where was a mistletoe when you needed one?

Knowing Oliver, he would undoubtedly appear out of nowhere with a camera and begin snapping pictures if Patrick and Cora kissed. Or Emily and Joe would enthusiastically wave again.

While Cora scanned the dessert menu, Patrick scanned the other tables.

When he and Cora had first entered the diner, he'd wondered if all the customers had purposefully put down their forks, spoons and cups to regard them, because the diner had become so quiet.

He'd been wrong.

Now he *knew* they'd been staring because when he made eye contact, people grinned. Some entertained rambunctious children. Others were couples—both young and old. In any event he felt like E.T., an extraterrestrial oddity who had landed on earth after living on the moon. Or wherever E.T. lived.

Olive's Diner definitely was, as Cora described, "a place

where all the patrons made it a point to know everyone else's business."

With a glib smile, he trained his gaze on the open case chock full of seasonal confections—mini cheesecakes, a classic red chiffon pound cake, and a triple layer chocolate torte iced with peppermint.

Although no one directly intruded, many people uttered hellos when they passed, and a youthful mother informed him, in a thick Germán accent, how she preferred his newscasts over the national media newscasters.

"*Danke*," Patrick responded.

"*Danke*?" Cora repeated when the woman had crossed to another booth.

"I spent my childhood with my parents and grew up overseas," he explained.

"Just you? No siblings?"

"Just me."

"Do you see your parents often?"

"Not often enough." He splashed a couple ounces of cream into his coffee and stirred. Hopefully, that would finally cool it. "They're currently vacationing in the Bahamas."

"So, you're fluent in German?"

"For the most part."

"Do you speak other languages?"

"French, Dutch and Italian."

"You've seen countless countries." She clasped her hands. "I've never ventured any farther than visiting my mother in Nevada."

I'll take you anywhere you want, either here or abroad.

The words had just come, and he pondered if saying them aloud was too bold. Their friendship was fragile and scarcely beginning to blossom.

In the midst of his musings, their plates arrived.

Cora prayed a simple grace, and Patrick kept his head down and quietly whispered words he hadn't uttered since he was a child.

"Bless us, oh Lord …" she uttered.

Then they relished a savory lunch, punctuated by the clinking of forks, laughter spilling from the counter where Emily and Joe sat, and Willie Nelson serenading the entire dining room with an upbeat rendition of "Deck the Halls."

An hour later. after they had declined dessert and chatted over coffee, Patrick placed two twenty-dollar bills on the table to ensure their waitress received a generous tip.

He thanked Oliver for the outstanding meal and top-notch service and claimed Cora's hand, pleased when she didn't object. He hadn't held a woman's hand since his divorce, and it felt good. It felt right.

Certainly, he'd dated, but dinners had consisted of polite exchanges with a woman over a meal. Nothing that would compel him to hold the woman's hand as they left a restaurant.

"You're lacking a mistletoe," Patrick mouthed when he caught Oliver's gaze. He tipped his head upward.

Oliver's eyes sparkled. "Excellent idea."

As Patrick and Oliver shared a wink, Cora asked him, "What's an excellent idea?"

Patrick didn't attempt to disguise his smirk. "Mistletoe hanging at the entrance to the diner."

"For kissing?"

"Why not?" He elected to go on a mistletoe hunt immediately.

She rewarded him with a spellbinding grin. There was nothing about her, he decided, that wasn't perfect.

"Instead of asking everyone in town where you lived," he joked as he held open the door for her to exit, "I should have hightailed it directly to Olive's Diner."

She chuckled. "Which is equivalent to placing a notice in the *New York Times*."

A WHILE LATER, they reached Bloomingfield. Patrick found an excellent parking spot in the town center, and, cooled by the afternoon air, he assisted Cora with donning her parka, then slipped on his jacket.

As they sauntered along, townspeople approached Patrick to discuss one particular news item or another. Others greeted him and Cora with a heartening smile and moved on.

He noted the way folks regarded him and Cora together, surmising they were a couple. He liked that. He hadn't expected to, but he did. A stroll with Cora resembled a free fall, bringing a wide-range of sensations—most notably his stomach bending into knots whenever she glanced at him.

She cared for children and clearly loved them when she described several funny, mindful moments. Her melodic voice reminded him of an angel, and she lived in an area of California that could have been lifted straight out of a storybook.

"Am I invisible?" Cora half-laughed as another group headed toward Patrick. "You've lived here a week and are already well known."

He swept an arm around her as if it were the most natural gesture in the world. "Local folks recognize me because of my broadcasts." Politely, he answered questions while he drew Cora closer.

An elderly woman scrutinized them. "You must be Cora," she finally said.

"I am," Cora replied.

"Finally, Patrick found you." The woman wiggled sparse

gray eyebrows, straight as pencils. "He asked everyone within a twenty-mile radius about you."

"Only twenty miles?" Cora twisted to him, her grin teasing.

"I'd search a thousand miles for you," he declared.

"Uh-huh." Cora rolled her eyes.

"When a man discovers a treasure, he will move mountains to find her," he said.

"Ooh, Miss Cora, he's a romantic guy," the elderly woman answered with a winsome grin. "I'd hold on to this anchorman if I were you. He's a keeper."

"Is there nothing secret in these towns?" Patrick chuckled.

"Absolutely nothing," Cora and the woman responded in unison.

After the woman waddled away, Cora paused. "Hold on. Rewind. I'm a treasure? No one ever called me that before."

He couldn't gauge her mood, but determined by her wide grin that she was truly charmed.

"A precious, wonderful treasure," he affirmed, tucking her hand in his.

She didn't pull away. An encouraging start. He could get used to strolling about this Norman Rockwell town holding Cora's delicate hand. She was gorgeous and hardworking, and her smiles came effortlessly. She was the essence of every trait that attracted him to a woman.

Besides, her scent brought whiffs of cinnamon and spicy vanilla, pure and fragrant. Wholesome as a bright winter day, he decided, as his pulse kicked up a notch.

She fell into an easy step beside him, their boots tapping on the sidewalk. On every street corner there was a gala celebration. To the marvel of the crowd, live reindeer pranced in a fenced in area near the town center.

"Fun fact," Patrick commented as they passed. "Reindeer don't fly, but some have a red nose."

"Wow. Brilliant." Cora giggled. "And you know this because …?"

"I'm a science nerd."

"You are?"

He brushed up against her with a friendly nudge. "Get to know me better and you'll find out even more."

Slightly, her lips parted. "Is that a fact?"

He lingered, caressing his fingers across her cheeks. "It's a promise."

Sleds were set beside the reindeer, along with stacks of colorfully wrapped presents. The squeal of clamoring children prompted Patrick to laugh out loud.

"Are you enjoying yourself?" Cora asked.

"Immensely." He faced her, grinning in satisfaction. "Thank you for agreeing to share this day with me."

"I couldn't resist the offer to ride in a Mustang convertible," she goaded.

"With me."

Her features sobered. "With you."

A rush of emotion went through him he couldn't explain. He smiled, nodded. He couldn't remember later on if he thanked her for bringing such euphoria to a December afternoon.

Her cheeks had reddened because of the brisk temperature, or perhaps because of his remarks. In any event, she looked like she could use someone's arm around her to warm her. Fortunately, he was up to the task.

Star-colored beams shone across shop windows, illuminated by a light machine in the square. A jaunty rendition of "Up On the Housetop" performed by a community flute choir, filled the streets with a high piping sound. A gigantic fir tree blazed with white lights and sparkled with glass snowmen ornaments. Trace scents of candy apples and caramel corn floated through the air.

Cora's grin went from one ear to the other. "You might grow to love this season if you live here long enough."

He blew out a lengthy breath. "I don't plan on moving anywhere else."

"I was referring to Christmas."

"Christmas? That'll take some work."

He couldn't promise anything more, even to this perky woman with the sassy smile who was slowly invading his heart. That last Christmas with his ex-wife had commenced in endless arguments, completed by a separation. A man's heart could only take so much.

"There are heaps of upcoming kid-friendly events, including a coloring contest," Cora said.

"Do you take any of your day-care children to Bloom-ingfield?"

"I mostly stay in Evanville."

"And Evanville offers the 5K race," he said. "You're partic-ipating, correct?"

"Yes, I've decided to, and afterward a singalong with Santa is scheduled."

He snuggled her closer. "Will Willie Nelson make an appearance?"

"I seriously doubt it. And you can only participate in the singalong if you run the 5K."

"Why is that?"

"I don't know." She shrugged. "Rules are rules."

He smiled at her solemn declaration. A rule-follower. He liked that too.

She lifted a perfectly arched brow. "I meant to ask you … you didn't sing with me when I sang in the diner."

"I sing … sometimes, but not often. Besides, instead of popular carols I prefer …" He faltered, trying to think of a high-brow piece of music. Brightening, he suggested Handel's *Messiah* again.

"You won't sing Willie Nelson but you'll sing the Hallelujah Chorus?"

"Certainly, at least in the shower." He tried to remember if he'd ever actually heard the 'Hallelujah Chorus.' He must have. It was a very famous piece.

"You sing all four-parts?" Cora inquired. "Soprano, alto, tenor and—"

"Soprano … usually."

"My word. You must have a high voice."

Evidently, he had gotten the sopranos mixed up with the tenors. Or was it the bass?

"I don't listen to a lot of holiday music," he replied, then changed the topic, hoping it would get him off the hook. "A certain someone suggested I remind them of Scrooge."

"Who?"

"You."

She granted another smile that caused his heart to beat double-time. They wended around a crowd of shoppers and Cora soon vanished into a candle store.

He waited outside. It allowed him to reflect on their day together.

Gradually, he was being led toward a beacon of hope— freshness and humor and goodness all rolled up into one beautiful woman. Whatever his former aspirations were in Raleigh, this was the day to realign them.

Cora reappeared, and they headed toward Bloomingfield Candy Shop.

The front window touted whimsical candy gifts molded into diverse shapes; and the signature chocolate-coffee fudge was arranged in bento boxes on a gold display shelf.

When they entered, the scent immediately transported Patrick back to his childhood. He drew in the heavenly sweetness and sugary bitterness, a chocolate-lover's dream.

Cora led him down the main aisle and introduced him to Sally, the owner who stood behind the counter. Strains of "We Wish You a Merry Christmas" played as a backdrop.

Sally's response was a jubilant "Hello. Wonderful to meet you, Patrick."

She wore a red velvet suit, and a red and white Santa hat. Instead of *Sally*, the name *Oliver* was embroidered on the hat.

"You're the famous chocolatier," Patrick said.

Sally crinkled her eyebrows. "And you're the famous new anchorman on the six o'clock news."

He grinned. "I saw a hat just like yours when Cora and I lunched at Olive's today."

"I wish I could visit the diner more often, but the holiday season is very busy for both of us."

Patrick couldn't tear his gaze away from her hat. "Did you and Oliver switch hats?"

Sally pushed a strand of springy blond hair from her forehead. "It's a secret joke between us."

"Not that secret. Your names are emblazoned on each other's hats."

She leaned forward. Her blue eyes were remarkably observing as her gaze alternated between Patrick and Cora. "You are a stunning couple. Has anyone told you that yet?"

"Not till now," he replied. He was beginning to like Sally more and more.

"We're not a couple," Cora swiftly countered.

"But we could be," Patrick said.

"But we aren't."

"I agree with Patrick," Sally broke in.

"Praise you, Sally." Energized by her compliment, he decided this was the ideal opportunity to kiss Cora. He tugged her closer and brushed his lips across hers.

Sally applauded.

Cora did not.

"What was that for?" she demanded as she stepped back.

"The moment called for it."

"The moment? We're in the middle of a candy shop, which is hardly romantic."

Their gazes locked. He read the emotions in her eyes—apprehension, embarrassment, and something else. Attraction? He sincerely hoped so.

"No one is here except for the three of us." He tried a smile. "Next time I'll ask permission before I kiss you."

"Okay." Cora returned the smile, although it seemed a bit forced.

"This kissing chat is lovely, and I happen to think my shop is extremely romantic." Sally's gaze relaxed as she continued to gaze at them. "Besides, Patrick couldn't help himself. He was swept away by the …"

"Chocolate," Cora put in.

"Charming woman beside me," Patrick affirmed.

He eyed Cora, who shook her head repeatedly.

"So," Sally motioned to the display case overflowing with sweets, "what can I help you with today?"

"I'm here to finish my holiday shopping," Cora said.

"Me too." Patrick gestured toward the doorway. "Sally, have you considered investing in a mistletoe? I suggested the same to Oliver when we were leaving his diner."

Cora rotated to face him. "If it were up to you, there would be mistletoe hanging all over town." She repressed a laugh which made Patrick breathe easier. Apparently he was forgiven for the spontaneous kiss.

Cora glanced at Sally and muttered, "He's impossible."

"Impossible men are the best kind," Sally said sagely.

"Are they?" Cora asked.

The opening of the shop's door interrupted the conversation.

Sally greeted the latest customer with a chirpy "Hello. Please browse and let me know if there's anything you'd like to purchase."

The woman bobbed her head. "Thank you. I will."

As Cora began her candy selection, Patrick leaned against the counter, content to admire her lovely profile and a glimpse of her tantalizing lips.

"Where's your brother, Ben?" Cora asked Sally.

"He took the week off to travel to Alaska with Maise," Sally replied. "They're visiting her family."

"Maise is the local food critic," Cora explained to Patrick. "She and Ben are newlyweds."

Patrick tapped a finger on his bottom lip. "Are they happy?"

"Blissfully."

With a high chin, he whistled along with the holiday background tune. He was surrounded by happy couples. Maybe he and Cora would soon join the ranks.

Perhaps it was the drinking water in this part of California, he contemplated jokingly, although he knew it was something more, something better—honest, hard-working folks raising their families and truly caring for each other.

"Ooh, what kind of sweets are these?" Cora pointed to dozens of cookies displayed in the center of the case.

"Church window cookies. See? They resemble stained glass. Tara, my newest employee, baked them," Sally said. "They're quite popular."

Cora peered at the festive cookies dusted with coconut. "I'll take a dozen."

"Are they a gift?" Sally opened a white box and began arranging the cookies in a neat row.

"Yes. For myself." Cora laughed. "I'll freeze them. It's

convenient to have extra cookies at the ready, especially when my brother returns from Nevada."

"Don't forget me," Patrick reminded.

"Never." She returned her attention to the display and Sally. "Jack likes peanut butter squares and I'll buy a box of caramels for my mother."

"What about your father?" Sally inquired rather loudly.

"He prefers dark chocolate." Cora's jaw clenched. She shrugged as if nothing was amiss, though something clearly was. "I'll purchase a pound. Regardless, it's not likely I'll see him."

"Where does he live?" Patrick asked.

"In Evanville."

"That's close. You'll probably see him."

"I probably won't." Her shoulders curled. "We had a disagreement."

Patrick searched her features. Clearly, she was upset. "Concerning what?"

She acknowledged his question with an airy wave. "Long story."

"Shall I ship the caramels to your mother?" Sally adeptly shifted the theme, before offering both Cora and Patrick a salted caramel sample. She then expounded on her recipe created with bittersweet chocolate.

"Infusion?" Patrick repeated. "Which means …"

"I have no idea." Sally grabbed a candy for herself. "Actually, I do. It's—"

"Remarkable. I've eaten them before." Cora popped the candy into her mouth.

Patrick did the same. The explosion of creamy roasted cocoa on his tongue led to one word. *Amazing.*

Bloomingfield was definitely growing on him.

"Jack will hand deliver my mother's gift to her," Cora said. "He's flying a plane to Nevada."

"Your brother owns a plane?"

"His instructor is allowing him to fly hers, and she'll accompany him. From what I've gathered, she might be a love interest, but it's too early to tell. Up till now, he's been a confirmed bachelor."

"There's no better time for romance than the holidays." Patrick stepped aside as the other customer sauntered over balancing a jeweled gift tower filled with wrapped candy. She set it on the counter, then started for the coffee fudge with the promise that her order wasn't finished.

"My parents owned a plane," Patrick said quietly.

Sally sucked in a short breath. "They did?"

"Yes, they were both diplomats."

"I'm definitely in the wrong profession." Sally groaned and leaned over the counter.

Cora froze in place and studied him.

He reached out to grab her hand.

She shook him off. "Wealthy diplomats?" Her gaze narrowed.

"My parents are well off. They own a home in the Bahamas."

Cora swallowed. "You told me they were vacationing there."

"They are. In their second home."

He recalled her comments about too much money being a bad thing. Nonetheless, he'd made it on his own and never sought financial help from his parents. They'd worked full time for years and deserved to reap the benefits of their hard-earned retirement in style.

"Patrick, I heard you dined at my sister's restaurant last night with Lorenzo." Sally stepped in.

"The Pasta Junction." He patted his stomach, answering Sally as Cora continued to watch him. "Lorenzo insisted I taste Julie's fettuccini, and I was more than happy to accommodate, although by the time we arrived the dinner hour was long over."

"That didn't stop you, though," Sally teased.

"I never refuse homemade pasta leftovers."

Sally's attention wavered between Patrick and Cora. She paused. "Why don't you both come to the Christmas Eve buffet?"

"I can't," Cora uttered quickly as Patrick replied, "Sounds marvelous."

He wished to see her, and his wish magnified as he gazed at her exquisite face. "Why not?" he urged. "The food is first class."

"I attend church service."

"So do we," Sally chimed in. "We'll dine together afterward. My daughter will be with me, of course, and Oliver will accompany us after he closes the diner."

"Sounds like an excellent plan, Cora," Patrick said. "After my broadcast, I'll drive to Evanville to pick you up. We can meet everyone there."

He smiled. Everything was being arranged perfectly. Except for convincing Cora.

"I can't," she said.

Sally boxed up the cookies and handed the package to Cora, her smile laced with irritation. "You won't be watching any children, correct?"

"On Christmas, all the kids will be with their parents."

"We've solved your church service conflict and you aren't working. Therefore ..." Patrick said optimistically.

"Sorry."

"Christmas Eve is special and I will not allow you to spend another Christmas alone." Hands on her hips and totally in her element behind the cash register, Sally looked completely self-assured. "That's an order from a dear friend."

Cora opened her mouth, then closed it.

"Super and settled. We'll have a festive and fun holiday." Sally spun to Patrick. "My store ships everywhere, by the way. May I suggest some boxes of coffee fudge with your order?"

"Your infusion candy is utter perfection. Make it two boxes."

"Of infusion candy?"

"Absolutely."

"And the fudge?"

"Sure."

Cora sent him a surprised look. "You're purchasing a lot of candy. I hope there are dentists open in the Bahamas during the holidays."

"There are. My parents love anything sweet and I obviously take after them." His gaze moved tellingly to her lips.

"Excellent." Sally's sweeping flourish got his attention. "Three boxes of infusion candy and two boxes of coffee fudge shipped to the Bahamas."

He nodded his assent.

Sally rang up his order and greeted the sum with a smile. "Ninety-five dollars."

He studied the receipt. "Does the total include the shipping charge?"

"Nope. In addition, I'll pack an extra dozen cookies— your choice—a treat your parents can indulge in."

"At no charge?"

"I'm a businesswoman. There's always a charge."

"Fine. Thanks."

His gaze found Cora's.

"You should be concentrating on your candy purchases, not me," she admonished.

"I have a unique talent. I can focus on numerous topics at once."

Sally rang up a new total and presented it to him with an effervescent smile.

He leaned forward and gasped.

"Are you certain about your focusing skills?" Cora goaded while Sally explained that shipping was expensive because chocolate required cushioning, packaging and refrigeration with cold packs.

Clearly outmaneuvered, he bobbed his head.

Sally was hands down the finest salesperson in the entire state of California.

What's more, maybe his concentration wasn't as good as he assumed, at least not when the lovely Cora was anywhere in the vicinity.

CHAPTER 5

On the return drive to Evanville, Patrick debated whether to broach the subject of the Christmas Eve buffet with Cora, and decided to wait a few days. Surely with Sally and her family in his corner, she wouldn't refuse.

Once they were on the road, Cora settled into the passenger seat and stretched out her legs. "Tell me more about yourself," she encouraged.

He described his newscasts in detail, minutely examining and evaluating his on-air segments.

"I want to gain a better understanding of you—the person," she stated when he finished.

He preferred learning more about her, but quickly explained that he'd decided to major in journalism as soon as he'd completed high school. After graduating from an Ivy League university with a master's degree, he spent the next ten years traveling around the world as a major news correspondent.

She sat straighter. "What countries?"

"The UK, Asia and Australia, mostly. Or, wherever there was a story." He'd accumulated a staggering amount of money in the process and had bequeathed a substantial amount to various children's' charities—most notably an organization that raised money for safe playgrounds that were also handicap accessible.

Casually, her hand touched his. "And then?"

"I was offered a studio position with a 24/7 cable news network." He slanted her a smile. "I applaud your interest, although all this talk centered around me is quite enough."

"I like learning about you."

He gave a crisp nod. "Why?"

"Because I like …*you*."

Her straightforward response made his heart pitch.

There was an attraction between them she obviously couldn't deny. Neither could he.

She glanced away when she recognized his appreciative gaze and studiously inspected her hands. "Sounds like you were rising the ladder of success."

"I certainly tried." He grinned in spite of himself. She'd summed up several years of his life accurately. "Nonetheless, I have complete confidence that the new anchorman in Raleigh who succeeded me is amassing an avid following."

"If you're correct," she noted with an infectious smile, "I assume his communication and improvisation skills are outstanding and he can think on his feet. Plus, he projects a professional image because you're the best newsman on television. I wouldn't want to be in his shoes and tread on the heels of your footsteps."

"Thank you, although you may be biased."

"For what reason?"

"Because we're on our first date, and I assume you wouldn't say anything negative about me."

"We're on a date?" Her eyebrows furrowed. "We had lunch and then Christmas shopped."

"We're enjoying our time together and therefore, this is a

successful date. Consequently, your opinion of my broadcasts are probably biased."

"True," she confirmed with an indulgent laugh.

He found her honesty welcoming and felt that familiar tilt of his heart.

"Thus, accepting this anchor position in Bloomingfield is a step up?" He heard the unexpected sensitivity in her tone and caught a glimpse of her puzzled expression.

"In truth, the position is exactly the opposite." He kept his hands on the steering wheel. Traffic was light and easy—another positive aspect of small-town living.

"I'm surprised," she said. "You seem like a go-getter."

"I am. I was." He considered how best to reply and chose forthrightness. "I prefer to report on the little things that touch the lives of people I knew, rather than massive world affairs that are overwhelming at times and seemingly impossible to cope with."

She studied him for a beat. "You willingly gave up an exciting career."

"I'm in a different season now." Not to mention that Cora fit into the new life he longed to find. She was energetic, attractive, and appreciative of what was right in front of her —not searching for an unattainable rainbow.

Wasn't joy found in the minute, everyday occurrences?

He needed to feel grounded again, calm again. He needed to breathe without the overwhelming strain of a fast-track lifestyle.

He darted a glance at her and imagined kissing her.

His hand grasped hers, and she smiled. He reciprocated, feeling a bit rash for his adolescent pleasure in the simple touch of her fingers.

Certainly, he wasn't falling in love. After a sorry marriage to a woman more interested in his connections and affluent lifestyle than in him, he was skeptical of anything remotely resembling love.

Cora switched on the radio and discovered a station featuring holiday tunes. Within minutes, "A Holly Jolly Christmas" blared from his Mustang's eight speakers, and she hummed along. "This is one of the songs my day care children are singing for our annual program," she managed to tell him between lyrics.

He maneuvered around a parked car, then stopped at a traffic light at the next intersection. "How many songs are you preparing?"

"Three. 'A Holly Jolly Christmas,' 'It Came Upon A Midnight Clear,' and 'Silent Night.' We rehearse every day and will present a concert to the parents before holiday break."

"The kids are memorizing all those words?"

"We keep it simple, holly and jolly." Her buoyant rejoinder was muffled as she turned the volume louder and sang the second stanza in a tone that was definitely easy on the ear.

The hours ticked by in a blink.

They exited the highway onto the two-lane road to Evanville, and his car topped the hill to her bungalow with ease. The afternoon had bowed to early nightfall. Bold hues of orange and gold stretched across the sky and Cora's features glowed, her gaze drifting upward to the first stars in the sky.

As they entered her driveway, her eyes widened and she raised her voice with an emphatic no!

"What's wrong?"

"I have motion detector lights."

"Really?" He motioned to her darkened house. "Where?"

"They aren't working and I need *new* ones." She let out a peal of laughter.

"Am I missing something?" He turned off the car's ignition. "Is needing new lights somehow funny?"

"Not the lights. The word *new*." She wiped tears of hilarity that had gathered at the corner of her eyes. "And I must figure out my wish before it's too late."

"What wish?"

She shook her head and refused to elaborate.

Her comment merely heightened his fascination. He'd never met a woman like her—car mechanic, businesswoman, and a loving daughter and sister.

He insisted on opening the passenger door for her, hoisted her packages from the trunk and walked beside her. The evening breeze was crisp, and he breathed in a lungful of refreshing air.

When they reached her porch, she lingered.

"Would you like to come inside for coffee?" She rushed her words, louder than usual. Her fingers touched her throat in an absent form of a question. Already, he was associating these subtle little movements to her.

"For coffee?" he repeated.

On the one hand, yes. On the other hand, definitely yes.

A puff of wind teased her hair. Absently, she pushed it aside. "Or tea or a soft drink, if you prefer."

"Coffee is fine." He preferred to crack open a cold soda, but settled on the coffee. He would have eaten a live octopus to spend more time with her. Casually, he slid his hands into his pockets so he wouldn't appear too eager. "Oliver has certainly mastered the art of hot coffee."

"Coffee is my specialty too."

"Hot?"

"Piping," she assured.

Inside the foyer, she peeled off her parka, and he shrugged off his wool coat. She hung them both in the closet.

While she placed her various Christmas gifts on closet shelves, he made amiable remarks about all the delicious candy she'd purchased, and she enthusiastically concurred.

They walked into her living room and she switched on a couple of side lamps, which cast a rosy glow into the room, and his appreciative gaze glided over her magnificent hair, and the glint of glossy russet highlights.

"You're staring at me," she said.

"I am?" He'd perfected his innocuous smile.

Her eyes twinkled. "Yes."

"I can't help it." He brushed a strand of hair from her temple.

He stepped back and scanned the room furnished with an overstuffed armchair, a rocker-recliner and a sofa, all covered in a tan plaid fabric and blanketed with knitted quilts. Warm and inviting without pretense, the room was ideal for holding a restless child or rocking a toddler to sleep.

Wall-mounted shelves held an assortment of toys, jigsaw puzzles, a pyramid of books and numerous teddy bears. Mittens and thick wool socks were folded beside a miniature pine tree arranged on a shelf.

"No holiday wreaths?" he asked. "You, the Christmas elf herself?"

"I'm mindful of tiny hands yanking down decorations and injuring themselves. I'll trim the outside of my house soon, but the inside can wait. Normally, I only put up a small tree, anyway." She gave a tiny laugh. "Will you decorate your place?"

"I'm still unpacking boxes in my apartment." He cocked his head. "Besides, Christmas isn't really my—"

"Your thing. Yes, so you've said. Please make yourself comfortable." She gestured to the sofa and disappeared into the kitchen.

Flanked by a pair of gray textured curtains, a sliver of moonlight shone through the window. Already understanding who she was—organized and disciplined—he wasn't surprised by the room's neatness. Those attributes, combined with understanding, altruism, and tenderness, were essential in running a successful day care.

He sank into the timeworn sofa, contemplating the great lengths Cora went through to clean her home every day after the children left.

His ex, on the other hand, had been the poster child for messiness, and he'd constantly tripped over her extravagant dresses and costly shoes strewn all over the floor. Certainly, her disregard for orderliness had underscored his overheavy work load.

Cora reappeared carrying a tray with two mugs of steaming brewed coffee, spoons, and napkins. She'd also included a glass creamer and sugar set. She drank her coffee black, but she'd obviously noticed his penchant for heaps of sugar and cream from their lunch in the diner.

He concealed his delight for her thoughtfulness with a heartfelt thank you.

She set down the tray and settled opposite him on the sofa.

"So, where were we?" she asked.

"About what?" He spooned three teaspoons of sugar into his mug, poured cream to the top and stirred.

"About you," she replied. "Your career move to Bloomingfield is hardly your entire life."

"I gave you my narrative and there's nothing else to tell." He took a gulp of coffee. Fragrant, delicious … and boiling hot. He blew on the coffee. It didn't help, and he scalded his tongue a second time.

"Everyone has more than one story."

He sat on the sofa's edge. "I haven't heard yours yet."

"As I mentioned, I've lived in Evanville my entire life and am thoroughly content." She raised her mug in a toast.

He heeded, and they clinked mugs.

"To contentment," she said.

"To contentment." He repeated. "Now tell me about yourself."

She wrapped her fingers around her mug. "I've always adored children, so opening my own business and tending to them is a dream come true." She inclined her head. "Now it's your turn."

"Again?"

"Absolutely."

"Okay. On one condition."

"Which is?"

"Sit closer."

He'd never shared his difficult years in grade school with anyone. In several he attended, he'd been teased for being overweight and frequently nicknamed Pudgy Patrick.

No, he decided. Not that story.

Perhaps he could muster up an amusing memory.

"Why?" she was asking.

"Why what?"

"Why sit closer?"

Involuntarily, he held his breath as a heartbeat went by. "Because I want to put my arm around you, and I can't if you're sitting on the other end of the sofa."

Warily, she swallowed coffee.

"You can trust me," he assured. "There's no mistletoe in sight. Which, in case you haven't noticed, seems to be the norm in this part of California."

A smothered half-laugh was his answer, resulting in her query, "How do I know for sure?"

"About a mistletoe? Look up."

She grinned. "How do I know about *you?*"

"I'll give you two reasons."

She waited. He liked the way her generous lips tilted up.

"First, you can always trust me. I'll ask your permission before I kiss you, and I never go back on my word."

She seemed to relax. "And the second reason?"

He leaned forward and lifted his mug. "I'm a man who holds hot coffee in high esteem."

"What?" She blinked. "You realize your explanation makes no sense."

He inflated his sigh. "You got me there."

Her shoulders shook with a choked laugh as she sat back.

His amber-eyed beauty. Every minute with her was a precious gift. And he craved more—endless hours—to ease into her approach to a slower-paced lifestyle.

In the ensuing hour, they discussed her childhood and her brother, Jack, who was a nurse at the hospital. A discussion came next regarding her parents' divorce.

Zoe, Cora's mother, lived in Nevada whereas Cora's father had always made his home in Evanville, much like Cora. Observing Cora's expression whenever she mentioned him, Patrick asked a question of his own.

"Are you and your father arguing about something?"

The upbeat mood of the previous hour vanished.

Briefly, she closed her eyes. "Why do you ask?"

He slipped an arm around her shoulders. "You're somber all of a sudden."

"We had a disagreement." Her cheeks reddened. She plucked a tiny loose thread from the sofa. "Actually, we've had numerous arguments—especially in the last few years."

Alerted to her studied nonchalance, Patrick tipped up her head. She blinked back the tears filling her eyes.

"What do you need?" he asked.

"I'm not sure."

"You're not alone. I'm here."

"I don't know where to begin."

"I care about you, Cora. I'll listen if you want to talk.""

Her features eased, though her chin lifted, as if defending herself. "Recently, he called me an unkind name and told me in no uncertain terms that I was desperate."

"Desperate about what?"

"Dating. Men." Her small hands fisted. "Since he and my mother divorced, his remarks have become snide and unsettling—especially about my being so thin. They hurt."

Inwardly, Patrick winced. "You're lovely."

Her fists relaxed. "Hardly ..."

Almost too stunned to speak, Patrick replied, "You're his precious daughter. Surely he argued in anger."

"His remarks still hurt."

"I'm sorry. Truly."

"Our most recent argument involved a guy I was dating." She rubbed her arms. "My father hated him."

"Why?" Patrick didn't expect the jealous pang in his chest at the image of Cora with another man. "Did this guy abuse you?"

"I never met him."

Patrick frowned. "You dated a guy you never met?"

"We corresponded through a dating website."

"Who is he?"

"No one important." She clasped her fingers together and avoided his gaze.

"Does he have a name?"

"Sure. Con man." Her laugh was strained. Her hands fell limp in her lap. "In retrospect, I should have known. The warning signs flashed loud and clear, and my father offered countless objections and cautionary advice."

"Which apparently you didn't heed."

"On top of that, he hired an investigator to prove to me that the guy wasn't real."

"Was he right?"

"Yes."

"Your father truly cares about you."

"It's just that he's always so hard on me, you know? My guard went up." She rolled her shoulders. A tiny scowl marred her features.

"Understandable."

With a slow, unsure head shake, she asked, "Have you ever read the story, *A Christmas Carol*?"

Taken aback, he gazed at her. "Uh, huh. Why?"

"The ghost of the future made Scrooge realize he only cared about himself."

"If you're referring to your father, then remember the end of the story. Scrooge changed and became the most beloved man in town."

"Meaning?"

"People change. People are forgiven, especially if they genuinely love you."

"Forgiveness is hard." She exhaled. "Any advice?"

"Wipe the slate clean and let go of your resentments."

She didn't move. Neither did Patrick.

Finally, he whispered, "May I?"

She lifted her head. A tear trickled down her cheek. They were so close he heard her pounding heart and his own thudded in response.

Gently, he brushed her tear away and kissed her forehead, before his lips moved smoothly over hers.

When she broke the kiss, he didn't press her further.

"So now you know my sad story," she said in a low voice.

"And I'm here for you."

He gazed at her perfect profile and righteous anger flooded through him. She had experienced betrayal, then embarrassment, all because a con man had taken unfair advantage of her. He could scarcely imagine Cora's disbelief when she discovered the truth.

He grazed his lips over her fragrant hair. "A word of advice from someone who doesn't know all the answers, or, in reality, any of them."

She grinned, and he took that as an encouraging sign to continue.

"Your relationship with your father is important. If you hold on to anger, it will build resentment and eventually harm you, not your offender."

She dipped her head. Sighed. "You could be a counselor, you know that? You're good to talk to."

"I'm happy being a small-town newscaster."

"Now it's time for you to tell me more about yourself."

"More? Again?"

"Totally."

He took a sip of coffee.

He wasn't sure how to begin. But he was here with Cora, and he knew he could tell her anything and she would be understanding.

Beneath the brilliance of her sweet smile, he fixed his gaze on his hands.

"I realized a hard lesson when I discovered my wife was cheating on me," he began.

His lawyer had used the word *cuckolded*. It had seemed ridiculous at the time, (who used that word?) but resonated 100 percent true.

"I'm sorry, Patrick."

"Don't be. It was eye opening, though our marriage hadn't been good for several years. I ignored the discontent because I was so bent on reporting."

"You didn't try to resolve your differences?"

"Of course. Then again, it takes two people. I wanted the

all-American dream life. She chose high society and incessant travel."

"Define it. The dream life."

Living a life with you, he thought as he gazed at her. Her sweetness was a gift to be embraced.

Aloud, he replied, "After my divorce, I assumed a happily-ever-after was elusive."

"And now?"

Quietly, he brushed his knuckles across her cheek. "Now I'm beginning to believe that true happiness is within reach."

Her face colored, and his heart curved toward her as it always did when she regarded him like that.

For a long moment she rested her head on his shoulder. Soothingly, he rubbed her back. She fit perfectly beside him, as if they had always been together.

The room was quiet. Church bells pealed in the distance. From her window, sparkling silver lights from the neighbors' houses twinkled.

Words weren't required, only the comfort of companionship.

Soon she fell asleep, and he wrapped his arms around her. He regarded her exquisite face in repose, and his fingers eased the dark hair from her temples.

Sometime later she awoke with a start, blinked up at him and rubbed her eyes. "Oh, Patrick, I'm sorry. I'm obviously not a good hostess."

"Don't apologize." He smiled at the disconcertment in her voice. "You slept a half hour at most."

"Still—" She shifted and his arms tightened protectively around her.

"You work too hard," he said.

"Not any harder than you." She slid from his grasp. "'Tis the season for busyness and obviously in my case, exhaustion."

"I thought it was the most wonderful time of the year."

She smiled. "Of course, but it's also crazy and stressful."

"I hope to simplify my life and focus on what really matters," he said. "That's the reason why I moved here."

"Here's a secret," she informed him with a sparkle in her deep-colored eyes. "Stay positive, no matter what."

"Like you?"

She nodded several times. "I try."

He basked in the enthusiasm of her gaze, then reluctantly checked his watch. "I overstayed my welcome. Sorry."

"No, not at all. Thanks for the company."

He stood when she did, and she walked with him to the entryway.

He wanted to see her again. That's all there was to it. But how? They both worked full-time Monday-through-Friday jobs, and he oftentimes worked extra hours depending on breaking news.

Still, where there was a will …

"Cora," he started. "When can—"

Her cellphone chirped, and she excused herself to retrieve it. She glanced at the caller ID and paled.

"It's my father," she announced quietly.

"Take the call."

"I'm not prepared to talk." Her voice caught. "Should I?" Her gaze drifted to Patrick and then back to the phone.

He nodded. "Definitely."

As she clicked the phone on and launched into a discussion, Patrick retrieved his coat and opened the door to let himself out. He had hoped the evening would end with another kiss. The spontaneous kiss in the candy shop hardly counted, and the one on the sofa hadn't lasted nearly long enough.

He glimpsed her, standing at the window, her body rigid in conversation.

Could she mend the differences with her father?

Once more, he reflected on the book, *A Christmas Carol*. Well-loved and timeless, the tale was one of forgiveness and repairing broken bonds.

Peace and harmony. What better season than the holidays?

CHAPTER 6

How long could a plain woman like her hold his interest?

Cora couldn't. She was average—someone who did everyday chores and led an everyday life.

Patrick's silver-spoon background had been enriched by foreign cultures. Furthermore, his job offered him entrée to the powerful, wealthy and distinguished. Hers gave her chattering kids playing catch in her enclosed backyard. Or tugging on her arm. Or whispering in her ear.

Consequently, as much as she'd enjoyed her shopping day with him, she was wary.

Wary because she found herself falling in love with him.

Her soulmate. Her partner. The right man.

It had happened quickly and without explanation. Now, her mind focused on him when she should be concentrating on other things—namely giving the children her unflagging attention, or the thousand chores begging to be accomplished.

She was confronted with chaotic days, her hours filled with a wailing twin who sounded like he'd been mortally wounded when he'd merely been egged on by his brother. Or, a pig-tailed girl screaming bloody murder when a freckled-faced boy chased her around the yard waving a grasshopper. Which, incidentally, turned out to be a leaf.

For the most part, though, the children were amazingly obedient. Nevertheless, by day's end, both Cora and Molly were tired.

As the week progressed, three youngsters had meltdowns from holiday overload; cookie baking to be finished with the older children; and a couple of parents dropped by unexpectedly, begging Cora to watch their child for an hour or two between Christmas and New Year's.

She never refused, though she worked out a schedule that was also fair for her. Per her exchange with Patrick, she'd decided the upcoming break was essential for her sanity and well-being.

Every night after the news aired on television, he would phone her.

The first night he inquired about her phone discussion with her father.

"We're taking it slow and easing back into our relationship," Cora summarized. "I've established boundaries beginning with no name calling or personal attacks."

"You're off to a good start," Patrick encouraged. "Remember, no parent is perfect, so strive for honesty."

"I am. We both are. I want stable, healthy communication and my father agrees."

"Stick with reaching a common ground and keep your expectations realistic."

Patrick was right, and she grinned. "You really should consider counseling in your spare time."

His chuckle was deep. "Thanks, but I'll pass."

The next evening, he cut their talk short because of a news story.

The following evening, he interrupted their phone conversation mid-way with, "Hang on, Cora." He murmured to someone in the background, then came back on the line.

"You're still at the station? It's nine o'clock at night." She kept her tone neutral, refusing to criticize him for working constant overtime.

"I arrive early and stay late. Tonight, I edited a story right up until I was on the air."

"The one about the local health-care industry?" she asked. "Your questions and ideas were spot-on."

"Thanks. Community commitment will generate a tremendous difference and—"

As she'd learned from earlier discussions, he reviewed his news hour almost as if it were a complicated sculpture to be painstakingly assessed. In fact, he was so critical of himself, she'd perfected the excuse of using the weather to change the subject.

"Hang on. Someone is insisting on an answer to a story question." Patrick muffled the receiver, returning a minute later. "Sorry. I gotta run. I'll call you tomorrow, okay? I'm looking forward to seeing you."

"Sure."

"Sure? You can do better than that. I think about you constantly."

And I think about you. But she didn't tell him that. Instead, she wished him a restful night and clicked off.

In the silence of her living room, Cora asked aloud, "Why don't our calls ever last longer than fifteen minutes?"

The answer rang as loud as a silver steel bell. Their spheres were simply too different.

When next he phoned, his voice was heavy. "Sometimes categorizing a new job as demanding is an understatement," he said.

Her heart twisted in frustration. "Bloomingfield isn't bringing the satisfactory life you imagined?"

"I'm to blame, not the town." He drew in a sharp breath. "I'm finding it hard to let things go and let anyone else do my job."

"Ah, you're unquestionably a perfectionist," she noted.

"The holidays, combined with a brand-new station and the move …" She envisioned his handsome face, his eyebrows furrowed into a troubled frown. "Cora, I can't wait to see you, but I don't want to schedule a date I'll have to cancel."

UNFORTUNATELY, that was exactly what happened.

The next day, he asked her to dine with him at The Pasta Junction on Friday because he was only working the afternoon shift.

She agreed.

After she had taken extra care to wear a silver sequined top and black wool slacks, secured her freshly washed hair in place with a satin headband, and teetered in four-inch heels (that she knew she wouldn't be able to walk in for more than an hour), he apologetically phoned and explained in a direct, but awkward manner that he was forced to cancel. He'd been called on assignment to Bloomingfield's town center to conduct spontaneous, on-camera interviews with local shoppers and couldn't refuse.

Fearful her disappointment might show, she blithely told him she understood and not to fret, refusing to sound pathetic.

"I'm sorry," he murmured.

She nodded into the phone.

"I miss you."

She squeezed her eyes closed. "I miss you too."

Sensing his sense of urgency to go, she swallowed. "Good night, Patrick."

"Sweet dreams, beautiful."

When the call ended, she yanked off her heels and sank onto the floor. Restlessly, she fidgeted with the silver bracelets on her wrist.

She'd chosen an outfit other than jeans and a sweatshirt, partly to dress appropriately for the exclusive Italian restaurant, partly to impress him.

With a grim, short laugh, she slumped against the wall. Although she shook her head in denial, the realism was that she was beginning to care too much for him. And caring for a man led to regret, and a bruised heart.

The hard fact was that he'd chosen his work over their date, and, after ruminating over that for a while, her pride forced her chin up.

She straightened, flew into the kitchen and combed the freezer. Quickly, she polished off the entire box of church window cookies from Sally's chocolate shop, allowing a thaw for only a few seconds in the microwave first.

Yes, the eating was emotional, but the occasion called for a sugar rush. Her father had once suggested she was too skinny, anyway.

BECAUSE THEIR FRIDAY night date hadn't panned out, Patrick promised himself he would echo the previous Saturday and spontaneously show up at Cora's house. However, a breaking news report on a mudslide in the mountains occurred before dawn, and he headed to the on-site location.

The mudslide situation was resolved by midafternoon, and he got into his Mustang and drove straight to Evanville. He still wore the tailored gray slacks, long-sleeved green polo, and a twill jacket, and didn't bother to change.

When he pulled into Cora's driveway, he found her stringing net lights around her outside bushes.

"Surprise!" He rushed forward and almost collided with her as she spun.

"Patrick … hello." She smoothed her candy-cane-striped sweatshirt over worn jeans. A pair of silver star earrings dangled from her ears. "I didn't expect to see you this weekend."

"I should have called first, but last Saturday's plans worked out and I hoped this Saturday would as well. I'm sorry about canceling last night."

"I understand. I'm thrilled you're here." A smile flickered across her expressive face—no trace of anything but happiness. He imagined sealing that happiness with a kiss.

The connection between them was real, and he knew she sensed it too.

With an absolute strength of willpower, he stayed where he was and didn't sweep her into his arms. He'd just arrived and the entire afternoon stretched ahead of them. Besides, there was no mistletoe in sight.

"The lights look good." He motioned to the bushes, then to her. "And you look even better."

She looked better than better. She looked exquisite. He cleared his throat, aware of the husky romanticism in his voice.

"I haven't plugged the lights in yet," she reminded.

He ducked his head. "Oh, right."

Once, he'd believed himself a talented conversationalist. Apparently, he was wrong because he was comparing Cora to a set of darkened lights.

"I bought *new* lights and a *new* motion detector." She laughed, exactly as she had the week before.

He was about to inquire about the funniness of all things new when she plugged in the lights. They illuminated her house with a silvery-white glow, and she smiled with a radiance that brought his self-control to a standstill.

He stepped closer.

She regarded him with wide-eyed innocence. "Did you want to say something about the lights?"

"I wanted to say something about you." He brushed his lips on hers. "Thanks for being so forgiving and patient."

"You're welcome." She shifted her gaze from him to her house. "I'd offer dinner, though I'm not much of a cook."

"My specialty is frozen pizzas."

"Grocery shopping is my least favorite chore and my kitchen is essentially food-less," she said.

"I'll treat you to Olive's Diner, providing there's a Saturday special."

"You're extremely generous, Mr. Gervez." She swallowed a burst of laughter. "Allow me a few minutes to change, and I'll take you up on your offer."

When they arrived at the diner, they chose their customary booth by the window.

Several customers' eyebrows rose, particularly Oliver's. "You're becoming my new regulars, and I sense a romance blooming." He set down menus. "Our special this evening is a mistletoe offering—barbecued chicken, marinated mushrooms, your choice of two sides and a slice of red velvet cake."

"A mistletoe menu?" Patrick peered at the ceiling. "Where's the mistletoe?"

Oliver chuckled. "I concentrate on the food."

"Some things never change," Patrick muttered.

Stifling a laugh, Cora headed for the jukebox. The diner was packed with people she obviously recognized, and she paused to chat with friends.

When she made her way back to their booth, a woman shouted their names.

Sally waved from behind the counter.

Oliver might not have gotten around to the mistletoe, but he'd placed a miniature white snowman clad in a green jacket and scarf beside the cash register. "I'm assisting Oliver," Sally declared, "because he's busy on Saturday evenings and my candy shop closes early."

"Is your daughter here?" Cora called out.

"Clarissa is in the kitchen helping a waitress sort red velvet cakes. I'll send her over for a quick hello."

Patrick turned to Cora. Her crisp white blouse, black jeans, and decorative wide red belt around her slim waist suited her. With tousled hair skimming her shoulders in velvety-smooth waves and festive star earrings, she emanated holiday perfection.

He stretched out his legs, relishing a pleasant evening. Christmas in a tiny community was special, especially when he shared it with Cora.

When their meal was finished, they spent a few minutes at the counter conversing with Oliver, Sally, and Sally's adorable daughter, Clarissa. Judging from the number of customers who came over to chat, Cora was a well-loved caregiver. Likewise, their admiration for her seemed to embrace him.

He rapped his fingers to the beat of Willie Nelson's "Winter Wonderland" and grinned.

"Let me snap a photo of you two." Sally grabbed her cellphone. "Stand by the snowman."

Patrick fixed his arm around Cora, snuggled her closer, and they smiled for the flash of the camera.

On the return drive, Patrick repeated his thoughts aloud.

"I prefer this life compared to my prior one in Raleigh," he announced. "I'm no longer in the thick of world-shattering events, or off to interview a president or prime minister, or attend a swanky dinner with movers and shakers, and I couldn't be happier."

She met his sideways smile with a grin of her own. "Our one traffic-light communities suit you?"

"Budget friendly and slower pace. Loads of living space to sprawl out. The comfort of driving instead of relying on public transportation, and no sirens blaring in the middle of the night to wake me."

"Anything else?"

He glanced at her. "I love this ordinary way of living with an ordinary woman at my side."

"Ordinary?"

"Common people."

Her gaze narrowed. "As in average and unexceptional?"

"I didn't say that."

No reply.

For years, he'd prided himself on being articulate. He improvised spur of the moment comments on television with ease.

But now …

Another pregnant pause.

"Cora, I—"

"Actually, you did say that." Her wounded tone scarcely hidden behind sarcasm, she murmured, "Thanks for clarifying how you honestly regard me."

When they crossed the town line for Evanville, he drew to the side of the road and held up his hands in regret. "You're not ordinary at all. I admire your traditional values."

Her face remained expressionless.

"You're valued and exquisite."

She wouldn't meet his stare.

This was worse than any outburst. Much worse.

"You're extraordinary, Cora." She made him feel strong,

wise, and loved, but he couldn't find the words to tell her. He reached out to brush his fingers over her beautiful cheek.

She jerked back.

Her home was still a mile away. It could have been ten miles, because they drove the rest of the way in silence.

When they reached her driveway, he switched off his car.

Cora shoved open the passenger door and raced toward the house.

She spun as he followed her.

"Can we talk?" he asked.

"Sorry, Mr. Big Shot Anchorman, but this *ordinary* woman has *ordinary* things to do, beginning with laundry."

"Please. I didn't mean it that way."

"It sure sounded like it."

"May I explain?"

She shook her head. Her creamy complexion reddened. "Patrick, I'm pleased you found a better home for yourself here. However, I don't appreciate being categorized into a slot marked 'Plain Ordinary Woman' to round out your lifestyle."

He rubbed a hand over his face. "What I meant was how content—"

She stepped inside.

"It came out all wrong." He blew out an exasperated sigh. "Look, Cora. You're the best thing that has ever happened to me."

But he was explaining to a slammed front door.

CHAPTER 7

The following week was a brief one at the daycare.

On Wednesday, the children presented their annual program. Cora requested the parents and children to don their favorite holiday ugly sweater, and styles ranged from motorcycle-riding elves to sparkly blue unicorns. The youngsters sang three beloved Christmas carols, their voices bell-light and enthusiastic, their exuberance warming the audience's hearts.

Afterwards, appreciating the sugar cookies Cora had baked ahead of time, thrilled parents commented that their offspring sounded like a choir of heavenly angels, and wished Molly and Cora a joyous holiday.

"Christmas Eve is tomorrow," Molly reminded after everyone had left. "Your brother flew off to Nevada with his instructor and you ran the 5K. Cheers for raising money for a worthy cause."

"And Jack won the candy cane eating contest for the fourth year in a row," Cora added.

"He must still be on a sugar high," Molly said.

"My guess is he's recovering nicely. He's with Olivia, his pretty auburn-haired pilot instructor."

"Therefore, all's well that *might've* ended well." Molly cleared the toys and arranged them in a bin. "Agreed?"

"All's well that *ends* well," Cora corrected.

"Indeed?" Molly paused and scrutinized Cora's face. "This holiday ended well for you?"

Cora ignored Molly's insinuation. "Christmas is only two days away, so technically the holiday hasn't started yet. If you're referring to my disagreement with my father, we're having dinner together on Christmas Day at his house."

"A suitable beginning to mending your relationship."

In an accomplished issue change, Molly motioned to the floral bouquet on the kitchen table. Crimson carnations, holly berries, and frosted pinecones were designed in a white wicker basket tied with a pink velvet ribbon. "Where are all the candy canes I saw in there yesterday?" Molly peered into the basket and fished out a broken candy cane.

"I ate them," Cora replied flatly. "I'm becoming more and more like my brother because sugar is my current best friend."

"Why? Never mind, I'll answer my own question." Molly's expression empathized. "You're eating comfort foods because you miss him, right?"

No name. They both knew who.

"I miss him," Cora repeated.

A silent sadness swept through the room.

Lightly, Molly touched Cora's shoulder. "The flowers are beautiful."

"Gorgeous, but they're wilting." Cora offered a trembly smile. "I should discard them."

But she couldn't bear to.

"Who are they from?" Molly asked. "Patrick?"

"Yes."

"Any chance you're seeing him again?"

Cora shook her head. She couldn't voice any words save for a broken laugh.

He'd called. She hadn't acknowledged.

He'd texted. She'd deleted his texts without reading them.

It was better this way. A clean break with no regrets, no heartbreak. Perhaps in days or months, she would recover her equilibrium.

Why, then, were her lungs sore when she breathed, her arms heavy as if she carried a massive weight?

"Well, we're done cleaning." Molly shrugged a parka over her fuzzy penguin sweater. "I'm off to celebrate with Harry for our first Christmas together."

Cora shook off her self-pity and offered a heartfelt, "Bask in every precious minute and Merry Christmas."

"Merry Christmas." Molly dragged Cora close and patted her hair. "Hey, if you want to talk—"

"I'm fine." Through a blur of tears, Cora stared down at her reindeer sweater. "I'll manage. I always do."

HOURS LATER, Cora sank onto the sofa with a cup of green tea and surveyed the two-foot "Charlie-Brown" tree she'd put up earlier that evening. Some might label the tree as pathetic—a skinny, two-foot tall fresh sapling.

For her, the tree symbolized the season. Real and authentic, trimmed with photo ornaments of the children she cared for. The tree reminded her of her peaceful childhood, before her parents had divorced and her father had hardened.

She grinned as she viewed the top of the tree, where she'd fixed an amusing ornament. A Scrooge that she'd found in town, complete with a pointed nose and narrow chin.

Patrick's handsome face flashed through her mind. He'd

referred to himself as Scrooge, except he didn't resemble Scrooge in looks or actions.

"*Bah, humbug,*" he'd said. "*Perhaps there's a chance.*"

Was he truly so awful because of a statement he'd apologized for?

In fairness, no.

If weighing in impartially, though, then yes. For a journalist, he hadn't chosen his words wisely.

She blinked and gulped in a mouthful of air.

Their hours together had been wonderful—more than wonderful—for the couple of weeks it had lasted. She drank her tea and let the tears fall. Wasn't this typical for her—a brief connection that soon fell apart because she'd misjudged a man?

She set down her cup and went to stand by the window.

"'*To err is human; to forgive, divine,*'" he'd quoted. She remembered the fondness in his gaze, his tone a rich caress.

She recalled the day they'd first met, which must have been a difficult time for him. After packing and leaving everything behind in Raleigh—his career, his home, and his ex-wife—his elation at arriving in California had been dashed when his car had broken down. Yet, he'd been gracious and respectful and thankful of her efforts to help him.

None of it mattered now. Their situation commanded that she forget their pleasant hours together—his entertaining, lighthearted mannerisms, his romantic kisses and quips about the lack of mistletoe.

He was a man who smiled for the television camera.

And somehow, however feigned, she must learn to smile again too.

.   .   .

THE DAWN of Christmas Eve day brought guilt. In spite of her brother's good-natured teasing regarding a Christmas wish, she'd never actually thought of any.

In the afternoon, she attended a church service in Evanville, and then returned to her bungalow. While she wrapped a final gift, a miniature princess castle for Sally's daughter, Clarissa, her thoughts drifted back to the wish. She still had time to come up with one before her brother phoned on Christmas day.

Speaking of a phone, an alert on her cellphone made her pause. Molly had sent a link to the local television station and texted:

Watch the last five minutes. He's love-struck.

Who? Cora typed back.

You'll see.

Cora wavered. Since their disagreement, she hadn't watched Patrick's broadcasts.

Slightly unnerved, she opened the text. A video of the previous night's Bloomingfield news report began. Per Molly's instructions, Cora scrolled to the last five minutes and turned up the volume as the camera focused on Patrick behind the news desk. Her breath caught at how athletic he looked in a gray blazer emphasizing his broad shoulders, his forest-green shirt and an amusing Santa Claus tie.

He was concluding a weather-report chat with Lorenzo. His banter was concise and clever, yet elegantly all male.

"Before I take a few days off, I'd like to thank everyone for their guidance and good will," Patrick said. "Already, I've made friends with a number of people." The camera panned to a grinning Lorenzo who provided a thumbs-up, then swung back to Patrick. "I expect those friendships will last despite the fact I sometimes say incredibly stupid things. I sincerely hope I'll be forgiven."

Lorenzo took a seat beside Patrick. "Go on," he encouraged. "Anything else you want to say to the thousands who are watching?"

"Yes." Suddenly somber, Patrick's eyes welled with emotion. "There is nothing ordinary about this community. Merry Christmas to our entire viewing audience—including a very special woman who lives in Evanville."

Open-mouthed, Cora dropped onto a chair and stared at her cellphone screen.

Patrick was reaching out to her on live television. There was no trace of anything on his handsome, expressive face except sincerity. Thin lines of fatigue underscored his eyes. He looked drained, and she wondered if anyone besides her had noticed.

Her chest lightened. Her limbs relaxed. She took in a lengthy, shaky breath and brushed away unbidden tears.

Her Christmas wish had been apparent all along—ever since she'd met Patrick: a renewed attitude toward love and romance, and the ability to trust her own heart.

Laughing aloud, she phoned her father. "Dad?" she inquired quickly when he answered. "Merry Christmas Eve. A special man might accompany me tomorrow for dinner at your house. Is that okay? He's real, I promise."

"Do I know him?

She beamed. "In a way, you probably do. He's the new anchorman on our local station."

"Patrick Gervez?"

"Yes."

"Sure, I'd like to meet him. He seems like a great guy on TV."

"He's a great guy in person too."

"Does he know anything about cars?"

"Not a thing." She chuckled. "But he's an old car enthusiast, just like you."

Within fifteen minutes, Cora had changed into a silver

sequined top and tweed wool skirt. She applied cream blusher in a berry shade, a touch of rosy lip gloss, and slipped on her four-inch heels. Instead of a headband, she clipped back her hair with a dazzling rhinestone barrette. At the last minute, she added gold translucent petal earrings for a dash of glamour.

She drew on her jacket, grabbed her gift for Clarissa, and headed to Bloomingfield for the buffet. She just hoped Patrick would be there.

AFTER CHURCH SERVICES, which Patrick had attended with Oliver, Sally, and her daughter, he cruised directly to The Pasta Junction.

Upon arrival, scents of fragrant basil, garlic bread and olive oil prompted an appreciative sniff as he stepped in the doorway. Platters of antipasti with assorted cold meats and sharp cheeses, and a tempting display of dishes were set beneath warmers. Additional offerings included pasta carbonara, a creamy dish in which Julie's homemade fettuccini was the focal point, along with an array of flavorful stone-oven pizzas.

Holiday instrumental music strummed in the background, and Patrick wondered if Willie Nelson was on the playlist. Noting the restaurant's sophisticated ambiance, he doubted it.

"Do you like the songs I selected?" Cora had asked him when she'd chosen a medley of Willie Nelson tunes on their first date in the diner.

He hadn't liked holiday music. Hadn't liked anything that screamed *Christmas* since his divorce. But his mindset had changed, and he was embracing the season for how it was intended—a jubilant celebration, a positive attitude, and spiritual reflection.

Cora would be pleased.

Oh.

He recalled the inflection in her one word when he announced he wasn't a churchgoer, and the sadness that had crept into her voice.

After the church service that evening, he'd proclaimed to an elated Sally that he'd like to attend church every week, and had texted Cora to tell her as much. A glance at his cellphone displayed no response from her.

He sighed, signaled a passing waiter, and requested coffee.

"You'll be awake all night," Lorenzo wisecracked as he sauntered behind Julie, a tall slim blond woman, into the kitchen.

"I assure you, I won't," Patrick responded.

"This week has been chaotic." Lorenzo paused. "You must be as depleted as I am."

Patrick gave a curt nod, though sleep had eluded him the past several days, and the reason had nothing to do with work. Ever since his final conversation with Cora, he hadn't slept more than a few hours.

He scrolled to the photo Sally had sent of him and Cora in the diner. Aware he was tormenting himself, he enlarged the photo and ran a finger over Cora's cheek. She was smiling, her cheeks flushed. Her dark hair was a stark contrast against her white blouse and shiny earrings.

How was she spending Christmas Eve? Was she smiling?

He hoped so. She deserved to be happy.

"Cora," he murmured. "Please give me a chance to talk to you."

WITHIN A HALF HOUR, Patrick was seated at one of several eight-foot tables, observing Lorenzo's twin nieces and Sally's daughter as they danced. Each of the little girls wore lace sweater dresses with knitted snowflakes around the hem, and he presumed the mothers had chosen the matching outfits for fun photos.

Sweet-smelling garland, entwined with snowy roses and clusters of wine-red berries, centered each table. Thick cream napkins were folded beside each emerald-green charger, and claret water goblets and sprigs of pine created a picture-perfect stage.

Cora would have loved this. She didn't care to cook, but adored dining out.

He grabbed his cellphone from the pocket of his navy blazer. It didn't hurt to try again, did it? If she replied, he'd happily volunteer to drive to Evanville, then back to the restaurant, although the distance involved might mean they'd miss the buffet entirely.

Maybe Julie offered takeout. He could buy dinner, then he and Cora could relish a cozy meal at her house.

If only she responded to him.

As he wondered how to phrase his latest text, he was dimly aware of the conversation from his nearest tablemates, Sally and Oliver. He absently replied to Oliver's question as he typed, *I miss you, Cora. Please let me make amends for my thoughtlessness.*

"Lorenzo's family is a jovial bunch," Oliver was saying. "His sister sent her daughter ahead so she and her husband could finish wrapping gifts from Santa."

Patrick picked a sprig of holly from the centerpiece and rolled it between his fingers. All that mattered was that Cora still cared about him, although he knew it was time to accept the circumstances. She wasn't interested in him anymore.

Sally got up, muttering something about helping Julie, leaving Oliver, who was commenting on ... Patrick didn't know what. He hadn't been listening.

Oliver studied Patrick with a perceptive grin and then glanced to the side. Lorenzo stood in the doorway and both men exchanged amused smirks.

"It's okay." Lorenzo clapped Patrick on the back. "We understand." With that, Lorenzo and Oliver started for the buffet line.

Patrick dragged out his cellphone, hoping against hope that Cora had answered.

She hadn't, and he shoved his phone back into his pocket.

Armed with a heaping plate of pasta, Oliver returned. "Any word from Cora?" he inquired casually. A bit too casually.

Patrick cut Oliver a dismissive glance. "As you well know, I haven't seen her since we ate dinner at your diner."

"A week without seeing the woman you love? It must be difficult for you both, especially at Christmastime."

"For her? Or for me?"

"She's obviously in love with you, judging by the way she looked at you while you were enjoying my mistletoe special," Oliver replied. "Is there a chance she's coming tonight? Sally mentioned ..."

The restaurant stilled, and Patrick stopped listening.

Slowly, he stood.

Cora had walked into the restaurant.

Her silver top and form-fitting skirt skimmed her trim figure, and high heels emphasized shapely legs and undeniable femininity. She scanned the tables, evidently searching for someone, clutching a wrapped gift embossed with reindeers.

Afraid to move, Patrick stood mesmerized for a moment, hearing her lilting laughter as she spoke with the hostess. Had she finally read his texts, his apologies, and appeared at last to talk to him in person?

He raced forward, and the overwhelming love for her

made his throat ache. He disregarded the exchanged murmurs from the other diners.

"You're here." He stood inches away from Cora, almost touching. His gaze fixed on her beautiful face. "Why?"

"Because I couldn't face another tomorrow without you."

"I called. I texted. In fact, I just sent you another text."

"I haven't read it. I've been driving."

He opened his arms. She set down the gift and stepped into his embrace.

"You bought me a gift?" he asked.

"Not unless you like princess castles. It's for Clarissa." He loved her quiet laugh.

A burst of merriment from the children as they spun in a circle made him want to join them. This comfort and serenity only happened at Christmas, with the woman who meant more to him than anyone in the world in his arms.

"I must tell you some things." He took in a breath. "Many things."

"Right here? In the middle of the restaurant?"

"Yes. Beginning with, I'm sorry."

"I accept your apology. I realized you didn't intend to hurt me."

"And I love you," he continued. "Thank you for making my Christmas special by showing up here tonight. More than special."

Her gaze was warm and affectionate. "I love you too."

He glanced around. Plates in hand, friends and strangers alike were staring as Cora pressed a hand to his heart.

"I realized you are my Christmas wish," she said softly.

"And you're mine." He stroked his fingers over her face, her lips. "You're all I want. You're all I need." He peered upward, hoping for a mistletoe.

Alas, nothing.

He bent his head and kissed her, gentle and loving. Who needed a mistletoe, anyway?

For the first time in forever, he'd found a town he could call home.

"A wish means you want something," he murmured.

She gazed up at him. "And that something is you?" Her smile was infectious. The same familiar smile that had brought gladness to his days.

"That something is us," he assured, kissing her again.

Because Cora Carpenter was his love, his happiness, and his Christmas wish.

The End

A NOTE FROM JOSIE

Dear Reader,

Thank you for reading *A Chocolate-Box Christmas Wish.*

I wanted to write another story centering around the characters in the "Chocolate-Box" series, and chose a character from a previous book, plus a new character—Cora and Patrick—to share a winter holiday romance with you.

If you loved this sweet romance as much as I loved writing it, please help other people find *A Chocolate-Box Christmas Wish* by posting your review. This book is available in ebook, paperback, audiobook, Hardcover, and Large Print paperback.

My Spotify Play List for A Chocolate-Box Christmas Wish is here.

RECIPE FOR TARA'S CHURCH WINDOW COOKIES

Ingredients:

12 ounce package of chocolate chips
    1 stick butter
    1 package flaked coconut
    1 package colored miniature marshmallows
    1 cup chopped nuts (optional)

Directions:

Melt chocolate chips and butter in a saucepan. Let cool. Mix marshmallows and nuts (if desired) into chocolate. Take a large piece of wax paper and sprinkle with flaked coconut. Spoon chocolate and marshmallow mixture onto the wax paper and roll into a log. Makes three logs. When sliced, the cookies look like church windows.

Enjoy!

USA TODAY BEST-SELLING AUTHOR

JOSIE RIVIERA

a

Chocolate-Box

Irish Wedding

PRAISE AND AWARDS

USA TODAY bestselling author

CHAPTER 1

Colum O' Brien didn't believe in Ireland's much-heralded mythology. Aye, he was Irish to the core, but there wasn't a wee bit of truth to mischievous leprechauns guarding pots of gold. Gold buried by fairies, no less. Goaded by skeptical amusement, he shook his head. He didn't put much stock in ancient Irish folklore.

Which led him to another thought: Dreams. Did they mean anything?

In any event, he wasn't looking forward to sleeping in his childhood bedroom tonight. He wondered if he'd have the same dream that had plagued him for months on end.

Over and over, just before waking, he'd gotten lost while driving on a shadowy, winding road, never finding his destination no matter how hard he tried.

Well, that assuredly wouldn't happen on this trip.

With a dismissive smile, he switched on the car radio, humming along to the folksy acoustics of "Wild Mountain Thyme," a Scottish tune.

The weather proved fine and clear for an Irish December afternoon, soon to glow with the dregs of sunset before the sky turned blue black. He opened the car window a crack, inhaling the earthy fragrance of peat smoke mingling with the bracing air of the Irish Sea. He flicked a glance toward the neighboring hills, marveling at the flicker of twinkling white lights in cottage windows—heralding the holiday season—then returned his focus to the zigzag coastal road.

A sign noted the final turnoff to a precarious, narrow two-lane road. Soon, he'd reach his family homestead in Wexford.

Thirty years ago, Colum could have accomplished this drive from his former Dublin ballet studio with one eye closed, but not anymore. His fifty-year-old eyes didn't see as well as they once did.

Unexpectedly, heavy clouds began lowering over the surrounding hay pastures. Rain spattered his windshield.

He slowed his speed. It was as if he'd driven off into a different country with no recognizable landmarks. The sudden storm had even shut off his GPS.

Where was he?

The mist thickened. Road signs became unreadable. He lowered the volume on the radio.

Instinct told him he must be nearing the last tiny village on the outskirts of Wexford. Thankfully, the taillights of another car appeared ahead.

Perhaps a long-lost relative?

Colum's widowed father had insisted on a gathering at his seaside home for his wedding celebration and asked Colum to be the best man. His father was marrying a dear friend and set a December wedding.

At first, Colum had made excuses for not attending; he taught numerous dance classes, plus was helping Sean, a troubled young man in his twenties. Years earlier, he'd met the lad at a volunteer performance in Dublin. A feature story by an American newsman, Patrick Gervez, had spotlighted how Colum's ballet troupe had given back to the city by inviting underprivileged teens to watch free productions. Since then, he'd claimed Sean as his nephew, relocated him to Farthing, and helped whenever possible.

Thus, it was difficult to get away.

This trip was an eleventh-hour decision. Not that Colum didn't love his father—though in truth, he'd been resistant to return to Wexford. The longer time passed, the more he'd lost touch with his hometown. And whenever he drove these roads, his heart remembered Keira, his high school sweetheart.

Now it was her mother who would be his father's bride.

Would Keira be there? Wexford was the last place Colum had seen her several decades earlier. But no, she lived in London now, and his father would have mentioned her attending the wedding.

Perhaps. Perhaps not. He and his father didn't converse much.

The car ahead accelerated around a sharp curve, slid off the main road, then skidded to a stop on a gravel lane.

Colum's heartbeat slowed, his fingers tightened on the steering wheel. He stomped on the brakes and swerved onto the shoulder. Quickly shutting off the engine, he dashed from his car.

As suddenly as it started, the rain quit. The clouds thinned; then slunk away.

He dragged in a breath as the driver stepped out of the car.

A woman. A fair-skinned, willowy woman. And with her came a whisper of a memory: Their shared childhood and his love for her.

"Are you all right?" Anxiety brought a tremor to his voice. Fresh breezes cooled his heated cheeks.

"I'm brilliant." She peered at him with keen blue eyes.

Blond hair, threaded with silver, tumbled down her back. The ends were tipped in . . . pink?

"Colum O'Brien. Is that you?" She touched a hand to her full, inviting lips—lips he well remembered.

He froze, his gaze fixed on her. He couldn't reply.

Keira Murphy. Here. He'd never expected to see her again.

"Aye. It's me." He strode closer; a tongue-tied moment.

She offered that same heart-shattering smile he'd thought about for decades.

"I'm delighted to see you, my long-lost friend," she said.

He couldn't stop gazing at her—her vivid blue eyes, sooty-black lashes and lovely slim figure. There were so many things he wanted to say, so many times he'd longed to hear her voice again.

"I'm happy to see you too." He cleared his throat. "You look grand."

More than grand. She looked exquisite.

He took both her hands in his and kissed her, a fleeting, polite brush of his lips on her cheek. Casual, yet intimate.

Her hair smelled like lilies, her skin soft and silky.

She breathed in a slight inhale, then pulled away.

He drew a shaky breath and ordered himself not to question why he'd been reduced to a long-lost friend status when they'd shared so much more.

Without another word, she moved to her car, her motions graceful. He held open the door for her and ensured she was settled. Then he headed back to his car and followed her to Wexford.

CHAPTER 2

The following morning, Keira sat in an oversized Adirondack chair on the O'Brien's spacious lawn. Moss grew on the weathered walls of the house, and the thatched roof drooped at the eaves. A string of holiday lights wound around each window, a cheerful reminder of the upcoming festivities. The scent of dew hung in the air, the grass damp from an earlier rain.

She regarded the stone markings at the front of the O'Brien property, the adjacent fields dotted by sheep, the sparkling waters of the Irish Sea.

"Hello, Keira," a deep voice called. Colum came from behind, covered her eyes with his hands, then immediately removed them. "Guess who?"

Her stomach fluttered, and she bit down on her lips to hide her smile. She admired his easy-going walk as he stepped around to face her. He was a man comfortable in his own skin, whereas she considered herself too tall and ungainly.

"That was easy," she teased. "You could've given me another minute to guess."

"I assumed you'd know it was me right away." He grinned. "May I begin our day by complimenting you, because you are gorgeous?"

"Thank you." She'd dressed in jeans and a red wool sweater, and twisted her hair back into a casual bun. She'd fussed with her appearance in anticipation of seeing him. "Were you comfortable sleeping in your childhood bedroom again?" she asked.

"The sea air is a balm. Without fail, I sleep well in Wexford." He dropped into the chair beside her and yanked out a cigarette. "It's a surprise, aye?"

"The fact you're still smoking? You vowed to quit when you were a teen."

"Over three decades later, and I constantly try to quit, although it's obvious I'm unsuccessful." He granted a rueful smile. "You never liked it."

"Still don't."

"I defer to your wishes, then." He slipped the cigarette back into his pocket, then rolled up the sleeves of his jean jacket.

"How can you dance and do that to your lungs?" As he smirked at her response, she studied him. His arms were athletic and muscular, his physique toned and fit in slim-fitting black pants and a grey knit sweater. She remembered when he'd held her at this very spot, on a similar breezy morning—a few days before she'd departed for London—a few days before New Year's Eve.

She shifted her gaze to the water. "So what's a surprise?"

"Your mum is marrying my dad," he said. "A gala event to begin the holidays."

"The best time of the year."

"Christmas?"

"And New Year's," she replied. "In fact, the entire month of December."

"The season isn't special for me . . . although I'm thankful for the adorable children I teach. The look on their faces is priceless because they're so excited."

She gestured to the O'Brien's home. The natural holly wreath hung on the back door. "We used to leave sacks by the fireplace on Christmas Eve, remember?"

"In the hopes the sacks would be filled with toys on Christmas Day." He chuckled. "Then we'd set out milk and bread on the kitchen table."

"In our house, we'd opt for a pint of Guinness and mince pies." She sighed, the memories poignant. "My mum has been alone since my father died."

"Similarly for my dad when my mum passed away."

"I recall that day." Keira had searched for Colum and discovered him sitting by the shore, his arms around his knees, his face wet with tears. At fourteen years old he'd been embarrassed she'd found him crying, for he despised weakness in himself. His shoulders were drooped, and his voice a whisper, but he'd finally relented and invited her to stay. In return, she'd offered consolation and her undying loyalty.

"Boys don't cry," he'd stated.

"But men do," she'd assured. *"Real men aren't ashamed to shed tears and show their emotions."*

"Our parents have been friends for years," Colum was saying.

"Like us." She folded her lips together. Why had she spoken the words aloud?

Until you left.

Colum hadn't uttered a sound, but, judging from his tightened expression, she could read his thoughts. They'd been inseparable. That's what happened when you were next-door neighbors.

She fingered the sleeves of her sweater. "I realize my departure from Wexford was sudden."

He shrugged.

"You know why." Too edgy to sit still, she shifted. "There were goals I wanted to accomplish before we settled down."

"Shall we give it a name?" he asked.

"What?" She sat straighter. "Me leaving?"

"Let's call it the demise of a friendship."

She flinched, as if his statement was a physical blow, even more so because of the slight catch in his tone. He'd been hurt.

For years, they'd planned to attend the same university in a neighboring town. That had only taken place for one semester. They'd pledged to stay in touch, although the busyness of life had taken hold.

"I said I would wait for you." His voice was quiet and solemn. "However, it was you who declared that we were young and couldn't plan our lives around a final commitment."

"Not once did you demand that I abandon my dreams."

"I wanted you to ride your rising career to the top," he said. "I never would've taken your achievements away."

Why? Did he love her so much that her happiness was more important than his?

She waited for him to say more. When he didn't, she searched his handsome face, although his features were remarkably bland. "You accomplished your dream," she finally said.

"Which dream was that?"

"Dancing professionally. You lifted those ballerinas effortlessly into the air. How many dancers can claim that?"

"All credited to thousands of hours of rehearsals; and workouts." He quirked a silvery-grey eyebrow. "Did you ever attend any of my performances?"

"No, not live, but I discovered YouTube."

He looked pleased. Something stirred in the fathomless depths of his green eyes, and her heart rate doubled.

"You watched clips?" he inquired.

"Aye."

More than clips. She'd watched his full performances.

"And you?" He shoved his hands into his pockets. "Did you find what you were looking for?"

"For a while, until I grew too old to model."

"You're not old."

"High fashion modeling is extremely competitive." The wind pushed her hair back. "When I was awarded a generous contract from an exclusive agency, I couldn't turn it down."

"And off to England you went. You hightailed it out of here before the New Year's bells rang."

She should've felt cornered by his statement—defensive. But this was Colum. She'd known him since they were children. She knew his nature. He was her constant companion, and she'd confided everything to him.

"You're asking me to apologize?" She fixed him with a level gaze. "I did on numerous occasions. How could I start our life in Wexford when London beckoned?"

"True." He watched the sea, and she followed his stare. The water was calm, the salty breeze conjuring images of picnics—wicker hampers stuffed with sausage sandwiches, sliced apples, and spice cake—while herring gulls squawked overhead.

"Fame and fortune, Kiki," he said. "Both are heady sensations."

Kiki. Her cheeks warmed. She'd nearly forgotten his nickname for her.

"I craved more." She swallowed and lifted her chin. "The excitement of a sizable city and glamorous occupation. Wexford is . . ."

He swept out his hands. "Adorable."

"You didn't stick around, either," she pointed out.

"No reason to."

Because of her? She pondered whether she should ask him. She didn't.

"I never congratulated you on your success," he went on. "Or rather, I did, but you didn't respond."

"I'm sorry. I was wrong not to answer your letters." Those precious letters—every word had broken her heart—but she couldn't write back, it would have only broken *his* heart. She'd established a new world—so different from his in only a matter of months. Nonetheless, his letters had slid from her fingers as she'd sat in her tiny London flat and wept. Joy to hear from him, bittersweet longing for leaving him behind, and the injustice of a demanding career that had initiated their separation.

She sighed. "My work was exhausting, and I hardly had a moment to breathe."

He greeted her explanation with a quick nod.

They'd been best friends. No. More than that. They'd been first loves.

"I'm standing up in the wedding." Keira navigated to a safer subject and offered a modest bow. "I'm the matron of honor."

"I'm the best man."

"Your father spoke of your obligations in Farthing," she said. "I wasn't expecting to see you."

Colum's occasional trips to Wexford over the years never had seemed to correspond with hers.

"Sean, a young lad who is like a nephew to me, continually needs my help," Colum replied. "I met him through Patrick Gervez, an American newsman who traveled to Dublin to feature a story on an outreach ballet program. Nowadays, Sean's graphic design business is doing fairly well, and he moved into his own flat. I packed his fridge with food, a matter of great importance to a twenty-something."

Typical Colum, she reflected. Forever helping people whenever possible.

"Is Sean independent?" she asked.

"He's getting there." Colum pulled his hands from his pockets and stared down at them. "I worry for him, though. I want him to be successful."

"I remember how you repeatedly volunteered at the homeless shelter in town and then organized plays for the children. You gave graciously of your expertise and talents."

"I tried."

"Help Sean, but don't give him handouts."

He grinned. "Advice now, Keira?"

"I speak from experience as a mother of two adult daughters who are often headstrong. I continued to indulge them for years, which was a mistake." She ran a hand through her hair. "Do you own a home in Farthing?"

"Renting is better for me," Colum replied. "My savings are stable, although I'm not wealthy."

"I just bought my own place."

"Congratulations! Where?"

"Take a glance to your right."

He turned. "Your mum's grand cottage?"

"She's moving in with your dad after the wedding, so, I figured, why not? It's my childhood home. Plus, I'm here to care for our parents as they age."

He leaned toward her and gave a heavy nod. "Aging is definitely a fact of everyday life, and it will be a comfort for them to have you next door."

"Their well-being is important, both physical and emotional."

"Aye." He shot a rueful grin. "And convenient when you need a cup of sugar."

"I don't bake." Keira beamed. "I sew."

"Right. How could I forget?" Colum offered a bemused chuckle. "I rang my father about my change of plans—before he requested someone else to be the best man."

"Who would he ask?"

"A cousin, maybe. Can't think of anyone who is suitable, though."

"You work in Farthing?" She'd already asked too many questions. She had at least a dozen more. She was so comfortable, so at ease conversing with him.

"I'm an instructor at Miss Clara's School of Dance," he replied. "Primarily, I teach preschoolers, and I love that age."

"Sweet ages."

"Someday, I fancy directing a public theater for adults and children."

"Underprivileged?"

"Aye, and also open to anyone in the community."

"In Farthing?"

"I haven't decided."

"You never married," she said. "Never had children."

"My longest relationship lasted all of eight months. I wasn't a particularly attentive partner while I concentrated on my career." With a noncommittal nod, he added, "Wexford was abuzz when you wed your agent in London. You were only twenty at the time."

"Henry was several years older."

"By two decades," Colum corrected. "A sophisticated man, I assume?"

Her face heated with the pain of the recollection. "He introduced me to a glittery circle. I thought of you when I met his friends at posh parties. We would've had a laugh at their uppity airs."

He grinned and leaned closer. "And your daughters are now . . ."

"Almost thirty."

"I always wanted children," he said.

"Twin daughters?"

"One would've been fine." His tone softened. "Two are better."

"Yet you never married . . ." Keira stammered with her response. When Colum studied her with those mesmerizing eyes, she forgot all rational thought. "You'll meet my girls. They're flying in from London. They'll miss the ceremony because of work, but will stay for a while afterwards."

"Through Christmas and New Year's?"

"They both have significant others in London, so I doubt it."

"I'm leaving a couple days after the service. I'm teaching several dance classes, then overseeing a holiday recital for the little ones after Christmas. The students have been preparing for months."

"You'll miss Christmas in Wexford, then. I hope to decorate my shop and my new home as soon as our parents are wed." Her brows knitted. "Will you return for New Year's?"

"Perhaps." Assiduously, he avoided her gaze.

"Remember the fun we had on New Year's Eve?"

Gently, he touched her arm. "Our families would visit for nibbles and drinks."

"And beforehand, my mum would clean the house from top to bottom."

"To signify a fresh start for the upcoming year."

"May I confess something?" she asked.

Colum automatically seemed to tense at her question. "Of course."

"On New Year's Eve, I placed a mistletoe under my pillow," she said.

"In the hopes of seeing your future partner in your

dreams." He peeked at her left hand. She'd taken her wedding band off years ago. "Is your husband . . .?"

"Henry and I divorced when our daughters finished primary school." Keira rubbed the back of her neck. "We only stayed in a polite agreement that long for the children's sake."

"Was it the right decision?"

"Each couple's choice is personal and involves many factors. From my experience, I should've left him sooner." Her marriage had been a slow deterioration of her self-confidence. As soon as her career had fallen to a standstill, Henry lost interest in her. He'd also worn away her independence and monitored her calories.

Colum glanced up and motioned toward the shore, extending a wave and a smile.

She followed his gaze to their parents. Cheryl and Richard, both in their late seventies, strolled arm and arm by the water's edge. Her mum wore a wide brimmed straw hat and billowy yellow-floral dress. Colum's father was stout and fit, as well as green-eyed, good-humored, and engaging. It gladdened Keira's heart to see their smiles. Love occurred at any age, she supposed. Just not for her.

She'd never been content in her marriage—even before Henry's verbal abuse. Had she been forever seeking the right man? She'd dated after her divorce, but no sparks.

Her chest filled with regret as she met Colum's gaze. He'd been her first love. Had he been her true love?

"Divine weather," he was saying.

"No rain in the forecast." She managed a radiant smile. "Let's hope the sun shines for the wedding."

"It's risky planning an outdoor ceremony in December," Colum noted.

"Wexford is considered the sunny southeast of Ireland. Besides, they're renting a tent with heaters for the reception. They can dash inside if need be."

"Good thing. There is constantly a threat of showers in an Irish forecast."

"Or a downpour," she inserted.

He stood and peered at the blue sky, the stretch of wispy white clouds. "Will you join me for a coffee in town? Just like we used to."

"When we were supposed to be in class."

"We'd have the craic—a good laugh and loads of fun." He chuckled. She remembered that chuckle—rich and pure and inviting. "We were a rascally pair,—ducking out of school early."

She held up a hand. "Speak for yourself."

"Hah! Half the time, you'd initiate our adventures. We'd pool our lunch money, hop on a bus, and eventually land at Michael D's whiling away the afternoon over scones and coffee and homework."

"Homework?"

He smiled. "Once in a while."

"I dine at Michael D's often."

His smile wavered. "I'm trying to get my head around the fact that all this time I assumed you still lived in London."

"I own a dressmaker's shop a few doors down from Michael D's," she explained. "In fact, I designed my mum's wedding dress. Care to take a peek?"

"Isn't it bad luck to see the bride's dress before the wedding?"

"Only if you're the groom." She accepted his extended hand and got to her feet. "Don't take any photos to show your dad."

"You're the one who could never keep a secret. Chatterbox."

She gave his shoulder a playful nudge as they began walking. "And you were quiet."

"So many memories." Conflicting emotions flashed across

his well-defined features—his sharp cheekbones that reminded her of a proud Roman warrior. His gaze locked with hers, a silent communication. He knew her so well. She'd never been at a loss for words, and they'd sit for hours. Colum, attentive and encouraging, while she chatted endlessly. She'd become a famous designer, and he'd continue volunteering and open a performing arts school. Perhaps they'd marry in the winter. A Christmas wedding, or New Year's . . .

Their lives had taken such different paths.

But what if . . .

No, no, no. She refused to play the "what if" game.

"What's the name of your shop?" Colum asked.

"Keira's Wexford Boutique."

They stepped onto a stone path, lingering to appreciate the buds of holly and pansies blooming up from the cold ground.

"You loved fashion." Colum paused to pick a bouquet, handing the flowers to her. "You made me a shirt once."

She sniffed, savoring the fragrant scent. He'd frequently slip her a spray of cowslip or clover or shamrocks—depending on the season.

"I sewed the shirt from jersey cotton fabric and a pre-made sewing pattern," she replied. "It was tight on you."

"I wore it often."

"Only so you wouldn't hurt my feelings."

He'd ignored teasing from the other boys and had worn her handmade shirt with pride. He constantly looked out for her. Her protector. He wanted to make her happy.

"You sewed this for me, Kiki?" he'd asked with a broad smile when she'd presented it to him. *"It's brilliant."*

He'd tugged it over his dog-eared t-shirt. He was tanned and muscular by then—on the cusp of adulthood—nearing eighteen.

The shirt hadn't been brilliant—an amateur's attempt at sewing and design—boasting a bold Hawaiian pattern of multicolored birds and leaves. Nevertheless, her interest in fashion, encouraged by Colum, had thrived.

"Is your shop successful?" He stood so close, the warmth of his skin heated her own. She inhaled the crisp scent of the sea. Knowing him, he'd probably gone for a swim at sunup.

He still had the muscular build of his younger self, his profile lithe, yet solid. His eyes were a mossy green—reminding her of the color of the forest after a hard rain. His hair was salt and pepper, raked short and side-swept.

"I'm happy," she acknowledged. "I've come to realize this idyllic wee town is my home. For me, happiness constitutes success."

"Ahh, living in Wexford."

She frowned. "Is there a problem?"

"Little towns are ideal for many chaps." He exhaled. "However, the country character here, coupled with my recollections of the old ways . . ."

"You find fault with our traditions? Our folklore?"

"Some of it. Nevertheless, a large city offers more theater and restaurant choices." He winked. "Plus, no one remembers me as an awkward adolescent."

"You were a pro in every sport. Whereas I—all legs and arms—"

CHAPTER 3

"You're exquisitely perfect." Colum blurted the words before he could stop himself. He scanned Keira's delicate profile—the curve of her nose, her flawless complexion with a sprinkling of freckles, and heard the sincerity in her tone. She actually didn't realize how attractive she was.

However, her blue eyes shone with a spirit that hadn't been diminished by hardship.

Her youthful features had matured, fulfilling the certainty of loveliness, enriched with a mellowness that had developed with maturing. Her posture was straight, her figure slender.

His only desire was to touch her, kiss her, cherish the delightful feelings intensifying inside him—the first true emotions he'd felt in decades.

He cupped her cheek. "Numerous points in my life have reminded me of you. I wondered if our mutual memories ever caused you to smile."

He braced himself for her reply. When she finally dragged her gaze to his, she drew a wobbly breath. "I laughed a lot in London whenever I remembered our adventures."

He bent his head and his lips grazed hers. So delicious, so inviting. "You're my precious Kiki," he murmured. "You've been my forever—"

"No." She tugged free. Her complexion was flushed, her eyes wet. "You're leaving in a few days."

"Aye, but there's no reason why I can't return. I've never stopped thinking about you." He brushed the shiny hair from her forehead and grinned at the pink highlighted tips. In her teens she'd been the town nonconformist, experimenting with bizarre fashions. However, the bright makeup and outlandish feather hats had never diminished the beauty of her high cheekbones and expressive eyes. No wonder a London modeling agency had signed her on the spot.

"Words are easy, Colum." He respected the proud grace of her walk as she stepped away. "Circumstances may prevent a person from following through—no matter their intentions."

When they reached her driveway, Keira insisted on driving them to town, vowing to take the curves slowly in light of the previous evening's mishap. She didn't. If anything, she accelerated during the ten-minute drive, while he gripped the edge of the passenger seat. When they arrived at her shop, she rummaged in her handbag for the keys.

He squinted through the wavy glass window of the vacant building next door. The exterior paint flaked at random, the interior was dust-coated, the walls cracked.

"What business was here previously?" Colum asked.

"Nothing for years," she answered. "There was talk of converting the space into a high-class hotel, but the funds never came through."

She finally found the key, and they stepped inside her shop.

It was tidy and spotless, and scents of cedar and mint lingered in the air. Clothes racks sported fine woolens and tweeds, hand knit scarves and cable stitch cream sweaters tagged to sell.

"Do you employ a staff?" he asked.

"Recently, I hired a mother and her adult daughter. They're smart, efficient, and excellent seamstresses." Keira walked to a back room and brought out a knee-length lace dress in a champagne shade, along with a flowered crown headpiece. She illustrated how she'd sewn each delicate button by hand.

"Tasteful for your mum." He applauded. "May I ask what the daughter of the bride is wearing?"

Keira winked. "It's a surprise."

"In secondary school, I'd ask what you planned to wear the following day, and you'd consistently say—"

"It's a surprise," they chimed in unison.

"Why did you forever ask me the same question, Colum?"

"To prepare myself." He attempted to keep his features straight. "I never knew what newfangled outfit you'd come up with."

"Fashion is fun. An adventure."

He rolled his eyes. "You found enough for both of us." He'd willingly gone anywhere she'd dragged him and felt fortunate just to be with her.

"I wished to dress better than those pretty girls in school who flirted with you," she said.

He chucked her under the chin. "I believe you were jealous."

"Believe whatever suits you."

"Were you . . . jealous?" He drew her near, held her close. He couldn't help himself. His yearning for her slowed his breathing.

As he gazed into her eyes, the seconds paused—becoming the shared remembrances of delightful hours, of days, of years.

He'd sought to deny it, but he'd never been able to resist her. When they were young, they'd fallen into an easy friendship—enjoyable and uncomplicated. By their teens, their relationship had changed. Romance began to bloom— although they'd both resisted the attraction to each other.

For decades afterward, his thoughts had gravitated toward her. How was she faring in London? Had she forgotten him? Undoubtedly, because she was married.

But now they were reunited, and the seasons apart were a mere moment in time.

"Jealous? Don't be ridiculous. You flatter yourself." Keira fussed with a tweed cape on a hanger, fumbling with the fabric. "The programs you choreographed at the Wexford homeless shelter were fun and uplifting, and you were only in your teens."

"Thank you. I love working with children." He wanted to congratulate her on navigating the subject change so seamlessly.

She turned toward him. "Do you still dance and perform?"

"There aren't many roles for fifty-something males," he replied.

"You were a key dancer with the Dublin ballet."

"Until I reached thirty. Then the younger, ambitious men were happy to replace me."

"Same in my occupation." She went back to fussing with the cape. "Runway models are most successful between the ages of sixteen and twenty-one."

"And afterwards?"

"I did catalogues. And sewing to make ends meet while raising two daughters."

"You're exceptional, Kiki. You lived on your own in London."

Tears welled in her eyes. He didn't expect them.

"My ex-husband, Henry, considered me obsolete when I aged out of working the runway." The cape fell off the hanger. She bent to pick it up. "After our divorce, I continued to question my self-worth."

"Did he abuse you?

"Not physically. His abuse was emotional." She lifted her hands, then let them drop. "I should've divorced him sooner, but I was trapped. Two young daughters and no way to support us."

"Now you're successful and content."

"I am." She laughed, unforced and laid-back. "This tiny slice of the world is my lifeline, and I'm not relocating anytime soon."

Life in a microscopic town was ideal for some people, just not for him. He dismissed the unspoken thought and sought a more manageable topic. Absently, he fingered a velvet hanger, while he relished spending the day with her. Finally, the Keira he recognized was emerging from behind her careful wall. Honestly explaining her hardships, without sugarcoating what he'd imagined had been her opulent London lifestyle.

"Ready to lead the way to Michael D's?" he suggested.

"Considering the coffee shop is a few doors down, it's not difficult."

"Do they still serve tea cakes?"

"Aye. And buttered scones with strawberry jam. Your favorite. The new owner kept the same menu."

He patted his stomach. "Your mum baked superb scones with lemon curd and whipped cream. You brought them to me after my ballet practice, rolled up in foil and topped with a silver bow."

"She still bakes over a turf fire. Batches of soda bread sit on our kitchen counter as I speak."

"Thus a delightful afternoon awaits."

She narrowed her gaze. "Colum O'Brien, you can't sample desserts and bread all day."

"Watch me." He laced his fingers through hers and led her out of the shop.

They passed McKay's jewelers and peered through the display case window. As was customary in many of Ireland's shops, the Claddagh Ring took center stage.

"Love, loyalty, and friendship." Keira admired an array of sterling silver and gold bands.

"Did your mum hand her wedding ring down to you?"

"I married in London, and she didn't attend because my father was sick. He died a year later, and she continued to wear the ring on her right hand. Now that she's marrying your father, she placed it in her bedroom drawer for safe-keeping."

Colum hooked his arm around her shoulders. "Awaiting you."

"I won't marry again."

"Why ever not?" he asked.

"Once was enough. I'm obviously not good at marriage." Her tone thickened, and she clasped her hands together. "Perhaps one of my daughters will wear it someday."

He swallowed the dull ache in his throat. He could still visualize Keira planning their future all those years ago.

"And after we graduate from university, Colum, we'll marry," she'd declared. Her color was high, her joy bubbling and infectious. *"Won't it be grand?"*

"Aye." He'd cradled her in his arms. *"Grand, indeed."*

CHAPTER 4

When they reached the O'Brien's cottage, Keira invited Colum into her home. The comforting scent of buttermilk and raisins and freshly baked Irish soda bread greeted him as they entered the light-filled kitchen. The walls were painted a dove gray, and a bold patterned rug covered the ancient tiled floor. Photographs littered a side bureau. Several were black and white photos of him and Keira. In one, they stood by the shore. He displayed a wiggling fish—their only catch that day—while she beamed, her light-blond hair in a long braid over her shoulder, and proudly held up the fishing pole. They were eight years old.

Keira gestured to the loaves stacked beneath numerous glass containers. "All ready for the reception."

"Your mum shouldn't bake for her own wedding."

"Why not? Baking is therapy."

He lifted a lid. "May I?"

"Sure. I'll slice a loaf and brew a pot of tea."

A few minutes later, she poured two steaming cups of robust breakfast tea and combined loads of milk and sugar into her cup. Once she settled, he seated across from her. The expansive bay window boasted an unobstructed view of the craggy hills and sea beyond.

"Thus, our parents are out and about today," he said.

"They drove to Waterford." Keira set the white porcelain teapot on the table. "My mum wished to speak with the DJ in person."

Colum sat back in joking amazement. "No bagpipes tomorrow?"

"The piper will perform when guests arrive and leave the ceremony." She sipped her tea and gazed at him over the rim of her cup. "At the reception, she insists on traditional Irish folk music."

Colum lifted his teacup in a salute. "She is a wise woman."

"I agree. She allowed me to make my own mistakes." Keira poured more tea. "The rehearsal begins in a couple hours, and the pastor arrives at five o'clock."

"What rehearsal?"

"We'll practice walking in and out, and where we'll stand during the ceremony. Didn't your father mention anything?"

Colum drummed his fingers on the wooden table. "Men don't talk much."

"My mum requested that you and I plan an impromptu party for afterwards."

"Did she now?" he asked. "I could do with more warning."

"Are you busy?"

"Not at all."

"Good." Keira smiled. She was gorgeous when she smiled. Her face was all gentle curves, her silky hair tumbling over her shoulders. "I'll ring a few places in town."

She made quick work of the arrangements, then picked up their tea cups and placed them in the sink. After she finished, she remained silent for a beat.

"When, exactly, do you return to Farthing?" she inquired.

The anticipation of a commitment was unmistakable. The speculation of "what If" he didn't have to leave.

But he did. He'd created another life. He leased a flat and had resided in Farthing for ages.

He traced his fingers along the sides of her face and smoothed back her blond hair. She turned her cheek nearer his palm before she slipped away.

Did his remembrances of their former years—when they'd finished each other's sentences—bring her the same pangs of heartfelt longing? He'd presumed his reminiscences were embellished by the idealism of youth. Now he wasn't so sure.

"My preschoolers await my return," he said.

"Do you enjoy teaching the younger age group?"

"Absolutely. I use distraction and positive feedback. And I heap on the compliments when the children point their toes."

"Do they . . . point their toes?"

"Hardly ever." He grinned as she laughed out loud.

Keira's radiance brightened his mood. When he'd lost his mum, he'd wept, his sorrow unbearable. Keira had been there—quietly consoling, encouraging him to express his grief. She'd put aside her sewing that day, changed her plans. Comrades till the end, they'd vowed. They'd sat tight for hours until the sky darkened.

He was her priority, she'd assured him. As she'd been his.

"My American friends, Patrick and Cora Gervez, have flown to Ireland for a holiday," Colum continued. "He's the newsman who introduced me to Sean in Dublin. In any case, I want to show him and his wife, Cora, around Farthing. As soon as the recital is over, I'll return to Wexford."

"Is that a promise?"

"A promise and then some." He kissed her temple. "That is, unless you're traveling somewhere for New Year's Eve?"

"Have you forgotten, Colum?" Lightly, she stroked his hand. Or maybe he stroked hers. "I'm not going anywhere."

CHAPTER 5

Although rehearsal dinners in Ireland weren't standard, Keira opted for a casual soiree with hors d'oeuvres, oysters, and pints of beer at sunset. They arranged tables and chairs under a canopied pergola on the sandy beach, and Colum and his father built a smoldering bonfire between the sand dunes. The fire whispered hisses, the flames flickering, and the air smelled of smoke and pine.

Bottles of water were plentiful, along with a marble board laden with a wheel of moist blue cheese, sharp cheddar, goat's cheese, soda crackers and crusty baguettes.

Keira reached for a handful of grapes as she admired the blade-leaf potted plants adorning the tables. The men had secured strings of subdued vintage light bulbs to the pergola.

Colum came to stand beside her, his arm brushing hers. He wore slim-fitting swimming trunks and a striped polo shirt, and his smile enhanced his good-looking face.

"May I?" he asked.

"May you what?" Her chest surged with excitement. She couldn't refute the unmistakable magnetism whenever he neared, as if an electrical arc sizzled between them.

He touched a finger to his bottom lip, a teasing gesture she fondly recalled. "May I have your grapes?"

"There's plenty where these came from, and I can assure they're all the same." She motioned toward the tables. "We requested the caterer bring fresh figs and dried apricots too. Remember?"

"You did most of the arranging."

"Correction. *All* the arranging."

"Right." Her remark earned a chuckle. "Well, I'd prefer your grapes."

"You constantly stole my food when we were young."

He swept an arm around her waist. "Not stealing. I asked first."

With an exaggerated sigh, she handed him the grapes. "Help yourself."

"I'd like nothing better than to help myself . . . to a kiss." His soft breath brushed her cheek. His green eyes smoldered as he bent his head and pressed his lips on hers.

The kiss deepened, and she wound her hands around his shoulders.

Somewhere near the house, her mum called. Colum broke the kiss, and an unexpected loneliness filled Keira's heart. With a sigh, she encouraged herself to yield to reason. Too many years had passed. Was it too late to start their romance again—simply pick up where they left off?

A possibility. But life, she'd discovered, was seldom simple. Twists and turns were encountered around every bend.

She plucked his arm from her waist and turned. "We're coming, mum," she called back.

Colum held her hand as they started toward the house. "I always admired your generous nature," he said.

"As if I had a choice," she joked.

He polished off her entire sprig of grapes and they shared a laugh.

He had laugh lines now. So did she.

As they walked, she reflected on their day. She liked sitting at the kitchen table with him and planning a rehearsal dinner celebration. She liked everything about this charming man with rock solid arms and sturdy shoulders.

"My two favorite young people," her mum declared when Keira and Colum approached. "You make a stunning couple."

"We're hardly a couple," Keira replied. "And we're hardly young."

Colum's father strode over. "Could've fooled me on both counts."

Their smiling approval was so contagious that Keira couldn't curb her grin.

"Your mum and my father are wise." Colum followed his declaration with a throaty laugh. She glanced at him, startled to see the love shining in his eyes, and her heart soared.

After chatting about the wedding and wishing their parents "good night," Colum kept his fingers firmly around Keira's and led her to the waterfront.

Those who chose to swim after the rehearsal had been encouraged to wear their swimsuits, and Keira had arranged a basket of towels on the beach. The full moon rose, a deep silver disc, steady and true, much like the fine-looking man smiling down at her.

Colum gestured with his chin. "Lots of folks are enjoying the water this evening. Are you up for a swim?"

"They're mental. The sea is freezing."

He chuckled. "It'll get even colder in January."

She pointed to the waves slicing across the rocks. "Is your judgement clouded? Have you been drinking?

"I don't drink alcohol."

She knew that about him. He'd never changed.

A sparkle lit his eyes. "We Irish are a hardy people."

"Uh, huh."

"Invariably, I swam faster once we reached our teens."

"Invariably?" She placed her hands on her hips, her legs slightly apart. "Is your fancy word a dare?"

"Absolutely." He shrugged off his shirt. His chest was firm and well-defined. Graceful and compelling. A man who devoted his life striving for beauty and artistry.

"As you may recall," she said, "I'm an exceptional swimmer."

"You should be." Wryly, he grinned. "You live by the sea."

She bumped up against him. "So did you." She untied her white shimmer lace coverup and set it on a chair. Her vivid-purple swimsuit sported a sweetheart neckline and revealed a peek of fair skin.

His admiring stare wasn't lost on her and her cheeks heated.

He grabbed her hand, and they dashed into the frigid water—the spray soaking their faces. Total immersion brought her teeth to chattering within minutes. They splashed each other before Keira admitted defeat and they headed for shore.

Colum snatched several thick towels and wrapped one around her. He arranged another on the sand close to the bonfire and beckoned her to sit.

With a lightness in her limbs, she obliged.

He sat beside her, tucked the towel nearer her shoulders, and cuddled her. Bits of sand clung to his cheeks, and she brushed it off.

"I would've stayed in the water longer," he declared.

"Uh, huh." She still shivered, but the heat of the fire, the warmth of Colum's body, offered pure pleasure. "Then why are your lips blue?"

"Yours are bluer." A relaxed smile worked across his

features. She recalled how his eyes darkened whenever he'd contemplated kissing her after a swim, and her pulse quickened. The scent of salt water and his damp skin brought wants and misgivings.

He bent his head, cupped her face and kissed her with aching tenderness. Oh, the taste of him, the gentleness of an unstoppable kiss. She didn't want it to end—like their youthful declarations. Only her emotions were different now. Deeper and sounder.

She pressed her forehead against his chest, her hands flattened on his shoulders. "I wish you could stay in Wexford permanently," she whispered. "This is your home."

"For many years, but not anymore." He gathered a deep breath. "In all honesty, I can't risk being hurt again."

"You're referring to me?"

"Aye."

She blinked, focusing on his words. "I wouldn't do that." She drew back, attempting to understand the overwhelming emotions he awakened in her. Had she hidden behind outward merriment and animation in London—a vigilant emotional balance that numbed her feelings? She'd clung to that balance for years, thankful for her two cherished daughters to love and care for.

"I realize you wouldn't intentionally." Colum kissed her forehead. "Though, please understand that my heart can only take so much."

She went to stand, and he kept his arm firmly around her. "May I hold you a while longer?"

Why? He'd hedged about continuing their relationship. Maybe he'd never been interested. Still, his affectionate smile melted her insides, and she relaxed. She regarded him and fingered the greying hairs at his temple. His lashes were black and spiky, his features well-defined.

She stirred, and he drew her closer, and the instinctively

protective gesture prompted her to smile. He buried his face in her hair, and she leaned back and briefly squeezed her eyes closed. Two people reconnecting on a windswept Irish beach. Two sweethearts. Tonight, she felt wholly at peace with herself, and in seamless accord with the universe.

"There's a family of otters. I saw them earlier when I took a swim. And kingfishers." He pointed toward the water, a sheet of indigo-blue silk. The moon rose higher, reflecting a milky glow across the hills. A chorus of crickets and the sizzling pops of the fire serenaded them, the murmurs of the departing guests fading away. "Do you recall when we'd spend the day intent on spotting an otter?"

"Aye. You'd spin their water frolics into fairy tales." Her throat clogged with tears. She inhaled a deep breath to compose herself.

"Once upon a time," he'd often recited in their youth, *"there was a girl named Kiki, and a guy named Colum."*

A fairytale. A happily ever after.

What happiness had she missed while she'd worn blinders —all to achieve success in a fickle career?

THE FOLLOWING morning dawned pleasant and clear. Keira drew open her lace curtains and gazed out her second-floor bedroom window, smirking as her mum directed the workers on the placement of the large white tent and the cathedral windows on the sidewalls. Colum's father guided other workmen on the location of the portable heaters.

Further down the shore, Colum emerged from the water. His swimming trunks draped low on his hips, his muscular chest glistened with drops of water. The sun glinted behind him, outlining his athletic physique.

He slung a towel around his neck and padded over to their parents.

Watching him, Keira's thoughts emptied of everything except him.

He raised his head, as if he felt her gaze.

"Aren't you chilly?" she teased.

He gave a look of lighthearted superiority. "Not a bit."

"You aren't serious. The temperature of the water is fifty degrees Fahrenheit."

"In truth, I'm frozen."

Her shout of hilarity almost drowned out his next remark.

"Can't wait to see what you'll wear to the wedding, Kiki," he said.

Kiki again.

She ignored the unexpected knot in her chest. Or, at least, she tried. A memory of their mutual years flashed through her mind—holding hands at sunset, shared secrets in the dark. Despite her anticipation of an exciting lifestyle beyond Wexford, she couldn't pretend the flood of emotions whenever he was near didn't exist.

"It'll bring tears to your eyes," she called back.

She assumed she'd moved on with her life. She hadn't. For decades, she'd searched to fill the void in her heart. And she'd fallen in love, once again, with the man she'd left behind.

AN HOUR LATER, Keira donned a knee-length, carnation red dress with a polka-dotted sash that she'd fashioned and sewn. The ends of her hair boasted a ruby hue, and she styled her heavy curls to the side with a pearl clip. She opted for braided jute sandals, satisfied that her outfit was tasteful and sensible.

As she gazed at her reflection in her full-length mirror, she recalled the conversation with her mum from the previous evening, after Keira and Colum had parted.

She'd knocked on Keira's bedroom door and entered. "I wanted to speak to you about Colum," she'd begun. "Day in and day out through the years, you looked splendid as a couple, but especially tonight."

"We're great friends."

"So you've made known. Nonetheless, I see the way he looks at you."

"I haven't noticed anything of the sort," Keira had replied.

"He can't stop staring, and you dissolve whenever you meet his gaze."

"He's leaving in mere days."

"Encourage him to stay. You've never gotten over each other. The sooner you both admit the truth, the better."

Her mother had known how difficult it was for Keira to leave him and Wexford all those decades ago. It hadn't been an easy decision.

"He has work and obligations in Farthing," Keira replied.

Even now, she longed for the tenderness of his embrace, the gentle insistence of his kiss. She'd appreciated the precious hours they'd spent in each other's company, and she sensed Colum felt the same. But what would tomorrow evening bring? Or the following? Would they finally celebrate a New Year's side by side again?

All those decades ago, she'd departed the day after Christmas, intent on securing a flat in London before her modeling contract began the first of January.

"New Year's is symbolic, Kiki," Colum had explained. They'd spent every holiday never more than a stone's throw from each other. *"Let's reflect on the past year, then look forward."*

By the time they were teens, they'd toasted, their sparkling grape juice glasses clinking as they cozied in Colum's living room by a fire in the hearth, while their parents celebrated at the local pub. They'd return well before midnight and switch the television on for a communal countdown.

"Why do folks insist on coming in the front door, then leaving out the back door?" Keira had asked him.

"It's touted to bring good luck." His lips had deepened into an exasperated smile. *"Another one of Ireland's traditions."*

Laughing, she'd refuted, *"Many traditions have a purpose behind them. Rituals are performed for hundreds of years, although few folks can recall why."*

His look implied a struggle between seriousness and humor. *"Here's a tradition that will last. Come what may, we'll spend New Year's with one another every year."*

Keira blinked back tears at the remembrance. That was the last New Year's she'd seen him.

"Sometimes the pathway to the person you cherish is a twisty and lengthy road," her mum was saying. Her eyes had misted, although her smile offered encouragement.

Keira snapped up her bouquet, a fragrant mix of snap-dragons and sunflowers, then walked to the window. Laughing and chatting, in a kaleidoscope of vibrant dresses and navy suits, ushers were seating the guests in rows of white chairs facing the sea. The pastor fixed himself at the altar, a classic wooden archway decorated with purple sea asters.

Her veins tingled with excitement at the enthusiasm of the guests. Today was a glorious, sunny day, the rugged land-scape dusted with snow on the highest mountain peaks. The stark blue skies promised joyfulness and enchantment.

At noon, the ceremony began with a lone bagpiper playing Mendelssohn's Wedding March. A ripple went through the crowd as Keira and Colum took their places, and the bride walked down the aisle to her groom.

Her mum's champagne lace dress complemented her rosy complexion. The flowered crown headpiece brought a statement of romance to her wavy gray hair. Her closely set blue eyes brimmed with happiness.

Colum's father, dressed in a black notched tuxedo, stood ruddy faced and noble, beaming as his bride approached.

Keira gazed at the two men, father and son. Their resemblance was astounding. The square jawlines and eye color were the same, as were their natures. Attentive and charismatic, both men forever wore a smile.

"You're beautiful," Colum said softly to her. His green eyes glistened with tears.

Her stomach flipped and she smiled—craving all things Colum. The boy he was, and the man he'd become.

Behind him, the sea shimmered—sparkles under the sun. In her teens, she'd imagined the shimmers as magical fairy dust, and that the magic would lead to an enchanted life with him.

After the wedding, they'd sing and dance at the reception. The lively melody of Galway Girl, an Irish tune. Or a romantic waltz, and he'd hold her in his arms.

Her pulse thrummed with the anticipation of another day with him.

She'd suggest he stay a wee bit longer. She wanted him to meet her daughters. She was so proud of them.

"All Those Endearing Young Charms," closed the ceremony. The emotional lyrics about a woman's youth fading away, encouraged the guests to join in.

Dozens offered congratulations, circling the bride and groom as they stepped toward the tent. Traditional Irish pub fare—hearty fish and chips, shepherd's pie, and seafood chowder, would be served buffet-style.

Keira caught up to Colum, who was speaking on his cellphone. His eyebrows crinkled in concern.

"Are you coming?" she asked.

He clicked off the phone. "I can't. I must leave."

"Now?"

"The young man in Farthing I told you about—"

"Sean? You loaded up his refrigerator."

Colum rubbed his jaw. "He hit a rough patch and was thrown out of his flat."

"He recently moved in."

"Correct, but he needs me. Patrick Gervez and his wife, Cora, are also in Farthing. They flew over from America for a visit to Ireland in the wintertime."

"Can't they handle Sean's problems?"

"They're on holiday. They're good friends, but Sean is my responsibility."

"He really isn't."

"He is, though." Colum's tone was strained, his chin high. "I won't shirk my obligation and ask my American friends to shoulder my burdens. I'll extend my congratulatory wishes to our parents and go pack."

What obligation? she thought. You're not even technically related. I need you too.

She respected that Colum always placed the welfare of others before himself, but she wanted him to be a part of her life too.

"Then . . . this is goodbye?" she asked aloud.

"Kiki, I've been thinking. Maybe it's better this way." He strode closer, his gaze locked on hers. "Our friendship has lasted decades, and neither of us can ignore our first love. But we shouldn't complicate our relationship with anything else."

Like romance? Like love? Like kisses under the moonlight?

Her vision blurred, her chest ached. "Aye. Friends till the end." She swiveled. She wouldn't let him see her cry. Keeping her shoulders straight, she quickened her pace to the tent.

She remained out of sight when Colum got into his car a

few minutes later. He'd changed into jeans and a button down blue shirt, and shrugged on a jacket. For a moment he waffled, glancing around.

"I'm right here," she was tempted to shout. But she didn't, and the stab of regret pierced deeper as he drove away. She'd never see his lopsided smile, nor hear his easy-going chuckle, again.

HER MUM APPEARED—KEIRA wasn't sure when.

"He left early because someone needed him." Tears clogged Keira's throat. She trembled, despite the sun's warmth.

"He apologized for his hasty departure. He always was the first in line to come to everyone else's aid." She gave Keira's hand a mild squeeze. "You'll see him again."

When? Keira's fingers were cold, but her mum didn't seem to mind.

CHAPTER 6

wo weeks later, and the day after Christmas, Colum flicked warning glances at his four-year-old ballerina students, but they paid him no heed. They knew he was a marshmallow when it came to disciplining them. Dressed in pink tights and black leotards, their hair tugged back in classic buns, they raced around his studio like it was a preschool gym. They should've been practicing their pitter patter turns by the barre. Instead, they practiced . . . running.

He clapped his hands to bring their attention to him. Alas, no such luck. He hunkered down to tie a tiny ballet slipper, reminded them to work at their dances for the upcoming recital, and then shepherded them to their waiting parents.

After speaking assurances to several anxious mothers, and thanking them for bringing their children for a last-minute practice, he arranged his gear in his locker and leaned his head against the wall. Since resuming his everyday life, he'd grown weary of the town of Farthing—and even his surrogate nephew.

After attending a morning church service the day before, their Christmas dinner had consisted of takeout boxty, potato pancakes stuffed with meat and vegetables. For the remainder of the day, Colum had volunteered at a soup kitchen while his nephew created a custom logo for a local shop.

In addition, Colum's dreams had started again—driving on a shadowy road and being lost.

He grasped a cigarette, then shoved it back into his pocket. He craved a coffee, or tea . . . but he'd have to sit in traffic forever first. In Wexford, everything was a mere ten minutes away.

"*I dine at Michael D's often,*" Keira had declared.

Keira—eternally in his heart, eternally in his mind. He'd assumed he was over her. He'd assumed he'd secured her in a safe, secret place. Returning to Wexford had been bittersweet, but memories of her and their years together had struck him at every turn. He'd even jogged along the beach the morning after his arrival and discovered the oak tree where they'd carved their initials when they were twelve.

But in a forty-eight-hour period, how could he reunite with his teenage sweetheart? He was a bachelor in his fifties and wasn't about to leave everything he'd worked so hard for, to move back to his hometown. Plus, could he truly contemplate settling down?

He blew out a breath. He'd tried to forget her. If anything, his feelings had grown stronger.

With a cheery nod to the straggling parents, he shrugged on his twill jacket and exited the studio.

Restless, he wandered the bustling city streets as people hurried home from work. Bright icicle lights illuminated the shops, and aromatic pine filled the air. Daylight had dwindled, and a purple dusk came earlier than expected. The days, the years, passed too quickly, and each hour was precious.

He paused. So what was he doing in Farthing?

He'd told himself not to care, citing a myriad of reasons, expecting his feelings would fade.

She'd left at eighteen, and he'd been devastated. Nevertheless, he loved her—a love so powerful it exploded within him. Surely, she felt the same.

He needed to take the right path and find his way home. Back to Keira and Wexford.

He drew out his cellphone to contact his father, then Keira's mum.

He hesitated.

Texts were a start. In person was better.

Decision made, he rang Sean, and offered his flat to sublet. Colum had secured a part-time job to enable Sean to get his finances in order and hoped the lad would be responsible. He'd shared his knowledge and been a sounding board. Now was a chance for the young man to transition to independence.

Then Colum enlisted the help of his father and Keira's mum.

Next came a phone call to Patrick Gervez and his wife, Cora, inviting them to visit the southern part of Ireland and Colum's hometown for a special event.

His fourth request was to Clara, his employer and long-time friend. She assured she'd find a suitable teacher replacement, that the recital would go off without a hitch, and encouraged Colum to follow his heart.

His heart. He pressed a hand to his chest.

He hurried to his flat to attend to last-minute details and pack a suitcase.

Then he drove to Wexford as if his life depended on it.

CHAPTER 7

Keira wrapped her fingers around a fresh mug of tea, leaned back in the oversized Adirondack chair on the O'Brien's lawn, and gazed at the blue-grey ripples of the water, a reflection of the sky. Today, she wore a one-piece V-neck jumpsuit, a snuggly knit in a bold fuchsia, and draped a thick woolen cape over her shoulders to ward off the chill.

The end of December carried a chilly, overcast day, and the holiday had occurred in a blur. Colum had texted every day—and they'd kept the topics neutral.

After a Christmas church service in town, she'd prepared roast turkey, stuffing, and buttery carrots, and dined with their parents. Colum had phoned, wishing them all a "Merry Christmas." He'd perfected his friendly, amiable tone.

Her eyes burned, but she didn't blame it on the smoke from the turf fires.

She blamed it on the tears she'd shed since he'd departed. All that remained were precious snapshots of their youth that she safeguarded in her mind. Many years ago, he'd unknowingly set the bar high. His likable character, wit, and intelligence had become the standard she'd unwittingly measured every man by since. They were so compatible—pieces of a puzzle fitting in perfect agreement.

"Hello, Kiki, my love," a deep, beloved voice came from behind her.

She gasped. The shattering gentleness of Colum's words sent a jolt through her.

She set her mug on the grass and slowly rose. Now he stood in front of her—his tall frame clad in dark jeans, a flannel shirt, and his familiar twill jacket. She assumed she was still breathing. She couldn't be sure.

"Colum." Her thoughts reeled. His presence was a solid force, mesmeric and undeniable. "Why . . . why are you here?"

"I missed you." His tone was whispered, raw with emotion. "And, I'm here to stay. Do you know any place for rent?"

"In Wexford?" Her gaze lifted to the man who held her heart. "For whatever reason?"

"For you. Only for you." He captured her in his arms. His lips pressed hungrily with an aching desire that would forever remain in her memory.

She molded nearer to him. "I've missed you too." Their breaths mingled. She returned his kiss with all the yearning in her soul.

His hands slid up and down her back. "I came to tell you that I love you. Everything you do—everything you say—everything you represent."

The taste of his lips brought unbearable happiness. She didn't want him to stop, fearful he might disappear.

"My precious Kiki, you're goodness, decency, and all that's true in the world," he said. "You're the treasure of my life."

She pressed a trembling finger to his mouth. "And you're

the treasure of mine." Heat radiated through her body. Her heartbeat raced so loud, surely he heard it.

Tears glistened at the corner of his eyes as he kept her firmly in his embrace. "I was fearful of having my heart broken anew and ordered myself not to love you."

She wiped away his tears. "And?"

"It didn't work." He cradled her face in his hands. "When we were apart, I realized we'd missed out on love once, and I won't allow it to happen again."

"I can't believe you're here. I'm speechless."

"All I need is a single word." He pulled a small black velvet box from his pocket and handed it to her.

She opened the box, which revealed a sterling Claddagh ring. "When did you—?"

"The ring is your mum's. She's a grand woman."

Keira ran her palm along the gleaming silver. The crown symbolized loyalty, friendship, and the heart represented love. Tenderness pulsed through her. He'd returned, determined to recover the love they'd begun decades earlier.

"Do you like it?" In his eagerness, his features appeared almost boyish.

"Nothing can ever mean more."

"If you don't . . . I'll buy you a new ring, although it's bad luck."

"You don't believe in Irish folklore."

"I'm changing my mind about many beliefs, especially if it ensures your happiness."

His response made her throat ache. Her Colum, ever wanting to please her.

"The ring is perfect," she said.

"Keira Moira Murphy." Colum brushed his lips over her forehead, her cheeks, her mouth. "Will you marry me?"

"I can't wait to be your wife." She looped her fingers

around his nape. Her lips parted for his lengthy, loving kiss. "Aye. Aye. Aye."

"Let's plan a New Year's Eve wedding, if you agree."

"New Year's is only a few days from now."

"That'll do."

"Our engagement will last less than a week?"

"Our engagement has survived decades." He glanced at her cottage. "We'll make our home there."

"You'll be living with me?"

"When we're married. Aye. A place next door to our parents is ideal, as we can care for them as they grow older. We have a responsibility to ensure they are secure, protected, and we're providing the help they may require."

"It's more than a responsibility. I consider it a privilege."

"Well stated. Plus, it's convenient whenever your recipes call for a cup of sugar." He winked.

"I don't bake. I sew."

"So we'll dine at Michael D's a lot."

She smiled. "A definite improvement over my cooking."

"I remember you were never much of a cook."

"What else do you remember?"

"I recall you always fired my heart into a tailspin." He tossed her one of his lopsided smiles. "And, I remembered the vacant building in town. I located the owner, and I've secured a lease on the place adjacent to your shop. This little town needs more culture and a community theater is an excellent beginning."

"You mentioned you preferred bigger cities."

He quirked an eyebrow. "Can a man adjust his opinions, or is that a woman's prerogative?"

"Both." She laughed. "Colum O'Brien, you've made me so happy."

"Kiki, I've only just begun."

EPILOGUE

$\mathcal{N}$ew Year's Eve day brought a brisk breeze and threat of showers. Outside, a huge white tent had been erected near the Irish Sea, and both the ceremony and reception would be held inside. Large propane portable heaters had been set up to take away the bite in the air.

Keira gave a last glance at herself in the mirror at her light-peach lace wedding dress, pleased with her appearance. The ivory netting veil with a feather and tulle flower; accented the feminine, flowing lines. She'd dipped the ends of her hair in a subtle shade of dusty yellow.

At two o'clock, the ceremony opened with the swell of keyboard music, and a hush went through the crowd. The tent glowed with candlelight, perfumed with rich bouquets of shamrock and crimson roses, tied with red satin ribbons. She savored every second, giving a special nod to her two beautiful daughters and her new friends, Patrick and Cora Gervez.

Colum had introduced her to them when they'd arrived from Farthing for the wedding, and they'd immediately invited her and Colum to America—enthusiastically chatting about their colleagues and family in Bloomingfield, California.

"You'll enjoy Julie Rossi's restaurant, The Pasta Junction, because she makes her own homemade pasta every day," Cora had gushed, as she tucked a dark-brown curl behind her ear. "Her husband, Lorenzo, is the local weatherman."

'We work together at the television studio." Patrick's blue eyes gleamed with pride as he beamed down at his wife.

Keira and Colum assured they'd love to see America.

"Perhaps for our honeymoon?" Colum asked her. "January weather in California is mild and has it all—beaches, mountains, and, from what Patrick has described—Bloomingfield Candy Shop—the finest chocolate shop in the world."

"Aye, it sounds grand," she'd replied.

As Keira started down the aisle, she carried a photo in her mind of this day—her true wedding day, exquisite and with the promise of a lifetime of love.

When she approached the altar, she grinned at her mum, her matron of honor, and Colum's father, the best man.

Then her gaze locked with her tall, handsome groom, resplendent in a dove-gray suit and emerald-green tie that matched his eyes.

Colum gazed at her with quiet joy. "Hello, my love," he whispered.

She recalled everything they'd been through, their decades apart. Love had emerged from friendship and taken hold. In harmony, their journey had led them back to exactly where they'd begun, and truly, this was the happiest of New Year's. Welcoming the future and letting go of the past, in the company of her loved ones.

With her hands laced with his, she repeated her wedding vows with him. They commenced the ceremony by reciting a traditional Irish blessing, an ancient Celtic prayer:

"May the road rise up to meet you.

May the wind be always at your back.

May the sun shine warm upon your face; the rains fall soft upon your fields and until we meet again, may God hold you in the palm of His hand."

And then she silently added to herself:

Once upon a time, there was a girl named Kiki, and a guy named Colum.

A fairytale. A happily ever after.

THE END

A NOTE FROM JOSIE

Dear Reader,

Thank you for reading *A Chocolate-Box Irish Wedding.*

I wanted to write another story loosely connected to the "Chocolate-Box" series, and located the story to Ireland during the holidays and New Year's. I chose Colum, a character from Oh Danny Boy and also brought two characters from A Chocolate-Box Christmas Wish—Cora and Patrick—to share a winter romance with you.

If you loved this sweet romance as much as I loved writing it, please help other people find *A Chocolate-Box Irish Wedding* by posting your review.

A Chocolate-Box Irish Wedding is available in ebook, paperback, Large Print paperback, Hardcover, and audiobook.

My Spotify Play List for A Chocolate-Box Irish Wedding is here.

With sincere appreciation,
Josie Riviera

Love sweet romance Irish romances?

Irish Hearts Sweet Romance Bundle

RECIPE FOR CHERYL'S IRISH SODA BREAD

Ingredients:

2 1/2 cups all-purpose flour

3 tablespoons sugar

2 teaspoons baking powder

1 teaspoon baking soda

1/2 teaspoon salt

1/3 cup cold butter, cut into chunks

1 1/4 cups buttermilk

1/2 cup currants or raisins

Substitute 4 teaspoons vinegar or lemon juice plus enough milk to equal 1 1/4 cups. Let stand 5 minutes.

Preparation:

STEP 1

Heat oven to 375°F. Line baking sheet with parchment paper; set aside.

STEP 2

Combine all ingredients except buttermilk and currants in bowl; cut in butter until mixture resembles coarse crumbs. Stir in buttermilk and currants just until moistened.

STEP 3

Turn dough onto lightly floured surface; knead gently 10 times. Shape into a ball. Place onto the prepared baking sheet. Pat into 6-inch circle. Cut 1/2 inch deep "X" in top of dough with sharp knife.

STEP 4

Bake 30-35 minutes or until golden brown. Serve warm. Enjoy!

ABOUT THE AUTHOR

Josie Riviera is a *USA TODAY* bestselling author of contemporary, inspirational, and historical sweet romances that read like Hallmark movies. She lives in the Charlotte, NC, area with her wonderfully supportive husband. They share their home with an adorable shih tzu, who constantly needs grooming, and live in an old house forever needing renovations.

To receive my Newsletter and your free sweet romance novella ebook as a thank you gift, sign up HERE.

Become a member of my
 Read and Review VIP Facebook
 group for exclusive giveaways and FREE ARC's.

josieriviera.com/
josieriviera1@gmail.com

Cherished Hearts Six Book Volume

Aloha To Love

Sweet Peppermint Kisses

Valentine Hearts Boxed Set

1-800-CUPID

1-800-CHRISTMAS

1-800-IRELAND

1-800-SUMMER

1-800-NEW YEAR

The 1-800-Series Sweet Contemporary Romance Bundle

Irish Hearts Sweet Romance Bundle

Holly's Gift

A Chocolate-Box Christmas

A Chocolate-Box New Years

A Chocolate-Box Valentine

A Chocolate-Box Summer Breeze

A Chocolate-Box Christmas Wish

A Chocolate-Box Irish Wedding

Chocolate-Box Hearts

Chocolate-Box Hearts Volume Two

Chocolate-Box Double Hearts

Recipes From The Heart

Leading Hearts

New Year Hearts

SENIOR HEARTS

Summer Hearts

Christmas in the Air (1-800-Book)

A Very Christian Christmas

The 1-800-Series Volume Two

The 1-800-Series Complete

Christmas Tails of the Heart

Pawfect Christmas Hearts

Pink Coral Island

Most books are available in ebook, audiobook, paperback, Large Print paperback and Hardcover.

Many are FREE on Kindle Unlimited!